House of Death

Sarah Royce Weldon

Snow Leopard Publishing

House of Death
Copyright © 2016 Sarah Royce Weldon.

All rights reserved. Printed in the United States of America. No part of this book may be used or reproduced in any manner whatsoever without written permission except in the case of brief quotations em- bodied in critical articles or reviews.

This book is a work of fiction. Names, characters, businesses, organiza- tions, places, events and incidents either are the product of the author's imagination or are used fictitiously. Any resemblance to actual persons, living or dead, events, or locales is entirely coincidental.

For information contact :
Snow Leopard Publishing
http://www.snowleopardpublishing.com
email: info@snowleopardpublishing.com

Cover Image by Claire Elaine Shaw
Cover design by J Asheley Designs

ISBN: 978-1-94436100-6 (paperback)
    978-1-94436101-3 (hardcover)
    978-1-94436102-0 (ebook)

LCCN: 2015955462

First Edition: January 2016

10 9 8 7 6 5 4 3 2 1

For Sophie, in the hope that one day she may read
House of Death…

ACKNOWLEDGEMENTS

Special thanks go to fellow Goodreads member Irene Ivy, for reading through my first draft of House of Death without complaint, and whose words of encouragement were invaluable.

A massive thank you to Marc Estes, and Christian Lee at Snow Leopard, for all their words of encouragement over the past few months. My editing team, without whose help and guidance I surely would have given up, and pushed the manuscript back in the draw to gather dust for another year.

Many thanks also to my many Twitter followers for re-tweeting excerpts from the book, and their kind words of encouragement. Of course, there have been times when instead of writing I was off playing on Twitter—but that's another story!

Finally my sister, Claire, for the wonderful cover design. Though I'm still not sure how she managed to get the ghosts into the tree, including the dog at the bottom!

Prologue

 Amelia squatted on the blanket as another contraction washed over her. She bit her lip to stop herself from crying out. And, as the pain subsided, she exhaled. It would soon be over. She hoped. One thing was certain; she was never doing this again. If he wanted more children he could have them—and besides, they had nowhere to live and very little money, and she couldn't see her parents helping them out with anything.
 Her face contorting in pain as another contraction hit her—stronger than before. She began checking the contents of the cardboard box by her side to take her mind off the pain. Inside were a large bowl, several clean towels, baby soap, two new clothes pegs in a sealed pack, antiseptic, and a pair of scissors. Two large thermos flasks of hot water sat on an old coffee table with a small lamp, and the baby's clothes and nappies were in an old suitcase underneath.
 Everything was ready; she even had some painkillers for af-

ter the birth. She'd sneaked them out of her mother's bedroom that morning when she'd left for work, and with luck it would all be over before her mother came home.

Feeding him or her would be the next hurdle to overcome. She couldn't risk taking the baby down to her room, nor could she stay in the attic. She'd think of something. She would cope. Not because she wanted to, but because she had no choice. It was no good feeling sorry for herself; she'd known the risks of indulging in unprotected sex. Antonio too, but because he was older, and as she mistakenly thought, wiser, she had trusted him.

The next contraction caught her unawares; her breath coming in short gasps as the muscles in her stomach contracted. This was a different pain. The final stage of labour. Reaching down between her legs she could feel the baby's head, and with the next contraction she gave one almighty push and baby Daniel took his first breath.

Taking the clothes pegs from their wrapper she placed one as near to the baby's stomach as she could, and the other a few centimetres away. And, calmly taking hold of the scissors, she cut the cord, wrapping the baby in one of the clean towels. Carefully she poured the now lukewarm water into the bowl, and with cotton wool began to clean the mucus from his eyes and nose.

He was perfect. The image of Antonio—with jet black curly hair, and eyes the colour of coal. She placed him in his makeshift crib—a cardboard box lined with a small cushion she'd stolen from the lounge. He didn't make a sound, a good omen, or so she thought. Amelia knew from the books she'd read that the afterbirth was yet to follow, and that she had to inspect it carefully. If just a small piece broke away and lodged inside her she would have to go to the hospital—and hospital would mean telling her parents and then all hell would break loose.

The front door opened and closed quietly. Annie took off her coat and hung it in the cupboard under the stairs. Sebastian had gone too far this time, she was sick of moving house. Tired of his crazy get rich quick schemes. All the money her parents had left her was gone, frittered away by her spendthrift husband. Her employers had called her in to the office that morning and said they'd be sorry to lose her, but wished her well in America. Flustered, she had thanked them and walked away. Sebastian had sent a letter terminating her employment.

They were on the move again but this time she would be leaving him, taking the children, and moving in with Antoine.

Annie made her way wearily upstairs to begin packing. The suitcases were in the attic, but so were the spiders. She hated spiders. Her hand poised on the doorknob, hesitating. Get a grip woman they're harmless, and taking a deep breath she opened the door.

Amelia froze. Someone was coming upstairs. Hurriedly she pushed the box containing her newborn son under the eaves. And scooping up the dirty towels, shoved them inside a black plastic sack, and picked up the brush and started to sweep the floor.

"Amelia. You startled me. Why aren't you at school?"

"We have a study day today; I thought I mentioned it last night, sorry. I was looking through the old photographs over there, I'm doing a project on photography at school and the teacher asked if we could bring in any old black and white photos we had."

So far so good, just a few minutes longer Daniel. She prayed her son would stay quiet until her mother went downstairs but it was not to be. Hungry now, the baby cried out.

"What was that?" Annie said, suspiciously.

"What—I didn't hear anything."

Annie put the suitcases she was carrying back on the floor, tilting her head to where the noise was seemingly coming from. The baby started to cry again. Amelia moved in front of the table.

"It sounded like a baby crying, and furthermore it seemed to be coming from behind you." Eyeing Amelia suspiciously, Annie leaned forward.

"Probably someone in the street below." Said Amelia, crossing her fingers behind her back she stepped forward in a vain attempt to stop her mother investigating further.

"You're hiding something Amelia." The baby started wailing piteously, and this time he didn't stop. Annie pushed her daughter out of the way and knelt by the table. Pulling the box from its hiding place, and taking Daniel in her arms she turned to her daughter. "Yours, I presume?" Amelia nodded tearfully.

"I think you have some explaining to do young lady, don't you? Am I to take it you at least know who the father is?"

"Of course I know who he is. What do you take me for?"

"Do you really want me to answer that question? How could you, Amelia, after everything I told you. I take it 'this', was an accident?"

"Yes, it was an accident. I'm sorry, I know I should have told you before but I was frightened of what you'd say. By the time I realised I was pregnant it was too late to do anything about it. Antonio loves me; he'll take care of us."

Amelia moved to take the baby from her mother but she pushed her away.

"For pity's sake give him to me, he's hungry."

Amelia watched in horror as her mother put the baby back in the box and pushed it under the table. Springing forward to protect her son she collided with her mother, barring her way.

"You bitch; you couldn't stand to see me happy. You just had to spoil it for me didn't you? How could you throw yourself at the only man I have ever loved? Whore. Get packed, take your bastard child and get out of my house. You will never, ever, have Antonio—he's mine, do you hear me, mine!"

"No, it can't be, he loves me, he told me."

Annie said nothing; she simply turned and walked over to the cupboard at the far end of the attic. When she turned back she was holding a gun. Amelia watched in horror as her mother pulled the trigger.

"No, please, my baby needs me..." Catapulted into the table by the force of the blast Amelia collapsed, blood pouring from the wound. I have to stop my mother from hurting Daniel. It was no use; she had lost too much blood. Watching helplessly as her mother stuffed cotton wool into the baby's mouth, and then push the box back under the eaves.

"Now that's taken care of, I'll take these down." She picked up the suitcases again, muttering to herself. 'Inconsiderate bitch, always leaving everything to me, well not any more she won't, good riddance to bad rubbish.'

"Help me, please; you're my mother for god sake."

"You should have thought of that before you slept around. At least this way you won't cross me again bitch. I'll pick a nice spot in the garden for you before I leave, and I'll be sure to tell Antonio you said to say goodbye."

Amelia dragged herself over to the box and lifted the makeshift lid. Her baby was dead. Kissing him tenderly she closed his eyes and pulled out the ball of cotton wool. "Sleep now little one, mummy will be with you soon." Her life force ebbing slowly, and with every passing second she slipped further into the abyss.

"Follow the light, Amelia, for eternal peace awaits you both, come join us. You have a choice, stay and face eternity in limbo or follow the light. Quickly now, before the portal closes… Ameliaaaaaa…"

The white light faded and died, the two now trapped between two worlds. Destined to roam the house for all eternity, for now, only the truth could set them free.

The house is quiet now. It's once pristine exterior, shabby, and dilapidated. Unloved, unwanted, and uncared for, the sale board tattered and askew—the house overshadowed by death and sadness.

Of the hundreds of sale particulars requested in the years that passed not a soul had crossed its threshold. Every year they dropped the price but the fear of the unknown is by far the greatest to overcome. The events of that April night forever etched in the minds of young and old alike. And on the anniversary of their deaths, the house, alive once more, silhouetted in the evening sky. A shrine illuminated by candlelight. The air heavy with perfume from the bouquets of spring flowers from friends and strangers alike. In homage to the family who had perished within its' walls seven years past.

Neighbours lock their doors now well before dark and close their shutters tight to keep out the bogeyman. Tales of haunting cries, the sound of gunshots, and finally the laughter of a madman.

The house had stood by. Watching. Waiting. Silent. As they excavated the graves concealed beneath the terrace, and one by one the bodies removed. A whole family wiped out, the family pets too, but the father was missing. And that made him the prime suspect.

Now the house has a new family, and the battle starts again. There will be no sleep for the dead whilst the guilty roam free.

The fight for justice and deliverance their quest. Only then will the house and its occupants find love and eternal peace.

1

New Beginnings - Charlene

Charlene waited patiently in the Estate Agents office for the Agent to return. A quick appraisal of the office decor told her everything she needed to know. The ultra modern furniture, and abstract art, which hung on its walls, passé. The air of neglect apparent. Had she been hasty in her choice of Agency?

"How much longer are we going to be mum?" Her son had a date.

"I'm sure she'll wait for you."

Jason sat heavily on the chair, his auburn curls swirling angrily. Teenagers. The agent returned smiling.

"Good news. I've spoken to the owners and they're prepared to drop the price for a quick sale." He scribbled a figure on the paper before him and passed it to Charlene.

"Are you sure we're talking about the same house?"

"Of course. Would you like to view?"

"Please, today if it's convenient?"

"Mum. What part of 'I have to be elsewhere' didn't you understand?"

"I'm quite capable of going alone Jason. Off you go, and don't be late. Dinner will be at 7:30 precisely!"

A quick peck on the cheek and he was gone. "Do you have children?" Charlene enquired.

"Yes, twin girls, Mai-Lin and Su-Li." He handed Charlene a photograph from the desk.

"They're adorable. Hard work too I shouldn't wonder. I have three sons and a daughter, the eldest, Matt, has just turned 21, he's away at college. The sulky one is Jason, 13. Carly is almost 16 and Philip was 18 last week."

He shuddered—Charlene Hamilton-Davies bore an uncanny resemblance to the previous occupant of the house and her children were the same ages too. Spooky. Get a grip, it's just a house—and I'm selling it today. Everyone has a doppelganger somewhere, don't they? He straightened his shoulders and smiling he looked up.

"How do you cope with four?"

"They don't normally cause me grief; I think it may be a touch of cabin fever, living cooped up in a hotel can't be much fun for them."

"Do you have transport Madame Amilton-Davies?"

"No, my car is in the repair shop. I stupidly let Philip reverse the car out of the hotel parking lot. The bollard lived to fight another battle—my car wasn't so lucky."

"No problem, we'll take my car."

He grabbed the keys from the desk and a small black screen from the draw and locked the door after them.

"I'm parked around the back. Word of warning—it's a bit of a tip inside, I ought to empty the rubbish out occasionally." Charlene got into the car, carefully avoiding the pile of papers.

"You don't have to apologise, the inside of my car is worse. Four times so, thanks to my kids."

The white Renault Clio of Charles Dupont wove in and out of traffic—like a swan gliding gracefully down the fast flowing river of commuters. Charlene watched the passers by—no one seemed in a hurry, all sauntering merrily along. Their progress halted by the occasional friendly greeting, and polite chit-chat. The obligatory air kisses over, they continued, elegantly meandering through the crowds. Their movements relaxed, positively oozing confidence, finesse. The 'in crowd'. Oh how she wanted to belong in this cosmopolitan city a million miles from the hustle and bustle of her native Atlanta.

Perhaps she ought to invest in one of the little gismos the Agent was using. It, like those around them, seemed to know exactly where it was going.

The car came to a halt in front of a scruffy townhouse and the Agent got out, and with keys in hand he turned to Charlene, hesitating momentarily. Come on Charles, you can do this—'work it, think sale'. Just don't tell her about the five dead bodies they found under the patio.

"A lick of paint and it'll be as good as new."

Yep, and a new door and windows too. Charlene looked at the house and shivered. "Someone just walked over my grave."

The keys slipped from Charles DuPont's grasp and landed on the step. Bending to retrieve them, he pulled out a handkerchief from his trouser pocket, and wiped the beads of perspiration from his brow. He was so close to a sale, one he thought would never happen. After all who would want to live in the 'house of death'?

His wife had begged him not to take the house onto their books. A devout Catholic, she had refused to help with the measurements and photographs. No-one at the agency was prepared to set foot inside, terrified by the ghostly tales. The house, silently biding its time. For hidden somewhere beneath its rugged granite facade lay the truth behind the slaying of Annie Delamare and her children.

Recovering his composure Charles Dupont opened the front door and went inside. The team of cleaners he had employed had eradicated all traces of the house's former macabre history. All that remained was the telltale musty odour of rising damp coming from the cellar below.

He caught hold of the silver cross on the chain around his neck and said a silent prayer. Now he was getting paranoid too. It was an empty house, one of many properties he had for sale, nothing more. Charlene faltered briefly on the threshold, and sensing her reluctance the Agent took charge.

"I'll open the shutters and let some light in. The musty smell will soon go. We normally advise clients to use a dehumidifier but the electricity has been turned off for some time."

True, the electricity was off but neighbours still reported seeing lights burning in the house. The police had roused him from his bed on several occasions. Each time he'd accompanied them to the house, and each time the house was empty. The murderer wouldn't be stupid enough to return to the scene of the crime would he?

"Are they costly to run, the dehumidifiers?"

"Uh, no, they work on the same principle as a refrigerator, and using one would actually save you money. Damp is costly to treat once it takes hold."

Charlene wandered into the kitchen. Sparse was the first word that sprang to mind. Minimalism. Lacking in cupboard space of any kind, other than the sink it was empty. How did people cope? Where did they prepare their meals? Minimalism in Charlene's world meant fitted cupboards, with everything hidden from view. A show kitchen.

"I rather hoped there would be a fitted kitchen."

"Fitted kitchens are rare in rental properties. It does have a dumb waiter."

Charlene suppressed a giggle; hopefully it would soon have a dumb cook too.

"It's a relic from days gone by when the kitchen or scullery would have been in the basement. Every grand house like this had servants. At the very least a cook, a tweenie, and a parlour maid. I bet the house could tell some tales, if only it could speak. Damn right it could. The house has been in the same family for well over a hundred years but the previous owner never married. By all accounts she never got over the death of her fiancé during the Second World War. She'd been in a nursing home for several years before her death and the revenue from the rental paid for her care."

"I'm glad she didn't die in the house. I couldn't live in a house where someone had died. It wouldn't feel right."

Ignoring her comments he followed her into the lounge. Pushing open the double doors to the adjoining dining room, and out onto the patio. The huge garden was now a tangle of brambles and bushes that had run wild over the years, obscuring it completely from the adjoining houses.

Charlene looked at the expanse of wilderness before her. It was rare to find a house of this size on the outskirts of town with a large garden—rarer still its price.

If she could get them to agree to refurbish the kitchen and cut back the garden a little. She could afford to splash out on a garden room. Here on the patio would be the perfect spot.

"How many bedrooms does it have?"

"There are three decent size bedrooms and a bathroom on the first floor. The spacious attic is ripe for conversion into two large en-suite rooms."

"And a downstairs toilet?"

"No, but the cupboard under the stairs would be ideal as it's directly under the bathroom. It does have a large cellar, which would be perfect for a games room." She was wavering. Crossing his fingers behind his back he took a deep breath, one last little effort and it would be a done deal. "Perhaps if I spoke to the family's solicitor he would be able to get them to agree to tidy the garden up. Maybe do something with the kitchen." If it meant the difference between selling and not selling he would pay for it himself out of his commission.

"Can you ring him now?"

"Err; yes of course, I'll get my telephone I left it in the car. I won't be a minute." He opened the door letting it swing to behind him and took out his telephone. Conversations of this type were always productive—the speaking clock never said no! "I will convey the details of the offer to the prospective buyer. Thank you for your time."

He went back inside—his face fixed in what he hoped was a pleasant smile. Dupont was deceiving her in order to secure the sale, but that was between him, and his conscience. Scruples wouldn't pay the bills, and keep the twins in nappies—lying would. "Good news, they agreed, providing you sign the contract immediately and complete the sale by the end of the month."

Charlene took one last look around her. Her gaze resting on the patio. Could they transfer the money that quickly? "In that case consider the house sold. I'll contact the bank tomorrow and have the funds transferred into my account. Will my husband need to sign the papers too?"

"Depends who's paying? It might be advisable for the property to be put into joint ownership, but I'm sure under the circumstances they will accept your husband's proxy for you to act on his behalf." He thrust the contract into her hand. "Just sign and date it at the bottom."

Charlene took a pen from her bag, hesitating for a second. "What's today's date?"

"April 5th."

A gust of wind blew through the open door—the house whispering its secret to anyone who would listen. 'The anniversary of the death of Annie Delamare, her four children and the family pets.' The agent shivered, he hoped the house had released him now, his obligations fulfilled.

"Would you like me to drop you back at your hotel on my way back to my office, Madame Hamilton-Davies?"

"Yes that would be great, thank you. For everything."

As he closed the door and locked it he hoped for her sake she didn't live to regret her decision.

2

The tramp sat down wearily on the steps of the house. Nervously looking about him. A final check assured him the coast was clear, and with that he took the key from his pocket, opened the door, and went inside.

It was risky coming here—but where else was there for him to go. The money in the bank account he'd inherited along with the car was long gone. The house was his safe haven. It would never sell. Who in their right mind would want to live in 'the house of death'? No one, but what if the unthinkable happened? What would he do then?

With candle in hand he opened the door to the cellar and descended into the bowels of the earth. Here he was safe, but winter was just around the corner. He had no money, no home—the newspapers had branded him a fugitive and a monster. In a moment of madness he had lost everything.

Lying down on the old couch in the corner he closed his eyes, pulling the rough woollen blanket around his shoulders. In his dreams he watched as the man loaded the suitcases into the boot of his car, and taking a roll of tape from his pocket he sealed the mail box. There was no forwarding address, only a curt message to return all correspondence to the sender.

The man had been most insistent, and extremely generous. The car had been in good condition, and would have fetched a decent price. Instead he had handed him the keys and told him to drive it away. There was a map inside the glove box and a letter. Instructions, he said, and then the man had walked off into the night.

He'd sat on the bench for hours, watching, but the man did not return. Morning came and went and still he'd sat. Darkness descended and one by one the lights extinguished, and all was silent. It was now or never. Taking the keys from his pocket he had walked to the car, opened the door and sat inside. The memory etched in his subconscious. He'd placed the key in the ignition and turned it clockwise. The engine had sprung into life and he had driven off.

He'd waited several days before opening the glove box and taken out the map and letter. The letter had made him infamous. The events that followed—an accomplice to murder.

Awake now, he sat up. Why had the man chosen him? Had he really killed his family like the papers said? But where was the gun? Surely he would have had a gun—and the blood what had happened to the blood. The house had been clean, the cupboards bare. The family had disappeared leaving behind a mass of unpaid debts.

The owner's representative had re-possessed the house and immediately called the police. Minute traces of human blood found, the dogs bought in and the carnage uncovered.

The kind, generous, man had duped him. He had dangled the bait in front of him and naively he had swallowed it whole. Metaphorically speaking that is, and now they were chasing him.

They were following the trail. His trail. The one he had unwittingly left as he followed the route the nice man had mapped out for him. He'd become a pawn in an intricate game of cat and mouse, and the net was drawing in.

It would be light soon. Time to leave. Making his way up the steps he quietly opened the door. A blood curdling scream stopped him dead—the sound reverberating off the walls. He peered nervously about before stepping into the hallway. As he did so an icy current of air rushed past him—the hairs on the back of his neck rigid. Standing motionless he waited, hardly daring to breathe. He could make a run for the door, if only his legs and brain would obey the command. In all the time he had been coming to the house nothing had ever happened before. So what had changed?

Bang! Thud! Crash! Particles of dust swirling in the air, like a sandstorm in the desert. Unearthly sounds assailed his every sense and still he was incapable of moving. A drowning man in a sea of noise. If he lived through this night he would go to the police and tell them everything.

The minutes passed and the sound of screaming had subsided only to be replaced with that of howling dogs. Covering his ears he shouted. "Please stop, it wasn't me. I'm not the one you should be punishing—I was used too." The noises stopped. The house was quiet. Nothing had been broken. Nothing had moved. There were no dogs. He was alone in the hallway.

He dropped the candle and ran for the door—not stopping to look behind him. Down the steps he ran, and out into the night.

The door to the house swung silently in the breeze for several seconds and then slammed shut.

~

"Jim. Jim, wake up! Did you hear that?"

"What? Go back to sleep woman. One of us has to be at work in the morning." Turning over he pulled the blankets over his head. He'd heard the noise alright, and knew all too well his wife wouldn't let it rest until he'd gone downstairs to investigate. Complaining bitterly he switched on the lamp and looked at the clock. 4.30 In the frigging morning. Reaching for his dressing gown he'd stuck his feet in his slippers, and still cursing his wife, had made his way downstairs.

Halfway down the second flight he stopped. What if there was someone in the house? He was unarmed. Okay, he was built like a brick shithouse, but that wouldn't stop a bullet, would it? He turned to go back upstairs and collided with his wife.

"What the fuck are you doing? I thought I told you to stay put and lock the door. You'll get us both killed!" Somewhere in the house a door opened and the pair froze.

"Mum. Dad. What are you doing on the stairs in the middle of the night? I heard a noise, and now I know what caused it I'm going back to bed. Some of us are trying to sleep around here you know." Jem added indignantly as she stomped across the landing back to her room, slamming the door loudly.

"Well, I guess we don't need to worry about anyone being in the house now. With all the noise she made I daresay any self respecting burglar will be long gone."

Jean turned and headed downstairs and switching on the hall light he pulled a club from his golf bag behind the front door. Just in case. Brandishing the club in the air he went from room to room checking for signs of a break in. Satisfied there was no one in the house he put the club down on the kitchen table and filled the kettle. He may as well have a cup of tea now he was up. His wife followed him into the kitchen, took two mugs off the draining board and dropped a tea bag in each.

"Piece of cake?"

"No thanks. Come and sit down, there's no one in the house. And yes, I checked all the doors and windows. And yes, they're all locked; no one broke in. And before you ask, yes, I heard the bang. It sounded as if it came from next door. In fact it sounded very much like the door slamming shut. And no—I'm not going to be ringing the police, tonight, or any other night. Remember what happened last time we thought we heard noises next door!"

Clara shivered and put her hands around the mug in an effort to stop the shaking. She remembered all too clearly, she still had the nightmares. The whole neighbourhood had been shocked with the grisly discovery of the bodies buried under the patio of the house next door. She hadn't known them well. No one had. The children were always polite, well dressed, and well cared for. The mother worked part time at the local primary school—so the newspapers said, as a lunchtime playground monitor.

Clara had bumped into her once in the local supermarket. She was with her husband. The same man who had apparently cold bloodedly slain his entire family and then buried them under the patio in hessian sacks filled with quick lime. The family's dogs too.

That was the last time she'd spoken to her. It was probably the last time anyone had spoken to her. Clara had seen the Bailiffs knocking at the door on several occasions. Each time they went away empty handed, the shutters remaining firmly closed.

Her daughter, Jem, had been sure she'd seen on her on the Saturday—the day before her death. She'd told the police about it, done her bit. But had she? Had any of them?

Perhaps they should have made more of an effort. Maybe if they had the family might still be alive. As her old dad used to say, 'there's lots of might's in a pound of cheese'. She never did understand what he meant. In fact there were many things in life Clara didn't understand. The episode next door being a prime example.

History, however, has an uncanny knack for repeating itself. What goes around comes around. Another one of her father's old sayings, there was hardly a day went by that she didn't miss her father.

Her mother had fallen apart when he'd died. All that remained of the vibrant woman her mother had once been, lost forever. Leaving behind a forgetful, frail old woman, trapped in a world of her own. Alone with her memories, and the little dog her father had fished out of the river. A few minutes later and it would have been curtains for the bedraggled young pup. As it was it cost them a small fortune in vets fees nursing it back to health.

Clara knew, without Daisy, her mother would have given in long ago. The dog was the only thing keeping her alive, and she had no intention of ending up like her mother.

"Clara, come on now, don't go all maudlin on me. I think the time has come to start thinking about a change of scenery. We could look for that place by the sea we're always talking about. The kids are grown up and Jem is getting married in the summer. What do you say? Shall we go away this weekend to the coast and see what's on offer?"

"Why not, what harm can looking do? Though you know as well as I do we'll not get a fair price for the house because of what happened next door. No one in the street will."

"Talking of the house next door I forgot to tell you. I

saw the Agent selling next door the other day. He was with a woman, and they went inside. Maybe he got lucky. If people move in next door we'll get him to value ours and get it on the market quick."

"Yeah, pigs might fly and the price of bacon will go up. There's about as much chance of someone buying next door as there is of me becoming the next President of France! I'm going back to bed. You coming? Or are you going to sit there drinking tea and telling fairy stories all night?"

He put his arm around Clara's waist. "I really did see the agent. I wasn't making it up honest cross my heart. Come here and give your old man a hug. He loves you, even though you are a grumpy old sod."

Clara flicked him around the ear lightly with the back of her hand. "I know you do, you miserable old fart. Come on back to bed or you'll look like death tomorrow."

"It's tomorrow already, and has been for the last five and a half hours. It's not worth me going back to bed now. I'll go online and book a hotel for the weekend. Maybe e-mail a couple of agencies, get a feel for the market. You go on up, no point in both of us missing out on our beauty sleep."

"Okay, if you're sure. See you at lunch." Clara closed the kitchen door and went upstairs. She peered out of the window at the top of the landing into the garden next door, but she couldn't see anything for the trees. She hoped Jean was right and that they had sold next door. A new start was just what they needed.

3

Charlene thanked the man repeatedly for repairing the car so quickly. Though she had the sneaking suspicion he had ulterior motives, and could practically feel his eyes boring through her clothes. He wasn't exactly unattractive; and she supposed if you stripped back the dirt and grime he would pass muster... In a crowd of a thousand people, and dirty nails was one of her pet hates.

She had a hundred and one things to do today before the appointment to sign the papers for the house. Troy had seen his attorney and signed the proxy and they had faxed it directly to the solicitor. The money was in the bank. The furniture out of storage. Everything was arranged.

The house was theirs, and she was on her way to the showroom to choose her new kitchen. The Agent had given her a voucher for fifteen hundred Euros, anything over that was her problem. That had been the figure agreed by the vendors. The garden was getting its makeover today too. Trees trimmed, grass cut, window boxes planted and fences repainted.

Troy had been his usual condescending self, agreeing to the Garden Room on one condition. His sauna went in the basement. As according to him, it was 'his money' she was frittering away. Cheeky bastard. Who'd done all the negotiating and running about? If there was any money left after she'd decorated and furnished the house, paid the kennel fees, and the kid's school fees she'd look into it. Maybe.

Charlene pulled into the parking lot in front of the kitchen showroom, it was tiny compared to the company they had used in Atlanta.

"Madame Amilton-Davies?"

"Yes, sorry I'm late I had to pick the car up from the repair shop." The salesman looked puzzled.

"The man from the agency said to give you this." She handed over the envelope. The salesman quickly tucked it into the book he was carrying and invited Charlene into the office.

He opened the envelope and peeked inside—a cheque for Fifteen hundred Euros. The man passed it to his secretary who scuttled out of the door, disappearing from view. Time to earn his keep.

"Have you any idea of the type of kitchen you would like madam? Traditional, contemporary, free standing?"

"Not exactly, do you have a catalogue I can look at, or any kitchens on display?"

"Of course, the showroom is downstairs. This way please."

He said, leading her down the corridor to a spiral staircase. Very 'a la mode apparently here in France.' Anyone who was someone had a spiral staircase in the house. Everyone except Charlene. She had been adamant, no spiral staircase. The damn things were dangerous.

"Are you alright madam?"

"Yes. Sorry, I don't like spiral staircases." Grasping hold of the banister as if her life depended on it, Charlene made her way downstairs, and began wandering aimlessly through the kitchens on display. She was about to give up when she spied a brochure, open on the desk.

"That's the kitchen I want!"

The salesman picked up the brochure and smiled, it was the most expensive in the showroom. Her fifteen hundred wouldn't go far at all.

"Madam has good taste. It's our 'executive model'."

Charlene winced. Their most expensive too no doubt. Oh well, easy come, easy go. Troy's sauna would definitely have to wait until after Christmas now. The kitchen was essential, unless they were going to eat at McDonalds every day for the rest of their lives.

"Monsieur Dupont emailed a photograph of the kitchen, and the dimensions of the room. I took the liberty of preparing several designs for your perusal." Opening his laptop he tapped in the design number and the kitchen appeared in 3D. "This design is very popular, and the central island will give you an extra four square metres of work area and cupboard space."

Charlene dreaded to think how much it would cost per square metre. "And the cost would be …?"

The salesman tapped in another code and the price appeared on the screen.

"Is that with or without appliances?"

"With, of course."

"It's a tad on the high side can you deduct the price of the appliances? I have everything from my old kitchen in storage."

He smiled weakly and tapped in a second set of numbers.

"That's the best I can do."

Charlene looked at the screen. Troy would go spare, if he ever found out that is. After all she still had her inheritance. What the hell, it was only money. Her money! "How soon can you fit it?"

Taken by surprise he reached for his diary, flicking quickly through the pages of the book in front of him. He had been sure the American lady would ask for time to think.
"How about the 15th of this month?" He'd omitted to add that another client had ordered the kitchen, and paid the deposit. Unfortunately his final cheque had bounced and the sale annulled—his loss was the American's gain.

"That should be fine; it will give us chance to repaint the kitchen. Do you have a sample I can give to the interior designer?" Charlene asked nonchalantly.

"Of course, I'll give you one of the doors. Take care not to lose it or we'll have to re-order and that could lead to a delay in fitting the kitchen."

"I'll guard it with my life." Charlene looked at her watch.

"Oh my, just look at the time, I take it you will bill me for the outstanding balance after the kitchen is in situ?"

"Of course, madam. If you have any queries between now and the 15th please don't hesitate to call." Handing her a business card he let her out of the side door, thus avoiding the staircase from hell.

Thank goodness the staircase in the house was normal. It was a rich, dark oak, with ornately carved newel posts and barley twist risers. A quick rub down with white spirit and a coat of yacht varnish and it would be as good as new.

Charlene unlocked the car and drove back to the hotel. She'd promised Jason she'd drive him into town and she was late. He wouldn't be best pleased, mind these days nothing pleased him. In fact all the kids were getting stroppy. A fact she put down to living in a hotel for the past few months.

They were missing Troy. Hell even she was missing him. There was apparently, a first time for everything. They missed the dogs too, only another couple of weeks of quarantine and they would all be re-united in their new home.

That was another thing to add to her list of 'things to do'. Get a man in to build a dog run and shelter at the bottom of the garden. As much as she loved Luna and Juno she didn't consider their fur as part of her daily diet. They'd be happier outside anyway.

She pulled up in front of the hotel. Jason didn't look at all happy. He flung open the car door, threw his bag into the back seat, and slammed the door.

"You're late!"

"Yes, sorry. Sorting the kitchen took longer than I anticipated."

"Humph. Well now you are here do you think we can get a move on or we'll miss the beginning of the film?"

"Excuse me. I think an apology is in order young man. I have a hundred and one things to do today and playing taxi for you isn't even on the bottom of the list. Don't make any arrangements for the rest of the week because I expect every member of this family to help with the decorating. Understood?"

"Aw, mum, do we have too?"

"Yes, 'we do' if 'we' expect to have the house ready for the kitchen fitters, and of course we have to fetch Luna and Juno in two weeks time."

"Okay, okay, don't blow your stack, I'll do my bit. I really miss Luna and Juno. Do you think they miss us too?"

"I'm sure they do. Go on, Chloe's waiting, do you need any money?"

"No mum, dad paid my allowance into my account last week. I won't be late I promise. Chloe's dad promised to drop me back at the hotel later."

"Have fun. I'll be at the house until late; make sure you have something to eat."

"Yeah, yeah, whatever."

What a stupid thing to say to a thirteen year old boy. All he did besides whinge was eat. Troy called him their human waste disposal unit. He didn't eat food—he inhaled it!

Charlene glanced down at her shopping list, mostly cleaning products, and paint. She very much doubted if she would be able to pick up all the stuff in one shop. France had been a culture shock as regards shopping. It was unheard of for the supermarkets in Atlanta to close at all. Here they closed for lunch—for the best part of two hours. And Sunday you might as well stay in bed for the entire day because nothing opened except the bakers. It was like a time warp – transported back into the 1950's in the blink of an eye.

But time warp or not, it was home. A safe haven where nothing bad happened…Reassuring almost. A place where your kids could go out alone and you wouldn't have to worry about drive by shootings and drugs. She hoped.

Charlene pulled into the supermarket car park. They would open in 10 minutes and not a moment before. She turned on the radio and immediately turned it off again. There was no point pretending, she could understand what they were saying. As soon as the house was up and running she'd be taking French lessons. She had managed okay so far, with a little help from the children.

Thank goodness Troy had insisted they all had private lessons—she hated to admit it, but he'd been right this time. Though to hear him talk he was always right, and even when he wasn't he wouldn't own up to it—'the Gospel according to St Troy.'

It would piss him off 'big time' if he knew what she really thought about him. Twenty five years of being married to a man who thought he was perfect. If he only knew the half of it—Meg Ryan had nothing on her.

4

The doors to the supermarket slid silently open. Charlene wandered amongst the aisles in a daze. They sold paint. But, according to the English man who'd chatted on incessantly about Dulux, and sheep dogs. It was crap.

His advice was to go to the local DIY store, and even then not to buy the shop's own brand. As he'd made that mistake once, and had to drive all the way back and change it for some decent paint an hour later. 'Wouldn't stay on the walls' he said, 'and although the colour was supposed to be Cappuccino he was sure it shouldn't have been frothy.'

He went on, and on, until Charlene thought her head would explode. Until she was rescued by a sour faced woman who'd accused her of stealing her husband. Charlene laughed so hard she'd almost wet herself. He was fat, bald, and ugly. And as she'd told the woman, she already had one like him at home. Therefore why would she need another sorry specimen, incapable of getting it up and making out it was all her fault.

The last remark must have hit a raw nerve because the woman grabbed the man firmly by the arm and dragged him bodily to the checkout. She'd almost felt sorry for him. After all he'd only tried to help. That'd teach him.

At least he hadn't hit on her with a corny phrase. The previous one had asked for her autograph. Made out he'd thought she was Meg Ryan.

Sashaying through the aisles, scooping up dusters and cleaning products as she went. Pausing briefly at the deli counter to pick up a chicken sandwich, an obscenely large squashy cream bun with fresh strawberries, and a bottle of sparkling mineral water. She'd missed lunch playing taxi for Jason.

Passing through to the checkout she paused to grab a bottle of Champagne. As she was frittering Troy's money away again today, it was only right he should pay for the Baptism too. Shame he wouldn't be there to help her drink it. Though come Christmas he would be in her face and on her case daily.

The past six months without him had been liberating. She was afraid that after her taste of freedom she would rebel; and that wouldn't bode well for her, or the children. Funny, when they'd first started dating he'd seemed so normal. And then he'd 'found God' and banned everything he considered ungodly. Pity he hadn't included sex! She would have willingly accepted a ban on that. She hadn't missed the groping at all. Procreation was off her 'rainy day list.' That she'd left back in the hospital when they'd given back her freedom of choice.

No more babies. Doctor's orders. For the next baby, could, and probably would, be the death of her. That was good enough for her. She'd signed the consent form against Troy's wishes—and right after Jason had made his way into the world, her womb had exited via the same route.

Troy never forgave her for that. To her it had been a clear cut decision, and she'd chosen life. She already had four healthy children and they needed their mother more than they needed another sibling. And if Troy didn't like it tough.

If only she'd listened to her mother and married for love. Instead of the first person who'd asked because she was frightened of being 'left on the shelf.' Right now the shelf was looking very attractive, even if it was twenty five years too late.

Charlene made her way through the checkout, taking great

pleasure in using Troy's credit card. She checked her watch. The paint store would have to wait; she was due at the solicitors in half an hour. Lunch first; she wouldn't enjoy spending Troy's money half as much on an empty stomach.

Some things in life were sacred. Her mother in law being a prime example. If she'd lived in India they'd have been obliged to have her stuffed, mounted, and put on the mantelpiece when she'd died. Or was that cows? Either way as far as she was concerned it was good riddance.

She'd never go to heaven, not that she cared. One bible basher in the family was more than enough. She finished her sandwich and took a bite out of the cream bun. Why did the cream always shoot out from the side? It appeared to be irrelevant which side of the bun you bit into first. She knew about these things, she'd done the tests. She always ended with cream on her top, and today was no exception.

Damn, now she'd have to make a detour past the hotel and change. She was going to be late—again. Ten minutes later she was sat in the waiting room of the solicitor's office. Like Charlene, he too was running late. Though she hoped he wouldn't be too long or the removal men would have dumped her stuff on the doorstep. As it was she would be cutting it fine.

The door to the office opened and Charlene's mouth dropped open. George Clooney? No it couldn't be—could it?

"Mrs Hamilton-Davies?"

"Yes, and you must be…George Clooney?" Damn, now he'd think she was just another dumb blonde.

"Err no, sorry though I have been told several times recently that I bear an uncanny resemblance to him from a certain angle. Come in please and take a seat, I have the papers ready for your signature. Forgive me for asking, but are you and your husband separated?"

She wished. She'd quite happily part exchange Troy for him. For him she wouldn't need to fake it. Her colour rising, as her brain galloped away with the image of him lying stark naked across her bed.

"Mmm, sorry yes, I mean no, its' only temporary I'm afraid." He smiled playfully. He was hitting on her. "Shame. If you'd like to check through the documents to make sure everything is in order and then sign them where indicated in pencil." Walking around the desk he leaned over, so close she could smell his cologne. "Here, here, and one final one here."

His hand brushed hers' as he collected the documents. The charge was electric. She pulled her hand away quickly. Please, if there is a God, let him ask me out. One measly little 'close encounter of the sexual kind', after all, I've done my penance—I married it.

"All done, congratulations. I hope you won't think me forward but… If I were to ask you out? Dinner one night maybe, would you come?"

Oh God, yes, and how. More visions of him naked. Now what did she do? The right thing—and decline? Or what her groin was telling her and accept joyfully. Flinging herself on top of him, pinning him down on the desk, and having her wicked way with him right here and now. Get a hold of yourself woman. What about your husband? Who gives a flying fuck about their husband when there's an offer like this on the table? He's not coming, but I'm sure I will be, and soon, and how.

"Charlene, I hope you don't mind me using your Christian name."

"Mmm…No, not at all, and yes, I'd love to have dinner with you." Followed by pure, unadulterated, sex. There, she'd done it— she'd said yes. Though it was a good job he couldn't read her mind. Or maybe he could? Maybe that was why he'd asked her out?

"Good, that's settled then. I have your mobile number, I'll give you call later in the week. Give you time to get settled in your new home."

Home. She looked at her watch. She was going to be late. Again. "I'll look forward to it, but now I'm afraid I really must dash or the removal men will leave all my worldly goods on my doorstep!"

"Nice meeting you, take care."

"You too. Bye." She shot out of the door and ran down the steps to the car. Giddy with excitement. Charlene Hamilton-Davies, if you fell in a heap of manure today you'd probably come out smelling of roses.

5

Charlene sped across town. The smile she had worn when leaving 'George Clooney's' office still firmly in place. Stupid bitch. She muttered to herself under her breath. So caught up in the fantasy she'd forgotten to ask his name. A clear cut case of sex engaged before brain. Now what did she do? Ring his office and ask his secretary? Yeah, right, like she wasn't going to look like a moron by doing that. She could of course ask the agent. Thingy, the man who'd sold her the house. She was hopeless—she hadn't asked his name either.

~

"Marcie, did Mrs. Hamilton-Davies take the keys to the house when she left?"

"No sir, I ran after her but she'd already driven off. I daresay she'll be back soon. After all she won't get very far without them will she?"

"No, I suppose not. Do I have any more appointments this afternoon?" Marcie took out the diary from her desk drawer.

"No sir, Mrs. Hamilton-Davies was the only appointment this afternoon. You have a squash court booked for 4:30

though."

"Good, well in that case I'd better ring the lady in question and drop the keys in on my way to the club. I'll see you tomorrow, don't stay too late."

"No sir, I won't. Goodnight."

"Goodnight, Marcie." Bounding down the stairs two at a time—he'd deliberately held the keys back. The one's now jingling happily in his trouser pocket as he jumped into the car. He'd seen the way she looked at him, and experience told him there was only one way to scratch that itch.

He hit the speed dial on his mobile. "Charlene—Antoine Monroe, from the solicitors. You left something important behind on my desk. My secretary ran after you but you were nowhere to be found."

"The keys! Thank goodness, I thought I'd lost them. Luckily for me the agent must have forgotten to lock the door after the viewing. The removal men had already starting taking stuff in when I got here."

"That's not like Charles Dupont, he's normally very conscientious. But there's no need for you to drive all the way back. I have an appointment over the other side of town shortly; I'll drop them in as I pass."

"Oh thank you so much—so many things to do, and so little time in the day to achieve them. You can help with the baptism while you're here. I have a bottle of champagne cooling in the freezer and it seems a pity to waste it on the removal men." If she'd misread the signs she would know soon enough. Antoine. Mmm… very sexy! Running quickly up the stairs to the bedroom she had earmarked as hers, she rummaged through the boxes littering the floor.

Voila! Black or red? Basque or bra? She held the flimsy lace creations in the air, undecided. Thong or bikini?

"Corr blimey, you'll give your old man an 'eart' attack if you wear those. Personally I prefer the black basque, and definitely the thong. Though I can't imagine they make one big enough to cover my wife's arse!"

Charlene dropped them onto the bed, covering them quickly with the bedspread. "Was there anything else?"

"Err no, sorry, missus, only you did ask."

Charlene's face turned bright scarlet. She'd said it aloud.

The shame of it. She could hear the man and his colleague tittering downstairs. Great, she might as well take out a four page ad in the local newspaper while she was at it. Mind, he was right. It simply had to be the black.

Charlene quickly brushed her teeth, and took one last look at the mirror before putting on her skirt and top.

The men had finishing emptying the lorry and were waiting for her in the kitchen. Taking out her purse she reluctantly pulled out a couple of notes. Charlene felt they'd had enough extra's today already. They'd be dining out on this story for weeks as it was.

"Thanks missus. Don't do anything we wouldn't do."

The jovial man replied as he opened the front door

"Evening, sir, supper's warming!" Puzzled, Antoine knocked on the front door and went inside.

"Have they been at the alcohol?"

"Not as far as I'm aware, why?"

"Oh, nothing. Here are your keys, Charlene."

"Thank you so much, Antoine. I do hope you have time to join me in a glass of champagne now you're here. It's an old American custom, from way back." He smiled knowingly, taking the glass from her hand.

"Is the tour included or will I have to come back later?"

"Not at all, where would you like to start?"

"How about we start upstairs and work our way down to the basement?"

"I'll lead the way." Taking him by the hand she led him upstairs. Opening the door to the bedroom she hesitated. "I was a faithful wife, for what it's worth."

Antoine took her glass and set it down on the night stand, and taking her in his arms he kissed her tenderly. His hands caressed the small of her back, pulling her closer still.

Feeling him harden, she undid his trousers and they tumbled to the floor. Her tongue darting lightly across his lips, she reached down releasing his manhood from the confines of his shorts.

Charlene lay down pulling him on top of her. The vision she'd had in his office of him naked on her bed came to mind—she blushed. Had he read her mind?

She neither knew, nor cared. Lost in a moment of lust and

rampant passion. Her basque and thong discarded along with the rest of their clothing in an ungainly heap on the floor.

Covering her with kisses, his tongue strayed below. Charlene screamed out in pleasure. As his tongue flicked across the tight bud buried deep within the forest, now swollen with desire. Shuddering, as the blood coursed hotly through her veins.

Time as they knew it had ceased to exist, and when he could hold out no longer he entered her. Two became one, their bodies entwined, their movements' synchronised, sexual athletes running the ultimate race, teetering on the brink of ecstasy. His body tensed, his essence shooting deep within her, touching her very soul. Seeking out her inner core.

Tears of joy ran hotly down her face. They didn't speak, for words were unnecessary. In the twenty five years she had been married to Troy, sex, had never been like this. She had given herself to Antoine willingly and he in turn had reached deep down inside her and stolen her heart. Her soul.

Were all Frenchman schooled as thoroughly in the art of seduction? She wondered dreamily.

6

Charlene woke with a start. She was sure she heard someone moving around in the house. Sitting up she grabbed her clothes from the heap on the floor and went to the bathroom to dress. Antoine was sleeping peacefully, a satisfied smile on his face. With good reason, he had surpassed her wildest fantasies, and she knew without doubt he would be back for more.

The strange thing was she felt no remorse at having broken her marriage vows this time. All thoughts of Troy obliterated in an instant.

There it was again. Footsteps on the stairs. The third tread from the bottom creaked when you stepped in the middle. The footsteps continued, stopping at the door to the attic. Charlene froze. The door to the attic creaked open and then slammed shut. Footfalls above, light, like a child bouncing a ball across the floor. The tinkling of glass. A broken window maybe? The slapping of an arm or leg— punishment for their misdemeanour? The sad lament of a child crying softly. Heavier footsteps now, coming down the stairs, hesitating halfway, and the slamming of a door.

Exhaling sharply, as beads of perspiration trickled down her neck. The temperature in the room dropped, and Charlene's teeth chattered noisily, but still she could not move. She closed her eyes. 'Antoine.' She wanted to feel his arms around her now, protecting, soothing, comforting. The door to the bathroom slowly opened and Charlene screamed.

"Sorry, did I scare you? I thought you'd gone up to the attic. I heard footsteps so I dressed and came to find you. Are you okay? Only you look as if you're about to...."

Antoine gathered her into his arms as she crumpled to the floor. He carried her back to the bedroom and laid her on the bed. Merde! What did one do for fainting? Smelling salts, a cold flannel, slap one gently around the face. What? He searched through the bottles on the nightstand. Nothing. He sat on the floor by the side of the bed. Should he try to rouse her? Or leave her be? He could phone Marcie, she would know what to do.

Pulling his mobile from his pocket he dialled the office. The phone rang out. Damn, Marcie would be at home and he didn't have her home number in his phone.

Charlene stirred; her eyes fluttered wide open staring at the door. "Charlene, what happened in the bathroom? Are you alright? Do you want me to call a doctor?"

"Did you hear it? Tell me you heard it all—that I'm not going insane, please, Antoine."

"It's all right; of course you're not insane. I heard something but I thought I was dreaming. I turned over and you were gone. That's when I came to find you. These old houses creak and groan sometimes, and they're draughty. It's easy to let your imagination run away with you. Moving house is a stressful experience. Anyway it's too dark to go up into the attic now. You have no electricity until tomorrow."

"Yes I do, how do you think I chilled the champagne?"

"But that's not possible. Marcie arranged for the power and the water to be connected tomorrow morning. They've been off for years, probably soon after the house was put up for sale."

Antoine was sure Charles Dupont hadn't told her of the house's macabre history or she would never have bought it.

Studying her face in the half light—she reminded him of Annie. Reaching over she flicked on the light. Nothing. Replacing the bulb she tried again.

"Perhaps there's a fault with the wiring? Or maybe a fuse has blown?"

"Well if it's a fuse it will definitely have to wait till tomorrow. The fuse box is in the basement. Do you have a torch?"

"Somewhere in one of the boxes, but which one I haven't the foggiest."

"Well that's that then, it will keep until tomorrow. I'll ask an electrician friend of mine to pop round and check it out for you tomorrow. It might be advisable to have the whole place rewired, better safe than sorry. Life is precious, and you have four other lives dependant on you. Charlene, this afternoon—it wasn't a one off was it? I thought maybe we could get together occasionally. Perhaps spend a weekend together, just the two of us. What do you say?"

"I say, I'd like that very much. But we'll have to be careful, especially around the children. And before you ask, I don't love Troy. I haven't for a long while. I guess after twenty odd years of marriage things go stale. He found religion, and I found I didn't know him any more, let alone love him. You know what they say—marry in haste, repent at leisure. We've had separate rooms since Jason was born. You see I went against his wishes. The doctors said it would be dangerous for me to have another child. I signed the consent form for them to remove my womb and he never forgave me. They gave me back my freedom of choice, and he withdrew his love and everything that went with it. My loss was God's gain. He joined the hallelujah brigade—some Christian brotherhood sect. I don't know much about it, he goes off with them for weeks at a time. The kids make fun of him behind his back; and my mother thinks I should divorce him and find myself a nice man."

"So you think your mother would approve of me then?"

"Oh, God, yes."

They walked downstairs hand in hand, and pausing at the bottom they embraced. Charlene opened the door for Antoine and two strange faces stared back at her.

"Hello. Sorry we heard noises and thought we'd better investigate. Has the house had been sold?"

"Yes, and Mrs. Hamilton-Davies is the new owner." Stepping forward Charlene held out her hand.

"Charlene, please, Mrs. Hamilton-Davies sounds so formal. This is Antoine Monroe, my legal advisor."

"Clara and Jean Le Goffre. Welcome to the neighbourhood, we live next door."

Antoine headed down the steps to his car pausing for a second.

"I'll talk to the electrician first thing in the morning Mrs Hamilton-Davies, I'm sure it's nothing to worry about."

"Thank you, for everything."

Antoine waved goodbye; he would call her later to make sure she was okay. He started the engine, and drove away.

Charlene turned to her neighbours. "I do hope you don't think me rude, but it's been a long day and my children will be wondering where I am. We'll be here early in the morning. Pop round and have a coffee, Clara, and I'll give you the guided tour and you can give me the lowdown on the area."

"Of course, please excuse us, we didn't mean to intrude."

"No need to apologise, you weren't intruding, as I said it's been a very long day and what I need right now is a bath and a large glass of chardonnay, so if you'll excuse me I'll say goodnight—until tomorrow, Clara."

"I'll look forward to it."

Fate had a strange way of intervening. Clara recognised Antoine; she'd seen him in church on the day of Annie's funeral. A friend of hers he'd said. But Clara knew different, Jem had told her everything.

Annie hadn't told a soul she was on the verge of leaving her husband. That she was in love with Antoine Monroe, her late father's solicitor. Her children were happy with the arrangement, they hated the way their father forced his beliefs on them. A religious fanatic who described himself as a disciple of god. An android devoid of emotion. His wife and children, possessions, to use as he saw fit.

Annie and Antoine had been together on the evening of the 4th of April. Neither knowing it would be the last time. He'd waited for her around the corner as usual, and they hadn't noticed Jem pass by. That night fate had dealt them a vicious blow.

Antoine drove his Volvo into the garage, the electronically controlled doors closing with a swish as he climbed out of the car. Unlocking the connecting door he dropped his keys on the hall table as he passed through. And taking a bottle of red wine from the rack in the lounge he opened it. He picked up a glass from the shelf behind the bar and poured himself a drink, and then sat in the easy chair, in quiet contemplation of what might have been.

Their last evening together Annie had been distracted, hostile even, not like his Annie at all. He'd put her frigidity down to her husband's latest craziness. According to him the family were leaving France and going to live in America to start a new job- working for the CIA no less. He remembered telling Annie 'the man was mental if he expected people to believe that tale. What would the CIA want with a fifty year old bible bashing no hoper?' Sebastian had lied, again. Annie and her children had died, and life as Antoine knew it had changed forever.

Now history was repeating itself and he couldn't let that happen. This time he would intervene. He wouldn't stand by and let Charlene meet with the same fate.

This time he would fight back.

7

Jean and Clara waved goodbye to their neighbour.

"Would you like to explain what was going on back there old girl? You looked as though you'd seen a ghost."

"The man who was with her, he's been in the house before. With Annie. They were lovers."

"Have you been on the cooking sherry again? He said he was her legal advisor."

"No he didn't, she did. What legal advisor do you know makes house calls at this time of night? And he was improperly dressed."

"What exactly is that supposed to imply. That they were shagging all afternoon?"

"Do you have to be so uncouth? I saw him arrive. The removal men were just leaving so that would make it around 4.30. He had his tie on and his shirt was buttoned up correctly then. There can't be a mirror in the bedroom or he would have noticed one side of his collar was lower than the other."

"Bloody hell woman. Do you notice everything?"

"Only the important things. You forget I worked in continuity; it was my job to notice little things like that. People watching television notice if an actress was dressed in a blue spotted top in one scene and a plain blue one minutes later. When filming finished the top would be washed, dried, and ironed ready for the following day. An episode you see on your screens takes a week maybe longer to produce. But time on-screen remains the same; therefore the clothes would have to be the same. Observations, expressions, clothing, everything was meticulously noted and referred back to."

"Yeah, but that was a lifetime ago."

"Old habits are hard to break, Jean. Okay, so I'm a freak who notices lipstick smudges, loose threads, and wrongly buttoned clothing. If I'd have been more attentive back then maybe Annie Delamare and her children would be alive now."

"It wasn't your fault, Clara; no one could have foreseen what her husband would do. He was devious; you read the newspapers. He joined a gun club to learn how to shoot. It's compulsory to have a permit to buy a gun, and in order to get the permit you have to take an examination.   He told them he was interested in clay pigeon shooting. Hell, he could hardly tell them the truth could he. 'Yeah, I'm interested in guns. I'm thinking of buying one to massacre my wife and kids, and save on the child support.' They would have locked him up and thrown away the key."

Clara knew he was right, but something niggled away at the back of her mind. She had seen Sebastian in a cafe over the other side of town with a woman with long blonde hair a few days before he'd disappeared. They had been deep in discussion, and Clara was sure the woman had been crying. Sebastian had grabbed her roughly by the arm and they'd left together. Crossing the road to withdraw money from the hole in the wall. The woman had handed Sebastian the money and disappeared into the crowd. Sebastian had tucked the money in an inside pocket, looking up as he did so, as if he realised he was being watched. The expression on his face said it all. The man was evil—the Devil personified.

The newspapers said he had borrowed money from a friend, a blonde. And she had vanished too....Had the same fate befallen the blonde she'd seen him with that day? Would she be found buried in a shallow grave somewhere nearby? Or had she run away with him, afraid to say no for fear of becoming another victim. Where had he gone? Had he escaped the country—driven across the border and on until he reached Russia and from there crossed the Caucasus Mountains into Asia?

Would anyone there know of the atrocities this evil man had performed? And if they did would they care? Who would notice one more religious fanatic in a country filled with them?

She already knew the answer to her question. No one would care. Why should they? It hadn't happened to them, what did it matter to them if five more infidels died? 'Life sucks, and then you die.' One of her son's favourite expressions. She supposed one he'd picked up off American television.

Jean passed his hand in front of her face making her jump. "You okay old girl? You were miles away, one minute we were discussing our neighbour's lover, and the next silence."

"I'm fine; something you said triggered a memory from before the murders. I mentioned it to the police when they asked for information and nothing came of it."

"Well there you are then it couldn't have been that important or they would have come back to you. How about we have an early night? Open a bottle of bubbly and put old Frankie on for ambience and make out like we used to BC."

"BC, what are you on about Jean?"

"Before children came along and scuppered the romantic interludes. Take us back to the old days, with Frankie crooning in the background."

"I hate to burst your romantic bubble but I don't remember any of this."

"Are you sure?"

"Uh huh, I'm sure. But thanks for trying to take my mind off next door. You get the bottle; I'll get the glasses and nibbles. Let's live dangerously. Who gives a damn if we get crumbs in the bed? It's our bed, our safe haven, where nothing bad can happen."

~

Charlene parked in front of the hotel—that way she could

see the car from her window. She opened her purse and reached inside—lovingly caressing the cold metal object. She'd never had the misfortune to have to use it, and she wasn't sure if she even remembered how. The presence of the object, reassuring—like a life insurance policy.

Opening the mini bar, she took out some ice. Dropping a handful of ice into the glass she poured herself a shot from the bottle of malt she'd bought last week. Try as she might she couldn't forget the episode in the bathroom. Who, or what, had made the noise. Was it like Antoine had said that it was just stress, with the move and everything? Her mobile vibrated, and reaching across the bed she picked it up. A text from Troy. Laughing as she read it aloud. 'Don't drink alcohol.'

"Why? I didn't join your band of no hopers, and I'll do whatever I want, how I want, when I want. So there." She exclaimed loudly as she read on.

'Remember to hear the children's prayers, and don't forget their bible studies, and be sure to enrol them in the local church choir.' "Who does he think he is?" She exclaimed, and pouring herself another shot of whisky she sat down to compose her reply, and was halfway through when the telephone rang.

"Charlene? It's Antoine. I hope you don't mind me ringing this late, but I wanted to make sure you got home okay. I tried your mobile but I was redirected to your answering service and I didn't want to leave a message in case one of the children picked it up. Did your neighbours keep you long after I left?"

"No I left a few minutes after you. I was just replying to a text from 'he who must be obeyed'. The man's insane, he wants me to enrol our children into the local church choir and make sure they don't shirk their bible studies. He'll be lucky. I sent all the bibles in the house to the local charity shop before I left Atlanta. All twenty six of them."

"What will you tell him when he asks where they are?"

"That they got lost in transit."

"I suppose it would be un-Christian of me to hope he got lost in transit too?" Antoine said quietly.

"Why, I wish that and more on him on a daily basis. My latest fantasy is that he is eaten by a wolf when he's out in the wilderness with his loony friends. I have others would you care to hear them sometime? Matthew reckons I would make great mystery writer. A kind of Miss Marple meets Stephen King. What are you doing this evening?"

"Listening to music and talking to you."

"And what would you like to be doing?"

"Devouring you, not unlike earlier this evening, but next time I'll be better."

"Impossible, you were almost perfect."

"Oh, so what would I need to improve in order to qualify as perfect?"

"Ah, now that would be telling. It's for me to know, and for you to find out."

"Bitch! When can I see you again? Soon I hope, just talking to you has me horny as hell. The beast is stood to attention waiting orders."

Charlene giggled at the thought of his dick clothed in a tin hat and fatigues. Damn him, now she was aroused too. She looked at her watch if she went in and said goodnight to the children now, maybe.

"Are you still there?"

"Yes, I was just thinking."

"Ah, I thought it was a couple of kids playing football outside with a tin can I could hear. What were you thinking?"

"That it would be decidedly wicked if you visited me here in the hotel tonight. We would have to keep the noise down though. I wouldn't want the children coming in to investigate what their mother was up to. Do you think it's feasible?"

"I'm picking my keys up as we speak, what's your room number?"

"25, it's on the ground floor, and my car is parked directly in front of my window."

"Okay I'll be there in about 20 minutes' tops. Have supper warming, chérie."

"The ovens on and almost up to temperature."

Antoine groaned loudly. "Do you know how hard it is to walk with a hard-on—never mind concentrate on the road ahead?"

"Nope, never had that problem. Stop talking; just get in the car and drive. The sooner you get here, the sooner we can deal with it."

She put the phone down, quickly looking at her watch—

she would just have time for a shower and say goodnight to the kids before Antoine arrived.

She knocked on the door and went inside. Carly was in the shower, and Jason was sprawled across her bed eating a hamburger and fries whilst texting.

"Yo, mom! How'd the move go?"

"Fine, I just popped in to make sure everyone was present and correct. Is Philip in his room?"

"Nah, he's out with some French bird. Celine, I think he said was tonight's offering. He said to tell you not to wait up. Carly say's I can sleep in the spare bed in here tonight if I want, providing of course I don't snore."

"Okay, don't stay up too late I'm going to turn in, it's been a long day. Don't forget we have painting duty tomorrow, and that is all of us, including Philip so if you could just text him and remind him that his presence will be required at 8.30 sharp in the dining room and to wear his old clothes." She kissed Jason goodnight and knocked on the bathroom door opening it slightly. "Night sweetheart, don't forget scruffy gear tomorrow."

"Okay mum, night. Mum—can I choose the colour for my room. I promise to keep within the realms of normal."

"I don't see why not, after all you have to live with it. What the hell, you can all choose your own colours. Just don't make me live to regret my decision is all I ask."

"We won't, promise. Night, mum, you're a one in a million."

"Yes, I know, and roughly translated that means there's a sucker born every minute. Goodnight kids."

Cool, mum had chilled out from earlier in the day and Jason intended she stayed that way. And if that meant painting tomorrow so be it.

8

Charles Dupont celebrated his latest sale. Alone. The bitch had refused to join him, implying what he'd done was immoral. Well to hell with her, he didn't give a shit. The house of death was history—sold to the American lady. Another satisfied client.

Swaying slightly, Charles jabbed his key at the lock several times, each time missing its target. He toppled forward, colliding with the door. The house had been waiting patiently for him, and now he'd arrived—the door swung silently open and he fell inside. Searching for the light switch he tripped over a box in the middle of the hallway. Thud! He landed heavily, the box now crushed beneath him. He would have words with the bitch in the morning.

The front door slammed shut behind him. Trapped. Charles watched in horror as the dog moved stealthily into the hallway towards him. A dog. But they didn't have a dog, unless of course his wife had disobeyed him again. He'd teach her a lesson she would never forget. Disobedience would not be tolerated in his house.

Dupont shook his head, in an attempt to clear the alcohol induced fog. He knew he really should have refused that last drink—because now he was seeing double. Two ferocious, big, black dogs, growling menacingly. He shuffled backwards slowly. Merde. He was in the wrong house.

Terror now forcing him into instant sobriety. Rabid dogs. He scanned the semi-darkness for a weapon to defend himself, the door to his left creaking, as it swung slowly open. If he could make it to the door and close it again quickly he would be safe. He could explain everything to the owners of the house in the morning. He hoped.

Glancing nervously at the dogs crouching before him, and, sensing their imminent attack he bolted for the door. Realising too late, that this particular door opened onto the stairway to the cellar below. Tumbling awkwardly, he hit his head on the corner of the wall, as blood trickling from the wound formed a puddle around his head. And his last thoughts as he slipped into unconsciousness were those of regret.

The outer door swung silently shut and the house was once more silent. Justice had been served. For now.

~

Jolted awake by the banging of the door, Clara looked across at the clock. It was after midnight. Perhaps Mrs Hamilton-Davies had changed her mind and decided to spend the night in the house. Climbing out of bed she peered through the window.

There was a car parked in front of the house next door. Charles Dupont's car. What was the estate agent doing here in the middle of the night? He was a married man. Just what was the American woman up to? Lowering the tone of the neighbourhood like this. She would have a few harsh words to say to Mrs Hamilton-Davies when she saw her tomorrow.

Climbing back into bed she switched on the bedside lamp, and picked up her book, but try as she might she couldn't settle. She had a strong sense of foreboding—déjà vu… Or ghosts. She wasn't sure if she believed in life after death, or ghosts. What you couldn't see or touch wasn't real. Was it?

It was no use she was wide awake now. Reaching under the

bed for her slippers, Clara pulled her robe around her and made her way downstairs.

She quietly opened the front door. There was no sign of movement—and creeping down the steps she peered in through the cars side window. Dupont had been in such a hurry he'd left the keys in the ignition. However, there was no sign of the American's car. Strange.

Clara went back inside closing the door. A nice cup of tea was what she needed, maybe then she would be able to sleep. It would all become clearer in the morning. Maybe... Switching on the kettle she dropped a tea bag in a cup, sat down at the table, and waited for it to boil.

In the street outside the two youths crept stealthily up to the car, peering through the window.

"The keys are in the ignition, Jimmy. Looks like we found our ride home." He opened the door quietly and climbed in the driver's seat. "Come on what are you waiting for?"

"What if Dupont comes out and finds us in his car, Pete?"

"We drive off laughing. I don't understand you, Jimmy, last week you were ready to kill this guy. He sacked you remember. You don't owe him any loyalty. Now get in."

The car sped off at breakneck speed leaving a trail of rubber behind it.

~

Clara cocked her head to one side; she could have sworn she heard someone calling for help. She sat perfectly still waiting, listening. There it was again. It seemed to be coming from the cellar. She picked up the poker and quietly opened the cellar door and listened. So intent was she in her effort she didn't hear her husband come up behind her. He put out his hand and touched her on the shoulder and she swung quickly round.

Seeing the poker in her hand he jumped backwards, somehow avoiding being whacked over the head by his poker wielding wife.

"Bloody hell woman. You could have killed me. What the hell are you doing?"

She dropped the poker and ran to her husband flinging her arms around his neck. "Oh my God, Jean, are you okay? You frightened the living daylights out of me. Creeping up on me like that. I could have killed you."

"You might still; my heart is thumping away like a bass drum. What the hell are you doing down here in the middle of the night with the cellar door open wielding a poker?"

"I heard a bang; it sounded if it came from next door so I came downstairs to investigate. You were sound asleep and it seemed pointless both of us being disturbed. I went outside— Charles Dupont's car is outside the American's house with the keys in the ignition, but her car isn't there."

Jean stood up closing the door to the cellar and locked it, placing the key in his dressing gown pocket and marched to the front door.

"Now where are you going?"

"I'm going next door to get the American bitch out of bed and find out what the hell is going on. First the Solicitor, now the Estate Agent, what is she doing next door—running a brothel?" Flinging the front door wide open, Jean marched down the steps beckoning Clara to join him. "Whose car did you say you saw?"

Clara peered past her husband into the street. The car was gone.

"But it was there a few minutes ago. I swear to you, Jean. Charles Dupont's car was parked in front of the steps of number 55."

"Well as you can see it's not there now. Are you absolutely certain of what you saw?" Confused now, she sat down on the stairs. "I'll take that as a 'no' then shall I? What's got into you lately Clara. Ever since the house next door was sold you've been acting weird. But tonight you've excelled all previous records. I'm going back to bed. Alone. I would feel safer if you slept in the spare room tonight, and we'll continue this discussion in the morning. Goodnight."

Stomping back upstairs he slammed the bedroom door closed. Clara opened the cupboard, took out the bottle of cognac, and poured herself a large one. Her hands were shaking so much she almost dropped the bottle. What had come over her? Jean was right; she was losing the plot big time. She sat down at the kitchen table and took a large gulp of Cognac— the fiery liquid warming. She hadn't imagined it. Had she? Making her way wearily upstairs, she hesitated before opening the door to their bedroom.

"Well don't stand there dithering, woman, come and get back into bed where it's warm."

"I'm so sorry, Jean; I wouldn't hurt you for the world. You know that." Sobbing loudly she climbed into bed and snuggled up to her husband.

"It's okay, no real damage done. Come on dry your eyes. A weekend away will do us the world of good. Recharge the batteries. Why didn't you tell me the nightmares had come back? You should go and see someone, Clara, and find out what's causing them. Perhaps you saw or heard something that night that your mind is blocking out. Regression therapy might help. I was reading an article about it the other day."

"You're right I should see someone, and find out once and for all. I'll make an appointment with the doctor next week and get him to refer me to a specialist."

Jean switched off the light and pulled his wife closer. Kissing her lightly on her forehead he closed his eyes and fell into a deep sleep.

~

Back in the cellar next door Charles Dupont stirred, every bone in his body ached. At least the dogs were quiet now; they were probably asleep in front of the door, waiting for him to try to escape. Well they'd have a long wait. He was going nowhere.

Pulling his handkerchief from his trouser pocket he dabbed his forehead. It had at least stopped bleeding. Charles attempted to stand. "Aaaiiii!" Pain shot up his leg forcing him back to the ground. At a guess his leg was broken. Shuffling as best he could, he made it to the old couch in the far corner of the cellar. And pulling himself to his knees, keeping all his weight on his good leg, he hauled himself onto it.

Sweating profusely now from his exertions—his right leg throbbing painfully. Charles closed his eyes. He'd happily give his right arm for a glass of water and two Advil. Leaning back on the couch, he pulled the old woollen blanket around him. The temperature had dropped dramatically in the cellar in the last few minutes.

'Hello, Charles, does it hurt? Why did you lie, Charles?

She'll find out soon enough what happened. Someone is bound to tell her about us eventually...'

"Who's there? Why are you doing this? I don't understand. Show yourself."

'Are you sure you really want that Charles? It's not a pretty sight—I saw how you reacted to the puppies. I think he must have drugged them before he cut their throats. All because they tried to stop him, but they were no match for a gun. He killed my babiessss................ Why has he not been punished for his crimes?' The disembodied voice demanded angrily.

"Who are you?"

'I think you know the answer to that already Charles. I'll give you a clue shall I? There were five of us, he shot us, and then buried us under the terrace in sacks filled with quick lime. Close by, very, very close, and now we're trapped. Destined to roam the earth for all eternity. Unless you help us, Charles—you have to make him confess, and avenge our untimely demise.' The ghostly voice continued.

"You're not real. There are no such things as ghosts. You can't hurt me. I'm delirious. Yes, that's what it is, it's the pain—it's causing me to hear things."

'And did the pain make the dogs seem real? I can call them down to join us. Would you like that Charles?'

"Noooo. Please keep them away from me. I'm sorry, sorry I lied, sorry for your loss. Sorry, so very sorry."

'That's better; see – it wasn't difficult... was it. We'll talk again Charles, you and I...................'

Something icy cold touched his face and he froze. Huddling down in one corner of the couch, pulling the blanket over his head, and rocking back and forth.

The fabric of his suit pants clung to his legs. He'd been 5 years old the last time it had happened, or maybe it was yesterday. Mamma would beat him—she threatened him last time. If he ever wet himself again she'd said she would lock him in the cellar.

"No, mamma, no. Please, mamma, I don't like it in the dark. Please don't leave me in the dark. Mamma......................"

9

Sunlight streamed in through the open curtains. Clara groaned, she had tossed and turned all night and now it was time to get up. Climbing wearily out of the bed she dressed. Showering could wait until she'd finished packing for the weekend. She opened the window and stared out over the park below at the old tramp sat on the bench under the oak tree. Charlene looked up, and seeing her at the window waved hello, but Clara's attention was elsewhere. Suddenly she screamed aloud.

"No, no, no, not again. Please don't make me watch you again, Sebastian."

Annie and the boys lay on the ground—dead, and standing over them was Sebastian. Looking up at Clara—grinning sadistically. "They're dead, all of them, I told you they would die. I did it for God. The bitch deserved to die. God told me I wasn't their father so I killed them all. May they rot in hell!

The room spun out of control and Clara slumped to the floor. When she came to Jean and Charlene were standing over her.

"You gave me such a fright Clara. I waved to you and you screamed. You looked terrified. What happened?"

"A vision from my nightmare. When I saw you wave I thought it was Annie…"

"Who's Annie?"

"Annie used to live in your house, she's dead now her husband…" Clara hesitated.

"That's enough. Come on old girl climb back into bed. I'm going to ring the doctor—this has been going on long enough. Charlene, how about you put the kettle on and make us both a cup of tea. I'll be right down."

Charlene smiled weakly and went back downstairs into the kitchen. The agent had forgotten to warn her about the weird neighbours. Annie must have been the owner who died in the nursing home. Poor Clara, she'd go into town later and pick up some spring flowers to cheer her up. Jean came into the kitchen and sat down at the table.

"Sorry about that. She's not been herself lately; I caught her wandering around downstairs late last night. Were you at the house last night, Charlene?"

"No, I went straight back to the hotel when I left here. A friend was supposed to be coming to see me, but he never turned up. Why?"

"Clara said she heard someone banging about next door, and that Charles Dupont's car was parked outside your house too. But when I went outside to look there was no sign of him, or his car."

"I haven't seen Mr Dupont since I signed the contracts. Though it's funny Clara mentioned hearing noises because the front door was unlocked again this morning and a box I'd left in the hallway was squashed flat, as if something had fallen on it. And there was a trail of soil from the patio doors right through the lounge, which stopped at the door to the cellar. Though there was nothing missing that I could see. While I'm here Jean, do you know which of these keys is for the cellar?" Charlene said handing him the bunch of keys with the agency tag still attached. Jean examined them and handed them back.

"It's none of those. The key is identical to this one unless Sebastian changed the lock." He exclaimed, handing a large key to Charlene.

"Will this open the door to my cellar?"

"I would expect so unless of course Sebastian changed the lock. Here take it, and if it fits get a duplicate made in town."

"Thanks, I'll let you have it back this afternoon. Jean who was Annie? Only I got the impression Clara was frightened by what she saw and…" She was interrupted by a knock at the door.

"Sorry, Charlene, I would imagine that's the doctor, I'll pop round later if I get chance."

"Yes, sorry, of course. I'll leave you to it, and thanks for the loan of the key." Walking to the door Jean put his hand on Charlene's arm.

"Be careful, if someone has been in the house it could be they have a key. Personally, I would get a locksmith to come and change the locks to be safe." He opened the door for Charlene and welcomed the doctor inside.

What was with all the subterfuge? Was there something Charles Dupont should have told her about the house? Deep in thought she didn't notice Antoine's car parked outside the house.

"Hello Charlene."

"Antoine. What happened to you last night? Cold feet?"

"I was at the hospital. A hit and run. The callous bastard left her for dead at the side of the road. I called an ambulance but it was too late to save her. She died from her injuries on the way to the hospital."

"Oh, how awful, do they have any idea who did it?"

"No, but for a while they were trying me out for size. I've come straight from the police station. I'm afraid they need to speak to you, for verification of the time and my reason for being at the right place at the wrong time."

"You'd better come inside and I'll fix you some coffee I could rustle up something to eat too if you like. It's been one of those mornings. Word of warning–the children are here, so not a word about yesterday."

"Of course, I won't say a word."

She opened the door and they went inside closing the door.

Charlene shouted upstairs to the children. "Best behaviour kids, we have our first visitor." Three pairs of feet clattered noisily downstairs. The two youngest were the first to land, positively oozing hostility. Carly pushed her brother roughly and he retaliated.

"Mom, tell him the room next to yours is mine."

"No it's not. I bagged it first bitch."

"Jason Hamilton-Davies! That's enough of that. I will not tolerate the use of that type of language in my house. Go outside and cool off, and don't come back until you're ready to apologise."

"Aw, Mom, it's not fair, she started it."

"That's as maybe but now I'm finishing it. Get out, now." What an introduction. If that didn't make him run for the hills nothing would. "This is Antoine Monroe, the solicitor who dealt with the acquisition of the house for us, Carly."

Carly was busy trying to figure out where she'd seen him before.

"Where are your manners, Carly? What's got into you guy's today?"

Carly stepped forward and held out her hand. "Hi, I'm Carly. Are you really a Lawyer? Because you sure don't look like any of the lawyers we had back home."

"Carly. Don't be so rude."

Smiling, Antoine took her hand and kissed it lightly.

"Aw cool, that's a first. You're class-e! Wait till I tell the gals at school—they'll be mort-i-fied and so jealous."

"Carly. I'm the one who's mortified. Whatever will Mr. Monroe think of us? Acting like a bunch of savages the lot of you. Go on—get out of my sight. Sorry about that, Antoine, they aren't normally so rude. Ah here's Philip, I hope you aren't going to let me down too?"

"As if. Hi, Antoine, how's tricks?"

"Fine, I think. I dropped by to see if there is anything you guys needed."

"As a matter of fact there is, I wanted to take a look in the basement but it's locked."

Charlene took the key Jean had given her out of her pocket and handed it to Philip. "Try that for size. Jean next door said the key should be the same unless Sebastian changed the lock."

Philip put the key in the lock and opened the door. "Ugh it smells like something died down here. Pass me the torch, Mom."

Charlene stood torch in hand waiting for the appropriate response from her son. Antoine stepped in and took the torch from her.

"Thanks. Hang on a second, Philip. This is an old house and the stairs might not be safe. I'd better go first."

The men made their way cautiously down the rickety old staircase. Antoine shone the torch around the cellar—something glinted in the corner, and as he moved closer he caught sight of the body huddled under an old blanket. His eyes, wild, like a frightened rabbit caught in the light.

"Mon Dieu. Philip, I want you to go back upstairs and ask your mother to telephone the SAMU. You stay with Jason and Carly and send your mother down with a blanket and a glass of water. Now, Philip."

"Sorry, yeah, on my way. Who is that on the couch?"

"It looks like Charles Dupont, the estate agent who sold your mother the house."

Charlene hurried down the stairs into the basement. "They're on their way, how is he? And more to the point what's he doing in my cellar?"

"I have no idea and I don't think we'll be finding out for quite some time. He's completely out of it."

"Mom, the ambulance men are here."

"Send them down, and see if you can find a light bulb, and a mop and bucket, and fill it with hot water and disinfectant. Lots of disinfectant."

The paramedics made their way into the basement. "Have you any idea who he is?"

"Charles Dupont." Antoine replied.

"The estate agent from Riverside?" The paramedic demanded.

"Yes, and before you ask we have no idea how he got down here or why."

"Okay let's take a look at him. Mr. Dupont can you hear me? Are you hurt? Can you tell us how you got here?" Charles Dupont clung to the paramedic's arm, clutching the blanket tightly to him.

"Have they gone? You must have seen them, two big black dogs. I'm sure they were rabid."

"It's okay, Charles, they've gone. We'll soon have you out of here and into hospital. His leg looks as if it might be broken, and he has a nasty cut on his head. He probably hit his head on the wall as he fell down the stairs."

They worked on him for several minutes before strapping him into the chair. "Okay, let's get him upstairs and into the ambulance where there's a bit more light." Charlene held the door open for them. "How is he?"

"He'll live this time, but his liver will only take so much punishment. Do you have dogs? Only he said he was forced into the cellar by two rabid dogs."

"No, our dogs are still in quarantine. Did he say anything else? Like how he got in?"

"Nothing that made any sense. He asked us not to fetch his mother, because it was her that locked him in the cellar."

"That's hardly likely seeing as she's been dead for the past ten years." Antoine said wearily. "I'll get word to his wife right away. She must be out of her mind with worry, wondering where he is."

"Okay we'll leave that with you then, sir." The ambulance drove away with Charles Dupont inside, he wouldn't be selling houses for a while. Where he was headed everything was painted white and most of the rooms had padded walls and doors without handles.

"He must have kept a set of keys." Charlene said, as she picked up the box from the hall floor, under which lay a bunch of keys.

"The missing keys I presume, that solves part of the mystery." Antoine took the keys from her, comparing them with the house keys.

"They aren't the same, these must be his keys for his office, and this one's a car key. But where's his car?"

"Clara thought she saw his car outside last night with the keys in the ignition, but when Jean went to investigate there was no sign of it. He assumed she'd imagined seeing it there. The doctor was with her when I left. Is there something in the air around here? I'm beginning to wonder if I wasn't a little hasty in my choice of neighbourhood. You would tell me if there was anything wrong with the house, Antoine—wouldn't you?"

Now what did he do? Tell her the truth or lie? Which would be worse in the end? What were solicitors required to do when backed into a corner?

"Of course I would. You had a pre-purchase survey I take it?" He asked.

"No, I didn't think it necessary. Troy is going to kill me if there is anything major wrong with the house." Antoine winced. Her last remark was to near the actual history of the house for comfort. And something else was bothering him—Annie's dogs were black.

Was there such a thing as a haunted house?

10

Antoine sat in the easy chair with his back to the window. He couldn't bring himself to look through the doors to the patio—and the final resting place of Annie and her family. He shivered; it was cold in the house. In the last few minutes the temperature had plummeted to below freezing. Sensing he was not alone he turned around.

The apparition floated effortlessly in the breeze. The air heavy with the scent of Vanderbilt—Annie's favourite perfume. He shut his eyes but when he opened them again the apparition was still there.

'Hello Antoine, long time, no see. You thought we'd gone for good didn't you? Did you forget your promise to take care of us? My babies, my poor, poor, babies died. We all died. Slain like animals and then buried in shallow graves. I thought you loved us. Is she good in bed, your new lover? She looks a little like me don't you think—is that why you chose her? Nothing to say, Antoine? What's up—cat got your tongue?

Charles Dupont had that same expression on his face when he saw me too—a mixture of horror and disbelief. He won't be lying to anyone else for a while. And you, Antoine, will you be joining him I wonder? Well say something, anything. A solicitor lost for words. That's a first.'

His mind raced ahead; did ghosts really exist—or was he dreaming? He pinched himself hard on the arm. Ouch!

'Oh yes, I'm here, so the answer to your question is yes, ghosts exist. Don't you have any other questions? Charles had questions; I expected more from you Antoine.'

Why had she chosen now, after all these years? Just as he'd found the courage to start again with Charlene.

"What do you want from me, Annie? A part of me died that night or had you forgotten Benjamin was my son too. My flesh and blood. My hope for the future. How did Sebastian find out, who betrayed us, Annie?"

'I don't know. That's your task. Search for the truth, find Sebastian, and make him pay for his crimes. Only the truth can set us free, Antoine, remember that. Look under every rock from here to hell and back if you have to. We have a right to justice. Don't fail me a second time Antoine. We'll talk again, soon, very soon.'

The patio doors flew open and Annie was gone. If she was ever there at all. Antoine collapsed into the chair. Did he believe in ghosts now? The door to the hall opened and Carly bounded in.

"Oh, you're alone; I thought mum was in here with you." She said offhandedly.

"No Carly, your mother is in the kitchen making coffee I believe."

"Then who were you talking to... I distinctly heard you talking to someone." Pulling his telephone from his pocket he waved it at the youngster.

"I was talking to my secretary." Eyeing him suspiciously, she backed out of the room and bounded down the hall.

"Coffee's almost ready; oh, I thought Carly was in here too. Shall we have it out on the patio?"

Panicking Antoine stood up. He couldn't go out there. "Sorry, Charlene, I have to get back to the office, Marcie telephoned to say there's a problem with the computer." He stood up hurriedly and bolted for the door. "I'll ring you later, I promise."

"Okay, will the police get in touch with me direct or do I have to contact them?" Charlene asked.

"They'll be in touch later today I should imagine. Sorry I have to dash. How about dinner tomorrow evening?"

"Err… yes let me know the time and place. Are you sure you're okay, Antoine?"

"Fine, things to do that's all."

Had she imagined it or was Antoine acting strangely. What was it in the air around here? First Clara, and then Charles Dupont in her basement doing an impression of an escapee from an asylum. And now Antoine. Maybe she should change her perfume, and talking of perfume—she sniffed the air.

"Carly Hamilton-Davies have you been at my perfume again? I warned you what would happen the last time you messed with my stuff young lady." No answer. She peered around the kitchen door she wasn't in there. Charlene stomped upstairs to give her time to hide the evidence. She searched from room to room but found no sign of Carly or the others. They had all disappeared. The door to the attic was ajar. So that was where they were all hiding.

She opened the door wide and stared in horror. A spiral staircase. Now what did she do. "Carly, Jason, Philip—are you up there" With no reply forthcoming she put her foot on the first step. Come on scaredy cat, it's just a staircase. Okay so it's a spiral staircase, but this isn't Hill House'…There are no such things as haunted houses. There are no such things as ghosts. All you have to do is put one foot in front of the other and eventually you will arrive in the attic. It's no big deal.

"Boo!"

Charlene missed her footing and landed in a heap at the foot of the stairs. "Carly. What are you trying to do, scare me to death? Where were you, I searched everywhere for you? Have you been meddling with my stuff again young lady? It reeks of Vanderbilt in the lounge. I do hope you haven't broken the bottle."

"I haven't touched it mom, honest. Do you think I'd risk

the wrath of the mommy, a second time?" She opened the door to the attic wider. "Cool staircase. I thought you said you'd never buy a house with a spiral staircase?"

"I did, and I meant it, I didn't know it was here?"

Jason and Philip peered over Carly's shoulder. "What are you doing on the floor, mom? Wow—wicked staircase... But I thought you said...."

"We already had that conversation Jason; mom didn't know it was here." Carly said accusingly.

"How could you have not seen it?" Philip asked in amazement. "Don't tell me you didn't go up into the attic when you came with the Agent. Oh my, pop's gonna flip his lid." Philip continued. "If there's anything wrong with the roof you're toast—it could have woodworm or Death Watch Beetle or something."

"Half the slates could be missing and mum wouldn't know."

"Thank you, Jason, we get the picture. Help me up. Right what we're going to do now is go upstairs." Charlene said, as she dusted herself down.

"Is that 'we' as in all of us mom?" Philip replied.

"Yes it is, I would already be up there if Carly hadn't come along and scared me half to death."

"I'm sorry. I heard you calling but I was under the bed investigating where this came from." Carly held up a silver cross and chain. "It must have belonged to the people who lived here before. I saw the chain peeking out from in between the floorboards and when I pulled it the rest followed. Is it real silver mom?"

Charlene took the cross in her hand and examined it carefully before handing it back to her daughter. "Yes, it's hallmarked on the back."

"Can I keep it, you know, finders keepers, losers weepers and all that?"

"I don't see why not. If they'd wanted it back they would have contacted the agent long ago. My guess is they don't know it's missing, or they have no idea where they lost it."

"Cool, my first treasure trove. I wonder what we'll find hidden in the attic." Carly added eagerly.

"Huh! I hope it's better than what they found hiding in the basement. One blubbering idiot in the house is plenty."

"Jason that's enough. I thought I told you not to tell him about Charles Dupont, Philip." Charlene scolded.

"I didn't, he was hiding in the kitchen when they bought him up. He overheard you and the lawyer guy discussing how he'd got there." Philip replied.

"Yeah, mom, how did the whacko get to be lurking in our basement? The ambulance man said he thought he'd had one over the eight. Said 'he reeked of alcohol.'"

"That's alcohol, Jason." Philip retorted.

"So it's true then. The man was as pissed as a fart when he fell down the stairs into our cellar. Which leads nicely into my next question? Exactly what was he doing in our house in the middle of the night in the first place?" Jason enquired of his mother.

"I don't know, sweetie, and I don't think we're likely to get an answer for some time. It may remain one of life's unsolved mysteries. So rule number one applies here."

"We know—not a word to pops." The children replied in unison.

11

"C'mon I'll lead. Mom, you and Carly next and Jason can bring up the rear. 'Operation Attic' is green to go. Hey mom this would make a great pad for Matt and me."

"Aw mom, that is so not fair, first the bi…"

"Jason. I'm warning you." Charlene retorted sternly.

"Aw mom, I always get the raw deal."

"That's because you're the youngest bro."

"Let's take a look before we decide who gets first dibs. Your father may veto the lot of you and install himself up here."

It was no great secret—their parents didn't sleep together. Carly assumed it was because of pop's snoring, but Matt and Philip had figured out the real reason years ago. The four climbed the stairs in silence.

"Ugh gross. I just saw the biggest spider."

Philip laughed; his little brother was such a wuss. "Stop being such a girl, Jason. The thing's hardly likely to gobble you up whole now is it?" Philip replied.

Charlene wandered over to the window and looked out over the garden. The attic was huge, plenty of space for the two boys and their father. Matt rarely came home these days; he had friends and a life of his own. And who could blame him, when Troy joined them at Christmas he would be back on his case.

How simple life would be if Troy were to disappear. She still couldn't bring herself to use the 'D' word, but oh, how she wished it would happen. She knelt down in front of a pile of junk leaning against the gable wall. There was a draught coming from somewhere. Probably a missing slate. She'd ask Jean later if he knew of a good builder to give them a price for the conversion and check the roof.

"Well boy's it looks like you've got your work cut out up here. Plenty of space for all of you up here. I'm sure Matt won't mind sharing with you guys when he's home for visits."

"Wicked. You're the tops mom." Philip said excitedly.

"Right shrimp, here's what we're gonna do…"

"Okay guys we'll leave you to it. There are brushes and stuff in the basement. Come on, Carly, we can make a start on the painting. We only have a couple of days before the kitchen arrives."

Cleaning was women's work and Jason was crap at cleaning. He absentmindedly ran the brush over the pile of junk in the corner. Wondering what the probability of finding treasure buried amongst the junk would be. Nil he imagined. That's why it had been left behind. It wouldn't hurt to look though, would it?

Course it wouldn't. Kneeling down in front of the pile he started sorting through. Old photographs of the house, an old school book belonging to some kid called Benjamin and a game of some sort. The box was marked 'Ouija Board'. He pushed it back into the carrier bag and continued rummaging through the pile. More of the same: old photographs, some in black and white, and one with a sour faced man, a woman, and four children posing woodenly in front of the house.

He wondered which one was the former owner of the Ouija board, and was about to give it up as a bad job until he came across another box wrapped in brown paper, and wedged tightly under the eaves.

"Philip, give us a hand to get this out from under here."

"On one condition–if it's valuable we go halves."

"Yeah, whatever. It's probably only some more old photos that never made it into frames."

The two boys pulled at the box but still it wouldn't budge. "Do you think it's stuck to the floor?"

"Could be, or it's holding that part of the roof up and when it moves the whole thing will tumble down around our ears."

Jason stared worriedly at his older brother. "Just kidding bro. Here, slide this old knife under it." He passed the knife to Jason, who slid the knife carefully under the box from left to right and passed it back to Philip. One sharp tug and it was free. Jason laid the box on the floor and pushed it towards his brother.

"I think you should be the one to open it, Philip, being the oldest."

"Why? You're not scared are you, Jason?"

"No, of course not, but what if there's something bad inside?"

"Wuss."

Jason didn't care if he was being a wuss. He had a bad feeling about the box. Watching nervously as Philip removed the paper carefully and then lifting the lid off he peered inside. Jason's eyes widened in horror as the colour drained from his brother's face. Curiosity eventually getting the better of him as he reached for the box.

"You don't want to do that. Trust me on this one, Jason; it's not a pretty sight."

"What's in there? Is it—something dead?"

"Oh yeah, it's dead alright—has been for some time."

"It's not—human is it?" Philip nodded and Jason backed slowly away from the box.   "Shall I get mom?"

"Yep, and you stay down there with Carly okay. I don't want her to see this."

Jason hesitated, part of him wanted to know exactly what his big brother had seen that had frightened him so much. Common sense prevailed for once and he ran downstairs to the kitchen to where Carly and his mother where busy painting the ceiling.

"Mom, Philip needs you upstairs. Now."

"Jason, can't you see I'm busy? Can't Philip come down and talk to me here?"

Jason shook his head. Something was drastically wrong; the boy looked petrified. Charlene handed the roller to Jason and wiping her hands on a wet cloth she headed for the stairs. Carly went to follow her mother and Jason put his hand out to stop her.

"No. Philip said just mom. Please, Carly, don't go." His bottom lip trembled and Charlene turned and ran up the stairs.

"Philip, are you alright? Whatever's the matter with your brother? What is it? Tell me what's wrong." He pushed the box over toward his mother and lifted the lid slowly.

"Oh my God. Where did you find it?"

"Under the eaves. I think it's been there a while."

Charlene stared at the tiny body crammed into the shoe box. Who could have done such a thing? It was a boy; and she estimated the pregnancy had gone to term. There was only one thing left to do. Bring in the authorities.

"Leave the box where it is. You didn't touch it did you?"

"No, mom."

"And, Jason, did he see inside?"

"No, I told him not to look."

"And he didn't? That's a first. Are you okay?"

"A bit shaken. The smell was bad when I opened the box. Was it murdered, mom?"

"I don't know, Philip, that's for the authorities to determine. Come on there's nothing we can do for him now." Poor little mite. Who would do that to a baby? A young girl maybe, too scared to tell her parents she was pregnant. Had she been all alone when she'd given birth? The pain she must have suffered. Had the baby drawn its first breath only to be stuffed into the box to die of suffocation and hypothermia?

She would talk to the local priest about a blessing ceremony. Release the spirit of the child and send him on his way. Exorcise the house. Charlene followed her son downstairs and telephoned the police. She would be glad when today was over. There was only so much excitement a girl could take. And today was far from over, and she had the distinct feeling that it was going to be a long night. She glanced at her watch; the police would be here shortly and she didn't want the children here when they arrived.

"Feeding time I think. Philip, why don't the three of you take a walk down the road to the pizzeria, and I'll join you as soon as I've dealt with our little problem."

Carly looked from her mother to her brothers and back again. Family secrets. There would be no way mom would tell her what her brothers had found, therefore no point in pushing the issue.

"Come on guys, let's eat. I'm famished." Carly said as Charlene opened the door, to find a very surprised detective on the doorstep, his arm faltering in mid air.

"Madame Amilton-Davies? Detective Inspector Malestroit."

It had been several years since Malestroit had last visited the house. He'd hoped he would never have the misfortune to return. Fate, however, had decided otherwise.

Charlene turned to the children. "Everything's fine, I won't be long, off you go. Sorry detective, but the children haven't eaten yet. You'll have to speak to Philip later, if that's okay. As you can imagine he's a bit shaken. It's not everyday you make a discovery of this kind."

"I understand, Madame. I can take a statement from your son tomorrow. The pizzeria does a very good Bolognaise and the Pizza's are excellent. Say hello to Mario, for me." Malestroit added.

She watched from the doorstep until they entered the restaurant. Safely out of harm's way. "The box is in the attic. I thought it was best to leave it up there until you arrived. This way, detective." Charlene led Malestroit up to the attic. The detective put on a pair of gloves and carefully lifted the lid. "Jason my youngest found it when he moved the pile of junk. I think he was hoping to find a treasure trove."

"Did either of your son's touch the body Madame Amilton-Davies? Or remove anything from inside the box?"

"No. Once Philip realised what the box contained he closed it quickly so his brother wouldn't see it. He said it was wedged under the eaves by the gable wall. The paper it was wrapped in is probably in the bag of rubbish. The boys were cleaning up."

Malestroit examined the former resting place of the box—

and tucked in behind the beam he found several letters tied together with a red ribbon. And taking an evidence bag from his pocket he popped them inside.

"These may explain what happened. My guess is the baby's mother was no more than a child herself. She must have been terrified her father would find out."

"You talk as if you know the family concerned, detective. Do you ever get the feeling that something is not as it should be? I'm getting that feeling now. That people are keeping secrets, and those secrets somehow affect my family, and this house."

"Sorry Madame Amilton-Davies I can't help you there. I see and hear all sorts of strange things every day. So much so, nothing surprises me anymore. Whilst I'm here perhaps you could clear a little matter up for me. I spoke to Mr Monroe, your solicitor, this morning. He found a young woman by the side of the road. A hit and run, she died on her way to hospital I'm afraid. Mr. Monroe said he was on his way to meet you. Is this correct?"

"Yes, he was. I was expecting him to come to my hotel but he never arrived."

"About what time did you speak to him?"

"About 10:30 yesterday evening. He said it would take him about 20 minutes to get from his house to the hotel."

"Are you sure he was ringing from home, madam?"

"Yes, I'm sure, but you could check with the hotel switchboard to be certain. I believe they log all calls, both in, and out. It's the Ibis Hotel, room 25."

"Thank you, Madame Amilton-Davies, I'll do that, and thank you for your co-operation. I'll be in touch as soon as I have any news on this little chap. I imagine you would like to get on with the renovations as quickly as possible. I'll see myself out. Goodnight."

"Goodnight Detective Malestroit and thank you for being so prompt."

The detective stood in front of the house. The press had dubbed it 'the house of death', and once again it was living up to its title. The resemblance between the deceased former occupant, Annie Delamare, and the American woman was incredible. They could have almost been mistaken for sisters. And exactly what was the relationship between her and Antoine Monroe? There was something very fishy going on. He could feel it in his water.

He looked at the box in which the infant lay. He'd bet his pension the DNA would be a match to Annie Delamare's daughter, Amelia. The autopsy findings had shown that she had recently given birth. It would be interesting to see who the baby's father was too. It could have been the reason behind the murders.

Tucking the box under his arm he walked across the road to his car. He had the strangest feeling someone was watching him, but when turned there was no one in sight.

Too many late nights and excessive amounts of caffeine, he presumed.

12

The telephone rang out several times. Bloody woman. She was never around when he needed her, especially when he had something important to discuss. He slammed the telephone back into the dock and walked over to the bar.

Troy poured two fingers of Bourbon and dropped a couple of ice cubes in the glass. He walked to the window and looked out over the night sky and the city beneath him. This was his territory; his domain and Charlene was unaware of its existence. As far as his wife was concerned he lived in rented accommodation, end of discussion. They had separate bank accounts, separate beds, and separate lives. Hell, they didn't even reside in the same country.

He went back into the bedroom and poked the sleeping form huddled under the covers.

"What you do that for sugar? I was sleeping, why don't you just climb on in here and snuggle up at the side of me for a while?"

"Not tonight. I have work that won't get done if you stay. Get dressed, and I'll call you a cab."

"Sugar, that's the third time this week you've brought me over here and then half an hour later kicked me out on my pretty little ass. A girl has her limits."

Taking a wad of dollar bills from his wallet, he stuffed the bills into her purse and walked out onto the balcony. Money talked the talk. Always had. Always would. "Be sure to close the door on your way out."

The girl dressed quickly. He was a mean son of a bitch when he was crossed. It had cost her dearly the last time she'd asked too many questions. Three weeks sitting around, just waiting for the swelling to go down. Nope. she wouldn't be doing that again in a hurry.

Her friend wanted to call the cops—but that would have blown her cover. They'd have asked all kind of questions that she didn't need to be answering. Like what a girl of her persuasion was doin hanging around with the likes of 'the man'. Picking up her bag she headed for the door. "Bye sugar, call me when you're in the mood. I'm out of town next week for a few days, but you have my number."

She was talking to herself again. He was off in another world, and she didn't ask where, or who with. That was 'the man's' private business, and the man liked his privacy. She'd heard his marriage was on the rocks from an acquaintance, but that had been a while since. They'd sold their house down in the burbs and rumour had it she'd high tailed it over to France with their children and the family dogs. How true it was she didn't know.

Naomi guessed that was the little lady he'd been trying to reach on the telephone. She'd done geography at school; France was six hours ahead of Atlanta, and tomorrow, well that was already today for them.

Naomi Gibbs was nobody's fool. Amazonian in proportion, not an ounce of excess body fat. Standing some 5 feet 10 inches in her bare feet, and tonight she was wearing heels. With skin the colour of burnished amber—her hair, long, and as dark as the night. A picture of health and vitality as she sashayed into the lobby pausing momentarily to admire her reflection in the glass. The concierge falling over himself in his efforts to impress, he'd have kissed her feet, if only she'd asked. Such beauty was wasted on Troy Hamilton-Davies. He was old enough to be her grandfather.

Men like Hamilton-Davies had everything. Money, position, standing in the community, and Naomi Gibbs for arm candy. She was out of his league—with the pittance he earned he stood no chance. She was destined to remain forever in his dreams.

Bastian watched the young woman as she flirted mercilessly with the concierge. There was smart money to be made with a body like that. He'd met her type before. Beauty, as the saying went, was only skin deep. She was the current arm candy of one of his disciples, and a man it was unwise to cross. Especially when one was under the scrutiny of the IRS—and him your only hope of salvation.

Hiding in the shadows he watched as she climbed into the waiting cab. Prick-tease. A real class act too. What she needed was a lesson in humility and he knew just the person to deliver it.

He crossed the street entering the building discreetly by the side entrance. Once inside the lobby he headed for the stairs. One day, he too would have a penthouse and everything that went with it. Every dog would have its' day.

Opening the door he stepped inside the hallway and walked down the corridor. The door to the penthouse quietly opened and Bastian went inside—Troy Hamilton-Davies sat on the sofa, drink in hand.

"You're late, Bastian. Time is money in my business so I'd appreciate you being punctual if nothing else."

"I would have been if I hadn't stopped to watch the floor show in the lobby. Nice body and such long legs. Tell me, Troy, does she swallow?"

A flicker of a smile illuminating his face for an instant - Naomi strikes again. Walking to the bar he poured bourbon on the rocks and passed it to Bastian. "My private life is exactly that, Bastian. It's your 'monetary policies,' the 'infernal' Revenue is interested in, and rumour has it they aren't the only government department following you on Twitter. Have you been a naughty boy, Bastian? I do hope in doing you a favour I'm not leaving myself wide open for an investigation of some kind. You catch my drift?"

"Loud and clear, they've got nothing on me. And whoever 'they' are, they'd better be watching their backs."

Observing his reaction closely—Bastian's mouth may have been talking the talk, but his body language said otherwise. He'd been visibly spooked by the last remark. Perhaps Brother Johnson had a valid point, that their intrepid, esteemed leader was keeping secrets. Big, juicy, class 'A' secrets, other than the one he himself had uncovered. Bastian Lamare wasn't an employee of the Central Intelligence Agency at all. They were probably squelching around the swampland he called home at this very moment.

Troy had his doubts about their newest recruit, Brother Michaels too. He knew a rat when he smelled one. And not unlike English rock candy, this one had danger stamped all the way through. It would be interesting to see how long he'd be allowed to continue sniffing around.

He handed the package to Bastian. "Present this to the Revenue people at the next hearing and they should back off. They have nothing concrete on the Brotherhood. I think it's you, personally, they have the problem with."

"Why's that?"

"Some of the questions they asked were a little too vague. The IRS doesn't usually pussyfoot around like that. When they sense blood they go straight for the jugular."

"So it's nothing concrete, just a gut feeling, yeah?"

"Something like that. Or it could be because they found this photograph as interesting as I did." He said pushing the photograph across the table. Bastian studied it for a few seconds and threw it back onto the table.

"What's it got to do with me?"

"I think you know the answer to that already. Even without the beard and the long hair, Bastian, there is no doubt the man in the photograph is you. Do you want to talk about it, deny it maybe?"

"You're mad, it looks nothing like me. I'll see myself out and thanks for this I owe you one. Oh, and one final word of warning, if I find out you're telling tales out of school, Troy, someone close to you could regret it."

"Are you threatening me?"

"That my friend depends on your point of view. I prefer to call it friendly advice. See you at the weekend, Troy, and bring your camouflage gear. I hear tell its open season on conspirators, so every one of us needs to be on our guard." The door closed with a whoosh as it brushed over the thick pile carpet. Not one of his more intelligent moves. The off white carpet had looked spectacular, for approximately one week, and by that time it was too late to change his mind.

Replaying the strange conversation he'd just had in his head; surveillance was called for on Bastian Lamare. If, of course, that was his real name. The man had met his kind before and knew how to deal with 'men' like Bastian. And exactly who to call to get the job done proficiently, with the minimum of fuss.

13

The man moved silently between the shelves of books, he'd always found the personal approach paid dividends. He plucked a book at random from the shelf. The codeword for this particular meet and the title of the book he'd chosen were the same. Highly amusing.

Troy placed the book on the counter. "I wonder if you can help me, I was looking for other books by Paul Donovan. I believe the Ninja Warrior is the first in the trilogy. Is it possible to verify this please?" The assistant looked up from the magazine she was reading and scanned the book.

"Sorry, this is the only one we have. If you'd like to fill out this form we will contact the publishers and order any others that may be available. It could take a couple of weeks." She pushed a sheet of A4 and a pen over the counter.

"That'll be twelve dollars and eighty cents with tax." Troy handed the girl a twenty dollar bill and waited for his change.

She hastily stuffed the book inside a bag with the receipt and smiling she handed him the package. "Thank you for your custom. Have a nice day." She had a squeaky, high pitched voice, which grated on his already raw nerves. He'd still not managed to contact Charlene. She wasn't answering her mobile and the hotel said the family had checked out several days since.

Walking over to the bench in front of the bookstore he sat down with the package on his knee. He opened the bag and placed the book on the seat next to him. He didn't have to wait long for the arrival of his contact.

Chas Denman glided up to the bench. Six and a half feet of rippling muscle and dreadlocks, Denman towered over Troy. Jamaican by birth, his parents had died when he was small. An aunt living in Atlanta had taken him in and raised him as her own. A fine, upstanding American citizen, she had imposed the importance of honesty, diligence, and integrity on Chas. Her proudest moment had been when he'd joined the Central Intelligence Agency.

Un-orthodox in his approach to law enforcement, at times bordering on illegality. He got the job done, and that was all his employers asked. He'd been decorated several times for acts of heroism in service above and beyond the call of duty. Today however, he was moonlighting.

"Yo man! You a Ninja Warrior fan too? This bro's awesome!" He sat down beside Troy.

"Okay, Harold Finn, you can lay off the Jamaican accent."

"How you doin, Troy, my man, long time no see. What service do you have in mind today? Extortion, bribery, rape, pillage?"

"You don't change I see. Good to see you, Chas. Details are in here together with your fee. Half up front, and the rest when the jobs done."

Taking the envelope from Troy he sat down. His face devoid of expression, as he opened it up and looked inside. He studied the photographs for several seconds then casually shoved them in his inside pocket along with the envelope.

"See you next week. Same place, and Troy, be careful out there. I take it you're aware you're being followed. Don't turn round. Use this mirror, bookshop, third shelf from the right.

That's your right. Hold it there. That's the one. Know him?"

"No, can't say I do. You know what to do?"

"Usual bonus?"

"Double. I don't like complications. They cloud my judgment; and make me meaner than a coyote sitting on a prickly pear!"

"Nice doing business with you man. Have……"

"If you value your life don't finish that sentence friend. I've not had a good day since they assassinated the last President. Nothing but trouble, women, and then some."

Chas was wise enough not to ask. He'd seen what the man called entertaining. And they had the cheek to call him mercenary. Chas skated off into the distance. Waiting a good five minutes before making the call. "Worked like a dream, nice doing business with ya! You have a target in mind for a dunk in the swamp?"

"Naturally, it's being taken care of as we speak. All you have to do, Chas, is take the credit and of course the payment. Usual rates okay?"

"Sure, I'll see to it right away. See you around, metaphorically speaking that is—don't do anything I wouldn't do…" He was talking to himself again. Now to get down to the real work, but first a guy had to eat. Chas unbuckled his skates and threw them into the van. He never saw the bullet coming. Not something you expect in the middle of a parking lot in broad daylight.

The gunman unscrewed the silencer and shoved the pieces in his inside pocket. Pulling off his gloves and mask he strolled nonchalantly to the van, and checking the coast was clear he pushed the motionless form inside and closed the door. Driving off down the highway at a leisurely pace he headed for Lake Oconee. It would be imprudent of him to contravene the law and bring the highway patrol sniffing around—given the nature of his cargo.

One day people would listen attentively when he spoke and until that time he would be 'watching his back'. He would deal with the man in his own time. Make him suffer; he couldn't say he hadn't been warned. The mole would be rewarded for his efficiency this weekend. A little target practice in the woods, in the dark of course. Moles don't hog the limelight.

Talking of lime, he must remember to call in at the stores sometime and pick up another sack. He hadn't anticipated the demand to be this high so early in the season. Nothing concealed the smell of a rotting corpse better than good old quick lime.

Chas groaned and rolled over onto his side. The van was moving, which meant whoever had taken a shot at him was taking him out into the wilds to dispose of. He pulled out his mobile; thank heaven for silent keypads. You just never knew when your life might depend on one. He tapped out the standard message for agent down and pushed the send button. Immediately transmitting his position via the satellite link.

He pulled out his Taser. Wonders would never cease it was fully charged and ready for action. All he had to do now was wait until the man stopped the van, and hit him with a charge.

He checked on his wound, the bullet had passed clean through. Woohoo, aren't I the lucky one. A couple of inches to the right and he would have been pushing up daisies. As it was he'd be out of action for a while. Bummer.

They were slowing down. Chas rolled onto his stomach keeping the Taser out of sight and waited. He would get one shot at this—after that he'd be toast. Ouch, he must remember not to do that. Even laughing silently hurt like hell. What's he waiting for? He doesn't realize he's pressed for time stupid—dead bodies don't usually fight back.

The door to the van slid open; the man grabbed his ankles and pulled him out of the van. Chas bit down hard on his cheek to keep from screaming out. The pain from his wound, white hot. He prayed that the man would kneel to turn him over.

There is a God. As the man took hold of Chas's jacket to roll him over he quickly bought up his hand, catching the man off guard. The first burst of the Taser knocked him backwards, stunning him. Chas raised himself into position to hit him with a second shot.

This time his aim was perfect. His assailant's body twitched uncontrollably on the ground for several seconds. Chas checked his pulse—still alive. Just. He pulled the photograph Troy had given him out of his pocket, checking it against the man on the ground. It wasn't him. So who was he, and why did he want him dead?

Chas dragged himself to the van and pulling himself up to his knees he got into the car. He had painkilling spray in his bag for sports injuries. He figured it was better than nothing. Ripping open his shirt, and gritting his teeth he sprayed it liberally on the open wound. "Fuck, that bastard's cold." He exclaimed, exhaling. Holding his breath was a bad idea too, a person could die like that. The whole episode smacked of double cross. He didn't believe Troy would set him up so that left only one person. Why the dirty low down skunk. Shit, now he had a second even bigger problem. Exactly how long would it be before the clean up team landed? His phone would lead them straight to him. He had to think of something, and fast.

Backing the truck out of the clearing he headed for the highway driving as if the devil were behind him. A few hundred meters ahead was an open farm truck. The perfect diversion. He pulled into the outer lane, wound down the window, and calmly tossed his mobile in with the pigs. That should keep them busy whilst he made his way to Mary-Jo's.

Tata always said if you want to live see the veterinary man, doctors were for sick folk who didn't know any better!

14

Chas drove around to the back door of the vet's surgery. The euphoria of escaping death once again had long since passed and his every movement hurt like hell. He reached up for the buzzer and collapsed into the waiting arms of Mary-Jo.

"Huggie, quick, it's Chas, he's hurt real bad. Help me get him inside. What happened? Who did this to you?"

Why do people ask such stupid questions, couldn't they see he was bleeding to death! "Cold, lost a lot of the red stuff, might need a bit of help here."

"He's not making sense. Come on, Huggie—help me lift him onto the table; let the dog see the rabbit. Syringe. Antibiotics. Now."

Chas put up his hand to push it away. However, he was in no fit state to do battle with Mary-Jo, and as she skilfully jabbed the needle into his thigh he passed out.

"Still frightened of needles I see." She said sarcastically, and reaching for the scissors she started to cut away his shirt. "Antiseptic—and lots of it, Huggie." Pouring the liquid onto the open wound she started cleaning away the dirt as she rolled him onto his side. "He is one lucky son of a bitch, the bullet went clean through."

Huggie pushed the dressing trolley over to Mary Jo and handed her another syringe. "Thanks, he'll need a tetanus shot too. After spending all this time and effort patching him up it would be thoughtless of him to die on me just because he's afraid of a little prick."

"Wouldn't it just. Ouch! Mary-Jo we're gonna have to stop meeting like this."

"Is that so? Well if you'd stop fucking around and get a real job we wouldn't have to. Tell me—what does the other guy look like?"

"Last I saw he was on the ground twitching. Two bursts of the Taser, he'll think twice before jumping the Ninja Warrior again. He was still alive when I left him in the woods down by the Lake. I'd say if the bears don't get to him he has a 50/50 chance of being alive when he wakes up."

"What's with all this Ninja shit, Chas? And don't worry if the bears don't get him Big Foot might."

"Ouch! Please don't make me laugh; it hurts like hell when I do that."

"What did I say that was funny? If something hurt me that much I'd sure as hell refrain from doing it. How about you, Huggie? Huggie? I wish he wouldn't keep doing that, it's unnerving the way he vanishes."

"An old Injun trick I guess. Will I live?"

"Unfortunately, yes. Normal folk however would have high-tailed it to hospital or at the very least a doctor if they got shot. You go see the vet!"

"With good reason. They'd be required to report all shooting related injuries and you're not. I was set up and what's worrying me more is I never saw it coming. Do you reckon I'm losing my touch?"

"I reckon you're losing your marbles, never mind your touch. You should report the incident, Chas, next time you might not be so lucky. You'd better stay here for a few days so I can keep an eye on you. There was a load of dirt and stuff in it; I cleaned it up but there's always a chance something might have crawled inside."

"Ugh, gross, and thanks, I owe you. Can I use your phone? Only I inadvertently fed mine to a truck load of pigs. Don't ask; it would take to long to explain."

Mary-Jo handed him the telephone and went out to check on another patient. "Troy—Harold Finn, I'm afraid we have a slight problem. I'm going to be out of action for a few days, someone took a shot at me. Luckily for me they were wide of the mark; I'll get a friend to snoop around a little. See if he can't find out who's behind it, I'll be in touch when I have some news."

"Should I be doing something, maybe hire some protection, Chas?"

"Might be wise, just until we know who's behind it. Oh and Troy, stay out of the woods near Sukie's Hollow, might be a bit of bear activity round about."

"Understood, take care friend and don't worry about the extra costs, send me the bill and I'll take care of it." The conversation had confirmed his gut feeling. Troy wasn't behind the double cross, so all he had to do now was figure out who was. That narrowed down the field to just under a couple of hundred people, give or take a few. In his line of work one made the odd enemy, and being shot at was par for the course. And a few days in the cabin in the woods with Mary-Jo could be exactly what the doctor ordered. No one would think of looking for him out here.

He reckoned that the clean up team would have reported him as missing in action by now. Pigs will eat anything if they're hungry enough, even mobile phones! As it was, he'd be laying off the pork for a while, that's for sure. As for the guy back in the woods, at a guess that'd be where Huggie had disappeared. He'd be a checking on the bear's progress, and maybe helping them out a little. A quick flick of the wrist and it would be game over.

Troy looked at his watch it would be about lunchtime in France. He took the telephone from his pocket and dialled Charlene's mobile.

"Troy, thank goodness you've called, I tried your office and they said you were working from home. Jason's in hospital. He fell down the attic stairs last night. He's got a couple of cracked ribs and a broken wrist but he's gonna be fine. He should be home this evening if he behaves himself.

"Jesus, Charlene, what was he doing in the attic in the middle of the night?"

"He was playing with the Ouija board he found in amongst some junk earlier in the day. Something spooked him and he missed his footing on the stairs. Luckily for him the door was shut and it broke his fall. And before you asked I put it in the trash can when I got back from the hospital this morning. That way no-one else will be tempted to fool around with it."

"I take it you didn't know it was up there? You know the dangers in fooling around with the powers of evil."

"It was a child's board game, Troy, nothing else and it's gone now okay, and no, I had no idea of its existence."

"Well, all the same, I'd feel happier if you fetched the local preacher man in to sprinkle some Holy water, and wave his crucifix around. Just to be sure, okay. I hope you gave him a dressing down—stupid boy. Too much time on his hands, the devil makes work for idle hands you know Charlene."

"Yes, Troy, so you've said, but like I said he was just fooling around, nothing more." Charlene felt her temper rising, why did every conversation they had these days have to include God.

"So other than Jason how is everyone? I telephoned a couple of times yesterday and got no reply. I really miss you guys."

That was her cue to tell him she missed him too, but that would be a lie she figured was best left unsaid. "Yes, well that's only natural and I'm sure the kids miss you too; they've not seen you for months and likewise Luna and Juno. We have to fetch them from the kennels next Saturday their quarantine period is finally up. As we speak there's a man outside building them a cosy little home in the back garden. The kitchen's was fitted yesterday, and the builder is coming next week to make a start on the attic for you and the boys. I got him to quote for an air conditioning unit so you won't fry next summer holidays."

"That's good, are you okay, Charlene, only you sound a little stressed?"

"I'm just tired, I spent the night at the hospital with Jason and… sorry, Troy, there's someone at the door. I'll get Jason to call you this evening. Bye."

"Charlene, hello, are you still there?" She'd ended the call and that had unnerved him. His youngest son had been dabbling with the powers of darkness and his wife was avoiding all emotional contact. He'd lost the controlling interest of the one thing he'd wanted most in his life. His family, he'd let petty differences take priority and things had gotten out of hand, and that call had confirmed his worse fear. Their marriage was over, and had been for some time. Charlene and the kids were happier without him. Perhaps he shouldn't have agreed so readily to the move. He had known he would never leave Atlanta permanently, and he now knew that Charlene wouldn't be back. They were lost to him forever.

15

Troy put the telephone down on the table and made his way over to the bar. He took the bowl of oranges from under the counter and switched on the juice extractor. It was way too early in the morning to be thinking about Bourbon, that's how alcoholics got started, and he didn't intend to follow the route his father had taken. No, there was a time and a place for whisky and 6:30 in the morning wasn't it.

He needed to focus on matters closer to home; just what exactly was Bastian Lamare afraid of them finding out. What deep, dark secret was he keeping? He picked up the telephone; Brother Johnson would know exactly who to sweet talk to find out. He dialled his private line.

"Hi, Troy, it's a little early in the day for social chit chat, do I take it you've seen the news?"

"No, I've not been up long."

"Our neck of the woods has a bear problem it would seem. A courting couple found a half eaten body late last night and called the cops. The cops found tire tracks and a Taser; unfortunately the serial number's been removed so they've no way of tracing it. Our esteemed leader's been taken in for questioning; apparently the body was one of ours."

"Anyone I know?"

"The new guy, the creepy one with the funny eye, Brother Michaels, can't say he'll be sadly missed. I always thought he was a bit strange; he obviously pissed someone off big time. They're appealing for witnesses to come forward, and scouring the countryside for a white van they believe may have been in the area. It was seen late yesterday afternoon heading out from the lake towards Buckhead. I'll bet you any money it has nothing to do with the incident. Probably belongs to some poor old guy who was caught short and stopped to take a dump! What do you think, Troy?"

"I think I'll leave it up to the cops to do the detective work. That's why they're paid our tax dollars, for solving mysteries we poor dumb critters can't! Do we know if Bastian's contacted a lawyer?"

"Not a clue, in any case I expect you'll be the first person he contacts on matters of the law, with you being a lawyer an all."

"Great, I need this now like a hole in the head. My youngest, Jason, is in hospital in France. He fell down the attic stairs playing with an instrument of devil worship. Sorry, Dave shouldn't involve people in marital disputes, bloody women. See what you can find out for me please, Dave."

"About devil worship?"

"No, of course not, sorry, forget it. I'm sure Bastian will contact me when and if he requires my input."

Damn, that was all he needed, the brothers thinking he was losing the plot and the cops investigating the Brotherhood. Be interesting to see how Bastian got himself out of this one. Who exactly was Brother Michaels, and what was the connection between him and Chas? Chas hadn't recognized Michaels so it was a safe assumption he wasn't central intelligence.

He wondered if he'd seen this mornings' news, and in all the excitement he'd forgotten to ask Brother Johnson whose palm he needed to grease to get background information on Bastian. Today had started badly, and considering the manner of Brother Michaels' unfortunate demise perhaps he should think about quitting Bastian's band. Perhaps the Numerologists had it right and there really was something in a name. Doomed by name and by nature.

Troy wandered into the den and booted up his laptop he couldn't ring Chas but he could email him.

'Hey, Harold, you seen the morning's news?' He clicked the send button and then poured himself a second glass of juice and waited for the reply.

'Yo, man, yeah, never been a bear problem at the lake before. Been a few sightings of big foot in the past, mostly attributable to kids smoking weed or eating magic mushrooms. If your dog's sick you should take her to the vets.'

Okay now he knew where to find him. He dressed quickly and picking up his laptop and headed for the service stairs. The Mercedes was too conspicuous for a trip to the vets, Matt's battered jeep would do. It still had the cage they used to transport Luna and Juno around town in the back. He drove the jeep out of the garage and into the heavy stream of city bound traffic. Lucky for him he was headed in the opposite direction.

Half an hour later he pulled in to a clearing behind the vets and climbed out of the Jeep. He took the smaller carrying cage out of the trunk into the waiting room and placed it behind the door.

"Can I help you, sir?"

"Sick dog, Chas recommended that the man, I mean, that I brought the animal here."

"Follow me please; the dog will be fine there."

Troy followed the Indian through the empty surgery out into the forest to a small clearing. He whistled three times and waited. The vegetation in front of him slid silently back to reveal a small log cabin. The Indian bid him enter and then disappeared. Indubitably that was Huggie, Chas's right hand man.

The cabin inside was sparsely furnished with a couple of odd chairs and a wonky table. Troy wondered what he was expected to do now. So engrossed in his deliberations he didn't see Chas come in by the side door.

"Troy, my man, how you doin. Sorry about the cloak and dagger stuff. Huggies' idea I'm afraid. Sometimes he takes his position a little too seriously. Come on through to the house and I'll get Tata to make us some fresh coffee."

Troy followed Chas through the door into a tiled courtyard. Over to the right was an Olympic sized pool, to the left stables, and behind them a path leading down to the house overlooking the lake.

"Welcome to my humble abode, we'll have coffee on the deck I think, if that's okay by you, Troy?"

"Yeah it's fine by me. Wherever did you find this place?"

"Oh I didn't find it, I built it from scratch. The little old cabin in the front was all there was when I bought the property. I added bits as I got the money; the lake house was my first project. Tata lives there with Huggie and Mary-Jo, my ex-wife. I flit in and out depending on where the work takes me. You look a little stunned, Troy. What did you expect a tin shack?"

"No of course not, but I didn't expect a mini version of the White House neither, it's incredible. Charlene would kill to live in a place like this."

"Very droll, considering my line of work, Troy."

"Yeah, sorry, slip of the tongue, I take it you've seen the news. They found the man in the woods half eaten; they reckoned it's the work of a bear. They identified him as one John Michaels; he's a member of the Brothers of Doom, Bastian Lamare's happy band of followers, or rather he was. They've taken Bastian in for questioning. I spoke to Dave Johnson this morning he filled me in on the grizzly details. Sorry, no pun intended, they found your Taser at the scene too. Thank heaven you'd removed the serial number."

Chas turned to Huggie who disappeared, returning moments later carrying a small box. "It wasn't my Taser, Troy. Mine's here, and it's been on charge since last night. Whoever dropped the Taser was the last person to see Brother Michaels alive. And I'd go so far as to hazard a guess that he or she had more than a little to do with his untimely demise."

"That throws new light on the matter; Chas have you any idea who Michaels was working for? You said he wasn't one of yours?"

"No he wasn't CIA or FBI. If he'd been either of those the area would be crawling with men in black suits and Ray-Ban's by now. Whoever hired him to take me out must have been under the impression he was capable of the job. He was good, I never saw him, and the first I knew was when I woke up in the back of the van bleeding."

"Yeah, but obviously not good enough, you're still alive. I think Bastian knows more than he's telling. Michaels has been snooping around in Brotherhood business for a while and it was only a matter of time before he came a cropper."

"Put it down on the table please, Huggie, and tell Mary-Jo I won't be here for lunch."

He nodded and disappeared. "Does he have a habit of doing that…?"

"Old Indian trick. Shall we go?"

"Sorry, you've lost me Chas, go where?"

"Have a mooch around Bastian Lamare's place of course, that's why you came here today isn't it?"

"I suppose so, I'm sure he's hiding something. It's a gut feeling I have; something about the man gives me the creeps. It's his eyes, they're evil, and they bore right into your soul. He threatened me too, when I told him the revenue people weren't the only one's following him on Twitter. He threatened my family, and last night my son fell down the attic stairs while playing a board game."

"I thought your wife and kids had moved to France, Troy? In fact, I distinctly remember you said you'd be joining them at Christmas. You're not making sense, Troy, and that's not like you. Anyone would think you were scared, really scared. Why don't you start by telling me what you know about Bastian Lamare, and we'll take it from there." He looked up to see Mary-Jo. "Hi sweetheart, sorry change of plan, we'll be one extra for lunch and Troy will be staying with us for a few days. Troy, this is my ex, the vet who saves my butt when I get into scrapes."

"Hello, Troy, nice to meet you. Can you do me a favour please; try and keep him out of trouble until he heals properly this time?"

"I'll do my best I promise."

Mary-Jo eyed the two of them suspiciously; she knew when Chas was up to no good. His body language sent out warning signals, his way of keeping her safe. What she didn't know couldn't hurt her type of stuff.

"Lunch will be about five minutes, which will give you just enough time to wash your hands and head for the table. You know how Tata hates food going cold."

16

With lunch over the two men made their excuses and disappeared into the boatshed. Chas pushed the boat down the ramp and attached the outboard.

Bastian Lamare's place was lakeside, a small log cabin in the woods with a huge barn, in which they held their meetings. He'd named it 'The Retreat' and this he shared with a couple of goats, several rabbits and numerous chickens. His half-hearted attempt at self-sufficiency. He'd attempted a small garden too but had given up, as it was impossible to dig, he kept hitting tree roots and breaking the blades on the ancient plough.

Chas steered the small open craft to the shore about half a mile downstream of the retreat and Troy jumped out.

"I'll go on ahead and take a look around; and if the coast's clear I'll whistle."

"Okay but be careful I don't want to have to explain to your wife and kids that you've been arrested for breaking and entering or worse."

Troy unlatched the gate and crept silently across the courtyard and let himself into the cabin. The place was deserted. He whistled to Chas.

"I checked out back, it's clear, he must still be with the Cops. Let's rifle through a few draws and such, and see what we find." Opening the door to the bedroom he went inside; someone had beaten them to it. Whatever it was they'd been searching for he guessed they'd not found. He knelt down beside the bed and looked underneath.

"Someone's been here before us, Chas, the bedroom's trashed. You find anything?"

"This could be what they were searching for Troy." He held up a flash drive. "I think it would be best if we took it back to my place to look at it."

"Yeah this place gives me the creeps. I don't know if this is important, I found it taped under the bed, Chas."

"Bring it along; I saw plastic sacks under the sink." Troy pulled out a black sack, and shoved the file inside. Hidden behind some tins of paint at the back of the cupboard was a shoe box. He shoved it in the bag, the cops would be taking the blame for ransacking the place so what the hell.

"Time to make ourselves scarce, we don't want to be here when the weirdo comes back." Chas said calmly.

Making their way back towards the boat—Chas bent to tie his laces. An arrow whizzed over his head and thudded into a tree a few feet from where Troy had been standing only seconds before. He wasn't sure the pigeon attached to it had been the intended target. Either way they needed to haul ass before the owner of the arrow came to collect his prey.

Troy was already in the boat drifting downstream with the current. Pulling an old fishing rod from under the seat he dropped the line into the water. He would bluff his way out; give Chas the opportunity to find cover.

Chas dropped to the ground, and crawled towards a clump of bushes; if he could make it underneath before the hunter came close he'd be home free. He rolled under the brambles coming to rest in the middle of the thicket. Bastian Lamare saw the man sat in the boat and took a second arrow from his sheath, and placing it in the crossbow he aimed it at Troy.

"Can't you read? Sign back there say's this here is private

property. I could shoot you; I'd be within my rights."

"Well if you do that, Bastian, you'll need to find yourself another lawyer. I thought the Brothers were welcome anytime chez vous. I decided I needed a hobby so I borrowed this old boat from a friend over the other side of the lake."

"Troy Hamilton-Davies—fishing. Now I've seen everything. You stupid son of a bitch, I almost shot you back there, good job your laces came undone."

Bastian hadn't seen Chas, or rather he had, but he hadn't seen Troy jump in the boat. Thank god he'd not started the outboard. He put the rod back in the boat and jumped into the water. Tying the rope to the bush he walked over to where Bastian stood.

"You catch anything then?"

"Nah, nothing's biting."

"That's what I figured, come on up to the house and I'll fix us a drink. You saved me a trip to town; someone silenced Brother Michaels permanently last night, the cops had me answering questions all morning. Said I wasn't to leave town."

"They let you go, so they must be satisfied."

"Yeah, but if they come back I want to know my back's covered by the best attorney money could buy, if I had any that is."

"Sure, that's what friends are for; you mentioned a drink, make mine bourbon on the rocks and you're on." He followed Bastian to the house watching his reaction as he opened the door.

"Putain, espèce de merde, c'est quoi ce bordel! Looks like they decided to see if I was telling the truth."

"They sure were messy bastards, come on I'll help clear up."

"No. Its fine I'll do it later."

"If you're sure, look, forget the drink, you've got enough to do here and I should be getting back. I don't want my friend to think I've run off with his boat. You have my number if you need my professional advice, and in any case I'll be here at the weekend. Maybe you'll be straight by then."

"Peut-etre, sorry I forget myself sometimes and break into my native tongue."

"No problem, can't answer you though, never was any good with languages. No Comprendo."

"That's Spanish, Troy, I'm French, or at least I was in my

previous life."

"Were you married, Bastian? My wife and I recently separated, and this'll kill you. She left America and went to live in France; she just bought a house in Vannes. My kids are all enrolled in private schools and are now bilingual, hell she even took my dogs.... I really miss those dogs."

Laughing he clapped Troy on the back. "You're a scream; you'd make a great comedian?"

"You reckon? I'll keep that in mind if I ever need to change jobs in a hurry, and I'll be sure to look you up for a reference."

"In answer to your question, yes, I was married, had kids too, but that was a long time ago."

"Did she leave and take the kids too? Why should women get exactly what they want, when they want, and how they want? And what do we get? To pay for it, that's what. I'd better go or it'll be dark before I get back, we'll talk again. Charlene sent me photos of the new house I'll bring them at the weekend."

"Bring a bottle too, looks like mine took a tumble." Holding the broken bottle up for closer inspection.

"Shame that, it was a mighty fine whiskey too. How come you know about Four Roses, Bastian, I thought wine was a Frenchman's poison?" His expression changed to one of indifference in an instant, the amity Troy had sensed before disappearing along with the daylight.

"I'd better get on with my clearing up." He opened the door. "Stick to the paths Troy, the woods are dangerous places around nightfall, as brother Michaels found to his disadvantage."

"Thanks for the advice." The door closed and he was alone again. Strange man, Bastian. He had almost forgotten himself back there. Married with children, that had been a turn up for the books. Troy wondered what had happened to them. Maybe the stuff they'd found in the house would give him an insight into the former life of Bastian Lamare.

He walked down the path towards the boat. There was no sign of Chas, now what did he do?

"Psst! Troy, I'm in the bush behind you. Bring the boat downstream a little, did he suspect anything?"

"No, nothing. He's mighty pissed with whoever trashed

his place but he doesn't suspect me. He's a strange one; I'll tell you about it later when we're back on safe ground, it feels weird talking to a bush."

Hampered by the fading light, the journey back to Chas's place took forever coupled with his reluctance to use the outboard. He was almost certain they were being followed. He'd seen a flash of light, a torch perhaps and he'd stayed low in the boat. Unfortunately for him Troy was no champion oarsman, and he gave up hope of staying dry in the first few minutes.

"For Christ sake, Troy, start the outboard before you drown me."

"Sorry, never could get the hang of these things. Is he still tracking us?"

"I don't think so, but just in case I'll stay on the floor. Here put this on otherwise you'll not be able to see where you're going." Chas said handing him a head torch.

"Great. Tell me—are there any alligators in the lake?" Chas shrugged and continued scanning the shoreline for signs of movement.

"If I say yes you'll panic, and if I say no you might get cocky. Let's just say if you fall in I'm not gonna be the one to dive in and pull you out, and leave it at that."

"Geez, I can't think why I let you talk me into this lil'ol excursion. Err, I don't want to worry you, Chas, but there's a boat heading straight for us."

"You sure it's a boat and not a log or something?"

"Yes, quite sure, and if it's Bastian we're fucked. He's bound to see you down there when he comes alongside."

Chas lifted the night vision glasses and focused on the approaching craft, and laughed. "You can stop panicking, it's only Huggie. I daresay Mary-Jo sent him out to make sure we're not out here feeding the gaitors."

The canoe pulled alongside. "Tata says you got five minutes, before your dinners' in the dog. He said I was to make sure you stay out long enough for him to reap his reward for being a faithful old hound."

17

Mary-Jo and Tata watched as the three men made their way from the boathouse. This was the time of day she loved best, sat on the deck with a glass of chilled Chardonnay watching the sunset over the lake. Tata looked up from her knitting. "Looks like the gaitors missed out again, the dog too. Poor Sultan, come here boy, Tata has a special treat just for you. A nice juicy marrow bone, with pasta and trimmings."

"No wonder the dog's getting fat, Tata, you're spoiling him, he's had his biscuits for tonight."

"Biscuits. Them's no food for my Sultan, he needs nourishment not punishment."

"Tata, his biscuits are especially created for a dog of his weight and size. A balance of vitamins, minerals, meat, vegetables and cereal to help keep him in tip top condition."

"Yeah well he don't like em, he buries them in the garden under the Azaleas. Why do you think they keep dying?"

"You ain't gonna win this one, sweetheart. Tata's right I

watched him bury them."

Troy smiled; it was a pity Charlene wasn't here she would have enjoyed this. The past thirteen years together had been blighted by a war of words, followed by interminable silences sometimes lasting for weeks at a time. Neither party prepared to give in, resulting in the recent separation. What he hadn't bargained for was Charlene moving his family to the other side of the world and excluding him. She'd told the children he was coming out to join them at Christmas. What she'd omitted to tell them was that it was only for two weeks holiday.

A skiing holiday at that. He'd paid for four rooms, two singles, a twin and a double, hoping she would give their reconciliation a chance and not make a scene. Unfortunately his plan backfired when the hotel in question sent the confirmation of the booking to Charlene. She'd telephoned him and told him she did not intend to share a room with him and that Matthew wouldn't be coming with them. He preferred Christmas in Paris with his friends, to being with his father.

In the courtroom he reigned supreme, juries were putty in his hands, but his family, that was a different story altogether. Charlene had changed, she was no longer the sweet, naïve young girl he'd fallen in love with. Somewhere along the way she'd turned into her mother.

"Penny for them?"

"Uh, oh sorry, miles away. What happened between you and Mary-Jo to cause the split?"

"Nothing I can put my finger on, married too young I suppose. She wants kids, and a husband who'll still be alive when they graduate. Trouble is she spends all her time buried out here in the woods with Tata, Huggie, and the animals, instead of getting out there and finding herself a man."

"Perhaps she's having second thoughts? Tell me did she ask for a divorce, a settlement, custody of Sultan?"

"No, not as yet, you think she's having second thoughts?"

"I'd stake my reputation on it. If she ain't divorced you yet my friend it's because she still loves you. If I were you I'd give serious consideration to finding a steady job, one that won't get you shot at."

Chas looked over to where Mary-Jo sat. Everything he'd ever done had been for her. For the family, but work always got in the way. Maybe the man was right—there were desk jobs to be had in the agency, all he had to do was ask. He saw the arrow whistle past Troy's head to late too warn them. "Everyone on the deck now. Tata, Mary-Jo, you okay?"

"Sultan's not moving." Mary-Jo whispered.

"I think he's dead, Mary-Jo, I want you to quickly make your way inside and put the shutters down. You too, Troy."

"But, you'll need help, and I…"

"You'll help me best by staying with the girls. Mary-Jo, call the cops. I'll take Huggie with me, and when I find the son of a bitch that killed my dog… I'll tear his fucking head off. Now move, and that's an order."

Troy followed the two women, pausing to drop his jacket over the dog lying motionless on the deck. Poor Sultan, he hadn't even gotten his treat. He scooped the dog into his arms and dived under the metal shutters seconds before they clanged shut.

"Is there somewhere I can put him, Mary-Jo? I couldn't leave him out there all alone."

"We'll take him to the basement. Tata, call the cops please."

"Is he dead?" The old lady asked quietly,

"I'm afraid so."

Troy put the dog on the table and took out his telephone; he'd felt it vibrate as he rolled under the shutter. "Shit. Stop Tata calling the cops Mary-Jo. It's from the shooter; if we call the cops he'll kill the hostage."

"How did he get your number, Troy?"

"It's Bastian Lamare, he says we have something of his in our possession, and when we give it back the hostage will be released unharmed. If we call the cops he says he'll feed her to the gaitors."

He pulled out the package he'd found taped to the bed and emptied the contents on the floor. He picked up the pile of newspaper clippings and flicked through them. They were from French newspapers. There was a false passport and a bundle of money, mostly Euros. He turned to Mary-Jo who shook her head.

"Too late, Troy, she's already made the call, do you know who he has hostage?"

"At a guess, Naomi."

"A close friend?"

"You could say that, or at least she was. Do you speak French, Mary Jo?"

"A little, why?" He tossed her the bundle of newspaper clippings.

"See if you can make sense of these." She spread them out on the floor, and arranging them in date order, and then started to read.

"They're cuttings relating to a murder several years ago in Vannes. The Police are asking for help in tracing the whereabouts of someone called Sebastian Delamare. He's wanted in connection of the murder's of his wife Annie and their four children in early April 2011 in Vannes. It says he killed his wife, children, and the family dogs and then buried them under the terrace of their rented home. Apparently he stuffed them into hessian sacks filled with quick lime and buried them in shallow graves. The wife and three of the children were found in one grave, the eldest son and the dogs were found in a separate grave a few feet away."

Mary-Jo picked up another clipping. "This one tells of a woman they want to interview, they believe she was his lover. She disappeared after withdrawing a large sum of money from a bank account in the joint names of herself and her husband, and the police are concerned for her welfare. And this is the report of a body being found, a blonde, believed to be the missing woman, but there's no trace of the money. The police are said to have issued a Blue Alert through Interpol and are investigating sightings throughout France, America and Australia. They are all dated from 2011 except for this last one. It's from a notaire putting the house where the murders were committed up for sale at the request of the Estate of the late owner. There's a picture of the house too. Do you think the guy mentioned in here is Bastian Lamare?" Mary-Jo asked.

"I'd bet my pension on it. He's running scared—after the body turned up in his neck of the woods the police hauled him in for questioning."

"Whose body did they find, Troy?"

"A member of the cult Bastian runs, Brother Michaels, his half eaten body was found in the woods by a courting couple."

"Ugh! I bet that put them off their stroke. Sorry, bad

taste."

"Nah, thought crossed my mind too. You say there's a picture of the house where the murders took place, Mary-Jo?"

"Yep, it looks a bit run down though, I wonder if they ever found anyone stupid enough to buy it. Who in their right mind would want to live in a house where five people were murdered? Here…"

Troy studied the picture and then took out his telephone and scanned through the photographs in his telephone Charlene had sent him of the house. "It's Charlene's house—the house in the picture, look!"

"It looks similar, Troy. I daresay there are many houses in the area built by the same builder. The only sure fire way to find out would be to telephone the sales people and ask the address. They'll be bound to know if it's been sold and to whom. But it's way too early to telephone now. France is about six hours in front of us time wise."

"This is going to be a long night. I should never have let her go. I should have gone to France and looked the house over before she bought it; instead I gave her carte blanche. If anything happens to her or my kids because of my stupidity I'll never forgive myself."

"And, Naomi?" Troy shrugged.

"She's a diversion, we have sex, and I pay her, end of story. And what about you, for someone whose dog was just shot you don't look too upset."

"I see animals die on a daily basis, Troy, its part of my job. It doesn't mean I didn't care for Sultan. What's bothering me is why you think something bad could happen to Charlene and your family. This guy Sebastian only rented the house in France; he didn't own it, and who's to say this guy and Bastian are one and the same. It's supposition, and you of all people should know Troy that supposition isn't admissible as evidence. No point worrying about something that hasn't happened. What we should be worrying about is your friend, Naomi. Have you tried telephoning her at home?"

"No, but she said she was going out of town for a few days."

"Then phone her mobile, here, I'll do it if you like." Mary-Jo said, taking the telephone from Troy.

"You won't find her under Gibbs. She's listed under her

professional name, 'Sultry Spice'—she's a striptease artist. You gotta problem with that?"

"Sorry, was my disapproval that obvious? It's none of my business who you see in your spare time. You're a married man whose wife left him, you aren't the first man to take up with an exotic dancer type and you won't be the last. You must be lonely up there in the clouds."

"Why do you say that? I spend most of my time at work surrounded by people."

"Troy, your secretary in her office, the other partners, the odd private investigator, and cops, don't count as people. Here, it's ringing."

"No-ones picking up, and Naomi never goes anywhere without her mobile. Damn Bastian Lamare. The cops will be crawling all over the woods surrounding his place by now. He'll be long gone, but what about Naomi?

18

Bastian Lamare sat on the small wooden bench, watching, and waiting, safe within the cabin. He peered out through the grimy window; it had been dark for some time. They would have called the search off until first light; the swamp was a dangerous place at night. If the alligators didn't get you the bears might.

The girl lay on the bunk in the corner of the cabin sleeping; all trussed up like a Thanksgiving turkey. Her eye was badly swollen where he'd hit her. Her cheek cut by his wedding ring, ironically the only item of value he now possessed.

She was alive, for the time being, but only because she was worth more to him this way. He needed his passport and the money. Without it he would be going nowhere. He couldn't risk going back to the retreat, far too dangerous. His only hope lay with counselor Hamilton-Davies, and his attachment to the girl.

Licking his lips, lasciviously, he would have himself a little light entertainment before he decided her fate. If she was incredibly good he'd spare her, maybe. For nothing in life was certain.

Time to send another message, and seal her fate. Weighing up the odds, he reckoned they were in his favour, for now at least. He tapped out the message and pressed send, and sat back and waited for the reply.

One thing was certain he would have to leave Atlanta. As he saw it he had three choices, Canada, Cuba, or Mexico. He pulled out his map and spread it out across the table. Cuba would be furthest away and would entail a plane ride, which increased his chances of being picked up by the cops. Something he was keen to avoid for all kinds of reasons.

That left Mexico and Canada. He would have to make his way to Alabama and then on to Memphis. He'd never been to Memphis; he could visit Graceland and Elvis's final resting place. Get real. This is not a vacation you're planning stupid; it's an escape from a murder wrap. From Memphis he traced the route through Arkansas, Oklahoma and then on to Albuquerque, New Mexico. A long, long way, the distance graph marked it at almost 1400 miles, granted he'd have the chance of work along the way. But a long way just the same.

He sat back and looked at the phone, no reply. Counselor Hamilton-Davis should have got back to him by now. Turning back to the map, and Canada, Ontario to Georgia was a mere 735 miles. That clinched it. He would go to Canada. At least some of the people there spoke French, making it easier for him to blend in.

His mobile vibrated towards him across the shiny surface of the table. About time Counselor, I was beginning to think you didn't care about poor little Naomi. He picked it up and opened the mailbox; there were just three words on the screen.

"Screw you, Asshole." Well if that was the way he wanted to play it so be it. Slamming the mobile down, he picked up the bottle of water and walked over to where the girl slept and poured it over her. Her eyes flew open; the man was standing over her, staring wildly—the crazy man was going to kill her. Rocking back and forth, she tried to recall The Lord's Prayer, but the words wouldn't come. Bastian put out his hand and grabbed her by the throat. Pinning her to the wall, his mouth up close to her. His putrid breath was stomach-turning—someone should explain dental hygiene to him. A strange thing to think when one is about to die, even for a 'would be' hooker.

"Counselor Hamilton-Davies has declined my generous offer, so I'm afraid I'm gonna have to teach him a lesson. Nothing personal, Naomi, I can call you Naomi, can't I?" She lifted her tear stained face and spat in his eye.

"Screw you, asshole."

"That's exactly what your boyfriend said. Obviously hanging out with him has led you into bad habits my dear. You're supposed to beg my forgiveness and plead for your miserable life."

"In your dreams. I wouldn't give you the satisfaction. You're gonna kill me anyway so why don't you just get on with it?"

"Sorry, did I say I was going to kill you?"

"I-I, just assumed that's what would happen to me if Troy didn't give you back your stuff."

"Did no-one ever tell you that when you assume, you make an ass out of you and me. Too deep for you? Never mind, don't worry your pretty little head about it. Tell me, Naomi, do you swallow? I asked the counselor a few days back but he declined to comment. I have another question for you. What's he like in bed? Does he go down on you? C'mon don't come the innocent. Or maybe he's a wham, bam, thank you mam, kind of lover, come on, you can tell me. I won't tell a soul, I promise. I know, 'screw you'. Well as it happens, that's exactly what I intend to do. I'm going to do you every way you've ever been screwed and then some. You'll be begging for mercy before the days' out. You ever watched a lion at it. No? Well his sex is barbed, that's how he stays inside, that, and the hold he has on his beloved's neck while he's riding her." He rubbed his hand across his crotch. "Well looky here, all this talk of fornication got the old one eyed trouser snake here all stirred up."

Unzipping his jeans he let them slide to the floor exposing his swollen member. Kicking off his shoes, he stepped out of his jeans and tossed them into the corner. Weighing up the pros and cons he decided against getting himself a blow job. Too dangerous—she might decide to get even and bite his pecker off. And as tempting as it was to ram all eight, long, hard, inches of it down her throat and shoot his load, he declined.

Rolling her over, he sat on her whilst undoing the rope around her ankles and retied her to the bed posts. He then did the same with her wrists, as she bucked, wriggled, and squirmed beneath him. "My, oh my, feisty young thing aint ya, don't mind me, you just buck all you like, you aint going nowhere but heaven, lady. I'll just get you warmed up a little, don't want to tear the ass right out of you, not yet anyways. Now if you tense up like that, sugar, it's gonna hurt a whole lot more than it needs to."

Naomi bit her lip as he slid his fingers deep inside her. "You're hurting me. You could at least have cut your fingernails."

"My fingernails are the least of your worries lady; you just relax and enjoy what's to come." He exclaimed kneeling between her legs, as he thrust his throbbing member deep inside her with such force she screamed out in pain. "Arrête de crier. It's not like it's your first time, is it? This is just the beginning sugar. I'm just warming up, oh my, you got yourself a real tight hole there, and I just love it when you squeeze your butt together. Makes me wanna bang away faster. Gotta pace myself though don't want to leave you wanting. Soon you'll be a screaming, and hollering, and begging for more." Sliding out of her he wiped himself off on a towel.

"Would ya looky here, you're bleeding. Don't tell me I just fucked me my first virgin ass. You should have said sugar, and I'd have slapped a little lubricant on before I slid her up there. Tut, tut, shame on the counsellor, he doesn't know what he's been missing. I need a drink, and I got me a nice bottle of Bourbon—Four Roses, you want some?" He thrust the bottle to her lips and tilted it back. If she drank enough it might obliterate the pain.

"Doucement, sugar, I only got me one bottle of this here liquid gold." And taking the bottle from her he took a swig and wiping his mouth across his arm he put the top back on the bottle and set it down carefully on the table. He walked back to the bed and straddling her once more, slapping her hard on the ass.

"Get on your knees bitch! That there was just the entrée;

this here is the pièce de résistance. Come on bitch; get that ass higher. I want to be able to see where I'm a going, and I aint got all day. When old one eye here gets the urge I just gotta give her what she's craving. And right now she's craving pussy. All wet an' juicy and you aint in no position to deny her entry." Bracing herself for the onslaught to come she gripped the blanket in her hands and burying her head in the pillow. The pain was excruciating, as he pounded away. Closing her eyes, she tried to think of a way to stop him.

"I need the toilet; I can't hold it any longer. Please, I'm begging you."

"See, didn't I tell you, you'd be begging me sooner or later. Don't even think about going through the window sugar. Remember the gaitors are waiting right outside and they're not particular about what they eat, just as long as there's plenty of it." He slammed the bathroom door shut and walked over to the table, picked up the Bourbon, and took a long, hard swig.

Naomi slid to the floor. Dear Lord Jesus, help me out here, I know I've not been a good Christian, but even a 'would be' hooker deserves a break. I'll change jobs, hell; I'll even join a convent if you could just find it in your heart to cut me a little slack here. Pulling herself up she took a clean towel from the rail, ran it under the cold tap, and bathed her wounds. Death would be a welcome relief from the humiliation and pain—her insides torn, and bruised.

"You done yet girl?" He kicked open the door and grabbed her by the arm. "Put your clothes on, it would seem the counsellor changed his mind. Shame for you he didn't do it a couple of hours ago, Naomi. But I'm sure you'll find a way to make him pay for what he's put you through. At the very least he should pay your hospital bills don't ya think? Nothing to say? That's a first, a woman who knows when to keep her mouth shut. Here's what's gonna happen. You hear me gal, cos I's only gonna say it the once, okay?"

She nodded and sat on the edge of the bed with her legs tightly closed. Rivulets of blood trickled down her legs forming a puddle on the floor. Taking a towel from the shelf he grabbed her arm and pushed her back towards the bathroom.

"You got any sanitary towels in that there bag of yours?" She nodded, Bastian opened her bag and fished around inside.

"Here, you know what's to be done, or when we get outside them gaitors will be snapping at your heels. Real excitable they are, and I take it you want to avoid that if possible?" Nodding she went back into the bathroom.

"In a couple of minutes were gonna go out into the woods and I'm gonna exchange you for my belongings, and then I'll be on my way. Now you make sure you holler if you think your man is trying to double cross me. You hear me girl. Cos if you don't you're gonna find yourself with an arrow in your head like good old Sultan. Understood?" She nodded. Bastian grabbed her roughly by the arm, and using her as a human shield they left the cabin and walked towards the clearing.

As he tied her to a lone pine tree he leaned in close and whispered in her ear. "Remember sugar, one false move and you're dead." And with that he disappeared into the undergrowth.

19

They moved silently through the forest, the old Indian stopped suddenly scooping a handful of earth into his hand and examining it. The two men watched as Huggie sniffed the earth then let it fall to the floor.

"What's he doing now Chas?"

"Following the trail, he's a natural. Being part Apache helps, that and the gismo he has in his trouser pocket." Troy hit him hard on the arm. "Ouch, that hurt."

"It was meant to; we wouldn't be in this mess if you hadn't insisted we go snooping around Bastian's cabin."

"Okay, I admit it was a little rash."

"Let's just do as he says, Chas, and get Naomi to safety."

"Do I have a choice, Troy?"

"No you don't, not if you want to get out of these woods alive."

The old Indian stopped and crouched down, and the two men joined him. "The girl's tied to the tree; he has to be close by."

"You're sure this is the spot?"

"The co-ordinates match the ones he sent us."

"Okay so we wait for him to make the first move. Remember we're here to exchange the package for the girl, nothing else. You got that Troy. That means no heroics."

"Yeah I got it. I'm not happy about it, but I'll not jeopardise Naomi's life. She looks pretty beat up. If he's hurt her… I'll kill him."

"Not so fast, he killed my dog remember and that means I have first dibs."

Bastian stood stock-still watching the three men from a safe distance. Huh, there aint a chance in hell you're gonna get close enough, Denman. At least they could have the decency to credit me with a degree of intelligence.

Troy's mobile rang out and Chas scooped it up before the second ring. "You assholes finished your discussion? Good, now put me on speaker—I aint got all day. I have me an agenda, and time is money, ain't that right Counsellor. So listen good, one false move and the lady here dies. I booby trapped the area around the tree, if you move a muscle before I give the word she dies, you too. Got that?"

"Understood, tell us what you want us to do. I promise there'll be no heroics; all we want is the girl."

"You see him, Huggie?"

"Nope, he's covered his back well."

"Hey, Curly, Larry and Mo, are you listening to me?"

"Yeah, we're listening; so what happens now."

"If you girls will stop talking and let me explain. Troy, I want you to take the package and put it in your right hand, and hold your arm out to your side. Keep perfectly still, that way you won't get hurt when the messenger collects it. You got that?"

"Yes, we got it; just do as the man asks, Troy."

"But there's no one here but us."

"Quiet, Troy, just do as he asks."

"Yeah, counselor—shut your mouth and gives your ass a chance."

Troy sprang forward. "I'll kill the son of a bitch, so help me." Chas put out his arm to hold him back and handing the package to him he whispered. "Keep it buttoned Troy before you get us all killed. He won't get far, trust me." Glaring at Troy, Chas moved back several paces. "Okay, Bastian, the package is in place."

"Keep nice and still there, counsellor—I wouldn't want you to get hurt. Just a few seconds longer and you'll be relieved of your burden." They saw nothing out of the ordinary until the sky above him darkened, and the pulsating beat of a large bird in flight grew nearer. The bird of prey swooped down, snatching the parcel from Troy's outstretched hand and then flew off into the distance. "You can put your arm down now. And like I said at the beginning, I booby trapped the area before I tied the bitch to yonder tree. Here's what happens now, you're going to stay exactly where you are and wait for my call. If you try to cut her free beforehand, you all die."

Chas caught hold of Troy's arms and threw him to the floor, pinning him down with his knees until he stopped struggling. "I'm warning you, Troy, I know how frustrating this is but we need to do as he says, for Naomi's sake."

Chas switched on the transmitter, the target was on the move, and that meant the tracking device hadn't been located. Like he'd said—he wouldn't get far.

"How long's it been since he left, Chas?"

"A good hour, I think he duped us. Huggie what do you think, is it safe or what?"

"I'll check the area; if there is a booby trap here I'll find it." Huggie disappeared into the undergrowth. "Keep your heads down you two; I'm going to cut her loose. Naomi honey, I'm not going to hurt you. I'm a friend of Chas, the name's Huggie and I want you to listen very carefully to me. Okay?" She nodded. "Good girl, I'm going to cut the rope, and when I say 'now' I want you to drop to the ground and stay there until I tell you to move, okay?" She nodded and Huggie cut the rope. "Now. Good girl, do you see Chas and Troy in front of you?" She nodded once more. "Okay, now crawl slowly to them, remember to keep low."

Slowly she made her way towards the two men, every movement sending shockwaves of pain though her body, tears coursing down her face. "I can't, it hurts, help me please, Troy." He was on his feet and heading towards her before Chas could stop him.

"Troy, get down." The arrow whistled past grazing his temple before it reached its secondary target, splitting the sapling in two.

"Holy shit! I owe you one Huggie, a centimetre the other way and I'd be pushing up daisies. C'mon sugar, you're safe now, let's get you to the hospital."

"Medevac's on its way, Naomi." Chas gently squeezed her hand.

"And the debriefing?"

"Later, when you've been checked over by the doctor, there's no rush he isn't going anywhere we can't follow."

"Hold on a minute, debriefing – what's going on here?" Troy looked across at Chas and then back to Naomi.

"She's CIA, Troy. Her brief was stick close by you and she did. You're a member of the Brothers of Doom, and Bastian Lamare's legal advisor, and therefore a suspect. It's an alias, his real name's Sebastian Delamare, 58 years old, born and raised in the South of France by his mother, father unknown. Interpol are interested in talking to him about the murder of his wife and children, he's their number one suspect. Sorry, Troy, but we couldn't risk bringing you in the loop until now."

Troy turned to Naomi, hatred in his eyes. "You bitch; you mean to say I've been under surveillance all this time. I even thought about preparing the divorce papers for Charlene; it's what she's wanted for a while. I thought—I hoped, we could get together you and I, and all the time you were with me you were spying on me."

"I'm sorry, Troy—please don't be angry with me."

"She's not to blame Troy; she was just doing the job she's paid for and we have other things to worry about. Now Bastian's on the run there's a chance he might try to make his way back to France, and the house in Vannes. He left something hidden, something he'd tried to keep secret, but the police have it now. The person responsible for the contents started the cataclysmic chain of events that ended in the murders of five people. The house where the murders took place, Troy, is the house in which your ex-wife and children now live.

Your family may well be in danger…

20

THE FRENCH CONNECTION

Troy Hamilton-Davies stood in line waiting to board the Trans- Atlantic flight to Nantes. Having spent an hour on the telephone the previous evening trying to reassure Charlene that all he wanted was to spend some quality time with the children. Take them to Euro Disney maybe or Paris—if he'd told her the real reason behind his trip she would flip. He couldn't see how Chas could be wrong. They had conclusive evidence that Sebastian Delamare had killed his family and then fled the country using a false identity.

Before he left he'd telephoned the hospital to enquire after Naomi. The nurse on duty had said she was comfortable—the standard hospital response. Your head could have fallen off and been stitched on backwards and the response would be the same.

When he'd spoken to Chas last he'd told him she'd had surgery, but that she was doing fine. What had happened had been a direct result of her work. They were the ones responsible, not him, he'd not asked her to spy on him. He was sorry it had ended the way it had, but shit happens and life goes on, and he had other problems to deal with. Like keeping his family alive.

What Chas had omitted to say was that they had admitted her to a sanatorium, for intensive therapy. Furthermore it was uncertain if she would ever return to active field duty.

He'd made Troy promise that at the first sign of trouble, whatever form it took, to contact him. Bastian, he said 'had disappeared' somewhere in Ontario, but they had the full co-operation of the Canadian authorities. They were certain he hadn't left the country. All the airports were on full alert, and they were confident he would shortly be detained. Troy wasn't convinced. After all, Bastian Lamare, alias Sebastian Delamare, had successfully evaded capture for the last seven years.

Turning his attention back to the letter—according to the letter his sons had found a box containing the mummified remains of a new born infant in their attic. News to him, Charlene hadn't mentioned it when she'd telephoned to tell him Jason had fallen down the attic stairs. Which left him wondering how many other snippets of information she'd kept from him?

He glanced back to the covering letter with the report. Detective Inspector Malestroit of the Sûreté had taken the box containing the grisly remains found under the eaves in the attic to the morgue. Who in turn had sent them to the leading forensic anthropologist, Dr. Anne-Marie-Le Straad. And whose report he was planning to read once he was on the plane. It would take his mind off flying; long haul flights were so boring.

Reading between the lines, his wife was still unaware of the macabre history of the house. If she'd known she would have mentioned it before now. How long it would remain a secret would depend on his ability as a lawyer. What she didn't know couldn't hurt her; he loved his family and intended to protect them at all costs. But she wasn't making it easy for him. Charlene had insisted he stay at the Ibis in town. The house was a mess, so she said. She was keeping him at arms length.

It wasn't fair to let the children think there would be a chance of reconciliation because reading between the lines it wasn't going to happen. According to Charlene, Jason was unusually quiet. A couple of nights during the past week she'd heard voices in the early hours of the morning coming from the lounge. But when she'd confronted him at breakfast the first morning he'd said she must have imagined it.

Troy made a list of people he needed to contact on his arrival in Nantes and tucked it inside his briefcase on the seat beside him. The seatbelt sign illuminated and the plane taxied down the runway. He took a piece of candy out of his pocket, popped it into his mouth, and closed his eyes. Take-offs and landings were not his forte; but once the plane was up in the air he was fine.

The plane levelled out and Troy breathed a sigh of relief, and unbuckling his seat belt he picked up the report and started to read.

Pathology report of human mummified remains found in the attic of number 55 Rue St Anne, Vannes: - For an extensive report please contact Dr. Anne-Marie Le Straad.

Gender - Male
Age at time of death – New born, death occurred within the first hour of life.
Cause of death – Asphyxiation.
Time of death Approximate- between the 1st and 2nd of April 2011.
Post mortem shows the infant was full term, with no obvious abnormalities. It is believed that it was placed in the box immediately after his birth.
Small traces of cotton fibres were found inside the infant's mouth. DNA samples taken from the remains are a match to Amelia Delamare, DOB 3rd March 1995 deceased 5th April 2011. Whose body was recovered from 55 Rue St Anne, Vannes on the 7th April 2011 along with the bodies of her three brothers and mother. All the victims died from shotgun wounds.
The youngest victim Ben aged 13 and the infant share the same Y chromosome. No link was established with the other male members of the family.

Troy put the report down, picked up the letter, and read it through again.

My findings with regard to the father of the infant and the child known as Ben are inconclusive. The three other children all have the same DNA markers.

Sorry to leave you with yet another mystery, Inspector Malestroit, but unless you take DNA samples from all the men in Vannes I doubt if we will have a successful conclusion.

It's a very sad case, young Amelia had obviously hidden the pregnancy from her parents, and it is my belief she had given birth alone in the attic. Once the baby was delivered she was confronted by a second dilemma. What to do with the baby. Tragically her choices were limited. And from what you tell me of the father of the girl, she had no one to turn too, the result of which was the unlawful killing of her son.

Perhaps it was a factor in the slayings. If I can be of any further help please do not hesitate to contact me.

Yours sincerely,
Anne-Marie Le Straad

That meant that Sebastian wasn't the real father of his youngest son, but how did that tie in with the dead baby? Annie was the mother of all the children, but not the mother of the baby.

Unless, unless Annie Delamare had an affair, and that affair had resulted in the birth of a son. And whose paternity she had kept hidden from Sebastian for thirteen years. Had that same man betrayed her, and embarked on an affair with her then fifteen year old daughter? Did Annie know? Had she covered for her daughter? It was highly unlikely; a mother wouldn't knowingly protect the man who'd betrayed her by sleeping with her only daughter. Maybe Sebastian hadn't killed his family after all.

What if Annie had killed them to silence them, after killing Amelia and the baby? Or the baby's father, who in turn framed Sebastian to stop Annie going to the police and denouncing him?

The pathologist, anthropologist, or whatever was right. There were far too many 'what ifs'.

"Would you like something to drink sir?" Startled Troy looked up.

"Yes please, Five Roses on the rocks?"

"Certainly sir." She handed Troy a miniature bottle of Bourbon, spooned ice cubes into a plastic beaker, and put it on the tray in front of him. Troy leaned over admiring the view as she bent to serve another passenger. Did the airlines recruit from the Miss America pageants or what? Tall, blonde, slim, and elegant, his type of woman, she looked a lot like Charlene at that age. Perhaps that was the attraction.

'Hello. Just who do you think you are counsellor—Brad Pitt? Get a hold of yourself man. What makes you think she'd give you the time of day? Once you step off this plane she'll forget all about you, and all the other passengers she serves day in and day out. To her you're just another passenger. And while we're on the subject, have you looked in the mirror lately? You've let yourself go over the past year. Go on deny it. I dare you! When was the last time you worked out, I mean really worked out? Exactly, you can't remember. Listen to your inner voice, counsellor; it could save you from making a complete ass of yourself.'

Troy shifted uncomfortably in his seat. 'Don't do it, she'll blow you out, I'm telling you.' His inner voice was telling the truth. He'd let himself go, and he knew exactly when and why he'd stopped taking care of himself. The day Charlene had boarded the plane to France, taking his children—their children, with her. And in that instant he knew, that however long it took he would win her back. He needed her in his life. For without her life was meaningless—he merely existed.

He smiled at the girl as she passed by. His inner voice had won. This time.

21

What Comes around Goes Around

Jason pulled the covers up over his ears but the voices wouldn't stop. "Please, leave me alone, I can't help you. No one can help you, not now, not ever. You're dead, do you hear me, dead." He peeked over the top of the quilt at the young girl sat on the edge of the bed. She had a small bundle wrapped in a tatty old blanket in her arms, which she was rocking backwards and forwards. A baby, the one they'd found in the box.

'It's no use hiding under the covers, Jason, we can still see you, and we know you can see us. We only want to talk, and we won't hurt you. The baby's sleeping; he looks a bit like Ben, my brother. But that can't be, can it?'

Jason pulled the covers down and looked at the young girl. "I don't know. Are you a ghost?"

"Yes, Jason, we all are. Can you keep a secret?"

"Sure I can, I won't tell a soul, cross my heart and…"

"Hope to die? Be careful in your choice of words Jason.

You'd better not tell anyone what I'm about to tell you. Antonio said it was our special secret. He's my boyfriend. Or he was. He's the baby's father, no one knew about us. Mother found me in the attic after the baby was born, but I was too clever for her. I'd hidden Daniel in the shoebox. That's his name. I chose it myself; Antonio said I could. He was going to take me away. We were going to be a real family, but Mother found out and went loony. She said I was a whore and that I couldn't have Antonio because he was hers, all hers. I heard a bang then I don't remember anything else. I didn't mean to hurt the baby; I only put him in the box so she wouldn't find him. You believe me, don't you, Jason?"

"Sure, but how did you get to be a ghost? I mean, I know you must have died an all that, but how, and who, and why?"

"You ask a lot of questions for a boy. I don't remember who killed me, though I suspect the why is Daniel—and the how is easy to figure out." She lifted the hem of her dress. "Someone shot me, see. I have a big hole and it goes all the way through. You can put your hand through and out the other side. Look." She put her hand through the hole. "We all have them; even mother, in her chest, roundabout where her heart would be—if she'd had one. It's her fault my baby died. She wouldn't let me go to him. Said it was better that way, and that no-one would want me, not with a bastard child in tow. I told her I was going to live with Antonio and our baby and she pushed me, boy was she angry. She said she wished I'd never been born and that Antonio didn't really love me. That he was her lover—the bastard, I thought he loved me and all the time he was sleeping with my mother. Antonio lied to me Jason. He said I was the only one." She sat back down on the bed and started to cry, cradling the bundle close to her chest. Jason put out his hand to console her but when he looked up she'd vanished, just like the last time. But this time she'd told him about the baby, her family, and Antonio.

Jason wondered if Antonio from the Pizzeria and the Antonio the girl talked about was the same person. He couldn't imagine a man like him finding a teenage girl attractive.

He lay back down on the bed and closed his eyes. The girl looked to be the same age as his sister. And what kind of a man takes advantage of a kid. If there was one thing mom and dad had drilled into him, it was to watch out for Carly.

How had the girl kept the pregnancy hidden for nine months? Surely someone would have noticed her stomach swelling. He rolled over onto his side. His dad would be here tomorrow, he'd talk to him about the girl. Dad would know what to do, mom would just freak out. And he'd seen the way she acted when Antoine was around.

A kid he may be, but stupid he wasn't. He knew there was something going on between the two of them. When he'd mentioned it to Philip he laughed and suggested he stop reading Carly's girly magazines. Being thirteen sucked, because no one took a 'dumb assed kid' seriously. He'd show them! He'd solve this all by himself; then they'd have to give him the respect he deserved. But where to start?

Reaching under the bed, he pulled the carrier bag out and peeked inside. It was safe, thanks to Carly. She had rescued it from the trash for him when he was in hospital, while mom was talking to dad on the phone.   He might need it later to communicate with the girl and her family. It was kind of spooky coming face to face with a real live dead person. He toyed with the idea of telling Carly about the girl but he didn't want to risk her freaking out too! He'd forgotten to ask the girl her name, and he had meant to ask if the locket Carly had found had once belonged to her too.

He ought to make notes in order to keep track of the events. A good etective would have a notebook with him at all times he was sure. A knock on the door made Jason jump, stubbing his toe on the coffee table as he headed for the door.

"Ouch, who is it?"

"It's me, Carly; I need to talk to you."

"Can't it wait until tomorrow?"

"It is tomorrow if you hadn't noticed, Jason, and no, it can't."

"Oh alright then, come on in, it's not locked." Carly opened the door, closing it quietly behind her, and sat down on the bed in the exact spot the girl had occupied only minutes earlier."

"If I'd known it wasn't locked I would have come in before. Who were you talking to, Jason? Don't try denying it, I was outside, I heard you."

"You wouldn't believe me if I told you."

"Try me." She stared defiantly at him. "I won't tell mom if that's what you're worried about. Is she hiding under the bed or did she slip out the back?"

"You really want to know?"

"Yes, I really want to know."

"Okay. I was talking to the girl who used to live here, a long time ago. I forgot to ask her name. She's dead, and has been for some time. You remember the box we found in the attic. Well that was her baby in the box; his name was Daniel."

"That's not funny, Jason, now tell me who she is, or I will tell mom."

"I just told you, I don't know her name, and she really is dead. Scouts honour, Carly. I'm not making it up, she has a hole in her stomach that she can put her hand through. It's… it's not the first time I've seen her. I think I let her out, up in the attic the night I fell down the stairs. I was playing with the Ouija board and she suddenly appeared. She's the reason I fell down the stairs, I panicked and ran but I missed my footing. She… she cushioned my fall somehow, I don't know how, or why, or at least I didn't until tonight. She needs our help, Carly, to find out who killed her. All she can remember is fighting with her mom about the baby and his father. She told her mom she was leaving and taking the baby with her and going to live with him. The man, the baby's father was called Antonio."

"You're serious aren't you?" He nodded and sat down beside her.

"Yep, I wish I weren't, trust me. She scared the hell out of me up in the attic."

"And now? Are you still scared?"

"No, not any more. I want to help her."

"But how, Jason? It could be dangerous. Hold on a minute—what if her Antonio and mom's solicitor is the same person? You know moms' having a fling with him don't you."

"Yeah, I'm thirteen, not mentally deficient, but his name's Antoine, not Antonio. The way mom's floating around she's either using or scoring."

Carly smiled. "Yeah, she's acting like a love sick teenager; it's gross, and at her age too. Dad will put a stop to it; after all she is still his wife."

"In name only, Carly, both you and I know they haven't slept together in years."

"Thirteen to be exact, Jason. Something must have happened when you were born to change things. Mathew said that up until then they were a normal married couple."

"Oh right, so it's my fault they hate each other. No wonder I'm screwed up."

"Don't be silly, Jason; dad's the one to blame. The doctors said it was inadvisable for mom to have any more children. He refused to sign the papers so she signed them herself. When she came home he moved into the spare room, and that's how it's been ever since."

Carly leaned over and kissed her brother on the cheek. "Yuk. What was that for?"

"Because you're my bro, and I need to ask you a big favour. I have to meet someone tomorrow evening, and I know dad will expect us to eat as a family."

Jason said nothing for a few seconds. "If I cover for you I want your assurance that you'll not be getting up to any mischief. I don't want the same thing happening to you that happened to the girl."

Carly bit her lip, crossing her fingers behind her back. She hadn't lied, not really. "I promise, now get some sleep."

"I'll try, night, Carly."

Carly closed the door behind her and made her way to her room. She hated deceiving Jason this way, but the deed was done. This man had been the light in her dull and boring existence, and old enough to know better. Her candle, and she, the moth who'd flown too close to the flame.

She had known the risks of unprotected sex and now she would pay the price for her wantonness.

22

Carly sat up in bed; she'd hardly slept all night and her mother had called everyone down to breakfast ages ago. Breakfast, the thought of which sent her dashing to the bathroom for the second time in as many minutes. If this kept up her mom would be bound to notice.

"Carly. Get a move on or we'll be late. You haven't forgotten we're picking your father up from Nantes this morning have you?" Damn she was in no fit state for a family outing this morning. She needed to think of something and fast.

Charlene made her way down the garden to the dogs' enclosure. She opened the door and Luna and Juno lurched forward sending her crashing to the ground. The dogs pounced, reducing Charlene to fits of giggles, whilst they licked her to death. She stood up, plucking bits of straw and wood shavings from her hair. That'd teach her to get ready first. "Steady on girls. We have to go out for a while but I promise when we come back you can have the run of the garden." The Labradors looked up at Charlene; and wagging their tails happily they trotted off to see what goodies lay in wait.

She made her way back up to the house. Carly sat at the kitchen table, her hands curled around a piping hot mug of tea. "You look awful sweetheart, are you sickening for something?"

"I think I must be, because I don't feel at all well. Do you think dad will mind if I'm not at the airport to meet him?" Charlene put her hand on her daughter's forehead. "You don't seem to have a temperature, is your period due?"

If her temperature wasn't raised before, it sure as hell was now.

She picked up her mug and sipped her tea, desperately trying to think of a plausible answer. Her mum would have had a vague idea of the date of her period normally. But since they had been living in the hotel she'd not shared a bathroom with her. She crossed her fingers and lied.

"Yes, I think I must be due any day now, so perhaps it's that."

"I thought as much. No, I'm sure he'll understand, and you'll have all day to recuperate before tonight's homecoming celebration. I thought we'd eat at Giovanni's." Carly flushed, she still had to get a message to Antonio, and doing it when all the family were present would be impossible.

"Is Matthew coming home for the weekend?" A swift change of subject and one she knew would divert her mom temporarily.

"No, he has an important exam next week. He'll be cramming like crazy all weekend, and you know what a grouch he is when he's studying. If anyone makes the slightest noise he explodes, I don't know where he gets his temper from. I think they gave me the wrong baby when I left the hospital."

Carly turned a subtle shade of green; oh no she was going to puke again. Putting her hand over her mouth she ran outside and threw up in the bucket her mother used to feed the dogs. *This is not going to work; I am so stupid. Whatever made me think I could keep my condition hidden for any length of time?*

"It's back to bed for you young lady, and if you're no better this evening it's a trip to the doctors. Has anyone else been ill at school this last week?" A get out clause, thank heaven for small mercies.

"Now you come to mention it, mom, yes. Both Serena and Corinne were absent from school for a couple of days last week. They're fine now though, it was just a tummy bug." Crossing her fingers behind her back she said a silent prayer. She figured she'd be doing a lot of praying over the coming weeks. Amelia stood by the patio doors, her baby tucked up in the old blanket, watching.

Good, the others were going out. She would be alone with the girl. Thought she was going to steal my Antonio, and keep the cross and chain did she. Well think again, whore, he's mine, and the necklace too. Until later…

A gentle breeze blew through the open window and the girl vanished. "Who opened the window again? Jason, Philip we need to go now or we'll be late, and you know how your father hates to be kept waiting."

"Chill out mom, Carly's not ready yet."

"Carly's not coming—she's not feeling well. Right are we ready now? Remember, Carly, drink plenty of fluids and if you feel worse telephone the doctor straight away, and will someone please close that window."

"Mum stop fussing, she's a big girl now, you don't need to baby her." There it was again, the 'b' word.

Puzzled by Carly's sudden malaise Jason waited until the others were almost at the car before he spoke. "What's up, Carly? I thought you wanted me to cover for you this evening. You won't get away with the same act twice in one day; you know that don't you." Carly nodded. "Who is he, Carly? And how long have you been seeing him?" Carly gazed down at the carpet, if she looked up she'd cry and blurt it all out and she couldn't risk that, not yet. Not until she'd spoken to Antonio. "Just a guy, no one you know. He's a bit older than me." Damn, she'd already given him' way too' much information.

"Like how much older, Carly? Are we talking a couple of years or what?" Damn her brother, why'd he have to be so persistent? She knew that the longer she took to answer the more he would suspect she wasn't being honest with him. Her hair tumbled across her face, she pushed it back, and tucking it behind her ears she looked up at him.

"Just a couple of years okay, it's no big deal, it's not like he's dad's age if that's what you're thinking." Another lie, you'll not go to heaven if you keep this up girl, that's for sure.

Charlene tooted the horn and Jason headed for the door. "I have to go; look we'll talk again tonight after the others are in bed. Don't worry I'm not going to rat on you; I just want to make sure you're safe that's all. Mom's booked dad into the Ibis in town, which means that she will have to drive him to the hotel after our family get together. Go and lie down, you really do look awful—more so than usual."

He ducked as Carly clipped him around the ear. "Hey. That's not playing by the Queensbury rules—hitting a man with glasses." Waving nonchalantly he disappeared, the door closing quietly after him. Finally she was alone, and sobbing uncontrollably she made her way upstairs to her bedroom, flung herself on the bed, and cried herself to sleep.

Carly awoke with a start, shivering; her mom must have opened the window earlier. The girl sat on the edge of the bed. 'Hello, Carly, I thought you'd never wake up.' Screaming, Carly leapt out of bed.

"Who are you? And what are you doing in my bedroom, not to mention in my house?" The girl did not look up, but continued rocking back and forth.

'You have something belonging to me. A silver cross and chain, it was a present from Daniel's father, and I'd like it back please.'

"The necklace is yours? I found it between the floorboards under the bed. Was it your room when you lived here? I'm sorry I don't know your name."

'Amelia Delamare and this is Daniel. Are you going to tell your mother about your problem? You're wondering how I know. Doesn't take a genius to work it out. You've been sick all morning, and I know for a fact you lied to your mother about your friends at school being ill. I was watching you from the patio. Who's the father Carly?'

"I don't see that's any of your business. Here, take it and leave me in peace. I take it you can find your own way out."

Carly placed the silver cross and chain in the girls' hand but it slipped through, landing on the bed. "I thought 'that' was what you came for?"

'Yes and no. Is Antonio the baby's father?'

Bemused Carly replied. "I think you should mind your own business. You're not his wife so I suggest you butt out." Carly put out her arm to push the girl through the door, and looked on in disbelief as it went right through her. "You're a ghost!"

'There's not much gets past you is there. I dare bet you're top of the class at school. Now where were we, oh yes, I remember, I was warning you to stay away from Antonio. You can't hurt me Carly, but I, on the other hand can make your life hell, should I so wish.'

"You're the girl, who was in Jason's room last night, aren't you? Amelia, who killed you?"

The ghostly figure stared menacingly at Carly, and in that moment Carly understood the meaning behind the expression 'if looks could kill'. Fear gripped her heart, an eerie creeping cold coursing its way through her veins, chilling her to the marrow. Amelia closer now, her face contorted in anger, hissed venomously. "Like I said, I'm here to warn you. Stay away from Antonio. He belongs to me. You will never, ever, have him, you hear me. For both you and your bastard child will die if you do not heed this warning, understood?"

Carly nodded backing away from the girl as she walked towards the wall and disappeared once more.

23

Troy looked at his watch for the umpteenth time in as many minutes; Charlene was late. Stomping off towards the bar he sat down and beckoned the waiter.

"Bonjour Monsieur. Que c'est que vous désire? Damn, no phrase book. They had Bourbon, so how different could the word be in French.

"Bourbon on the rocks."

"Monsieur is American, yes? I recognise your accent; it is from the South I believe." Troy sighed, another wannabe Yank.

"Yes, Georgia."

"It is very beautiful part of America n'est ce pas? My sister, she is in Boston, she is learning your language whilst studying at the university."

Troy smiled wanly, he wished the man would fetch his Bourbon and have done with it. He was in no mood to exchange pleasantries. "The American lady at the desk is looking for her husband, perhaps it is you?" Troy turned and watched as his wife tried unsuccessfully to convince the girl behind the desk to check the passenger list.

Trying hard not to laugh, he nodded to the waiter while his wife frantically thumbed through her French phrase book for the appropriate response. Some things, it would seem, never changed. It was heart-warming to discover his beautiful wife of twenty five years was still as disorganised as ever. Of course, if he were a gentleman, he would by now have gallantly jumped on his white charger, and rescued his damsel in distress. But he was still mightily annoyed at having been left kicking his heels in the airport lounge for the last three quarters of an hour.

"Would Monsieur like for me to telephone the desk?"

"Yes please, I think perhaps your colleague has suffered enough." Taken aback by Troy's somewhat flippant remark, he picked up the telephone and spoke to the young girl at the desk. She gazed across at Troy who raised his glass. Smiling, she escorted Charlene and the boys over to the bar.

"Sorry, Troy, the traffic was horrendous and of course we were late setting off." She smiled at the barman and sat down at the table. "How was your flight?"

"Fine, I slept most of the way. You look, ravishing." Flustered, Charlene fidgeted with her bag.

"You don't have to flatter me, Troy, we're married remember."

"I remember fine, I was making sure you did." Charlene blushed. "Hello Philip, how's tricks? And Jason, you've grown since I saw you last. And what's with the acrobatics in the attic young man? You gave your old man a fright, your mom too I shouldn't wonder. Hey, there's someone's missing from my welcome committee, where's my baby girl?"

"Huh, its like this pops. Carly puked her guts up in the dog's bucket this morning, and mom said she could stay home."

Great, thanks for that Jason, drop me in it why don't you. "Nothing to worry about, Troy, she picked up a virus from school. She'll be fine for this evening. I booked a table at the Pizzeria down the road. Hope that's okay with you, Troy, only you know how difficult these guys are to please."

"Fine, it's been ages since I had pizza, we can do the fancy French restaurant when Carly's feeling better. Would be remiss of me to come all this way and then not sample the cuisine in a country renowned for its culinary excellence."

Charlene stood up, tapping her foot impatiently. "Shall we make a move? I'm sure you'd like to go to your hotel and freshen up before you see the house. Jason, Philip, help your father with his luggage. We're parked in the short stay parking."

"I'm in your hands, I might hire a car later in the week, give you a break, unless of course you'd like to join us at Euro Disney." Charlene was a terrible actress. Edgy, and distracted, she had almost jumped out of her skin when Jason spilt the beans on his sister. He'd coax it out of her over the next few days. Something or someone was bothering her. "We'll see. How long are you planning on staying?"

"Gee, Charlene, I missed you too. I just arrived and already you're asking when I'm going back. I might well decide to stay with my wife and children. As you were so keen to point out, we are still married. Enough of that, who's for a Big Mac?" Confrontation avoided, for the time being, he needed her onside to find out exactly what she knew.

Charlene parked in her usual spot in front of the Ibis. Getting out of the car she opened the trunk and helped Troy with his luggage. "Will you be okay?"

"I'm a big boy, Charlene; I came all the way from Atlanta by myself, so I'm sure I can manage booking into the hotel alone."

"Hey, pops, we'll stay with you if you like, help you sort out your hire car. That way mom will have time to go shopping, maybe buy herself a new dress, get her hair done, the works. What do you say?" Philip winked at his father hoping he would agree.

How could Charlene argue with a chance to spend lots of money with his blessing? It would give him the opportunity to talk to the boys, find out what they know about the baby in the box, amongst other things. Trying hard to suppress a smile he looked directly at his wife.

"I think that's an excellent idea, how about you Charlene? Are you happy with that arrangement?" If she refused it would go down as a round in his favour. And there was no way she was about to let that happen! Smiling sweetly she walked to the car and opened the door before answering. "How could I refuse such a generous offer? I'll see you boys later. I take it you won't need me to pick you up later if you have a hire car?"

Ha, round two to me, I believe. Climbing into the car she closed the door, started the engine, and drove off towards the city centre. Where she was going to take the greatest of pleasure spending her husband's hard earned cash. Parking the car in front of the first chic beauty salon she passed she went inside. An attractive blonde bobbed up from behind the desk, and Charlene squealed.

"Désolée, avez-vous un rendez-vous madame?"

In her eagerness to put one over on Troy she'd forgotten the language barrier. "No, is there anyone here who speaks English?" She was sure that everyone in the salon had stopped what they were doing to look at the stupid American woman. Charlene blushed.

"Of course, madame, it is not a problem. Would it be for a shampooing and cutting?"

"No, the works. My husband has generously given me carte blanche with his credit card and it would be foolish to let him off lightly. N'est ce pas?"

"Absolutely, madame, if you'd like to follow me. Please take a seat and Juliette our top stylist will be with you presently. Would madame care for a glass of champagne, or a cup of coffee?" Woohoo, champagne and their top stylist, this is going to cost Troy big time."

"Champagne would be lovely, thank you, and could I possibly trouble you for a magazine. I'm in need of inspiration—I need something special to wear for this evening."

"Would madame think it bold of me to suggest she visit the boutique of my sister? She has recently taken delivery of designer originals ordered from the Paris summer collections of several top designers. And she has the most marvellous collection of Jimmy Choo sandals. I will give you her card and call ahead and arrange a personal showing should you so desire."

"How wonderful, yes, please do. Thank you so much." Could her day get any better, such a pity Carly wasn't here to reap the benefits too. She picked up a magazine from the pile the blonde had left and started thumbing through. A pair of red sandals, but not just any sandal a Jimmy Choo's 'Linda sandal', and according to the writer, a snip at 549 Euros! Now all she needed was a dress to match, and just because Carly wasn't there didn't mean she shouldn't benefit from Troy's new found generosity. One never knew when, or if, it would ever surface again.

Two hours and a couple of hundred Euros later—with her blonde locks teased into the latest style. Her jewel encrusted finger nails glinting in the bright sunlight; Charlene stared back at the image in the mirror. Was that really her?

"Madame is pleased with the result?"

"Madame is not just pleased, she is ecstatic. I'm not sure my husband will recognise me."

Juliette smiled knowingly. She sincerely hoped the American lady would show her gratitude with an obscenely large tip. Charlene handed over Troy's American express card to the blonde, who disappeared into the office coming back minutes later with a machine for Charlene to tap in the code. Opening her wallet she saw she only had a 20 Euros note in change, she took it out and dropped it in the basket on the counter, smiling at Juliette as she did so. Extravagant, but worth it.

Two hours later Charlene made her way back to the car clutching several designer label bags, which contained everything from lacy underwear to her prized Jimmy Choo sandals. Troy would go ape when he got the bill for today's spree. Served him right.

~

Antoine kissed his mother goodbye at the door, and headed towards his office, and as he rounded the corner he collided with Charlene coming out of the boutique.

"Charlene, you look amazing! I was going to call you later to ask you if you'd like to have dinner with me tomorrow evening."

"Antoine, I'm sorry, my husband is over for a few days from Atlanta. He wants to spend some time with the children and take them to Paris. Jason and Philip want to go to Euro Disney."

"You haven't mentioned Carly, I take it she's well."

"As a matter of fact, no, she's picked up a tummy bug from school. I sent her back to bed this morning. Why do you ask?"

"I was sure I saw her last Thursday afternoon leaving the offices of a friend of mine, she's a gynaecologist—Dr Marie DiAngelo."

"You must have been mistaken, Antoine."

"If you say so, Charlene. Don't you have a son in Paris?" He demanded, changing the subject.

"Yes, Matt. He's studying law at the Sorbonne. I'm afraid he doesn't see eye to eye with his father. Troy is hoping to talk to him about his future. I think he wants him to go back to Atlanta when he qualifies and work with him. I should be getting home, Carly will be wondering where I am. I went a little overboard with Troy's credit card in there."

"So I see. I'm sure he'll agree it was money well spent. You look ravishing. I love your hair like this." Charlene blushed, as Antoine touched her hair. Looking deep into her eyes he took hold of her hand, and lightly kissed the tips of her fingers sending her libido into overdrive.

"Antoine, I have to go. I'll call you when Troy goes to Paris I promise." She opened the car and Antoine put her purchases on the back seat and closed the door.

"I'll be waiting for your call." He watched her drive away. It would be no use asking Marie why Carly had consulted her, client confidentiality wouldn't allow her to say. He'd seen Carly with Antonio Giovanni a couple of times too, and even to the untrained eye they were more than just good friends.

A married man with young children, he wouldn't like to be in his shoes if his wife found out. The lovely Sophia Giovanni, a hot headed Sicilian, whose father allegedly had mafia connections, and someone it would be unwise to cross by all accounts.

It had been a while since he'd eaten at Mario's, and the time had come to have a quiet word with Antonio Giovanni, before things got out of control. And tonight was as good a time as any.

24

Charlene unlocked the door to number 55 Rue St Anne. She kicked off her shoes and dropped her keys onto the table in the hall, the door closing quietly. Tilting her head to one side she examined the door's hinges. Bizarre, the door always swinging shut on its own like that.

"Carly, I'm home." Silence. Perhaps she was sleeping. Charlene dropped the bags on the sofa on her way through to the kitchen. What she needed now was a large glass of ice cold Chardonnay. She opened the fridge, took out the bottle, and poured a glass.

Taking her dress from its bag she hung it on the back of the door, and clutching the red sandals to her chest she danced around the room.

Carly stood in the doorway watching her mother. Whatever she was 'on' she wanted some. She cleared her throat bringing Charlene to an abrupt halt.

"Hello darling, sorry, I got a bit carried away there. Are you feeling better?"

"Yes, I'm fine now. You've changed your hair! And you've been shopping too I see." Irritated at missing a shopping spree she slumped into the now vacant chair.

"Don't worry, I didn't forget about you. Pops insisted I go shopping, so I thought it only fair to buy my baby girl a dazzling new outfit for this evening too."

Passing the bag to Carly she watched impatiently, as she opened it up and peeped inside. "Omigod, a Vera Wang. Is it a copy?" Charlene shook her head.

"Nope, it's an original; I had to guess your size though—come on, try it on." Carly quickly stripped down to her underwear and stepped into the dress.

"Mom, it's beautiful, it must have cost a fortune, are you sure pops is okay with how much it cost?" Casually glancing at the price ticket. "Thank you, thank you, thank you!" And squealing with delight, she bounced up and down on the spot.

"I think a different bra to this one though, don't you mom?"

"In the other bag, and to complete the ensemble, a pair of Jimmy Choo sandals."

Carly flung her arms around her mother's neck and smothering her with kisses. "The girls at school are going to be green with envy when I tell them I have a pair of Jimmy Choo's. Never mind the Vera Wang original, and underwear by Victoria's Secret. Can I wear them tonight?"

"That was the whole idea, I thought it was about time your father saw you in something other than jeans and T shirt. Tonight Cinderella shall go to the ball."

"Right young lady let's get this lot upstairs and shower quickly, I'll French plait your hair if you like, unless you'd rather wear it down."

"Which do you think would look better, Mom?"

"Whatever you want, make-up too if you like, but don't overdo it. We don't want to give pops heart failure before he pays the bill."

"I promise to go easy on the kohl."

She disappeared into the bathroom and Charlene smiled as she heard her daughter on the telephone describing in minute detail her latest acquisitions to her best friend.

Oh to be sixteen and know what I know now. Memories of the last years of innocence, of her first kiss. Of fumbled amorous advances by a never ending stream of pubescent, spotty faced youths. She had been nominated homecoming queen that year too. Her mother ensconced in her sewing room, night after night working on 'the gown'.

Thousands of crystal beads and seed pearls encrusted the bodice, the diaphanous layers of chiffon, iridescent, tantalising. Her mother had 'borrowed' the design from a book on Greek mythology, the dress of a Goddess. Her first grown up dress. A dress fit for a queen.

Charlene was sure 'the dress' had played a major part in securing the crown. Voted the student most likely to succeed, and succeed she did. In marrying into one of Atlanta's prestigious families she'd had the world at her feet. Invincible.

But that was a lifetime ago. Now facing the reality their marriage was over, and had been for a long time. Seeing him this morning had confirmed it, and the final nail in the coffin was Antoine. A man she had known for only hours before she'd taken him to her bed. Antoine signalled excitement, passion, and danger.

"Bathroom's free, mom." Carly hovered in the doorway. She could come clean now, and tell her mother everything let someone else make the decisions. Later maybe, after she'd spoken to Antonio, after all it was as much his fault. Thus being so, it was only fair he took his share of the blame.

"Is something bothering you, Carly? You know you can talk to me if you have a problem."

"No, I'm fine honest, I just wanted to… to say I love you mom."

"And I love you too, pumpkin. Now scoot, or pops and the boys will be here and we'll still be in our undies!"

Charlene took the red dress from its hanger. How she loved the feel of pure silk against her skin.

"Need a hand with that?"

Charlene turned. "Troy, you startled me. How long have you been standing there?"

"Long enough. You look a million dollars; and red always was your colour. Jimmy Choo, my, my, we have been pushing the boat out, does that mean I get to stay here tonight?" Pulling her close he took hold of the zipper, hesitating. "I'd much sooner be taking this off, you little minx. It's been a long time,

Charlene, and I've missed you." He said pulling her closer, his erection, hard against her back.

Shocked by his sudden display of affection Charlene pulled away. "Troy, we have to talk."

"This sounds serious." Sitting down on the bed he watched as his wife of twenty five years carefully applied her make-up. Well, I'm waiting, what is it you want to tell me? That you're having an affair? Is he good in bed, Charlene, your Antoine?" Charlene dropped the mascara in surprise. "That's better, now I have your full attention. How do I know? That would be telling tales, and you know I've never been one for telling tales. You're blushing, Charlene, a sure sign of guilt that. Did you make love to him here, in our bed, or did you sneak off to a hotel? I'm not giving you a divorce, Charlene, not now, not ever. It goes against my religious beliefs. Did you know that some religions still condone the stoning of adulterers? The Arabic word for it is 'Rajm', a friend of mine from the retreat told me all about it. Bastian Lamare, but of course that's not his real name. His real name's Sebastian Delamare, he's French too. Wanted for five maybe six counts of murder. He's on the run again, but the authorities lost him in Ontario. Remiss of them I know. You're very quiet, Charlene, aren't you going to deny it?"

"What would be the point, Troy? I'll get my divorce eventually, with or without your consent. You haven't changed; you're still the same old Troy. Well, blackmail won't work this time, Antoine has nothing to hide."

"I wouldn't be too sure about that if I were you. You hardly know the man; he could be a serial killer for all you know. Did you make him beg, like you have me? Or did you throw yourself at him like a whore? Well which was it, Charlene, vamp or whore?"

"It's none of your damn business, now get out of my bedroom and let me finish dressing. The table's booked for 7.30, and as for your earlier question, I think you already know the answer, don't you, counsellor!"

Carly had been listening at the door. Jason. Why could he not learn to keep his mouth shut? Wherever there was trouble, Jason would be there, lurking somewhere in the background. She made her way downstairs, and taking a deep breath she opened the door into the lounge.

"Wow, pumpkin, you look stunning." Carly bounded up to her father bouncing down on his knee.

"Thank you so much for my outfit pops. I am, by now, the envy of all my friends." She wiggled her Jimmy Choo clad feet. "On the catwalk this evening we have Carly Hamilton-Davies. Tonight Carly is wearing a Vera Wang original, shoes by Jimmy Choo, and underwear by Victoria's Secret. Ta daa." Planting a kiss on her father's cheek, she glared at her younger brother. Oh boy was he in trouble now. Pops had obviously had words with his mom, and Carly had been eavesdropping on their conversation. He was hopeless; he'd never been able to keep anything from his father. Carly was hopping mad, and he dreaded to think what his mother would do to him after pops left tonight.

"Aw pops I'm famished, what time are we eating?" Jason said, quickly changing the subject. Charlene opened the door to the lounge. "The table was booked for 7.30, and it's now 7.45, so could we please get a move on." Carly, Philip, and Troy were the first through the door—Jason tiptoed towards the door hoping to sneak past his mother.

"Not so fast young man, I think you owe me an explanation."

"What for?"

"You know what for, how could you, Jason? You told your father about Antoine visiting and your father put two and two together and came up with twenty two as per usual."

"No he didn't, you slept with Antoine—Philip knew, Carly too. You betrayed pops, and your vows. I hate you, and I won't stay another minute in this house. I want to live with pops."

"Fine, if that's how you feel you can go back to the hotel with your father tonight." Charlene pushed him through the door and closed it. Watching as her youngest ran off to join his father and the others. Why was life so difficult? Taking a deep breath she opened the door to Giovanni's and headed for the bar.

"Madame Hamilton-Davies, good to see you again. Are you settled in your new home?"

"Yes thank you, Antonio. Have they ordered yet?"

"No madame, they are waiting for you."

"Good, let them wait. I'll have a Cosmopolitan please, Antonio."

"Certainly, madame."

Antoine opened the door to the restaurant and made his way to the bar. And creeping up behind Charlene, he placed his hands over her eyes. "Guess who?"

Holy shit. "Antoine." This is not happening. Please if there is a god, make him disappear. "What the... what are you doing here?"

"Eating, and hopefully now not alone. Join me please."

"I can't. Troy and the children are in the restaurant. Antoine, you have to go! If Troy sees you talking to me he'll make a scene. He knows about us."

"Merde! How did he find out?"

"How did I find out what, may I ask?" Troy asked sarcastically. "So this is lover boy—I was expecting someone younger this time Charlene."

Pulling himself up to his full height Antoine stood; his arm protectively around Charlene. "If you don't mind, that's my wife you're mauling, kindly remove your arm."

"And if I don't?"

"Let's just say you don't want to go there, and leave it at that shall we."

Antonio looked nervously from one to the other and then back to Charlene. Testosterone alley. And my wife thinks her family is scary.

"Stop this now—both of you. Back off, Troy, I'm warning you, if you make a scene tonight I'll never forgive you. Now go back to the children and let me talk to Antoine alone." She pushed him towards the restaurant, hostility oozing from every pore, defying him to cross her. He turned and went through the doors colliding with Carly coming out.

"What's all the commotion out here? Holy Shit. Antoine—bad timing man, this is not the place to be this evening, trust me. Take him outside and explain mom, go now. I'll deal with pops."

"But Carly..."

"But nothing, just go talk to him outside, okay."

"Bravissimo! Bravo mio pica uno."

"Not now." She hissed, "Antoine, please, you're making

things worse than they already are." Carly watched as her mother and Antoine went outside, she turned, hissing at Antonio. "What the hell are you trying to do, Antonio? Start another world war. We need to talk later, in private. I'll sneak out when everyone's in bed, wait for me by the bench behind the tree, okay."

"Okay. Ti amo, Carly."

"Antonio, what is it with you, do you want to get caught?"

"Of course not, sorry—I wasn't thinking. Go, I will see you later okay."

Returning to the table Carly watched as her father ordered yet another drink, his third in as many minutes. Sensing his anger, and frustration—poor pops, he should never have come to France; their marriage was over long ago.

Her mother kissed Antoine goodbye. Carly prayed her father hadn't witnessed the floor-show. With the amount of Bourbon he'd imbibed it would be bound to end in bloodshed. She desperately needed the loo, that was where she had been heading when she'd found them all in the bar. It was no use if she didn't go now she would wet herself.

"Keep pops glass topped up, Philip, and whatever you do; don't let him out of your sight." Carly whispered to her elder brother. "I'm just going to the ladies pops—I won't be long. If Antonio comes to take the order I'll have the Hawaiian please, mom too, it's her favourite." She squeezed his hand. "Let her go, pops, for me, she deserves to be happy. You both do, it's the best for both of you. You'll always be my dad, no matter who mom is with, no matter who is in your life. Our love for you won't change because you and mom end the marriage. I just wanted you to know that."

Charlene stood behind the door listening, the tears flowing freely once more. She hugged her daughter tightly. "Thank you, sweetheart. Your dad and I will talk, okay."

Troy looked up and nodded his agreement. "I'll have the papers drawn up when I get back; let's keep this amicable, for their sake, as well as ours. Deal?"

"Deal. Let's eat."

"About time, I'm fading away with hunger. I'm sorry too, mum, and if you haven't let my room yet, I'd like to stay."

"Jason. Enough already."

25

Carly crept downstairs and quietly opened the front door and disappeared into the night. Jason waited until the door closed before creeping out into the hallway. What was Carly up to outside this late? Pulling on his trainers and a sweatshirt he opened the door and peered outside.

He could see Carly clearly, her slim silhouette, illuminated by the shimmering light of the moon, and the millions of stars shining brightly in the heavens above. He closed the door and slipped quietly into the shadows. There was only one way to find out who his sister was getting down and dirty with. And that was to follow her.

"Are you sure you weren't followed Carly?" Antonio asked, looking nervously around.

"Sure, I'm sure, everyone's asleep. Mom went straight to bed when she got in and Philip drove Pops back to his hotel. And you couldn't wake Jason if you set off an atomic charge under his bed.

"What about Sophia, won't she wonder why you're so late?"

"No, I play poker with the boys on Thursday night after I close up. The boy's will cover for me if she rings. Now, what was so important?" Pulling her into his arms he kissed her long and hard. One hand under her T shirt, fondling her unfettered breasts. The other fumbling with the zipper on her jeans. Carly caught hold of his hand placing it back on her waist. Pulling away from him she walked over to the bench under the tree behind the restaurant and sat down.

"We need to talk first, Antonio. Please, come and sit beside me, oh God, I don't know how to tell you. I thought you were taking care of things, Antonio." A tear trickled down her cheek.

"Taking care of what baby, you're not making sense. Here, dry your eyes, and tell me what's wrong. That's better, come on Carly, out with it."

"I'm pregnant Antonio! That's what's wrong."

"Santa Maria, Madre di Dio, ma non puo essere non e possibile. Is not possible, Carly, I was careful. Oh God, Sophia will kill us both if she finds out. Devi abortire il bambino, Carly. You must get rid of it; I will give you the money."

"But, Antonio, I thought you loved me? Surely you don't want me to kill this child, our child. A child created in love, Antonio. You said you would leave Sophia and the children, and take me to Italy and I believed you. You lied to me, Antonio. I was a virgin! How could you use me this way? No man will want me now, not carrying another man's bastard child. Omigod, it was you—you did this to Amelia Delamare too, didn't you! You promised her you would take her away when she'd had the baby. Daniel was your son!"

"Amelia's dead, Carly."

"I know she's dead. Her ghost haunts our house. She sought me out—said she would kill me and my baby if I saw you again."

"Amelia and the baby haunt your house? You've seen her, and my baby—but it was a secret, our secret. Her father would have killed us both if he'd known Amelia was with child. I swear. I didn't know she'd given birth, we were supposed to meet that night but she never showed up. I figured her father had given her a hard time for coming to meet me and locked her in her room again. I wanted to marry her, and bring up our child together. I loved her and that monster killed her and my baby. After she died I went back to Italy, and that's when I met Sophia. You reminded me of Amelia. I just wanted to feel loved, and wanted again, Carly. You have to believe me; I never meant to hurt you. I never meant for this to happen."

Jason leaned on the side of the building. Holy shit! What a mess. Poor Carly, how could Antonio do that to his sister? He stepped out from the shadows walking towards the couple. He tapped Antonio on the shoulder, and, as he swung around, hit him square on the jaw. "That's for knocking my sister up. You're old enough to be her father, Giovanni. You son of a bitch, she's sixteen years old. Be interesting to hear what your wife has to say about 'il bambino'. Don't ya think?"

"You wouldn't dare."

"Oh wouldn't I. Watch me. Would ya just look at that? I appear to have your mobile Antonio now I wonder how that happened. And if I scroll through the list, yep there she is." His nimble young fingers quickly tapping the keys, he turned to Antonio. "I wonder how long it will take her father's goons to get here. An hour, thirty minutes, or less?"

A car pulled up across the road. Antonio tried to get up off the floor but Jason was too quick for him. Pushing him back down with his foot. "Not so fast, I figure you have some explaining to do. Don't you?"

"Jason, please tell me you didn't text Sophia. She'll kill us both." Carly shrieked.

Antoine Monroe stepped quietly out of the shadows, and pulling the terrified Italian swiftly to his feet, he turned to Carly.

"No Carly, he messaged me. Your secrets safe—for now. What in the name of god were you thinking, Giovanni? She's just a baby, wasn't what happened to Amelia warning enough. You did the right thing calling me young man, god knows what would have happened if you'd called his wife."

"I kind of figured that, and as stupid as I think my sister is, she doesn't deserve to die because of scum like him."

Carly leapt into Antoine's arms, sobbing uncontrollably. "There, there, sweetheart, come on, everything will work out just fine, I promise. Let's go home. We need to bring your mom up to speed with what's happened. Then decide what to do from there. And you, you'd better go home, and start praying her father doesn't find out."

Antonio Giovanni snatched his mobile from Jason and went back inside the restaurant. He'd have some explaining to do when he got home, as to why his face looked as if he'd gone five rounds with Mike Tyson, for starters.

"You pack a mean punch young man. I'll have you on my team any time. Come; let's go wake your mother." He scooped Carly into his arms and carried her over the road and into the house. "Jason, go wake your mother please, while I put the kettle on and make some tea. I think this is going to be a long night. It'll be fine, Carly, don't worry in a week's time you'll have forgotten all about him. I take it you don't want to keep the baby…" Charlene appeared in the doorway. "Hi, honey, sorry to wake you, but I think Carly has a little confession to make. Sit yourself down while I make the tea. Do you take milk and sugar?"

"No, Antoine, as it comes, though not too strong, with a slice of lemon please, there should be some ready cut in the refrigerator.

Hey pumpkin, what's wrong? Why are you both dressed, and what's Antoine doing here?"

"I'm sorry, mom, I went to see Antonio. We had something to discuss—mom, I'm pregnant."

"Oh pumpkin, please don't cry, it's not the end of the world. Is Giovanni the father?"

"Yes, I'm so sorry mom, I've let you down, please don't hate me!"

"Aw honey, I don't hate you, it's not your fault. C'mon dry your eyes, why don't you go upstairs, have a nice hot bath, and then get into bed and I'll bring you up a cup of hot chocolate. While Antoine and I decide what to do next. I take it you don't want to keep the baby."

"No, I'll do whatever you think is best. He lied to me mom, he told me he loved me, and that I was beautiful, and tonight he pushed me away. He was so angry, like it was all my fault. I never want to see him again."

"You won't have to pumpkin. He was right about one thing,

you are beautiful, and precious, and if anything should happen to you… Go on, up you go, I'll be along soon." Antoine stood in the doorway he bent and placed a chastened kiss on Carly's forehead as she hugged him for the umpteenth time.

"Night beautiful, sweet dreams."

"Right young man, before I ground you for the rest of your natural life, would you care to explain what you were doing outside in the middle of the night?"

"Typical. Carly gets hot chocolate and sympathy, and what do I get for my troubles. Grounded! Life sucks!" Jason stomped up the stairs slamming his bedroom door behind him.

"Kids. Why me, why now, as everything in my life is finally getting back to normal. And wham, another tragedy. Troy agreed to the divorce, he said he'll file the papers when he returns to Atlanta. God knows what he'll do when he finds out about Carly's problem."

"Why should he find out, telling him will change nothing, except maybe he'll file for custody and make you out to be an unfit mother. And I think you were a little harsh on Jason. He was looking out for his sister. I'll have you know he floored Giovanni. He packs a mighty punch; Giovanni's face was black and blue."

"Good. Serves him right for messing with my baby girl. What happens now?"

"We take her back to see Dr DiAngelo, the Gynaecologist Carly saw last week, and get her to make the necessary arrangements. I'll get her to bill Giovanni, paying to put things right is the least he can do. You want that tea now?"

"No I want you, right here, right now. But I know it's not a good idea given the circumstances. This is why I'm going to settle for a whisky and a rain check. I'll pop upstairs with hot chocolate for the two reprobates and apologise to Jason while you pour us both a drink."

Charlene helped Carly into bed. "Is that what you were trying to tell me earlier?"

"Yes, but I figured it would keep until I'd spoken to Antonio."

"How far gone are you?"

"Seven or eight weeks, Dr DiAngelo said I had until my twelfth week to abort. I went to see her last week after school.

Antoine saw me didn't he?"

"Yes he did, I told him it couldn't have been you. Oh baby, promise me you'll not keep things from me again." Charlene said sadly.

"I promise. Mom we don't have to tell pops do we?"

"No honey, we don't have to tell him if you don't want too. I'll square it with Jason. Antoine said I was hard on him. Snuggle down and get some sleep. Night, night."

Closing the door she crossed the landing and knocked on Jason's door. "Can I come in; I have hot chocolate and humble pie to deliver." The door opened slowly and Charlene went inside. Jason lay on the bed, his suitcase half packed on the floor.

"Going somewhere?"

"Yeah, back to Atlanta with Pops. You don't want me, you made that clear."

"You silly boy, of course I want you. I was angry at you both sneaking out the house in the middle of the night. I didn't think before I yelled. Am I forgiven? Antoine told me what you did to Giovanni, I'm proud of you for defending your sister's honour like that. You haven't spoken to you father about tonight have you?"

"No, why?"

"Because I don't think it would help matters. You know what a temper pops has; he'd probably do something stupid. I think we should keep this between ourselves. What do say?"

"Okay mom, and for what it's worth, I'm sorry. Okay and I promise I won't do it again."

"Come here; give your mom a big hug. Now drink your chocolate and try to get some sleep."

"Night mom."

"Night sweetheart". Maybe coming to France had been a mistake. Perhaps she should let Troy take the children back to Atlanta with him; after all she hadn't done a good job of keeping them safe so far.

She flopped down on the sofa next to Antoine and picked up her glass. "To us, that is if you still want me, with all my excess baggage, and problems."

"What do you think? Of course I want you. I love you. Everyone has baggage. Carly will be as good as new in a few days, and we could take the kids away for a holiday when Troy leaves. What do you say?"

"Yes, I think that's a wonderful idea. Bermuda's quite nice at this time of year."

26

Antonio poured another Cognac, rubbing his chin. The kid Jason packed a mean punch, and he was smart with it. The ranch style doors leading into the restaurant swung back and forth.
"We're closed." But there was no-one there. One of the clients had obviously opened a window in the restaurant. Getting up from the chair hurt like hell, might be a good idea to drop in at the Hospital on his way home. He might have broken something when he fell. Anaesthetised by the cognac he shuffled into the restaurant. Strange, all the windows are closed. He checked the door. Satisfied the place was secure he shuffled back to the table and poured himself another drink.
'Better make it the last Antonio or 'wifey' will send her father's henchmen to come find you.' Amelia hissed.
"Carly, is that you? Stop playing games; I know you're mad at me; I have the bruises to prove it. Why are you hiding?"

'Oh, she's not hiding, Antonio; she's tucked up safe in bed across the road in my old bedroom. You disappoint me; I thought you would have known better than to cross me.'

"Amelia…no it can't be. It's not possible, you're dead."

'No shit, Sherlock! Does your wife know about me?'

"No. There was no reason to tell her, you were dead long before she came onto the scene. What do you want from me, Amelia?"

'Your DNA. I want you to go to the police and tell them what really happened, Antonio. They think papa was responsible for my death and they're wrong. My mother shot me and then suffocated our son. The callous bitch didn't even wait until I was dead before she buried me under the terrace. She was so angry. She called me a whore and accused me of taking the only man she had ever loved from her. At first I thought there had been a misunderstanding, and then I remembered. When we moved here papa would be gone for days, sometimes weeks. I was just a baby; you brought pizza every night for my mother. I saw you, in my mother's bed, naked. And a few months later Ben was born, my mother said he was premature, she lied to my father didn't she, Antonio. Ben was your son, and that's why she killed us. You betrayed her, you betrayed me, you betrayed your boys, and now you're going to pay.'

"No, it's not possible. I would have known. Your mother was a lonely woman, Amelia, she had needs. Needs your father chose to ignore. He was too busy with his hair brained schemes and keeping his mistress happy to bother with your mother. It was over between your mother and I long before I started seeing you, I swear on my daughter's life. I was a fifteen year old virgin with a permanent hard on. Your mother seduced me. I had no idea Ben was my son you have to believe me."

'Do I? Why? Give me one good reason to believe you. After all the lies you've told I'm not sure you'd know the truth if it slapped you in the face. Charlene knows you seduced her daughter, the solicitor told her. I get the feeling you could be in for a surprise. You'd do well to remember 'that hell hath no fury like a woman scorned', Antonio. And to think I was stupid enough to believe your lies. I rue the day I set eyes on you; I might be alive today if not for you, we all might. Tell the truth, Antonio, before it's too late. They say confession is good for the soul my darling, you should try it sometimes. Why not start with Sophia and her father, before someone else does. Remember, only the truth will set you free………………'

Giovanni poured himself another drink. Had he really seen Amelia? Or was the alcohol playing tricks on his fuddled brain? He knocked back the last of the Cognac, picked up his keys, and headed for the door.

He unlocked his car, hesitating briefly. If the police caught him he would lose his license for sure. But they had to catch him first.

The man moved stealthily from the shadows and quietly opened the back door of the car. Lying down in the well behind the seats he checked his weapon. He'd waited seven long years for this moment, and tonight Antonio Giovanni would pay for his sins. But not even in the wildest of his dreams, had he expected Sophia Giovanni to be so wilful.

He had followed Giovanni's wife, Sophia, to a sleazy bar one night a couple of months back. He'd plied her with alcohol, and then taken her out into the alley, and pushing her roughly against the wall he'd forced her legs apart. She'd fought like a tiger in the beginning—though it soon became evident the little minx was gagging for it!

His hand caressed her inner thigh—she was wearing stockings. Sebastian grinned—remembering a quip from his youth—his hand had strayed to the 'giggling gap'…and once you got past there you were laughing.

Sophia gasped as Sebastian's fingers worked their magic—every nerve ending in her lithe body screaming out in ecstasy—her hands clawing his back, as her juices overflowed—with orgasm after glorious orgasm. She wanted him inside her—had to have him. She hoped he was as good with his sex as he was with his hands. But the man, wasn't about to be rushed. Sophia rubbed against him—he was rock hard—his erection straining against the coarse fabric of his jeans.

He'd pleasured her long enough. Now it was his turn. And, taking her by the hand, he led her down the alley to his car, opened the door, and pushed her inside. "Take off your clothes." He commanded.

Sophia licked her lips lasciviously, slowly peeling off her

blouse, her firm, full breasts rising and falling with each breath, her nipples erect. Sebastian slid his fingers into her wetness, and taking her nipples between his fingers, caressed them until she begged for mercy—reducing her to a quivering wreck. She fumbled with the zipper on her skirt, and, regaining a little composure, she pulled it down over her head, casually dropping it onto the growing pile. Watching as Sebastian unzipped his jeans, freeing his burgeoning erection—undressing in the back of a car was something he hadn't done since his youth. Tugging clumsily at his jeans, he watched entranced as Sophia dipped her fingers in her wetness, playfully sucking them one by one—the little minx had turned the tables on him again.

"Come on then, show me what you're made of—fuck me senseless." Sophia said huskily. "Silly me, we've not been formally introduced and here we are all naked and about to get down and dirty..." She giggled.

"Is that so, Sophia?" Sebastian said brusquely, and taking his swollen member in his hand—shoved it roughly into her open mouth. "Name's Sebastian—now suck!"

Sebastian groaned; she was driving him wild—as her tongue flittered lightly across the tip of his rock hard member—he gasped—so much for him being in control. Sophia leaned back against the door, opening her legs wide.

"Wanna take it to level two? She said, as she pulled him towards her.

Sebastian seized her by the hair, winding it slowly around his hand and thrust deep inside her. Sophia retaliated, wrapping her long, slim, legs around his back, and with slow, circular movements—drove him deep inside her...he was lost, drowning in ecstasy, each movement sucking him deeper, and deeper inside her until he could hold back no longer, and shuddering violently as his demon seed exploded inside her.

~

Sebastian rubbed his crotch, his erection caught against the zipper of his jeans—just thinking about that night made him horny.

Impatient, he peered through the gap between the front seats. They should have been moving by now, surely...But the car remained stationary—silent, except for the sound of

Giovanni snoring. He was out cold. Damn, the man. Sebastian got out of the car and pushed him over to the passenger seat fastening the safety belt securely around the sleeping man. He didn't want Giovanni flying prematurely and spoiling his surprise. That would never do. He turned the key in the ignition and drove off into the night.

Jean woke with a start. Clara wasn't in bed. A ghostly figure stood silently by the window, staring. "Clara, what are you doing out of bed? You know what the doctor said. Are you alright?" Walking across the room she sat on the bed.

"He's back."

"Who's back, Clara?"

"The man next door, he just got into Antonio Giovanni's car and drove off. He'll be back for the others too before long." She climbed into bed. "Giovanni's been up to his old tricks again with the young American girl from number 55. I saw them earlier, she was crying. Another bastard child, which makes three. He made the mistake of thinking no one knew about Annie, and Amelia. But Sebastian knows everything."

"Sebastian disappeared years ago, Clara, for all the police know he may be dead. You're over tired; the doctor should have admitted you to the hospital for a few days, instead of handing out pills and potions. I'm going to call him in the morning and insist that you go to hospital."

"Have me committed you mean, like Charles Dupont. He's quite mad, you know. I overheard young Jason and his brother talking about him the other day."

"I'll fetch your medicine, come on snuggle down under the covers. Nobody's going to have you committed, I won't let them."

Jean went downstairs and put the kettle on the stove. Taking the bag of tablets from the cupboard, what had the doctor given her? If anything the hallucinations were worse. And despite his promise to Clara he was beginning to think the best place for her was the Asylum. There at least she would be properly looked after. He had work tomorrow, and Clara would be alone most of the day. What if she wandered off? The doctor warned him this could be the early onset of Alzheimer's.

The front door opened and swung too. Now what was she

doing? He ran to the door to see his wife disappear behind the restaurant. Grabbing his coat from the hook in the hall he ran down the steps and across the road.

There he found Clara sat on the bench staring vacantly across the park. He would ring the doctor first thing. "What are you doing out here, Clara? You'll catch your death. What will the neighbours make of you wandering around in the middle of the night in your night clothes?"

"I wanted to be sure."

"Sure of what, Clara? It's the middle of the night and there's no one here but you and I. What's that in your hand?"

"Antonio Giovanni's St Christopher, he must have lost it in the scuffle with young Jason. He was only looking out for his sister. I don't think he meant to hurt him."

"Did you see all this from the window tonight? How long were you watching?"

"I don't know—I didn't look at the clock." He placed his coat around her shoulders and pulled her closer. My poor Clara. What's to become of you? Of our plans for the future?

"We have to warn the American. Her family is in danger; promise me you'll help me find the courage Jean, before it's too late!"

27

Troy staggered into the bathroom. One day he would learn that jet lag and Bourbon don't mix! Exactly who had brought him home? Quietly opening the door, he tiptoed to the bed and lifted the covers back. Philip!

"Morning Pops. I feel honour bound too say 'you look like shit'. And you snore! I hardly got a wink of sleep last night. Around three this morning I put a pillow over your face to see if it would shut you up."

"And?"

"You snored louder than ever. Next time I'm calling you a cab and sleeping in my own bed."

"Why didn't you drop me off and drive back home?"

"Duh, because I haven't passed my test yet. And Mum only just got the car back from the repair shop. And before you go off on one—it was my fault. I backed into a bollard in the car park."

Troy smiled. Boys would be boys. Philip reminded him very much of himself at his age. Overconfident and full of fun.

"Why didn't you use the hire car?"

"Insurance. I couldn't remember if you'd added me to the list of drivers. I figured as mom has me on her insurance it would be best if we took her car."

"Good thinking. I'll get a shower and then I suppose I'd better buy you breakfast and take you and the car back to your mother. What do you say we pick up Carly and Jason and do ourselves a little exploring? Maybe hop on a boat over to Belle Isle?"

"Cool, mom's been too busy with the house of late to explore. There are some great beaches, and they surf here too. You up for that do you think old timer?"

"Less of the old, I'll take you on any day boy. Do you think your mom will mind if I call Atlanta from her place?"

"Nah, we have unlimited free calls to a hundred destinations worldwide with our internet package. Pops, can I ask you something?"

"Goes without saying."

"Last night before we went to the restaurant you told mom about a man you knew back in Atlanta. You said he was French. Why did you tell mom about him?"

"I was going to tell her something important, but I decided to wait until I had all the facts. Why?"

"Because I've heard that name before. Some of the guys at school reckoned he murdered his family and buried them under the terrace behind his house."

"Go on…"

"Pops, the word on the street is that he lived in our house. Which means the proposed site for mom's garden room was where he buried his entire family doesn't it?"

"I'm afraid it does, Philip. Do you think your mother knows?"

"No Pops, she wouldn't have bought the house if she'd known. There's something else too. Jason and I found a box in the attic; it contained the mummified remains of a newborn baby. Freaked me out, I can tell you. Mom called the police and they took it away. Do you think the man killed the baby too?"

"I don't know son. The dead baby and the youngest boy, Ben, shared the same Y chromosome."

"You talk as if you know all about this case pops. Is that the real reason you're here? You said this man was on the run, do you think he'll try to come back to the house?"

"Yes, I know him, and yes, it's possible. The authorities lost him in Ontario. Philip, the CIA thinks he's coming after my family. It's a long story, some of which I am not at liberty to disclose. Tell me, does your mom still have her gun?"

"Yes, she keeps it in a draw in her bedroom."

"Good. Anything else strange happened since you've lived there?"

"Yeah, we found the Agent who sold mom the house in our basement the day after mom signed. He was jabbering on about rabid dogs attacking him. They carted him off to the funny farm."

"Can you find out where he's being treated? Discretely, I don't want to alarm your mom until I'm sure the threat is real. Deal?"

"Deal. Now can we have breakfast? I'm famished."

With Philip in the role of collaborator he could relax a little. He could trust him to keep a watchful eye on Charlene and the others, whilst carrying on with his investigations.

Charlene had made it crystal clear he wasn't welcome to stay at the house last night. And he doubted very much if she would consent to the trip to Disneyland Paris. And unless he could get her onside again he stood no chance of persuading Matt to join the practice. Not to mention, he would be unable to relax with the kids in Paris knowing Charlene was in the house alone. The newspapers had nicknamed it the 'house of death'—the agent must have thought all his birthdays had come at once when Charlene agreed to buy it. He couldn't blame him. He would have done the same if he'd been in his shoes.

Philip finished the last of the croissants and pushed his plate away. "I'm suffed, I couldn't eat another mouthful."

"I'm glad to hear it. I think the Maitre D was getting worried too. Shall we make tracks? Before your mom thinks I've kidnapped you and whisked you back to Atlanta. And Philip, let's keep the stuff about the house between ourselves for now. Okay?"

"Sure, no point in upsetting mom unless we have to pops."

~

Carly looked at the clock. She supposed she ought to get up; she'd tossed and turned all night. She'd woken up in the middle of the night and found Amelia, in the rocking chair at the end of the bed, sobbing. She'd told Carly everything. About her mother and Antonio, about Ben. She made Carly promise to go to the authorities if anything happened to Antonio.

Though how she was supposed to convince the authorities the information she had was genuine she didn't know. She could hardly tell them a ghost had told her, or they'd lock her up and put her in a room next to Charles Dupont. She'd tried to ask Amelia about her brothers, but she'd simply said she was tired, and disappeared.

Carly sat up slowly. Eager to avoid a repeat performance of yesterday morning. She would be glad to get back to normal; sixteen was too young to be saddled with a baby. She had things to do, and places to visit. There'd be plenty of time later for marriage, and children.

Her mother had promised not to tell pops. It would, as her mother said, have only added to Carly's problems. He would only have gone after Antonio—and the last thing she needed now was Antonio's death on her conscience and her dad in jail for murder.

Charlene was in the kitchen preparing breakfast for Antoine. He had that 'just got out of bed look'. His hair tousled, and it didn't take a genius to work out whose bed he'd been in. In the immortal words of her friend, and mentor, Sara, her mother had the same 'just fucked look' too.

Standing in the doorway to the kitchen, she felt she was somehow intruding, on 'their intimate moment'. As if sensing she was being watched Charlene looked up.

"Hi honey, how are you feeling this morning? I took the liberty of telephoning Dr DiAngelo. She has a cancellation this morning, and in light of the time issue, I thought it was best to take the appointment."

"Its fine, mom, best to get it over with, and then everything can get back to normal."

Troy stood in the hallway listening. Now what were they

up too? He opened the front door and let it slam shut and walked into the kitchen. It was obvious Antoine had been here all night. He wanted to lash out. Punish her for her infidelity. But what would be the point. It wouldn't solve a thing; they would just go behind his back. After all he'd been doing much the same with Naomi since Charlene had left Atlanta. Naomi. He wondered how she was doing, if she missed him. He would telephone Chas later, ask for the number for the hospital, and maybe give her a call.

"Is this a private discussion or can anyone join in? Who's seeing the doctor?"

Damn, he must have been standing in the hallway, eavesdropping. "Carly has women's problems Troy." Charlene explained quickly. "And I'm sure you don't want to embarrass your daughter into giving you a full explanation." Smiling she walked up to Carly and squeezed her hand.

"You ready honey?"

"Yes, I'll get my bag."

"We'll see you at lunch, Antoine. What are you planning on doing today, Troy?"

"Phil and I talked about maybe catching the boat over to Belle Isle." He kissed his daughter on the cheek. "Maybe next time, pumpkin."

"I'll hold you to that, pops."

Carly was hiding something. Charlene too, he could read her like an open book—cover to cover.

Antoine looked from Charlene to Troy. If he didn't make a move now he would be trapped. And a confrontation with Charlene's ex was something he was hoping to avoid. Plus, he had an appointment with Sophia Giovanni and her father. He figured they had the right to know the truth. She could decide for herself where she went from there.

"I'll get my jacket and I'll be right with you. Sorry, Troy, much as I'd love to stay and chat, duty calls. Another time maybe."

Antoine grabbed his jacket from the sofa and followed Charlene and Carly out into the sunshine.

"Scaredy cat."

"Yep, that's me. You want me to come with you?"

"No, we'll be fine. You do whatever you have to do."

He checked his watch; he'd have just enough time to shower and change before meeting Sophia Giovanni and her father. He felt a bit like Androcles, entering the lion's den. Vulnerable.

28

Antonio Giovanni never knew what hit him. One minute he was minding his own business, happily sleeping off the after effects of his alcoholic stupor. And the next he was flying through the air.

However the euphoria was short lived, as the realisation hit home that he was hurtling towards the ground at phenomenal speed. Round about now under normal circumstances he should be seriously considering pulling on the toggles to open his parachute. But the circumstances today were far from 'normal'.

Desperately he yanked at the toggles but nothing happened. Someone had sabotaged the small pilot chute. Whoever pushed him out at 10,000 feet had also taken the liberty of rigging his main chute too. To quote the immortal words of his father in law, Mario Marcello, he was 'well and truly fucked!'

His pathetic, miserable life now flashing rapidly before his eyes. His time all those years ago with Amelia, and the realisation he was about to become a father for the first time. And sadness and despair at her untimely demise.

Of meeting Sophia whilst working in his uncle's restaurant—smiling as he remembered her father's reaction to their courtship and subsequent marriage. The birth of his twin daughters—Charlotte and Alicia. Their first steps, and the sound of their laughter. All the other firsts—their Holy Communion and subsequent Confirmation. Their first boyfriends, first cars, and the cruellest of all, their marriages. Some other man would give his daughters' away. That same man or one just like him would be the one to hold his grandchildren for the first time. Life was so unfair.

His tears running freely…only a matter of seconds before his body crashed to the earth. Mercifully he would be unconscious before he 'kissed mother earth' for the last time. The next pile of dirt his body saw would be the dirt thrown onto the coffin containing his battered and broken body at his graveside. There would be no open coffin for his funeral. No vigil by candlelight—no shroud of purest silk would clothe his body.

They would simply scoop up what they could find, pop it into a plastc box, and place it discreetly in the coffin—with the lid screwed tightly shut. So as not to offend the mourners.

"Goodbye cruel world, goodbye wife, goodbye Carly."

'And what of me, Antonio, and our son?'

"Amelia! Have you come to lead me to the other side?"

'Yes my darling, I'm here. Are you joyful at the thought of our reunion? Poor Antonio, you were cursed from the moment you touched me. Always just one step away from a premature death at the hands of my father.'

"Your father. Are you sure?"

'Yes, I'm sure. I watched him strap you into your harness and push you out of the plane. You are the first, but there will be others. My father is hell bent on vengeance. Against you and your family, he sees it as his divine right. He is, as you must now realise, quite mad. Close your eyes and sleep now my darling. Welcome to eternity.'

Sebastian steered the Cessna back to the landing strip, the death of his daughter, avenged. Watching had been the best fun he'd had since grandma caught her knickers in the mangle. Grandpa had whipped out his pocket knife and cut the elastic, a wicked grin on his face.

The body of Antonio Giovanni had hit the concrete with a distinct thud, somewhere near the old mill ruins. No doubt shattering every bone in his body as he landed. They would have to scrape up what was left of him.

He would have to move quickly if he wanted to recover the camcorder he'd fixed to the parachute before the emergency services found him. He sincerely hoped it hadn't been damaged as he landed. Marcello had been explicit in his demands, and proof of Giovanni's demise was non negotiable. Not if he wanted to be paid it wasn't.

The plane taxied down the runway and into Marcello's private hangar. Pulling off his gloves he shoved them into his pocket, pulled his cap down over his face, and strolled casually out of the hangar.

Finding the body proved more difficult than he'd envisaged. The disused lot was buried under a tangle of brambles and nettles. He was positive the body had fallen here. He walked alongside the one remaining wall of the derelict building almost tripping over the lifeless form that had been Antonio Giovanni. De-flowerer of virgins. Game over, Giovanni, justice served. For now.

Sebastian knelt beside Giovanni to retrieve the camcorder. Today was most certainly his lucky day, unlike Giovanni it had survived the fall. He pushed it into his pocket and walked away. Sirens wailed in the distance, some Good Samaritan had done their good deed of the day and telephoned the emergency services and reported 'the accident'. Bloody do-gooders! He took his mobile from his pocket and pushed redial. It rang out three times before a man with a heavy Italian accent answered.

"Yes."

"It's a done deed. The package was delivered at precisely 7.32 this morning, and proof of posting will be with you within the hour."

"I look forward to receiving it. Shall we say midday?"

"With pleasure, the usual place?"

"Naturally. I look forward to it."

The policeman watched as the man walked back towards his car. He looked familiar. He'd take a walk over to the aerodrome later and make enquiries.

"Sir—over here." Detective Inspector Malestroit turned and walked towards the perimeter wall.

"Looks like his chute failed to open sir." SOCO said as he searched the pockets of the dead man. "Jesus, Mary, mother of God—it's Antonio Giovanni. What in God's name was he doing jumping this early in the morning?"

"An accident?" The Inspector enquired.

"Can't say for sure, not until we get him back to the morgue and piece him back together, sir."

"Well what are you waiting for? I want the report on my desk like yesterday. Got it?"

"Yes sir. Sir? Who's going to break the news to his wife?"

"I'll do it. Contact her father and have him meet me at the house in an hour."

"Will do, anything else?"

"No. Yes, I want two of you to go over to the aerodrome, I saw a man in coveralls hanging around back there. Maybe he saw what happened. And get a statement from everyone over there. Someone must have seen who piloted the plane."

29

Antoine Monroe walked into the ostentatious foyer of MSC Industries, nothing but the best for the Marcello's. With its highly polished marble and glass interior, coupled with the state of the art stainless steel and glass staircase. Right down to the circular reception desk aquarium, with its array of brightly coloured tropical fish.

Exactly how much money the Marcello family had shelled out on refurbishing their city headquarters he wouldn't like to estimate. Walking up to the reception desk he couldn't help but notice one of the other 'wow' factors sitting behind the desk. One of the many dark haired, brown eyed, olive skinned Sicilian beauties the Marcello's employed looked up from her typing, smiling pleasantly at Antoine.

"May I help you, sir?"

"Yes, I have an appointment with Madame Giovanni and Monsieur Marcello Senior. Antoine Monroe, I'm afraid I'm running a little behind schedule, my last appointment over ran slightly." A slight exaggeration but better than having to admit to the goddess sat before him he was someone else's significant other.

"Please take a seat." The goddess said as she stood up—the view from behind tantalising. Oh to be twenty years younger and rich enough to afford the upkeep on 'this years' model. The heels of her stilettos clicking noisily on the marble floor as she walked. She returned moments later with a tall, well groomed young, man wearing a charcoal grey, double breasted, hand tailored suit. Italian designer no doubt and sporting a silver grey shirt with a striking red silk tie. Family for sure. He walked over to where Antoine sat.

"Mr Monroe?" The young man shook Antoine's hand. "I'm Carlo Marcello; my father has asked me to speak to you. This way please." Antoine followed the young man down the long corridor to a small, but immaculate office overlooking the garden. The floor to ceiling bookcases, furnished with hundreds of leather bound books, all perfectly placed—like soldiers on parade.

A huge dark oak bureau took pride of place in the centre of the room. The old world décor in complete contrast to the buildings ultra modern foyer. With its high backed, olive green leather swivel chair, adding sway to its Mafia image. One half expected 'The Godfather' himself to wander in and take his place behind the desk.

On the wall behind Marcello junior were the various accolades and awards received by the company's founder, Mario Marcello. A single oak framed photograph graced the desk, its image turned to face the occupant of the chair. This was, undoubtedly, the domain of Marcello Senior. Carlo Marcello sat down behind the desk.

"Please have a seat Mr Monroe. My father and sister have been unavoidably detained I'm afraid, a death in the family. He sends his sincere apologies and hopes you haven't been inconvenienced. Perhaps I may be of assistance?"

"I'm afraid not. Client confidentiality, I'm sure you understand. Someone close?"

"Yes, my brother-in-law, Antonio Giovanni. He was killed early this morning in a sky diving accident. A Detective Malestroit arrived at the house about an hour ago to break the news of the tragedy personally. My sister is, as you can imagine, deeply upset."

"That is very sad news. Antonio was a fine upstanding member of the community. He'll be sadly missed. Please be so kind as to convey my condolences to the family. And if there is anything I can do to help, please do not hesitate to contact me. Here's my card. If you would be so kind as to ask your father to let me know when the funeral is please. Thank you for your time." Antoine stood; and shaking hands with young Marcello he said his goodbyes.

And with one, last, lecherous peek at the receptionist, Antoine made his way outside into the bright sunshine. Well that was a turn up for the books. Suicide, in light of his latest faux pas? No, he didn't think so. Not his style at all. Antonio was too full of himself to take the coward's way out. He'd telephone Malestroit after lunch; and see what he could find out.

Once back in the city centre he headed directly to the consulting rooms of Maria DiAngelo. He needed to talk to Charlene alone. The last thing Carly needed to hear in her present state of mind was that the father of her unborn child was dead. Who knew what she would do when she found out. His greatest fear was that she would change her mind about the abortion out of some misguided sense of loyalty to the dead man. No, the sooner the problem was taken care of the better, for everyone's sake.

Locking the car he walked quickly across the courtyard. Charlene stood outside, cigarette in hand—he'd never seen her with a cigarette before. "Hi there. I didn't know you smoked."

"I don't, not any more, except in times of extreme stress."

"How's Carly?"

"She's being admitted. That's why I'm out here; they're taking blood and stuff. Dr DiAngelo is operating on her this afternoon. It's a simple procedure, it apparently only takes a few minutes and Carly should be able to come home tomorrow morning if there are no complications. I was about to telephone you. Do you mind if we take a rain check on lunch? She looks so sad; I don't want to leave her alone."

"No of course I don't mind. I've just come from a meeting with Carlo Marcello, Sophia's brother. Charlene, Antonio's dead. A sky diving accident early this morning."

"You don't think. I mean he didn't...you know..."

"No, I'm sure it was an accident. Antonio was too full of life to end it in such a violent manner."

"It would be hypocritical of me to say I'm sorry he's dead, given the circumstances. What he did to my daughter is despicable, not to mention illegal. She was fifteen years old when he seduced her, Antoine. I can never forgive him for what he did to her. Never. His death is a blessing in disguise."

"You don't have to convince me, I'm on your side. However it does mean that I will have to delay speaking to the old man until after the funeral."

"Surely there's no need to tell the old man. Now that Giovanni's dead the problem of him re-offending has been addressed. After all, it's not his fault his son-in-law was a pervert, who got his kicks seducing under age girls, is it."

"No, I suppose not, but it does mean that you will be left with the bill."

"It's not a problem Antoine, I have the money. And I would soon as not be beholden to the Marcello's for anything. I'd better be getting back; Carly will be wondering what's keeping me. Will you be able to pick me up later this evening? We can grab a bite to eat before I go home and face Troy and the boys. You can help me get my story straight, being a lawyer you should be able to come up with a tale even Troy would believe."

"I'll do my best. About 8 o'clock, okay. And now I really should be getting back to work or Marcie will be sending a search party out for me." Kissing her quickly on the cheek he made his way back to his car.

30

Detective Inspector Xavier Malestroit sat at his desk; having just received the report on the death of Antonio Giovanni he opened the file. Giovanni was just thirty eight years old. What a waste. He had broken the sad news to his widow and father in law that very morning, at their home overlooking the Gulf of Morbihan. The guy had everything to live for. A loving wife, two beautiful daughters, a house in Millionaires Row, no apparent money worries. It was a shame.

He skimmed quickly through the report. A tragic accident? But what in God's name was Giovanni doing in a plane ready to jump with a blood alcohol level of 3.65 mg/l! He'd heard of inexperienced jumpers needing Dutch courage, but that was taking the piss! But according to his wife he'd jumped hundreds of times, and always insisted on packing his own parachute. It was no wonder his parachute malfunctioned. With all the alcohol in his system he wouldn't have been able to co-ordinate his movements in order to pack it correctly.

He'd gotten the distinct feeling Marcello Senior wasn't surprised to hear of his son in law's sudden demise. More like he'd been expecting it. Something stank, like a pile of rotting fish. He'd be keeping a watchful eye on old Mario. Rumour in the city was that the Marcello's 'were connected'. How true it was he didn't know, but he figured a little poke around in MSC's company history was definitely in order, if he was ever to get at the truth.

The wife seemed Kosher enough; her tears were definitely those of grief. A widow at thirty five, left with twin girls and another baby on the way to raise alone. Sophia Giovanni had only found out about the baby the day before, she'd said, and as Thursday night was his night out with the boys, playing poker. Antonio Giovanni hadn't known about the new addition to his family, and now he never would. Apparently he always stayed out overnight because he didn't want to risk his license by drinking and driving. Conscientious guy it would seem.

They had drawn a blank with the man he'd seen hovering around the scene of the accident. No one matching his description had been at the aerodrome that day, if the statements were to be believed that is. The pilot of the plane was also conspicuous by his absence, not one person had seen him take off or land. Everyone on the premises that morning had either all nodded off at precisely the same time, or were telling him a pack of lies. But why? What were they covering up? And for whom?

Malestroit continued reading. Jesus. Every bone in his body fractured—shattered into tens of pieces. He hoped and prayed Giovanni had been unconscious before his body hit the ground. Reading on, he wrinkled his nose in disgust. His internal organs reduced to a pile of mush, his face virtually unrecognizable. It would be a closed coffin funeral for sure.

It was sheer luck he'd had his wallet in his pocket when he jumped. And that he was particular about his pearly whites, or they'd have had a hell of a job identifying him. His dentist it would seem was the only person who didn't have retrograde amnesia. Though just in case they'd taken DNA samples. He looked at his watch, damn, it was too late to stop the test now.

Oh well, at least they would be doubly sure it really was Antonio Giovanni, and not some poor old tramp dressed in his clothes. Not unheard of in cases where the 'said victim' had money worries. Death was the only acceptable excuse for loan sharks, and bullies, sometimes inadvertently at the hands of their own henchmen.

But Giovanni was solvent. His business a success, his restaurant one of the best pizzerias in Vannes. His father had transferred the business to Antonio on his return seven years ago.

Mario Giovanni reunited once more with his only son— Antonio, all smiles, with his beautiful Sicilian bride, Sophia, at his side.

That had been one hell of a party. The Champagne flowing freely, the street closed to traffic. The neighbours carried away with the spirit of conviviality at the impromptu celebrations. Each placing their contribution to the festivities on the large table set up in the park behind the restaurant. The party had continued well into the night. The sadness that had overshadowed the street after the slaying of the Delamare's forgotten. The house standing silent, once more relegated to the shadows.

Happier times, once more overshadowed with sadness. Mario Giovanni was his friend. And if there was anything suspicious about Antonio's death, however circumstantial, he would find it. The culprit would be brought to justice, he owed the old man that much.

The door to his office swung open. Malestroit peered over the top of his spectacles at the young policeman standing impatiently before him. "Well spit it out, what was so important to make you forget your manners?"

"Sorry sir, only they said that you might think this was urgent." Passing the detective a manila envelope he disappeared, closing the door quietly behind him.

Malestroit took out his letter opener, a gift from his late wife, on their last anniversary before the cancer rendered her incapable of speech. A week later she was dead. It had been his dear friend, Mario Giovanni, who had saved him from the depths of despair.

He slit the letter open and slid the contents out. Antonio Giovanni's DNA results, staring at the paper in disbelief, he placed it print side down on his desk. How had this gone unnoticed all these years? If Benjamin Delamare had been alive today he would have been some twenty two years old. It also meant Antonio Giovanni was the father of Amelia Delamare's baby—the mummified remains the Hamilton-Davies boys had found in their attic. Had someone else reached the same conclusion and put out a contract on Giovanni? His father in law maybe? Opening the bottom draw of the filing cabinet he pulled out the file of the Delamare murders. Its yellow band a constant reminder of his failure.

The Canadian police had contacted Malestroit only last week. They had a man fitting the description of Sebastian Delamare under surveillance. Unfortunately they'd lost him in Ontario a few days later, which meant that by now he could be anywhere. Pick a country, France maybe. In light of today's revelations he would take the file home with him and go through the evidence once more. He had a sneaky feeling Giovanni's death was somehow linked to the slaying of the Delamare's. Working out how and why was his problem, and for the time being he intended to keep it that way.

The telephone rang out. Damn he had been hoping to get away early tonight. Pay his last respects to the deceased's poor distraught father. He must be devastated, too lose his only son in such tragic circumstances. Xavier wondered what would become of the restaurant now that Antonio was dead. He picked up the telephone.

"Detective Malestroit? Antoine Monroe, can you spare me a few minutes of your valuable time, it's regarding the death of Antonio Giovanni." Malestroit sat up straight in his chair, Monroe now had his full and undivided attention.

"I'll drop by on my way home. You were lucky to catch me, Antoine, I was going to drop in on Mario Giovanni—express my condolences."

"In that case I'll get my secretary to make a fresh pot of coffee."

Xavier Malestroit picked up his keys, putting the reports inside the Delamare file. Make for interesting bedtime reading tonight. He wondered what information Monroe had. Only one way to find out and locking his office, he signed out at the front desk and walked across the square to the offices of Antoine Monroe.

Marcie, was just leaving as he arrived. "Mr. Monroe is in his office, Detective; he said to go straight in. Good Night."

"Night, Marcie." Nice girl, Marcie, pity she'd never married. Perhaps he'd give her a call, ask her out, and maybe take her for a meal. Who knows what might come of it. The door to the office opened.

"I thought it was you, Xavier. Has Marcie gone?"

"Yes, she was leaving as I arrived—very pleasant girl, Marcie."

"Yes, I suppose she is, not my type though, a little too reserved. Don't stand on ceremony, Xavier, take a seat. Coffee?"

"Why not, unless you have a little something tucked away in that drawer of yours."

"You know me too well. Pull up a chair. I have a tale to tell that might be of relevance to your case."

"Intriguing. Tell me more." Pouring two large measures of Edradour and two large coffees', Antoine perched on the corner of the desk.

"I may have been one of the last people to see Antonio Giovanni alive last night. I take it what I say will stay strictly within these walls."

"Of course, unless you killed him that is?"

"Drat, and there was me hoping to keep it secret. Joking aside, I received a telephone call last night late. I was just about to turn in for the night. It was young Jason Hamilton-Davies, and he'd used Giovanni's telephone to make the call. There'd been a slight altercation between Giovanni and the boy. He'd caught him with his sister in-flagrante delecto behind the restaurant. He'd followed Carly when she'd sneaked out of the house and he'd been eavesdropping for a while in the shadows. To cut a long story short, it would appear Giovanni had knocked his sister up. The boy was defending his sister's honour, albeit a little late in the day I admit. When I arrived Giovanni was lying on the floor with young Jason's foot on his chest. He packs a mean punch—he floored Giovanni with a solitary blow to the chin. He was bleeding from a cut to the chin but very much alive when we left a few minutes later. Giovanni must have gone back inside the restaurant, presumably to clean himself up before heading home. I heard a car drive off about an hour later. I stayed over with the family last night. Before I intervened I heard Carly accuse Giovanni of being the father of Amelia Delamare's baby, she called the baby Daniel. He verified it as the truth. He said he'd been devastated at hearing of Amelia's demise. I believed him; I don't think he had anything to do with the killing of the girl and the baby."

"We kind of figured that. So what's your point?"

"How did young Carly know about Amelia Delamare and the baby? The girl has been dead for seven years, Xavier. Please explain it to me, because I'm lost here."

"I can't explain it, Antoine. I'm a policeman, not a Clairvoyant. How Carly Hamilton-Davies came about her information I don't know, but she is correct. And not only that, Antonio Giovanni was the father of Amelia's little brother, Ben. It's all here, in black and white. His DNA is a positive match to both young Ben Delamare's and the baby the Hamilton-Davies boys found in their attic."

31

The colour drained from Antoine's face, as he replayed the last words spoken as his world fell apart. No, it wasn't possible. Ben was his son. Knocking the whisky back. The amber liquid tracing a fiery path all the way down to his stomach. Malestroit watched, bemused, what had caused the sudden change in his companion's manner? Was it something he'd said?

"Are you okay, Antoine?"

"Yes, sorry, I just remembered I have to pick Charlene up from the hospital."

"The daughter got rid of the baby then."

"Of course. Why would she want to ruin her life bringing up a child alone? She couldn't rely on Giovanni to protect her—and he made it quite clear she had to get rid of it before his wife found out."

"Seems young Antonio had been quite productive in the last few weeks of his life. His wife's up the duff too, only found out about it Thursday, which was Giovanni's poker night.

Never went home on Thursdays apparently."

"I bet he didn't. I wonder how many more girls there are out there all awaiting a happy event."

"Ah, now if you'd asked me that before today I'd have said none. But in light of recent revelations regarding Antonio Giovanni's sexual exploits I think I'll pass. Does young Carly know he's dead?"

"No, we thought it best not to tell her under the circumstances."

"Wise decision. I'd better be making tracks too." Xavier held the manila folder up. "I thought I ought to go over the Delamare file again, in light of recent events. We had a report of a possible sighting of Sebastian Delamare from the Canadian authorities. They had a man fitting his description under surveillance. Unfortunately they misplaced him in Ontario, remiss of them I know. Thanks for the drink and the company, Antoine, it get's lonely in that big house of mine at times. I'll see myself out, oh, and if I hear anything else I'll be sure to keep you in the loop."

"Thanks, Xavier, mind how you go."

Xavier Malestroit closed the front door behind him and walked back across the square to his car. Why had the news that Giovanni was young Ben Delamare's father upset Monroe like that? Unless...unless what? Get a life Xavier. Stop being such a dork, and for once in your life put you 'first'. Call Marcie, send her some flowers, and put a little romance back in your life. Before someone else beats you to it.

~

Antoine poured another whisky and telephoned Charlene. He was in no fit state to spend time in that house tonight. The call was automatically re-directed to her mailbox. That was good, at least this way she wouldn't know for sure he was avoiding her.

"Hi, Charlene. Antoine. I have to go away for a few days, sorry to leave you in the lurch at short notice. Give my love to Carly please, and I'll ring you when I get back." Placing the telephone back in its dock he banged his fists down hard on the desk. 'Why did you lie to me, Annie?'

'How do you think I feel knowing Tony toss-pot is my real father?'

Startled, Antoine looked around him, it sounded like young Ben, but that wasn't possible…was it? "Ben. Is that you?"

'The One and only, how you doing, Monroe. Mama knew you'd be angry with her when you found out the truth. Papa was angry that night too, I heard him shouting at her. He called her names, bad, bad names and him a disciple of god. Then the dogs dug Amelia's leg up and he went ballistic. It was mama, who killed Amelia and her baby, she was jealous of her relationship with Giovanni. I heard her tell papa. The baby was Giovanni's too, which makes him my half-brother. Old tosspot certainly 'put himself about a bit', didn't he. Papa pulled a gun from nowhere and shot mama in the chest, from real close. There was blood and guts everywhere. Gross. And then he turned the gun on me. He said he was sorry, but as I was Giovanni's bastard son, I deserved to die like Amelia and the baby had. I pleaded with him to let me live, there was a scuffle. Michel came in from work and tried to take the gun from him but it went off, and Michel fell down dead. I don't remember anything after that. Alexander died too didn't he, and the dogs. Why did he kill the dogs, Monroe?'

"I don't know, son, and yes, Alexander died too. Why did any of it happen? Your father is the only person who knows all the answers to this particular puzzle. And he could be anywhere. He could even be dead for all we know."

'That's why I'm here, Monroe; mama sent me to warn you. To make amends for her duplic…, damn, for not being honest with you. She uses all these big words and expects me to remember them. He's watching you; she says you have to go away, far away. That it's not safe for you at the American's house. The man who came the other day with the boy, Jason, is her husband?'

"Yes, Troy is her husband, her ex-husband actually."

"Mama says he's not to be trusted, he's keeping secrets, and he'll hurt you if he gets the chance. She says it's him that bought papa here, albeit inadvertently. I think she swallowed a dictionary for breakfast. Reckons he's in danger too, but not to let that worry you. He has big guns backing him up. Sometimes I worry about her, I really do. I'd say it was dementia setting in if it weren't for the fact she's already dead. Cos he wasn't carrying a piece last I saw of him when he took his boys over to Belle Isle. Papa never took us any place, except to church to pray for our sins. Amelia and the baby moved out of the basement and into the restaurant. She reckons now Giovanni's dead they can be a family like he promised. Good luck on that one, once a toss-pot always a toss-pot. She's not the only under-age girl he's knocked up, is he, Antoine?' Antoine shook his head. 'I thought as much. I'm off now—places to visit, people to see, you know how it is. When you're hot, you're hot. Being dead kills me. I'm thinking of doing a stint with Jamal whatshisname, you know, him who starred in the Marsupilami film. Mama's always telling me to stop being such a comedian. I keep telling her it's a good career move; I could make loads of dosh being the first ghost comedian. See you around.'

"Ben. Are you still there, Ben?" Damn. That was one of the more interesting conversations he'd had with young Benjamin. Pity it had to come seven years after his death. His instincts had told him to run, and his ghostly visitor had confirmed it.

Scribbling a quick note to Marcie to cancel all appointments until further notice he picked up his keys, mobile and laptop and headed for the door.

Sebastian is watching you stupid. Time to get streetwise, and use the tradesman's entrance. I suppose he knows what car I drive too. He could get a taxi, and get it to take him straight to Charles de Gaulle but that would cost him serious money. He'd no choice but to hire a car and drive to the airport. He needed his passport too, but where would he go? 'Bermuda's good at this time of the year.' That's what Charlene had said.

Opening his lap top and taking out his credit card Antoine booked the last available seat to Bermuda on the American Airways flight leaving Charles de Gaulle at 11.00 am the following morning, a direct to flight to New York's JFK Airport. He would have about 4 hours to kill there whilst waiting for his connecting flight to Bermuda, which was due out of JFK at 5.25 pm. And by 8.45 pm tomorrow evening he would be safely ensconced in a hotel somewhere on the island. Safe from harm.

32

Spending all day being the strong, reliable one, while her poor baby girl had fallen apart had taken its toll on both mother and daughter. Carly, heartbroken, and full of remorse. Charlene, angry, and frustrated, and if Giovanni wasn't already dead, she would have happily killed him herself.

How to keep Carly from finding out was her next problem. And heaven forbid that Troy should ever find out. What she needed right now was a large glass of chardonnay and a cuddle, and Antoine was late. She'd give him five minutes and then she was leaving.

Sebastian pulled the car to a halt across the road from where the American woman stood. Interesting. Monroe had stood her up too. He'd obviously slipped out unnoticed, but his car was still in its parking space. The only visitor he'd had was Detective Malestroit. He'd arrived as the lovely Marcie Le Gall, Antoine Monroe's secretary, finished work for the day.

Sebastian was positive he'd left alone. Though he had been

forced to hide behind a newspaper to avoid being recognised a second time in the day by the bumbling detective. He supposed Monroe could have slipped past him unnoticed, but that still left the problem of his car. A taxi pulled up kerbside and the American got in. Perhaps she was meeting lover boy somewhere for supper. Following at a discreet distance he watched as the taxi turned into Rue St Anne.

Another dead end. Time to call it quits for one day. Patience and fortitude he had in abundance. Tomorrow was another day, and what he needed right now was a long, cool, beer, swiftly followed by several other beers. The likes of which he had cooling back at the house he'd 'borrowed'. After all, its owners wouldn't need it where they'd gone.

Pulling in to the garage, he pushed the remote control on the dashboard, closing the doors behind him. What the world and his dog couldn't see wasn't happening. Mind no one had seen him last time except the tramp. The old man had kept the authorities tied in knots for months while he'd escaped over the border. And that was another loose end he'd yet to tie up.

He took the spade and quick lime from the boot and placed them in the wheelbarrow. He would bury the old couple tonight before they stunk the place out. Pushing open the door to the kitchen he cautiously peered inside. Everything was as he'd left it. The old couple sat at the kitchen table, their meal half finished. Turning up the air conditioning unit a little he helped himself to a can of beer from the fridge and sat down at the table.

"Cheers!" Pulling the ring pull he poured a little into the glass. "Chilled to perfection, I compliment you on your choice of beer, old man. Shame you had to die so I can drink it, but life's a bitch. You have to admit you had a good innings, and at least this way you'll be together forever. Not separated for months, years sometimes. Hanging around just waiting to die and join your beloved on the other side. Only to find that the woman you had mourned had found herself a 'Toy Boy' in yonder paradise while you'd been counting the days until you could be together again! What's that you say old man, she wouldn't dare? I wouldn't bet on it if I were you. Take my wife for instance, got herself knocked up by the pizza delivery boy and passed the kid off as mine for thirteen years. It's true I tell you. Like a mushroom I was, fed on shit and kept in the dark. And then to add insult to injury some years later the very same pizza delivery boy knocked my fifteen year old daughter up too. You can imagine how I felt. I wanted to kill them all. I ask you, what did Tony toss-pot have that I didn't? Oh sorry I'm forgetting my manners, would you care to join me in a beer? No? Okay, suit yourselves."

He took another beer from the fridge and swigging from the opencan he paused for a moment, belching loudly. "I'm beginning to feel a bit peckish; I skipped lunch. You know how it is. You have a job to do and before you know it, it's late and every where's closed. You know what I fancy—a big steak, with chips I think, don't you. Oh dear, not hungry? Never mind, I can manage, you just sit there and enjoy the rest."

Sebastian opened the freezer and poked around inside. Interesting, the old man must have been a hunter. He pulled out a slab of venison, and a duck; and finally a whole fillet of beef. I have died and gone to heaven. Hmmm, if this old couple had a fillet of beef in their freezer maybe they had money or valuables hidden. And a hunter would have guns too.

He stuck the beef in the microwave to defrost and opened a bottle of Bordeaux he'd found in the wine rack next to the freezer. A further search of the freezer had yielded a bag of frozen oven chips and a pack of chocolate éclairs.

Deciding to investigate the rest of the house whilst the beef defrosted Sebastian made his way upstairs. The décor upstairs was much the same as the rest of the house, the wallpaper, faded and peeling. He sniffed the air. Mildew. It had an unmistakeable odour. The old couple obviously didn't believe in fresh air.

He pushed open the door to the first bedroom it was empty except for a large ornately carved wardrobe. Oak he guessed, and by the look of it riddled with woodworm. Turning the heavy brass coloured key he opened the doors. Empty. Further inspection of the room yielded a door, cleverly disguised as part of the wall. The panels decorated with the same, hideous, rose covered wallpaper. He turned the door knob; locked.

The bell to the microwave pinged. The key would wait, his stomach wouldn't. Throwing open all the doors as he passed Sebastian made his way back to the kitchen.

Cutting the beef in half he put the biggest piece into the oven and switched it on. The other piece would make for a decent breakfast before he resumed his search for his next victim.

It would be dark soon—time to prepare the old couple. Starting with their valuables, he pulled at the old woman's wedding ring. Crack. That fixed that problem. He held the diamond encrusted ring up to the light. He'd get a fair whack for that at the pawnbrokers. Her clothes were next for the off. Finally he rolled her up in an old cotton bed sheet he'd found in the cupboard under the stairs. He'd burn the clothes later along with those of her husband. Placing the cadaver in the wheelbarrow he then turned to the old man.

Whistling his appreciation as he removed the old mans pocket watch, and unless he was very much mistaken it was solid gold. Old gold at that. Once the old man was naked he rolled him in an identical sheet, placed him in the wheelbarrow alongside his beloved, and wheeled it outside.

At least now he could eat his supper in peace, and pouring himself a glass of Bordeaux he sat down. The aroma of roast beef wafted enticingly around the tiny kitchen, while his stomach rumbled in anticipation of the banquet to come.

Opening the oven door he poked the meat with his knife. At last, supper was ready. Sliding the beef onto a plate he cut off a large piece, placing it between two slices of bread smothered in mustard. And biting into the enormous sandwich he sat down. Heavenly. Forking the last morsel of beef into his mouth he pushed the plate away, belching loudly. A sign of appreciation in Medieval times, so he'd read. Collecting the plates, he scraped the leftover food into a plastic bag, sealing it tight. He would wash up later and then sit down with a large cognac and a cigar from the old guy's stash of Havana's. The perfect end to an almost perfect day; but he had one more task to complete.

With spade in hand he stepped outside into the cool night air and started digging. Clang. He'd struck metal. Switching on the torch he shone it into the hole. Buried treasure maybe? Furiously he dug around the object until it was exposed, and lifting out the metal chest he placed it on the ground. Finish the hole stupid, it might be nothing more than a beloved pet inside.

The hole was deep enough he decided, and clambered out of the hole. He wheeled the barrow containing the old couple close to the edge, and tipped them in. All that was left to do now was empty the bag of quick lime over the area, fill in the hole, and plant the tree. Removing the hessian sack from the roots of the apple sapling he placed it in the centre of the grave. Firming the soil around the tree he proceeded to replace the turf, sprinkling grass seed over the area. A sprinkling of water and in a couple of days the new grass would have obliterated all signs of activity.

Sebastian rinsed his spade under the tap and dried it with an old towel he'd found on a hook outside. Brushing the remaining dirt from the box back onto the garden he picked up a small hatchet. One swift blow sent the padlock skimming across the garden. He opened the chest slowly. Holy Shit! So the information he'd received from his superiors had been correct. The lid clanged shut as Sebastian sank to his knees and kissed the ground. He would never want for anything again; he could buy himself a new identity, a new face, a new life.

A trip into town is in order I think. To celebrate my new found wealth, after all I've gone all day without killing anyone and a man has needs.

33

Charlene threw her bag and jacket on the sofa and headed for the kitchen. A note on the refrigerator caught her attention in passing. Troy and the boys were staying over on Belle Isle for a few days.

Pouring a large glass of ice cold chardonnay she wandered out onto the terrace and sat at the small table. Luna and Juno had been cooped up all day; she supposed she ought to let them out.

Closing the door to the kitchen she walked down to the enclosure and opened the door. The dogs were cowering in the far corner of their sleeping area. Strange. Normally they would have leapt all over her. "Hello girls, what's eating you two, are you sulking because we left you alone all day?"

Walking back up the garden she left the gate open and went back to the terrace. Several minutes later the two Labradors skulked out of their enclosure and bounded up the hill to where she sat. Stopping short of the terrace and crouching low to the ground, growling menacingly. "What's got into you two?" Frightened she turned around, imagining a crazed axe murderer was maybe standing behind her. But she was alone. "Stop it! You're spooking me girls." She shifted uneasily in her seat as the dogs continued howling piteously. Had they sensed her sadness?

'Shush now, your mistress cannot see me, she is not in tune with my world. I will have to wait for the boy, Jason, to come back. He's receptive, young Carly too, such a shame they're not here to see us reunited in death as we were in life don't you think, Antonio?'

'I don't think Carly will care one way or the other, I let everyone I care for down. First your mother and Ben, then you and Daniel, and now Carly.'

'Stop feeling sorry for yourself, Antonio. You should have known that one day my father would seek you out and punish you for your sins. You screwed with his master plan—his dreams for the future. Now he's evened the score. Are you aware your father in law was a party to your demise?'

'Are you sure?'

'Of course I'm sure, I was there when it was all arranged.'

'Bitch, you could have warned me.'

'No I couldn't. And even if it had been possible to warn you I wouldn't have because I was angry with you for sleeping with Carly—for betraying us. Here take your son a moment I want to try something with the woman.' Amelia drifted over to the chair, and leaning forward she clapped her hands. Charlene looked around, pulling her jumper around her shoulders. She'd felt a draught nothing else. Sighing she drifted back to Antonio.

'It's no use we're wasting our time with her, she can't help us she can't even help herself.'

'What's that supposed to mean?'

'She is in mortal danger, the solicitor too. Ben was dispatched to warn Antoine Monroe this evening. I was entrusted to do the same with her, let's hope Ben had better luck than I have. Come, you need to rest now, to gather your strength for the ordeal to come.'

The dogs sat up and wagging their tails bounded over to

Charlene almost knocking her off the chair. "Whoa... Not so fast girls, just a moment ago you were howling like wolves and now you want to play." The two dogs licked Charlene's face and hands. Picking up her empty glass she went inside in search of doggy treats. She shivered. Someone had walked across her grave again. Picking up her telephone she dialled the message service.

"Hi, Charlene sorry about earlier, I got caught up with a client. I need to see you now, urgently. Is it okay for me to come over?" Antoine sounded different, frightened almost. She pressed the number 4 to return the call and waited.

"Antoine Monroe."

"Hi, it's me, I'm all alone. The boys have gone off exploring with their father, the dogs are acting weird, and I for one would love some company. Have you eaten?"

"No. Charlene, go to the front door and look outside. Tell me is there a strange car in the street?" Charlene walked to the front door, opened it a little, and peered through the crack.

"Nope. The street's empty except for my car. Next door are in Auvergne, Clara had a nervous breakdown you know. She's out of hospital now I believe, and staying with her sister near Salers."

"No, I didn't know about Clara. I'll ring for a taxi, I had a drink with Detective Malestroit earlier and I didn't want to risk my license so I left my car at work."

"Supper will be waiting. Tell the taxi driver to put his foot down I'm calling in last night's rain check."

"Will do." Tonight was getting better by the second. Lifting her arm she sniffed tentatively. A quick shower is desperately required. And lingerie, the sexy lacy creation I bought yesterday afternoon will be perfect. Charlene bounded up the stairs into the bathroom, and stripping off her clothes she jumped into the shower. Ten minutes later she stood in front of the mirror putting the finishing touches to her hair and make-up. Ding-dong, ding-dong, ding-dong! Grabbing her robe she ran downstairs and flung open the door.

"Surprise." Sebastian exclaimed as he pushed her inside, and grabbing her by the arm, he slammed the door. "You ought to be careful who you open your door to lady. Move inside now. My, my, how the old homestead's changed. The benefits of having loads of dosh I suppose. Ah, I can see you're wondering how I know the old house."

"Who are you, and what do you want with me?"

"Mmm… depends what's on offer." He pulled at the tie holding her robe closed. "Nice underwear, bet that cost a pretty dollar. Lose the robe. Now. You'd better do as I say bitch or else." Charlene let the robe slip from her shoulders to the floor.

"Pull up a chair and sit down. No, not like that, the other way, like in the film. C'mon show me some pussy." Charlene turned the chair around and straddled the chair. Where was Antoine?

"That's better. You sure do smell good. Expecting someone special are we. I doubt if you'd be dressed like that for your old man would you. No. I think you're waiting for lover boy. Tell me, Charlene, how is Antoine? Well, I trust. He gave me the slip earlier. I think someone may have tipped him off. I know it can't have been Giovanni because he's no longer with us. Could have been the bungling detective I suppose. We'll find out soon enough though, won't we?" The man exclaimed menacingly.

"Who are you, what do you want, and how do you know Antoine?"

"That would be telling. You'll find out soon enough, we'll just sit here and relax and wait for lover boy. He has a thing about women that live in this house, does Antoine. Him and Giovanni alike."

"What do you mean by that?"

"Wouldn't you like to know?" Ding-dong, ding-dong, the doorbell chimed. "I wonder who that can be. Get up bitch. Go open the door, and remember—no funny business or you're dead. Got that?" Nodding Charlene stood up and walked towards the door. She felt the knife point in her back and stiffened. "Smile bitch, you're supposed to be pleased to see him." Biting her lip she opened the door.

"Charlene. You'll catch your death opening the door dressed like that. Where's your robe. He kicked the door shut and placed his suitcase on the floor, removing his jacket and placing it on the case he turned around.

"Nice to see you again, Monroe." The man said. "Come on in and join the party, the little lady here is dying to know why you have a thing about the women from this house."

"How did you get in?" Antoine demanded.

"Duh, the same way as you, thicko. The lady here flung open the door and welcomed me in. I gotta feeling she thought I was you, hence the welcome. Oh, and she did have a robe on when she opened the door but I had her take it off. It was obstructing my view. Not bad for her age, considering she's had four kids. Tell me, Antoine, how does she compare to my Annie in the sack?"

"None of your fucking business, Sebastian. Is that why you murdered your wife and family? Because you found out she was leaving you for me. You're sick."

"So the papers said. Tell me, did they ever catch the tramp? Ah, see, just then, when I asked if they'd caught the tramp you showed surprise. It's my latest party piece, reading peoples' faces to see if they lie. It's quite an art. The lady's longing to know who Annie is, Antoine, will you tell her or shall I? And what's with the suitcase, Antoine? You moving in with Charlene here? Not sure what her old man is going to say about that, got a bit of a temper has the Counsellor. Ain't that right, lady, he can be real mean. I have a sneaky feeling lover boy here was going to do a runner, just like last time, eh, Antoine. Where were you when Annie and Ben needed you eh?"

"Were you running away, Antoine?" Charlene asked quietly.

"It was my intention to leave France, yes, but my conscience got the better of me, which is why I'm here now. I came to warn you about him, in the hope I could get you to safety."

"And, Annie?"

"He didn't deserve Annie. She was too good for him, with his hair brained get rich quick schemes. I first met Annie after her father died; I was the Executor of his will. I advised her to invest the money but she said the family were in financial difficulties and asked me to transfer half of the money into their joint account. A few weeks later Annie came to my office after Marcie had gone home for the evening. She told me she needed the rest of the money. Her husband had threatened to leave her and take the children if she didn't give him the money to save his business. I advised her against it, but she insisted it was what she wanted."

"Too right, the bitch was sitting on a fortune, and what was hers was mine by rights. She was my wife—and he turned her against me."

"You did that yourself, Sebastian, and you know it. You destroyed her. You and your bible bashing friends were slowly sucking the life out of her. She was lonely and …"

"And you thought you'd just slip her a portion to cheer her up a bit. How gallant of you. The bitch hoodwinked the both of us over Ben though, didn't she? For thirteen years I looked out for that boy thinking he was my own flesh and blood. Only to find that all that time she'd been bonking you, and Giovanni. I saw red, but I swear I never meant to kill her, not at first."

"What do you mean, not at first?"

"I went home to have it out with her about the two of you. I found her in the garden and my gun was leaning against the tree. She said she'd been shooting pigeon. We had an almighty row. I told her I knew about the two of you and that I had my doubts about Ben being my son. I can see her face now; she laughed at me, and said that I was wrong about you being Ben's father. Said it had been an accident. I was in retreat with the Brothers, and I'd left her to move into the house here alone. She'd ordered pizza for supper and opened a bottle of wine. When Antonio Giovanni had eventually turned up with the pizza, she'd invited him in, and one thing had led to another. A few weeks later she'd discovered she was pregnant. When she told me Ben was Giovanni's son I hit her. One of the dogs attacked me, while the other dug up my little girl. The bitch had found out Amelia had been screwing the pizza man and that he'd knocked her up too. She'd given birth to Giovanni's bastard son that afternoon; Annie caught her in the attic trying to hide the baby. She shot my baby girl, suffocated the baby, and then calmly packed her bags before dragging our daughters' body down to the garden and burying it under the terrace. I picked up the gun and was about to shoot Annie as Michel came in from work, he tried to stop me. We fought and the gun went off, I didn't mean to kill him. Ben bounded in just as I pulled the trigger a second time, and shot Annie. I was so angry with her for deceiving me I turned the gun on Ben and shot him too. I buried them alongside Amelia and I fully intended to turn the gun on myself and end it all, but the dogs wouldn't leave them buried. So I slit their throats and dug another grave. I was just finishing it when Alexander came home unexpected. I had no choice but to kill him. He would have turned me in to the police. Ungrateful bastard, after everything I'd done for him. Do you know what my firstborn son thought of me? He thought I was a failure. He called me a Eunuch. So I shot him. God told me I should leave the house and go far away and never come back. And if it hadn't been for your meddling husband, lady, I would still be there now."

34

Charlene sat in stunned silence. All this killing had taken place in her house and no one had thought to tell her. "Why didn't you tell me about the house, Antoine?"

"I suppose for the same reason as Charles Dupont. I figured what you didn't know wouldn't harm you; I never vouched for this maniac coming back. For the past seven years I have blamed myself for Annie's death. That I had somehow let her and Ben down, and until today, I was convinced he was my son. Malestroit told me the truth. The baby the boys found in the attic and Ben had the same DNA markers; and his father was none other than Antonio Giovanni. I was devastated, and angry with Annie for deceiving me."

"My heart bleeds for you, Monroe. How do you think I felt when I found out?"

"I don't give a shit about you and your feelings, Sebastian, and if it's the last thing I do I'll see you behind bars. Can you forgive me, Charlene? I never meant to hurt you. You have to believe me. I love you, more than I have ever loved anyone in my life."

"And Annie, did you say the same thing to her too? Did you promise her the world on a stick too?" Charlene demanded tearfully. "I want to believe you Antoine I really do. But..."

"Please just give me one more chance, I promise you won't regret it. We can sell this place; buy a big house near the beach, get married. What do you say, Charlene? Will you marry me?"

"Stop right there, Monroe, before you have me in tears. For starters the two of you seemed to have overlooked one small thing—that I'm holding you hostage. So sit down over there, and shut the fuck up. That's better, now pay attention, cos I'm not gonna be repeating what I say. Okay lady, now why don't we start with you? I want to know where Counsellor Hamilton-Davies is. He's the man you're married to, remember."

"I'm not stupid. Why are you so interested in Troy?"

"He double crossed me, and now its payback time. He had a mistress back in Atlanta. Naomi Gibbs, young, vibrant, sexy, with skin the colour of burnished amber and the longest legs you've ever seen. Pity she was a Federal Agent. I should like to have been there when they informed him of that last snippet of information. He'll always wonder if she stayed because she had to. Some would call it 'poetic justice'. You see the man thought she wanted him for his animal magnetism, and all the time she was using him to get the low down on me. The bitch should have cut out the middle man, and come directly to the source. Who knows where that would have taken her? The last I saw of the delectable Ms Gibbs she was on her knees, with her ass in the air, and a mighty fine ass it was too."

"You're disgusting."

"So they tell me. I take it the man has a telephone with him wherever he is?" Charlene nodded. "Good, here's what we're going to do next. You are going to send him a message, and then we're going for a little ride, just you and me."

"And what do you intend to do with me?" Antoine demanded nervously.

"All in good time, Monroe, all in good time. You can start by getting dressed lady, something warm I suggest. After all I wouldn't want you to catch a cold would I? While I have a little talk with your boyfriend here—man to man like. And don't get any funny ideas of trying to escape. The doors are all locked and I have the keys right here."

He lifted his shirt up to reveal a large key ring to which were attached several sets of keys. He pushed Charlene out into the hall towards the stairs. She hesitated as she passed the hall table. The telephone wasn't in its dock. Had she taken it upstairs with her after Antoine had telephoned earlier?

She made her way slowly upstairs. Who could she call? If she telephoned the police she knew the madman in her lounge would kill one or both of them. But if she telephoned Troy it would put the boys at risk too. There was only one person she could call—Richard, he would understand the gravity of the situation and take whatever action was necessary to prevent bloodshed. Especially hers. When she'd taken Antoine to her bed that first afternoon she'd been a little economic with the truth. He hadn't been the first man in her bed, during her marriage. That honour she had bestowed on Richard Garner, one-time playboy, and business associate of Troy. And the real reason behind her moving to France.

Charlene picked up the telephone and crept quietly across the hallway and into the bathroom locking the door firmly behind her. Turning on the cold water tap to drown out the noise she pressed the speed dial.

"Davies and Garner Associates, how may I help you?" The voice replied cheerfully.

"Della? It's Charlene Hamilton-Davies; I need to speak to Mr Garner urgently."

"I'm sorry Charlene, Mr. Garner is with a client, and he specifically asked not to be interrupted."

"Please, Della; it's a matter of life and death."

"But…"

"Just transfer the fucking call, Della." The line went dead for a split second and then she heard Richard yelling at Della.

"Charlene, what a pleasant surprise, how are you?"

"In the shit about as deep as it gets. I need your help Richard, there's no time to explain everything. There's a man in my house wanted by the police here in France for murdering his family. He says he knows Troy, and that he double crossed him, his name's Sebastian."

"Never heard of him, you need to call the police, Charlene,

right now."

"No, if I call the police he'll kill us for certain."

"Us? Are the children with you?" Richard asked anxiously.

"No. Carly's in hospital and the boys are with Troy. My friend is downstairs with the man."

"Why not just come right out and say you're with your current lover, and have done with it, Charlene. We both know it's the truth. You've got a nerve calling me after what you put me through."

"What I put you through, Richard—really? Is that how you remember it?" Charlene was fuming, but there was no one else she could turn too. "I can't call Troy because that might put the boys in danger. Call whoever you have to, Richard, but do it now. Please, I'm begging you. I have to go…"

"Charlene, I still love you. Hello? Charlene, can you hear me? Damn that bloody woman. Della! Get your ass in here now. Get Chas Denman of the CIA on the phone for me right away. Why are you still standing there woman? It's a matter of life and death. Move it."

35

Charlene pulled an old track suit out of the cupboard in the bathroom. It was a little on the large side but she didn't have time to search for something more suitable, or the man would wonder what she'd been doing all this time. She buried the handset under a pile of dirty clothes at the bottom of the laundry basket.

The spare handset was in the kitchen cupboard, it wouldn't be charged up, but that didn't matter. It wasn't likely she would need to use it. She was glad Carly was safely ensconced in the hospital, safe from further harm. Her hopes now pinned firmly on Richard Garner. Creeping across the landing into her bedroom, she quietly opened the draw where their passports were kept, quickly scribbling the telephone number for the hospital were Carly was staying in the notes at the back of her passport, and closing the draw.

The door to the bedroom flew open. "Come on, bitch, you and I have things to do." He scanned the room. "Nice; it's certainly an improvement on Annie's décor. Pity we have to rush—that bed looks mighty comfortable. And I ain't ever had me a woman who smells as sweet as you." Sebastian grabbed her roughly by the arm and pulled her out onto the landing heading for the stairs.

"Wait here. There's something I need to get from the attic." Charlene sat on the top step looking down. She could see Antoine slumped in the chair; the bastard had beaten him, and knocked him unconscious while she'd been trying to get help. She stood and was about to go to his aid when Sebastian came down from the attic, carrying a small, brown paper parcel. "Where do you think you're going missy?"

"Nowhere. What have you done to Antoine? He's not moving. You haven't…"

"Don't worry; he's still alive, for now. Come on, you can help me get him downstairs into the cellar."

"And what if I refuse?"

"Then I'll have to kill him here. Which is it to be?"

"Why are you doing this? What will killing him achieve? Hasn't this house has seen enough death? Tell me, Sebastian, why did you come back? What was so important?" He held up the package.

"This, and to get even with lover boy for destroying my family. For trying to take what was mine by rights." Sebastian sneered.

"Annie was your wife, Sebastian, not a piece of furniture. Why didn't you just leave her when you found out she was having an affair."

"Because she deserved to be punished for her sins. Like I punished Antonio Giovanni for betraying his wife and children."

"But Giovanni wasn't married when he slept with Annie; he was only fifteen years old, and a minor. She was the one in the wrong; the one who should have known better."

"Yes, I know my wife was a slut, but my daughter wasn't, not until Giovanni impregnated her. And, Carly—is she a slut too? Giovanni refused to mend his ways and he paid for it with his life. End of story, his wife will be better off without him, his kids too."

"Even the new baby? If the shock of losing her husband

doesn't cause her to miscarry that is." Charlene whispered. The look of amazement on Sebastian's face told her he hadn't known about the baby. Exactly what was the connection between this man and the Marcello's? Were they implicated in Giovanni's murder too?

Sebastian pulled his knife from its sheath, placing the blade across Antoine's throat. "Are you helping, or do I cut his throat here and now?"

"I'll help. The key's in the kitchen cupboard."

"Then fetch it quickly, I haven't got all night." Charlene hurried into the kitchen and took the key of its hook along with the handset placing it quietly in the holder.

"Nice try lady, who were you going to call? The ex perhaps? Be my guest. You'll save me having to scour the country looking for him. Here." He thrust the telephone into her hand.

"I don't know his number, it's a new telephone. His other phone wouldn't work in France—if you don't believe me look in the drawer."

Sebastian opened the draw, took out the telephone, and flipped it open. He scrolled through the call list, and satisfied the telephone was in fact Troy's, he dropped it back in the drawer. Grabbing Charlene roughly by the arm he dragged her back into the hallway. Antoine was propped up against the wall, his lip swollen, and a rivulet of blood trickled down his cheek from the cut above his eye.

"Unlock the door. Now take hold of his feet—down you go lady."

"He's heavy, I can't hold him. Argh…" Charlene missed her footing and fell backwards. Sebastian let Antoine's inert body slide the rest of the way down the stairs and ran down to check on the woman, he couldn't find a pulse. Damn, he'd wanted the woman alive, for insurance, and now she was just another liability. He turned off the light and closed the door, locking it behind him and then disappeared into the night. The house, silent once more.

~

'Are they dead, Amelia?'

'I don't think so, Ben.'

'What are we going to do? We can't just leave them here like this, they need a doctor.'

'You think I don't know this, Ben. It's the 'how' that's the problem. We're dead and the only people that can see us are Carly, her brother, and Antoine. And Carly's in the hospital, Jason is off with his dad somewhere, and Antoine is somewhere between this life and the next. So who do you suggest we try first?'

'I suppose it will have to be Jason…Listen—did you hear that? I think he's back.'

The tramp waited until the man got into his car and drove off. He was hardly likely to forget, even with the beard and long hair; he knew it was him. Crossing the street, he stood on the steps to number 5, and knocked timidly on the door and waited. Taking the key from his inside pocket he slipped it into the lock—the door swung open. He hesitated for a second before crossing the threshold, the last time he had entered the house he'd vowed never to return. And here he was again.

"Hello? Is anybody here?" No answer. Torn between closing the door once more, walking away, and staying—it was as if some invisible force was willing him on. He sensed danger but no obvious signs of a struggle. No blood stained the expensive off-white carpet in the hallway. Braver now, he entered pushing open the door to the lounge. Hidden somewhere in the house was a body, of that he was certain. He tried the door to the cellar; it was locked. He tapped lightly on the cellar door. "Is anyone down there? Are you hurt?" He put his ear to the door and listened.

'Quickly, Ben, go and see who it is, and I'll see if I can make some sort of a noise, anything to keep him from leaving.'

'Okay, sis.' Ben stuck his head through the wall and watched the man as he listened at the door. He'd seen the old man before, sleeping on the old couch in the far corner of the cellar before the house was sold. He reached out and tapped him on the shoulder. 'Don't be afraid, I won't harm you, old man.'

The tramp looked around him. "Who's there?"

'My name's Ben, I used to live here before I died. Please don't be scared…we mean you no harm. We need your help, the man that just left was my father. He's a bad man. The American lady and her boyfriend are in the cellar and they're hurt badly. Will you help them?'

"Was it you the last time?"

'No. That was my mother with the dogs. She is doomed for all eternity because she killed my sister. We are the innocents, my sister, her baby, and I…we just want to help Antoine and the American lady and put an end to the killing. Will you help us, please?'

He looked nervously around him, was he going mad? Or did he just have a conversation with a ghost? "Why can't I see you?" The Old tramp asked.

'I don't know? Some people just sense our presence, while to others we appear as visions. I can't explain why it happens; only tell you that it does. Can you see the key to the door anywhere?'

He looked around the kitchen and found Charlene's keys on the counter top. "I found some keys, but I don't think the key to the cellar is on here." He tried several of the larger keys in the lock but the door remained tightly shut. "It's no use, I'm going to find the telephone and call the police. It's high time this ended, once and for all." He picked up the telephone and dialled the emergency services. The ball had been set in motion; the authorities were on their way. He'd have some major explaining to do when they got here, but he didn't care. He didn't want to meet his maker with the deaths of two more innocent people on his conscience.

"Are you still there, Ben?"

'Yes, I'm here, my sister too, don't beat yourself up about the car, you were duped by my father. The police will understand I'm sure. We will leave them in your care now, and thank you. You are a kind man; your sins will be forgiven.'

"How did you know I was worried about that, Ben? Ben? Are you still here?" He was alone again. He opened the front door, sat down on the steps, and waited for the police to arrive.

The sirens' wailing stopped as the police car came to a halt and the first policemen leapt out and ran to where the tramp sat. "Was it you that placed the call, sir?"

"Yes, officer, I have reason to believe there are two people trapped in thecellar, and they may be badly hurt. I'm afraid I can't find the key to the door, you'll have to break it down."

"Okay, sir, if you'd like to go with the constable he'll take a few details." He watched as the door was forced opened and then followed the constable; with any luck tonight he would have a bed somewhere warm and dry. Even if that meant spending the night in a police cell, at least his conscience would be clear, and he knew that for the first time in seven, long years, he would sleep well. He only hoped they were in time to save the young couple.

Xavier Malestroit descended the steps into the cellar of number 55.

"Will they be okay, sir?" The young constable enquired. "Hard to tell. Let's just say they're lucky to be alive, though I still can't work out how the tramp knew they were down here? Somewhat spooky down here though, I have the distinct impression someone was watching me." Malestroit exclaimed with a shiver.

"You've been watching too many late night movies, sir; you'll be telling me next this house is haunted." Ben and Amelia sniggered. Poor Inspector Malestroit, they'd make a believer out of him yet.

'Don't, Ben; Malestroit will get to the bottom of it eventually.'

'Yeah, with a little help from yours truly he will. It's time our old man paid for his sins I've had enough of purgatory and if we help things along a little…'

36

Richard looked at his watch for the second time in as many minutes what was keeping Della. It had been two hours since Charlene's frantic phone call, and a good ten minutes since he dispatched Della down to the front office to fetch Chas Denman.

He was about to pick up the telephone when the door opened, and in came Della, with a fresh pot of coffee and a plate of donuts, followed closely by a tall, muscular man, with skin the colour of dark chocolate. His shoulder length dreadlocks shining raven black in the sunlight; and who, he assumed, must be none other than Chas Denman.

"Sorry for the delay, Richard, only I thought you might appreciate the sugar boost as you missed lunch." Della said thoughtfully.

Richard pulled himself to his full height, and at a couple of inches short of six foot he was no midget, but Denman towered a good head above him. "Put it over on the table by the window please, Della, and can you try that number for me again. Mr Denman, please, take a seat. Coffee?

"Please. Tell me about the conversation you had with Troy's wife this morning."

"I haven't spoken to Charlene in well over six months until today, and she suddenly rings me up out of the blue asking for my help. She said there was a man in her house threatening her and her friend; she asked if I knew of him. I think she said his name was Sebastian. She seemed to be under the impression that he was an acquaintance of Troy's, and that Troy had double crossed him, over what she didn't say, and now he wanted his revenge. That's all there was, the line went dead, and I've been calling the number for the last two hours without success."

"And that was all she said? And how did she sound to you?"

"Stressed out, and frightened of whoever was in the house. I think she was calling from the bathroom, I could hear running water."

"Did you hear the man talk at all?"

"No. I told her she needed to call the police, but she was adamant the man would kill them both if she did that. Charlene and I didn't exactly part on the best of terms, I'm afraid I was a little sharp with her at first."

"Where did she say Troy was?"

"With the boys, off exploring somewhere. I've been trying his phone too, but all I get is the message service. I think Troy may have changed his telephone."

"May I? My stomach thinks my throat's been cut; I missed lunch too." Chas reached for a chocolate covered donut. "My wife tells me they're bad for my physique, but needs must." The door opened quietly with Della hovering nervously outside.

"I have an Inspector Malestroit on the telephone for you, Richard. He said it concerns Mrs Hamilton-Davies."

"Put it through please, Della." He pushed the button putting the call on speaker.

"Inspector Malestroit? Richard Garner speaking is Mrs Hamilton-Davies alright?"

"I'm afraid there's been a little accident, Madame Amilton-Davies and her friend were found locked in the cellar, unconscious. They're on their way to hospital as we speak; I believe Madame Amilton-Davies called you from this number earlier this evening. Is that correct, sir?"

"Yes, she asked for my assistance, she seemed frightened."

"Did she say what of?"

"Yes inspector she did, I'm going to pass you over to Agent Denman of the CIA and let him fill you in with the details; just a moment." He pushed the privacy button, handed the telephone to Denman, and sat down at his desk waiting for the call to end.

"Okay, Inspector, as soon as I have my flight details I will email them direct to you. Au revoir."

"Mr Garner, Interpol have issued a blue alert for the apprehension of Sebastian Delamare."

"Is Charlene badly hurt, Mr Denman?"

"They won't know for sure until they get the results of the tests. I'm leaving for France on the first available flight tonight. If you give me the number of your direct line I will keep you informed of Mrs Hamilton-Davies progress if you like. Don't worry Mr Garner, with the CIA, Interpol and the Sûreté Nationale on his tail he won't get far, I promise you." Richard handed him a business card.

"My home number is on there too, and don't worry about the time delay, I'm a light sleeper."

"Goodbye, Mr Garner. Don't get up I can see myself out. May I?" Chas said pointing to the donuts.

"Be my guest."

"Thanks, I don't mind if I do. I imagine the next meal I eat will be on the plane."

Richard sat back in his executive black leather recliner looking out over Atlanta; exactly what was his partner mixed up in? Was it the reason he had suddenly upped and left last week with only a day's notice? He logged on to the computer using Troy's password—had the man no imagination. He still used his date of birth as his code—a child of six could hack into his files without even breaking into a sweat.

Richard keyed in 'Sebastian' and 'all files' and then sat back and waited while the files uploaded onto the screen. He took out his pen drive, plugged it into the USB port, and downloaded the files; this would be his bedtime reading for this evening.

Charlene walking out on him had been a wake-up call;

and if he ever hoped to get her back into his life where she belonged he would need to convince her his womanising days were over. And for that he needed to be in France.

"Della, find out when the next flight is to Vannes, France, and book me a seat—Business Class naturally. Oh, and ring around the hospitals in Vannes and find out where Mrs Hamilton-Davies has been admitted, and then send flowers, chocolates, and fruit, the best money can buy."

"Anything else, Mr Garner?"

"No, Della that will be all for today, why don't you take a few days off and visit your mother."

"Thank you, Mr Garner, I might just do that." Della slammed the telephone down.

"Damn the Davies bitch." She had almost succeeded in wearing down Richard's defences, one more week and he would have been putty in her hands. And one bloody phone call and off he trots to France, like a little lap dog. Personally Della couldn't see the attraction; after all, the woman was almost prehistoric! And here was she, an intelligent, vivacious, caring young woman, crying out for love. Mother Nature wasn't playing fair. If she knew someone who practised Voodoo she'd give Charlene a taste of her 'alternative medicine'.

37

Malestroit sat in the interrogation room with the old man; and as he told of the events of that April night seven years ago, his blood ran cold. Sebastian Delamare had deliberately set out to confuse the police by implicating an innocent man. A man, who because of his actions had been persecuted—hunted down like a wild animal for being in the wrong place, at the wrong time. And without whose steadfast action earlier that evening, the American woman, and his friend Antoine would probably have died of their injuries.

He would talk to his superiors in the morning; hopefully he could persuade them to drop the charges of perverting the course of justice. The man hadn't known of the murders beforehand, he had simply taken advantage of an act of kindness. Sebastian was an accomplished liar, as his investigations would bear witness too. What would he himself have done in the man's place?

There for the grace of god and all that jazz. What agony he must have suffered, knowing, he had assisted a murderer to escape. For a while the police had eagerly chased the car and the tramp around the country, whilst Sebastian had slipped quietly away to safety.

"And so you see, detective, I had nothing to do with the murders, had I known of the heinous crimes the stranger had committed, I would have come directly to the police, and turned him in."

"Tell me, Henry, what changed your mind after all this time?"

"I saw the man leaving the house tonight, about half an hour before I telephoned for help."

"You're sure it was the same man?"

"I'd know him anywhere, even with his beard, and long hair."

"Did you see where he went, or what car he was using?"

"He turned left at the top of the road, towards the town centre. And I think the car was a Citroen Picasso, dark blue, or black. I couldn't see the number plate clearly I'm afraid; it was covered in mud."

"How come you happened to be there tonight, Henry?"

"I wanted to see if the house had really been sold, I used to sleep in the cellar until a few weeks ago….the key to the front door had been in the glove compartment of the car."

"Ah, so it was you in the house when the neighbours saw lights in the cellar at night."

"It may have been."

"Did something happen to frighten you, Henry?"

"I heard…noises—the spirits of the house are angry and frustrated, even the dogs."

"Dogs? Did you see the dogs?"

"No, but I heard their bloodcurdling cries."

Malestroit sat back rubbing his chin—Charles Dupont had mentioned the dogs—rabid, black dogs, when he'd questioned him after his accident.

Was there such an animal as a haunted house? Something Antoine had said to him about Amelia Delamare stuck in his mind… 'How did young Carly know about Amelia Delamare and the baby? The girl's been dead for seven years, Xavier.' How indeed.

"Are you going to charge me, Detective?"

"I'm afraid that's not up to me to decide, Henry. I'll speak to my superiors first thing tomorrow morning. Meanwhile I'll get someone to take you down to the cells. Have you eaten today?"

"I had a cup of lukewarm coffee and a stale croissant this morning."

"Okay, I'll send out for a takeaway for you; you're not vegetarian I take it?"

"Only when there's nothing else on offer. Clara, the lady who lives next door to the Delamare's, used to bring me a sandwich and a drink if she saw me on the bench and Mr Giovanni used to give me leftover pizza sometimes. But Clara's not been there for a few weeks now, and Giovanni's is closed. Is he ill?"

"No, Henry, Mr. Giovanni's dead. A tragic sky-diving accident yesterday morning; his parachute failed to open."

"You don't think it was an accident, do you Detective?"

"I'm not sure what to think now, Henry." A knock at the door halted their strange conversation. "Constable Lebrun; will you take Henry here down to the cells and make him as comfortable as you can, and send someone out for a take-away for him. Order something for me too; I think tonight is going to be a long one. Any news from the hospital yet?"

"Not sure sir would you like me to ring them."

"No thank you, constable, just see to it that Henry is taken care of."

"Will do, sir. Come on, Henry; let's see if we can't find you some books and stuff to help pass the time." The constable led the old tramp down the corridor towards the cells; he would sleep well tonight, his conscience clear. Xavier Malestroit picked up the telephone and dialled the number on file for the local hospital.

"Detective Malestroit here, is there any news on Madame Amilton Davies and Mr Monroe?"

"Madame Hamilton-Davies is off the critical list."

"And Mr Monroe?"

"Still in surgery, detective."

"When will I be able to speak to Madame Amilton-Davies?"

"Not until tomorrow afternoon, after the doctor's seen her, detective."

"Okay, will you ask someone to let me know as soon as Mr

Monroe comes out of surgery please?"

"Of course, I'll make a note and leave it on the desk." Malestroit put the phone down. His old friend was in a bad way, it didn't take a genius to work that out. Surgery meant problems.

Thinking back to his conversation earlier with Henry, tomorrow he would make an appointment with Charles Dupont's doctor. The forensic examination on his car had placed it at the scene of the hit and run accident Antoine Monroe had reported. He had been unable to speak to Dupont so far, to find out where he had been that night.

Clara Le Goffre, Charlene's neighbour, had been certain she had seen Dupont's car parked in front of next door at around midnight; and Antoine Monroe had telephoned for an ambulance at approximately 10: 45—and the car was found abandoned on waste ground near the station the following day by a routine patrol of the area. But how did it get there? Right now he had more questions than answers, as well as a thumping headache. He checked his in-box, satisfied there was nothing from Chas Denman he logged off the computer, tidied his desk, and headed for the door. Time to go home, damn he'd intended to pay his respects to Mario Giovanni this evening. He looked at his watch; he'd call round first thing in the morning—it was late, and he was hungry.

"Where's Lebrun?"

"Here sir, sorry, there was a queue." He handed him the brown paper bag—Malestroit peered inside. Hamburger—again.

"You off home, sir?"

"Yes, there's nothing much I can do tonight. Night all."

"Night sir." Malestroit waited for the constable to push the button to open the door; it was raining again. He pulled the collar of his jacket up, tucked the brown sack containing his meagre supper inside, and ran the hundred or so metres across the car park to where his battered old Volvo stood all alone.

Stopping in his tracks—he was sure his car had been closer to the building. Backing away slowly, he noticed a smudge of what appeared at first glance to be green Playdoh on the door sill. Jesus, Mary, mother of God—someone's booby trapped my car. He turned and ran back towards the safety of the Police station, banging on the doors for them to open up. Lebrun opened the door slowly.

"Can you not read, sir? Oh, sorry, sir, I didn't realise it was you. I thought you went home ages ago?"

"Call the bomb squad and get someone out to cordon off the area around my car." Lebrun didn't move. "Well, what are you waiting for Lebrun? Move it!"

"Jesus—you're serious?"

"Of course I'm bloody serious, man; someone's planted C4 under my car, and if I hadn't realised it wasn't where I'd left it earlier this evening I'd be playing a harp by now. Get me the video surveillance tapes of the car park from this evening."

"Yes sir."

Malestroit exhaled deeply—he was getting to old for all this. Reaching inside his jacket he pulled out the now flattened paper sack and threw it into the waste bin. No point in chancing a second near death experience.

"Sir, the bomb squad are asking to speak to you."

"Tell them I'm on my way. Did you find the video?"

"Yes, sir, it's set up in the conference room. I should imagine the men from the bomb squad will want to look at it too."

"Yes, I'm sure they will, open the door, Lebrun, there's a good chap—oh and Lebrun… you wouldn't like to see if someone could rustle up a quick sandwich would you?" Malestroit took a cigarette from his jacket pocket, searching his pockets for his lighter as he walked across the car park.

"I wouldn't light that if I were you, sir." Malestroit turned. An officer of the Bomb Squad stood guard, the area surrounding his car cordoned off with crime scene tape. He looked at the cigarette in his hand and nodded in agreement.

"Sorry, I wasn't thinking. Have you found the bomb yet?"

"Yes, sir, it was wired to the ignition. It was lucky you saw the putty on the door. There's enough explosive under there to launch it to the moon!"

"Will they be able to get it off without damaging my car?"

"No, sir, I'm afraid the safest way to deal with it is a controlled explosion. Looks like you'll be needing a new car, sir." He handed Malestroit a business card. "My brother will see you right, sir; just tell him Sergeant Benson sent you." Malestroit put the card in his wallet and thanked the sergeant; after all it was only an old car, it could have been worse, he could be dead.

Xavier pushed the buzzer and waited for the door to open; his number one priority now was to find out who hated him enough to want him dead? Heading directly for the conference room and the tapes that hopefully would give him the answer he needed. This time he'd been lucky but what if they tried again? Switching on the television he sat down, remote control in hand, fast forwarding the tape to the appropriate time slot. As the man walked away from his car, he turned towards the camera and looked up. Sebastian Delamare! It had to be him; old Henry had said his hair had grown long.

"Lebrun!"

"Sir? Is there a problem with the tape?"

"Go and fetch Henry please, and bring him directly to me."

"Yes, sir." Lebrun opened the door to the old man's cell stopping dead in his tracks.

"Oh, Henry, why here, and why on my watch?" The old man lay on the bed, his arms folded across his chest, an enigmatic smile on his wizened old face. He looked so peaceful, but Lebrun knew he was dead. He reached for the emergency cord, pulling it three times, and then sat down on the bed to wait for the cavalry to arrive. He'd been fine an hour ago when he'd given him his supper, said he was looking forward to a peaceful night's sleep. His first in almost eight, long, years. His wish granted, for now he'd sleep in peace for all eternity.

Malestroit was the first through the door; he slumped against the wall, crestfallen—the one person who could identify Sebastian Delamare was dead.

"I'm sorry, sir; he was fine an hour ago when I bought his supper. Said he was looking forward to a peaceful night's sleep. He got his wish, sir. He's at peace now."

"I guess it was his time, Lebrun. Close his eyes and cover him up, the doctor's on his way." More bloody paperwork.

"Was it important, sir? You know, what you had to ask him?"

"Yes, Lebrun, it was important, a matter of life or death—mine. I believe the man who planted the bomb under my car was none other than Sebastian Delamare."

"Wasn't he the man who murdered his family and then vanished?"

"The very same, Lebrun, the very same. We'll just have to hope Mr Monroe regains consciousness, and hope he can identify Delamare. Can you ring for a taxi to take me home, Lebrun? I'm tired. It's been a long day, a very long day indeed."

"Of course, sir." Dejected, the detective turned and headed for the door, and with one last look at the old man, lying quite still on the narrow bed he made his way back up to his office. Hesitating as the ground trembled beneath his feet—as outside his car exploded into a million pieces…

38

Charlene opened her eyes. Where was she? Antoine. What had happened to Antoine? The last thing she remembered was helping the man carry Antoine down the cellar steps, and then everything went black. The door to the room opened, and a nurse wheeled a medicine trolley to the side of the bed.

"How are you feeling, Mrs Hamilton-Davies? Do you have any pain?"

"My head hurts a little. How did I get here, where's Antoine?"

"All in good time, Mrs Hamilton-Davies, all in good time, first we need to get you well again." The nurse handed her a glass of water and two tablets; Charlene tried to sit up.

"Why can't I feel my legs?"

"You had a nasty fall, Mrs Hamilton-Davies; here these will help with the pain."

"I have to go, I can't stay here. You don't understand I have to pick my daughter, Carly, up from the Clinic, she'll be wondering where I am. Where are my clothes?"

"Your clothes were ruined I'm afraid; we had to cut them off."

"And, Antoine; is he alright?"

"I'm sorry, Mrs. Hamilton-Davies; you'll have to ask the Doctor about Mr Monroe. Is there someone you could call who can fetch your daughter for you?"

"No, her father doesn't know where she is, and I don't have his new mobile number." The nurse smiled reassuringly as she wheeled the trolley towards the open door.

"I'll get someone from Social Services to come and talk to you, I'm sure they will be able to arrange for your daughter to be picked up and brought here." Charlene lay back, the medicine weaving its' magic spell as she drifted off to sleep. The nurse raised the cot sides on the bed and turned off the light closing the door quietly behind her. Yawning as she pushed the trolley back to the office.

"Everything okay, Chloe?"

"Yes fine, the new patient was asking after the man she was brought in with." The older woman peered over the top of her spectacles.

"You didn't tell her anything did you?"

"Of course not. Can you make a note for the day staff to contact Social Services; her daughter is in a Clinic somewhere. Let them sort it out, it's what they're paid for."

"You wouldn't like to make the policeman a coffee would you Chloe, he asked me ages ago, but you were on your rounds."

"Sure thing, you want one, Mary?"

"Yes please, strong, and dark as the night, it might help me stay awake until the day shift turns up. I hate the graveyard shift, nothing interesting ever happens."

"You're weird. I prefer the night shift because it's quieter; and I can catch up on my studies without too many interruptions. Okay, three black coffees coming up, does he have sugar?"

"I didn't think to ask, sorry."

Chloe went into the kitchen; Mary smiled, could hear the young nurse singing away to herself. She was definitely no threat to Madonna, as she gave her rendition of 'Material Girl' her all—karaoke nights had a lot to answer for.

"You took your time; I thought you'd gone to Brazil with Madonna for the coffee."

"Funny ha ha. Here, I raided the biscuit tin while I was waiting for the kettle to boil."

"You're a star! Mind you don't eat all the chocolate digestives while I take the policeman his coffee."

Mary picked up the third cup of coffee and a couple of plain digestive biscuits, and headed for the double doors leading to Intensive Care.

Chloe sat down and took her text books out of her bag—an ear piercing shriek broke the silence as Mary came crashing back through the doors.

"Chloe, get security and a crash team to Mr Monroe's room now." Chloe pressed the panic button, picked up the telephone, and dialled security and then ran to help the other nurse.

"Jesus, is he going to be alright? Did you see who did this?"

"Yes, where the hell is the crash team?"

"Here, give us a hand with the door." The security guards arrived seconds after the crash team.

"Who's in charge here?" The security officer demanded curtly.

"I am—Staff Nurse Mary O'Brien."

"Okay, Mary, tell me what happened?"

"I was bringing the policeman a cup of coffee, and as I came through the doors he was coming out of Mr Monroe's room, knife in hand. I screamed and he ran off towards the stairs."

"Are you absolutely certain it was the policeman on duty outside Mr Monroe's room you saw running off Staff Nurse O'Brien?" The older woman thought carefully for a couple of seconds before speaking.

"No, it wasn't the same man, his hair was long and he had beard too."

"Okay, guys, we need to search all the rooms on this floor, the real policeman is here somewhere and he may be hurt." The security guards dispersed.

"The patient's condition has been stabilised for now, but we won't know the extent of the damage until we run a fresh battery of tests. Staff, can you make sure Mrs Hamilton-Davies is okay. Security is checking the hospital grounds, and I'll notify

Detective Malestroit of the breach in his security arrangements. Fun here isn't it!" The doctor said sarcastically.

The policeman had vanished—but he couldn't have disappeared into thin air. There was one place left to check—the men's toilets. Chloe knocked on the outer door and listened—and pushing the inner door open with her foot, she peered inside. "Hello?" She was just about to give up when she heard a muffled groan coming from the far cubicle. "Doctor Mackie—I think I've found him."

"Well what are you waiting for nurse? Go help him."

"What if it's the assassin's still in there?"

"A valid point, I'll call security and get an armed guard up here. If he's moaning he's alive, for now." She could hear the doctor on the telephone to security, but what she couldn't hear now was the man. She was a nurse, and the man was hurt, she hesitated for a split second and then sprinted to the far cubicle pushing the door open a little.

"Get a crash team here quickly. I can't find a pulse." The policeman's head was wedged behind the toilet, his body contorted at an awkward angle. She fished around in her pocket, pulled out her Swiss army knife, searched for the flat head screw driver attachment, and started to dismantle the wall panel. They'd need room to work on him. She was just unscrewing the last of the screws when the doctor burst through the door with the crash cart accompanied by two nurses.

"Good thinking nurse, here, let me give you a hand with the panel." Between them they carried the heavy melamine panel over to the wall and propped it up next to the sinks. "Fetch a trolley, and don't forget the back board and neck brace. And call maintenance tell them to get a plumber up here quickly." The doctor said.

"On my way." What was it Mary had said earlier? 'Nothing exciting ever happens on the graveyard shift!' Grabbing a trolley, she yelled to Mary to telephone maintenance for a plumber, and then ran back to the injured policeman.

"We won't need the backboard, nurse, he's gone. Go back to the ward and get staff to make you a cup of coffee, you'll be off duty in half an hour or so. We'll take it from here." The outer door opened and the plumber sauntered nonchalantly inside.

"What the fuck? What's that panel doing over there? They said you needed a plumber not a carpenter." The maintenance man peered over the doctors' shoulder at the body wedged behind the toilet.

"Is he…?"

"Yep, very."

"How the fuck did he get stuck in there?"

"We don't know, and now we have to wait until the police arrive before we move him, so I'm afraid you've had a wasted trip up here."

"Not your fault, doc. Will I be needed later?"

"I imagine so; do you need your time sheet signing?"

"Please, you know what sticklers they are in Admin."

"Tell me about it."

39

Malestroit had tossed and turned for hours, until finally he'd fallen asleep. Only to be dragged back to reality by the incessant ringing of the telephone. He picked up the clock—six thirty, he'd been asleep at the most for three hours. His head was throbbing—maybe if he ignored it whoever was calling would give up, and annoy someone else. Torn between a sense of duty, and lack of sleep, he hesitated a couple of seconds then grabbed the telephone. This call had better be important.

"Malestroit."

"Sorry to wake you, sir, but the hospital called; they said it was urgent..." Wide awake now he sat up, searching under the bed for his slippers.

"Okay, give me the number." He scribbled the number on the pad on the nightstand and then disconnected the call. A doctor Mackie—he hadn't dealt with him before. He dialled the number, sat back, and waited patiently for someone to answer.

"Intensive Care—Staff nurse O'Brien speaking how can I

help?"

"Inspector Xavier Malestroit, for Doctor Mackie."

"Good morning Inspector—hold the line please while I find him." He heard the clacking of heels on the tiled floor and the opening and closing of a door. At least she hadn't put him on hold with that infernal music. He heard her tell the doctor to take his telephone off divert. Smiling to himself—he was always forgetting to do that—it was good to know he wasn't alone.

"Inspector Malestroit—thank you for getting back to me so promptly. I'm afraid I have bad news...."

~

Malestroit put the telephone back on the nightstand; the body count was mounting rapidly—first Antonio Giovanni, then the tramp, and now the constable guarding his old friend was dead too. And according to the doctor, Antoine was hovering between this world and the next. A host of tests would now have to be performed to reveal the extent of the damage caused by the intruder. The doctor had been blatantly honest with him; there was little hope for his recovery. But a little hope was better than none at all wasn't it? Charlene Hamilton-Davies was paralysed from the waist down—though according to the doctor it might only be temporary.

In his line of work good news was something of an anomaly; no one could say his work was a labour of love. His day began with visits to mortuaries, prisons, and crime scenes, not necessarily in any particular order. The people he passed his days with ranging from the victims of crime, to the dregs of society. He really needed to get out more, see the world, smell the flowers—and whatever normal people did when they had time on their hands—retirement had been on his mind recently.

Why did that one small word put the fear of God in his heart? What would he do with his days? He'd never been one for DIY or gardening; he'd never had the time. There had always been a case to solve, a criminal to track down, and another body to bury. And now here he was at fifty seven years of age facing a retirement alone. When his wife died he'd simply refused to deal with the reality of life without her and thrown himself headlong into his work. It became his saviour, his reason for living, his port in the storm. But the storm was rapidly turning into a hurricane and he was powerless to stop it.

He shuffled into the bathroom and turned on the shower. Ten minutes later he was dressed and ready to face the world again. He had plenty to do at the office today. The chief would want a report on the death of old Henry—forensics had promised him the autopsy report today and he still needed to address his transport problem and find himself a new car.

His eyes strayed to the set of car keys on the nightstand; his wife's Porsche sat unused in the garage. He had given it to her for her birthday the week before her diagnosis was confirmed. It seemed silly it sitting there gathering dust when he needed a car. Walking over to the nightstand, Xavier's fingers hovered above the keys, the dust motes swirling in the shafts of light filtering in through the net curtains at the bedroom window—he really ought to wash them. Marion would be horrified at the colour of them.

'Take them; use the car, Xavier, please. Use it for me…'
The ghostly voice whispered softly.

"Marion? Is that you?" He stood motionless. Waiting, hoping for a sign—a faint breeze blowing from the open window, the air heavy with the scent of freesias—his wife's favourite flowers.

Sighing he picked up the keys. "God bless you, Marion. Wherever you are, and I promise I'll take good care of her." Better care than I did of the last one. From now on he'd be parking in the secure underground parking. Had he really heard her voice? And if he had, did he believe in life after death—in ghosts?

~

Lebrun grabbed his bag from the front seat; if he was late again Malestroit would have his hide. He couldn't help but feel the inspector blamed him for old Henry dying on his watch. Slamming the car door shut he headed for the stairs, stopping while a flashy, red sports job pulled into the space next to him. One of the top brass he supposed. Imagine his surprise when the door opened and out climbed Malestroit.

"Err, morning, sir. Nice car." Malestroit smiled to himself. No one had ever envied his transport before. He knew it would be all around the building that he'd won the lottery by lunchtime, for sure. Running his hand across the bonnet he turned to face the constable.

"Yes, it is rather, isn't it—it was my late wife's. It's been sitting in the garage at home gathering dust since she passed away. I figured it was high time I did something other than clean it, given my current lack of transport." Malestroit locked the car and followed Constable Lebrun to the stairs. He had a killer on the loose, and a mystery to unravel; he couldn't, wouldn't retire, not until the Delamare's killer was behind bars.

He opened the door to his office, sat down at the desk, and opened the report. Slamming it down hard on the desk he jumped up and headed for the door. "Lebrun! Get in here, now." Lebrun picked up his hat and tucking it under his arm he headed for Malestroit's office.

"Sir?"

"Come in—sit down and read this." He took the report from Malestroit and read the opening paragraph. "Well, Lebrun, how do you think Henry came by the poison?"

"I have no idea sir. The only thing that Henry ate yesterday evening was the hamburger and fries from McDonalds and you had the same, and you're fine."

Malestroit leaned over and poked around in the waste bin under his desk; pulling out a brown paper bag covered in grease stains and placed it before the constable. "I didn't eat it." Opening his drawer he pulled out an evidence bag, opened it, and carefully put the grease stained bag inside, sealed it, and handed it to the constable. "I want you to go directly to the lab with it. Do not give it to anyone other than the man himself; and don't let that bag out of your sight, not even for a second—understood, Lebrun?"

"Yes sir, right away sir. Do you think the old boy was the intended target?"

"I don't know, Lebrun, and until such time as I do everyone connected with this case needs to be on their guard. And, Lebrun, tell them I want the results yesterday—understood?"

"Yes, sir, perfectly, sir."

"Close the door on your way out." Malestroit waited until the door closed behind the departing constable before taking out the folder. Now more determined than ever to solve the crime that had haunted him for the past seven years, and put the ghosts of the Delamare's to rest.

40

Sebastian parked around the corner from the house—creeping silently through the park, and taking care to stay hidden in the shadows. Watching, as the scruffy man sat down on the steps of number 55. He'd seen him out of the corner of his eye as he sped away, his intention being to head back to the old couple's place for the night. To sleep, perchance to dream and all that crap, but curiosity had gotten the better of him.

The eerie lament of police sirens could be heard in the distance. Had the old man called the police? Was that why he was sat on the steps waiting. Figuring it would be best not to hang around long enough to find out—and as the first police car screeched to a halt Sebastian was already back in the car. He slid down in the seat and waited before driving off at a sedate speed so as not to bring attention to himself.

He would deal with the meddling tramp after he'd attended to Malestroit—and he had the perfect solution to that particular problem innocently disguised in brown paper on the passenger seat next to him. His favourite type of 'Play Doh'; the only kind he'd ever had the pleasure of modelling with—even though its modelling properties were limited to destruction, rather than construction. But in the end Malestroit had handed him the tramp on a platter, metaphorically speaking of course.

He'd parked as near as he dared to the police station, and sat in the bushes waiting for Malestroit to return. His patience was rewarded an hour or so later when the errant detective drove into the car park, and then made his way up the steps into the police station with the handcuffed tramp. Interesting. Even more interesting the bumbling detective had left his keys in the ignition, he deserved to die for his stupidity, if nothing else.

Planting the bomb had been relatively easy, killing the tramp easier still. He'd followed the young constable at a safe distance on a hunch. One that had paid dividends—he'd followed him to McDonalds. Sebastian overheard him tell the girl behind the counter to charge them to the Police account, as he didn't see why he should fork out money to pay for his boss's supper—let alone that of the man bought in for questioning. He had swiftly ordered two of the same, sprinkled the poison onto the hamburgers, and waited until the constable headed for the door. The rest was a piece of cake.

He figured one way or another, the policeman and the tramp would die that very evening. What he hadn't figured on was the policeman being so observant, or so clumsy—he must have either dropped the burger in his panic to get back into the police station or thrown it in the bin because it had gone cold. Or maybe he'd just lost his appetite—almost being blown up would do that to a person.

Damn the man—what the fuck did he have to do in order for him to die? Shoot him? Send him Anthrax in the mail—what? Maybe he was losing his touch—or maybe he'd allowed himself to become complacent. After all, dispatching Giovanni to the hereafter had been almost too easy. Everything would become clearer with a good night's sleep. He hoped!

~

Malestroit rubbed his forehead; his migraine was getting worse. Damn, he didn't have time to be ill. He fumbled in his jacket pocket for the bottle of tablets; and flipping the lid open with one hand, he shook a couple onto his desk. He popped them into his mouth, washing them down with a swig of water. Leaning back in his chair, he closed his eyes, desperately hoping to rid himself of the pesky little man with the hammer running amok inside his head—if he could have unscrewed it and swapped it for another he would have happily done so.

Constable Lebrun knocked on the office door; there was no response. He stood for several seconds wondering what he should do next; Malestroit had given him explicit instructions not to let the report out of his sight.

"Anyone know where Inspector Malestroit went?" The duty sergeant checked the register.

"He's still signed in so he can't be far away. Jack."

"What now?" Jack bellowed sticking his head around the door of the office.

"Is Malestroit in with you?" The policeman stuck two fingers up at the duty sergeant and went back to his desk. "I'll take that as a no then; sorry Lebrun. Have you tried knocking?"

"No, I thought I'd just stand here like a twat until he realised I was here. What do you think?"

"No need to be like that. I only asked."

Shaking his head, Lebrun knocked loudly on the door to his boss's office once again before going inside. Malestroit was slumped over the desk, snoring gently. "Sir… Inspector Malestroit, are you okay?" The Detective stirred, looking up at the constable through sleep filled eyes; and yawning, he sat up.

"Sorry Lebrun, I must have dozed off there for a second. I didn't get much sleep last night. Is that the report?"

"Yes, sir. I stood over them while they tested it, seemed to have the desired effect. That has got to be the fastest they've worked in a long time." Malestroit smiled, partly at the thought of the young constable standing behind the lab technicians, but mostly because his headache had gone.

"Holy Shit." Malestroit exclaimed.

"Was it…poisoned sir?"

"Yep, you could say that. It would seem that my hamburger had enough poison to kill a cow, ironic really, as it was already dead. A distillation of the root of the Hemlock Water Dropwort plant, it produces a neurotoxin, which, when ingested causes death—and the victim appears to have died with a 'smile' on his face."

"The old tramp was smiling. And there was me thinking it was because he'd come clean and confessed. Poor old bugger, after everything he'd been through, to die like that...."

"Exactly, Lebrun, a horrible way to die, and whoever killed him was intenton getting me too. I want you to think back to yesterday evening Lebrun; did anything unusual happen at McDonalds? Did you see anyone touch, or tamper with the burgers after you'd paid for them?"

"No, sir, the girl put them into the bag and then handed it to me, just the same as she did with everyone. No wait…as I was leaving a man bumped into me—he knocked the bag out of my hand."

"Think carefully, Lebrun—who picked the bag up?"

"He did sir, he bent down and picked it up and said he was sorry for being so clumsy. He was slurring his words; I remember thinking he was either a drunk or a druggie."

"Did you get a good look at him Lebrun—it's important, think man, think."

"No, sir, he had a baseball cap pulled down over his eyes, the only thing I remember was he had long hair and a scruffy long beard, and was hippie like in appearance."

"Sebastian Delamare! Henry said he'd recognise the man anywhere, even with his beard and long hair—I think the man at McDonalds and the man Henry saw leaving the American woman's house were one and the same. All we have to do now is find out where he's hiding, before he tries again."

41

The woman from Social Services waited impatiently for the nurse to finish her briefing. As if she hadn't enough on her plate; now she had to play nursemaid to the American's daughter. She looked at her watch for the umpteenth time; she had another appointment in an hour.

"Sorry to keep you waiting, we had a bit of a drama here last night. The patient should be awake now. This way please."

"Thank you. What information do we have on the daughter's whereabouts?"

"Not very much I'm afraid, just that she's in a clinic somewhere in town and Mrs Hamilton-Davies was to have picked her up this morning. Here we are." The nurse pushed open the door to Charlene's room. "Morning Mrs Hamilton-Davies, how are you feeling today…?" Madeline Champlain stepped forward; she needed to speed things up a little here if she was to get to her next appointment on time.

"Hello, I'm Madeline Champlain from Social Services. The nurse tells me your daughter, Carly, is in a clinic in the city, and you need someone to pick her up for you, is that correct?"

"Yes, that's correct. Here's the address and a letter for the Doctor giving you permission to remove Carly from their care. I'm grateful for your help, Madame Champlain. I'm afraid I don't have anyone else I could ask. My husband is off with my boys over on Belle Isle, and he recently changed his mobile. I haven't had time to put the number in my contacts, remiss of me I know, but the last thing I expected was to end up in hospital."

"It's not a problem; I'll telephone the clinic and arrange to pick Carly up after my next appointment and bring her here."

"Thank you."

"Until later then. I'll see myself out."

Charlene lay back. "How's Antoine today nurse?"

"I haven't seen Mr Monroe today as yet, Mrs Hamilton-Davies. The Doctor will be in to see you later, maybe you should ask him."

"He's not dead is he? You would tell me if that happened, wouldn't you?" Charlene choked back the tears; everyone she had ever loved had either turned against her, or died. The nurse took hold of her hand and squeezed it gently.

"Ask the doctor when he does his rounds; he's better qualified to explain than I. I'll be back with your medication shortly, and I have it on good authority breakfast is on its way. I took the liberty of ordering for you for today, bacon and eggs, it's my favourite and one I should resist if I'm ever going to get into my bathing suit again."

Charlene smiled weakly; the nurse would have told her not to worry if Antoine was out of danger surely? The nurse closed the door quietly behind her and made her way back to the office.

"How's Mrs Hamilton-Davies?"

"Fine, she was asking after Mr Monroe again. It's such a shame; I hope they find the man that did this to him soon. It's making me nervous; every time someone buzzes I hesitate before letting them in. He could try again."

"I'm sure he won't, he almost got caught in the act last night. That poor policeman's family. He has two young children and another on the way, so the security guard said. Are the test results in from the lab for Mr Monroe yet Chloe?"

"Yes, I put them in the file for the doctor."

"Did you look at them?"

"No, I couldn't bring myself to open it. Ignorance is bliss and all that bullshit, and my looking won't change the results, will it."

"No, it won't. What will be, will be. She's young and attractive, she'll get over him—women like her always do." The buzzer sounded and the two nurses looked at each other for reassurance, before answering.

"Delivery for Ms Hamilton-Davies—come on, open up, I haven't got all day here."

"We'll need to see some ID please otherwise you can't come in, new security rules."

"What is it with you people? I already bared my body and soul in reception to one of the hospital's pet gorillas. Ring down and check with the front desk if you don't believe me."

"Don't worry, I will, and in the meantime you can wait there, those 'pet gorillas' will have my hide if I let you in unchecked."

Pet gorillas indeed, they were all pussycats, except maybe the one they called 'Rambo', she supposed he didn't get nicknamed that name by being a pushover.

"Hi, Chloe Philbert from the ICU. We have a delivery man asking for Mrs. Hamilton-Davies has he been cleared by your guys?"

"If it's a scrawny looking guy with thick horn rimmed glasses yes, he's been cleared—Rambo gave him the once over." Chloe sniggered.

"Just a second while I check." She put the phone down and peered through the window at the man, and satisfied, buzzed to release the lock. "Yep, it's him, thanks."

"Who have you got in here? Royalty or something? Here sign this." He thrust a dog-eared book and a pen at her and waited while she signed it. "Can someone give me a hand with this stuff?"

"You missed a word out of that sentence—Donald." She said acidly, as she read the name tag on his jacket.

"Sorry. Please, thank you, have a nice day…kiss my ass." He muttered through gritted teeth, the smile not quite making it to his lips. "Someone must really love her."

He handed Chloe a huge bunch of flowers, an enormous, beautifully presented basket of fruit, and put the biggest box of chocolates Chloe had ever seen on the corner of her desk.

"Don't eat them all at once, will you." And with that he shot out the door before Chloe had time to reply. Cheeky beggar! She sneaked a look at the card with the flowers, opening the envelope carefully.

Forgive me please, Charlene.
Richard xxx

"My goodness, who are these beautiful flowers for Chloe?"

"Mrs Hamilton-Davies. There's fruit and chocolates too. Looks like you were right too—I sneaked a peak at the card, they're from another man. Some people have all the luck! I'd better take them through I suppose."

"This I have to see; I'm right behind you with the chocolates and fruit. I wonder if she'd notice if we borrowed a couple of kiwi's and a banana."

"Shush…she'll hear you!" Chloe tapped lightly on the door and opened it wide. "Aren't you a lucky lady, today?" Chloe breezed, as she handed the bouquet to Charlene. "There's a card too." She waited while Charlene opened the envelope and took out the card; she looked at it briefly before pushing it back into the envelope, tossing it onto the bed.

"There's more."

"Surely not?"

"Yes, a huge box of chocolates and a basket of fruit."

"You'd better put them over there on the table I suppose. Would you like some fruit? It seems a pity to waste it…it must of cost my friend a small fortune. A guilty conscience I suppose." The nurses looked from one to the other, made their excuses, and went about their business.

"What do you make of that little outburst Chloe?"

"No idea, but I wish someone I knew felt guilty enough to send me flowers—never mind the fruit and chocolates."

"Me too." The older woman sighed, and sat down heavily on the desk. "I can smell bacon and eggs." The buzzer sounded three short bursts followed by one long indicating that breakfast had indeed arrived and with it the day staff.

"Anything interesting happen during the night ladies?"

"Do you want to tell her, or should I, Chloe?"

"I think you should Mary. After all it was you that discovered the man running from the patient's room."

"Yes, Chloe, but it was you who found the poor policeman at deaths door in the Gents toilets." The three nurses looked from one to the other; and then the Staff nurse laughed.

"You had us going there for a moment. Dead policeman indeed. You'll be telling me next the Pope's not Catholic. Right, let's get to work ladies so that these two can get off home to their beds."

Chloe picked up her text books from the desk, stuffing them hastily into her back pack. Mary shook her head, but said nothing. Let them find out the hard way.

42

Madeleine Champlain walked into the foyer of the DiAngelo Clinic, and waited whilst the receptionist telephoned the good lady herself. The door to reception opened, and a petite woman walked up to where she stood, her long, dark hair, tucked neatly behind her ears.

"Madame Champlain? Marie DiAngelo, I understand you are here to pick up Mademoiselle Hamilton-Davies."

"That's correct. Here is a letter from Mrs Hamilton-Davies, authorising me to collect Carly. I'm afraid her mother was involved in an incident at her home yesterday evening and is in the hospital."

"Oh dear, I do hope she isn't badly injured. I'll get the nurse to fetch Carly. Sylvie, can you organise a coffee please for Madame Champlain."

"Certainly, Doctor." The receptionist poured coffee into a delicate china cup, and passed it to Madeleine.

"Cream and sugar?"

"No thank you, this is fine." Madeleine Champlain looked

at her watch. She would have to cancel her next appointment. She flipped open her organiser and dialled her office.

"Celine. It's Madeleine. I'm not going to be back in time for my next appointment I'm afraid, would you please give Monsieur Dubois my apologies and make another appointment."

"Certainly, Madeleine. Will you be back before lunch?"

"I sincerely hope so." She disconnected the call and sat down. The door to her left opened.

"Here we are, Madame Champlain." Madeleine picked up her bag, walked towards the young girl, and held out her hand.

"Hello, Carly, my name is Madeleine; I work for the Social Services. Your mother asked me to collect you and take you to her."

Eying the woman suspiciously Carly spoke. "Dr DiAngelo said my mother was in hospital. Is she badly hurt?"

"I'm not sure of the nature of the injuries your mother sustained I'm afraid Carly. When I saw her earlier this morning she was sitting up in bed though, and her main concern was you. Would you like to speak to her?" She held out her mobile for the young girl.

"Just push the speed dial, and if my memory serves me well the hospital is the third on the list." Carly took the telephone from Madeleine, hesitating for a second before handing it back to her.

"No, it's fine." She turned to the nurse, and taking her overnight bag from her, followed Madeleine Champlain outside to the car park.

Madeleine Champlain studied the girl closely—she looked very much like her mother. The same fine bone structure, but she looked so miserable, as if she had all the worries of the world on her shoulders. She opened the passenger door for the girl moving the newspaper from the seat.

"Here, let me take that." Carly sat down placing the newspaper on her lap. She turned it over, and there in full view was a photograph of Antonio. The words jumped out at her—the late Antonio Giovanni. Antonio was dead. An accident, it said…

"Nooooo…No, it can't be true, tell me it's not so."

"Carly, are you alright? What can't be true?"

"Antonio Giovanni, he can't be dead. He just can't be..." Sobbing uncontrollably now, Carly let the newspaper slide to the floor and Madeleine picked it up and read the article.

"Did you know Monsieur Giovanni well, Carly?" Carly simply nodded, and lifting her tear stained face to the heavens she said: "It's all my fault. I'm sorry, Antonio; I shouldn't have murdered our baby." Rocking back and forth now, Madeleine took her in her arms and held her tight.

"Cherie, this man had no right to take your innocence, my poor child. It's not your fault, it says he died after his parachute failed to open, it was an accident, Carly." But the girl wasn't listening, nor was she making sense.

"Papa must have found out, about the baby, about Antonio and..."

"And what Carly? Your father is on Belle Isle with your brothers, and has been since yesterday morning. You're distressed, you have just suffered a terrible ordeal, it's only natural you would feel bad about this mans' death. C'mon let's get you back to your mother, maybe she can explain what happened better than I."

Carly slid down in the seat—it was all her fault, Antonio was dead, her baby was dead, and it was all down to her.

Charlene looked at the clock on the wall, what was keeping the woman from Social Services? She had promised to have Carly here for lunchtime, and it was past midday. She picked up her buzzer and pressed it. Where was everyone today? She pressed it a second time and waited.

The nurse looked up from her desk, the American woman was buzzing again. She closed the folder in front of her and stood up, smoothing down her apron. If she was going to keep this up all day she'd be confiscating her buzzer before long. "You rang, Mrs Hamilton-Davies?" The nurse peered over the top of her spectacles at the American woman, dangling helplessly over the side rail of the bed. "Oh dear, we have gotten ourselves into a state, haven't we. What were you trying to do?"

Charlene scowled at the nurse; and as tempted as she was to say she was training for the high hurdles at the next Olympics she refrained. "I was trying to reach the telephone. The woman from Social Services promised to have my daughter here before lunch, and there's still no sign of her." The nurse sighed, and taking hold of Charlene's arm she helped her back into bed.

"Would you like me to telephone Madame Champlain for you Mrs. Hamilton-Davies? The traffic is probably bad—with everyone rushing home for lunch…" The door to the room opened; the nurse looked up to see Madeleine Champlain, and a very sad young girl, whom she presumed was the missing daughter, Carly.

"Momma! What happened to you?" Carly flung herself onto the bed, sobbing.

"There, there, pumpkin, it's not as bad as it looks—honestly, it doesn't hurt at all. How about you, are you okay?" Carly dried her eyes on her sleeve and sat up.

"Why didn't you tell me Antonio was dead momma?"

"You had enough on your mind, Carly, and I didn't want to upset you. It was an accident, his parachute failed to open. He was dead long before he hit the ground, I'm sure he didn't suffer." Charlene looked at the nurse for reassurance.

"Your mother's correct Carly, he wouldn't have been conscious at the end, thankfully. C'mon, dry your eyes and sit down here. Would you like to have lunch with your mother?"

"Please, if it's not too much trouble." Charlene exhaled, mouthing a silent thank you to the nurse who was already heading for the door. Crisis avoided…for now. Charlene turned her attention to Madeleine Champlain.

"Thank you for collecting Carly, Madame Champlain, it's much appreciated. I do hope we didn't put you to too much trouble."

"Not at all Madame, Carly, but if you'll excuse me I'll be off now. I have a lunch appointment over the other side of town. Take care, Carly, Madame." Closing the door quietly behind her Madeleine Champlain hurried down the corridor towards the exit. If she didn't get a move on her lunch date would assume she had stood him up—again!

~

Carly sat down beside her mother. A solitary tear trickled down her nose, and dripped onto her mother's hand.

"I'm sorry for your loss pumpkin; I can't say I'm sorry he's no longer a threat to my family, because that would be a lie. How are you feeling now?"

"Two days ago I had a life growing inside me, and a man who I thought loved me…and now, now I just feel kind of empty and sad."

Charlene pulled Carly to her, and held her tight. "I should have protected you better Carly, and I failed you, and for that I am truly sorry. Can you forgive me?" Drying her eyes on the tissue her mother handed her, she took hold of her mother's hands in hers.

"Momma, you did nothing wrong. I'm the one who needs to ask for forgiveness—I let you down, and however long it takes I'll make it up to you. I promise. Did you tell pops?"

"No. I haven't told him, nor am I likely too. As Antoine pointed out it would achieve nothing. On the contrary, he would have you and Jason on the next plane back to Georgia, before I could say custody battle. Matt and Philip are old enough to make their own minds up as to with who and where they want to live, but you and Jason would have no choice but to obey. Maybe I have been a bad mother, and perhaps I should let him take you back to Georgia to live with him, but I'd rather die than be separated from any of my children, so if you go, I go too—so there you have it. Talking of pops, we need to contact him; after all you're not well enough to be alone in 'that house'. I take it you know Jason's mobile number, because I didn't get around to putting your father's new number in my book, and he left the old phone in the kitchen draw."

"Of course, but you're wrong mum, I'd be fine on my own in the house it doesn't scare me at all. I know about the ghosts—I've spoken to Amelia, that's her name, and the baby Jason and Philip found in the attic's name is Daniel—Jason's spoken to her too, several times. In fact Amelia saved Jason from breaking his neck when he fell down the attic stairs. Though it was her fault he fell in the first place—she scared the daylights out of him when she suddenly appeared when he was playing with the stupid Ouija board."

"Trust me Carly; it's worse than you think. This girl, Amelia, did she say how she died or mention who killed her?"

"No, not to me she didn't. Momma, has something bad happened? Is that why you're here?"

Charlene hesitated for a moment before continuing. "Yes, Carly, something bad happened last night at the house. A man forced his way into the house. He said he used to live there with his family, and that his family were dead. He held Antoine and I hostage. His intention was to kidnap me and leave Antoine to die in the cellar."

"So how come you escaped?"

"I don't know. The last thing I remember was being forced by the man to carry Antoine down the cellar steps. I must have fallen because the next thing I know I'm in hospital, Antoine too. I can't seem to get anyone to tell me how he is; they keep fobbing me off with excuses. I think he may be dead."

43

Carly jumped up and headed for the door. "Where are you going now Carly?" Hesitating she turned to her mother.

"I'm going to find out how Antoine is, and if they won't tell me I'll scream the place down. They have no right to do this to you momma, you and Antoine are more than just friends." With that she flounced out of the door letting it slam shut. Leaving a stunned Charlene staring at the now closed door. One way or another it looked like she would find out what was wrong with Antoine.

Carly stood in the corridor wondering what to do next; and what had seemed like the right thing to do at the time didn't seem so appealing now. The nurses' station was un-manned so she crept up to the desk, searching the whiteboard for Antoine's name. Awaiting test results—so he was alive! Now if she could just find where he was…

"May I be so bold as to enquire what you are doing young lady?"

Carly turned to find a man in a white coat sporting a stethoscope staring intently at her. Damn. "Sorry I was looking for a pen, but there doesn't seem to be anyone around." It was a feeble excuse, and the first thing that popped into her head. He fished around in his top pocket and handed her a pen.

"Here, take mine."

"Thank you; I'm Carly Hamilton-Davis." Carly said as she held out her hand, and leant forward in an attempt to read his name tag.

"Dr James Marsh—are you a patient or just visiting?"

"Just visiting. I wonder if you could tell me which room Mr Monroe is in please, only I promised my mother I would pop in and see how he is." The doctor leaned over the counter and studied the whiteboard.

"He's in room 472, but I'm afraid he's not allowed visitors."

Carly swayed—now is not the time to faint girl. "Are you okay? Perhaps you should come and sit down for a moment while I fetch you a glass of water." He disappeared into the room behind the nurses' station and came back with a glass of water. "Here you are Carly." He put the back of his hand on her forehead, and frowning, took hold of her wrist. "You have a slight temperature, and your pulse is racing."

Damn—Dr DiAngelo had warned her about over-exerting herself today. The last thing she needed was to be admitted to hospital again. Though it did have one advantage, she could stay close to her mother. She didn't like the idea of going back to the house, because despite her bravado she was scared of Amelia. And who knew how many more ghosts were trapped inside there.

"Dr Marsh—how is Antoine really? My mother has asked several times but she keeps getting fobbed off with feeble excuses and she's really worried that he may be dead, or worse." Carly couldn't think of anything actually worse than being dead…but it sounded more dramatic in that context.

"No, Carly, he isn't dead—he's in a coma. There was a problem in the early hours of this morning and his condition has deteriorated since admission. I shouldn't really be telling you this, as you're not his next of kin, so mum's the word, okay?" Carly nodded, and blinded by tears, stumbled back into her mother's room followed by the doctor.

"Good afternoon Mrs Hamilton-Davies, and how are we feeling today?" Dr Marsh took the chart from the bottom of the bed, and frowning he put it down on the bed. The American lady seemed to be extremely agitated.

"Sore, and very annoyed. I have been trying to find out how Mr Monroe is all morning, but no one will give me any answers. They keep fobbing me off with platitudes, and I'm sick of it. Will you please tell me what the problem is?"

"As I told your daughter, Mr Monroe's condition deteriorated overnight and we are awaiting the results of tests carried out after the incident." Carly looked puzzled, Dr Marsh hadn't told her about any incident.

"What kind of incident?"

"I'm not at liberty to say Mrs Hamilton-Davies—I've already said too much, and now if you'll excuse me I have other patients to see."

"Not so fast, Doctor Marsh. The police found us both unconscious in the cellar of my house—how they knew we were down there is a mystery. One I intend to get to the bottom of. Now, please, tell me what happened to Antoine."

"Do you remember anything at all?"

"Yes, a man forced his way into my house and threatened me with a knife—he said his name was Sebastian and that he used to live there with his family. He claimed to have killed his wife and sons and then buried them under the patio...the dogs too...He said my husband double crossed him and that now it was payback time. My husband is on Belle Isle with my sons and I haven't been able to contact him. Naturally I'm worried; I've seen what this man is capable of first hand."

"I can assure you that Security has been put on a red alert after last nights incident. I believe the man you just described tried to finish what he started last night—and unfortunately the policeman appointed to guard you and Mr Monroe was killed in the line of duty. Would you like to see Mr Monroe if I can arrange it?"

"Yes please, even if it's only for a few minutes."

"Leave it with me; I'll see what I can do." The Doctor opened the door to leave and collided with a nurse.

"Sorry, Doctor. Um...there's a gentleman to see Mrs Hamilton-Davis—he says it's a matter of some urgency..."

"Does he have a name, Nurse Bertrand?"

"Oh yes, sorry it's a Mr Denman, and he says he's from the CIA."

"Then you'd better send him in, we don't want to leave him standing out in the corridor if he's from the CIA—do we nurse." He wondered how some of them managed to pass their examinations. "I'll come back later." He held the door open for the visitor—he wouldn't like to meet him in a dark alley. The man was huge, towering a good head and shoulders over him.

Chas Denman took out his wallet containing his ID and passed it to Charlene. Carly gasped—she had never met a real live CIA operative before. Her face coloured, as she realised he was watching her with some amusement.

"Good afternoon ladies. Chas Denman at your service—I'm here in response to a conversation you had with Mr Richard Garner M'am. May I?" He indicated to the basket of fruit on the far table.

"Be my guest." Charlene watched as he took a peach from the middle of the display and bit into it. The juice dripping down his long, dark fingers. She licked her lips.

"Momma! Where are your manners?" Charlene blushed, as her daughter handed the Adonis before her the box of tissues. Chas took the box from her and pulled out several tissues, and after wiping his hands and mouth, tossed them into the waste bin.

Chas Denman was a remarkable sight. And the words tall, dark, and handsome, had just taken on a new meaning. Dreadlocks framed his ruggedly handsome face, his skin unblemished, and as dark as the darkest ebony. With eyes the colour of roasted coffee beans, and lusciously, kissable lips. Charlene had an overwhelming urge to leap out of bed and launch herself into his arms. All of which hadn't gone entirely un-noticed by Carly—geez whatever medicine her mother was taking she wanted some.

Chas Denman had been observing their reactions with amusement. He had never been able to figure out why women drooled over him. To him it was just a body—his body. Okay, so he worked out regularly, and he watched what he ate, or rather Mary-Jo did. Well most of the time anyways. He smiled, remembering the chocolate covered doughnuts he'd eaten before leaving Richard Garners office. His last square meal too, as he'd slept all the way from Atlanta to Vannes.

He wondered if the Counsellor's wife would mind very much if he had himself another peach, and maybe a banana or two. As soon as he'd finished interviewing the delectable Charlene, and her equally attractive young daughter, he would get directions to a café and have himself a slap up meal. After all he was in France, home of gastronomy, and the CIA were footing the bill.

"May I? Sorry, but I slept all the way from Atlanta, and the flight attendant didn't like to wake me; and my last meal consisted of doughnuts in Mr Garner's office prior to leaving for the airport."

"Please help yourself; Carly, see if you can find a bag to put some fruit in for Mr Denman—I'm sure the nurse on the desk will have one somewhere." Carly got up and headed for the door. It was so annoying when adults did that, because now she'd never get to hear the full story. Not unless she eavesdropped. She leaned close to the door—just her luck. The room was soundproofed.

~

"Have you managed to contact your husband Mrs. Hamilton- Davies?"

"No. Not yet, and please, call me Charlene. Mrs Hamilton-Davies sounds so stuffy and formal."

"Sorry, Charlene. Do you know where he is exactly?"

"He's somewhere on Belle Isle; he has our sons Philip and Jason with him too. Sorry to sound so vague but we didn't actually part amicably yesterday morning. You see I had the audacity to ask him for a divorce the night before, and as you can imagine, it went down like a hooker in bible class. If you'll pardon the pun."

Denman tried hard to suppress the smile threatening to escape, without success. Charlene Hamilton-Davies was one feisty lady; and he pitied the man that tried to tie her down— metaphorically speaking of course.

"Okay, I'm seeing Inspector Malestroit of the Surete later; I'll ask him to see if he can't locate Troy and the boys, and bring them back as a matter of urgency. We can't have Carly alone in the house, not with a lunatic on the loose. Do you feel up to answering a few questions Charlene?"

"Of course, what would you like to know?"

"Let's start by getting a description of the man who attacked you, so the Inspector will be able to issue a photo-fit of him to the newspapers and television. You know the sort of stuff, height, weight and so on." Chas took out his sketch pad and pencils and sat down in the chair at the side of the bed. "Okay, try closing your eyes and picturing the man. Let's start with his face…any scars or birthmarks that you noticed?"

Charlene closed her eyes for a moment. "He had a scar on his left cheek, just under his eye. It was jagged and raised. And a scruffy beard, his hair was long and tied back in a pony tail with an elastic band; and it is difficult to say what the actual colour was. It didn't look as if it had been washed in a while—a bit like the rest of him. He hadn't cleaned his teeth either. They were stained, and his breath smelled faintly of alcohol. His eyes were bloodshot and dark brown I think."

"Can you remember what shape his face was?"

"Yes, it was long, and gaunt, as if he'd lost weight recently, with a greyish tint, but that could have been because he was dirty. He was tall and slim—but not as tall as you, I'd say about 5'10, he had long finger nails—they were the only bit of him that actually looked well kept—almost manicured. I don't think he was used to manual labour either, because his hands were smooth. I think he wears spectacles too. Although he didn't have them on, but the bridge of his nose was marked from spectacles being worn regularly." Chas put the final alterations to his drawing and then turned it slowly towards Charlene.

"Oh my Lord, it's him…well almost—his eyebrows were thicker and bushy and they almost joined in the middle. And his face was leathery; as though he'd spent a long time in the sun in recent years." Chas made the alterations and held it up for Charlene's approval.

"That's him. That's Sebastian Delamare." Chas studied the drawing closely. The drawing made it official, Bastian Lamare and Sebastian Delamare were the same person.

"Right, I'll give this to Inspector Malestroit this afternoon, and set the wheels in motion. It's high time this man paid for his crimes, both here and in the US. I'll send a copy of this over to Naomi Gibbs; get her to verify him as the man who kidnapped her."

"The man mentioned her; he said she'd been assigned to my husband, to spy on him. Is it true? Was she spying on Troy, or was she his girl like he said?"

"Sorry, Charlene. No can tell, Ms Gibbs was part of an undercover operation, and as such, all information relating to that operation is classified."

"Can't blame a girl for trying. You see if Troy's been playing away from home too, it will make for a more amicable divorce. He can't expect me to stay faithful if he hasn't—now can he. No matter how the said 'indiscretion' occurred. It would be a bit like the pot, calling the kettle black, don't you think?"

"I'm not here to think, or to discuss your marital problems Charlene. I'm just here to glean a little information, and to assist in the capture of a wanted fugitive—should the need arise. You will have to ask Counsellor Hamilton-Davis about the 'alleged indiscretions'. And your source could hardly be described as a fine, upstanding citizen, now could he. In fact your source is wanted in connection of the murders of eight people, and the attempted murder of at least two people of which I may be one of." Chas lifted his shirt to show off his latest scar. Charlene smiled sympathetically.

"I bet that hurt like hell."

"Only when I laughed; and of course when Mary-Jo stuck me with the hypodermic, shot me full of antibiotics and topped it off with a Tetanus vaccine. My ass was so sore the next day; I had to think twice before sitting down. And Mary-Jo's my wife before you ask."

"It must be handy having a doctor for a wife in your line of work—cuts out the middle man at least."

"Mary-Jo's a vet'nary Charlene, not a Doctor, and a mighty fine one at that. She's saved my ass on more than one occasion. And yes, I know, normal folk visit the doctor when they've been shot at, but the doc would have to report the incident. Let's just say I'm not above bending the law a little, if needs must, and leave it at that shall we."

Chas pushed his sketch pad back into his backpack and stood up, he pointed to the basket of fruit. "Is it still okay to mis-appropriate some of your lovely display Charlene?" His stomach rumbling loudly in protest.

"Of course, though it sounds like you could do with something a little more substantial than fruit." He grinned boyishly, revealing a perfect set of gleaming white teeth.

"I think you could be right. I'll ask the doc if he can recommend a decent restaurant nearby, unless of course you know of one."

"No sorry, I'm afraid I don't know this area of Vannes, and eating out with three teenagers usually ends at the nearest KFC, McDonalds, or a pizzeria! I'm afraid that part of their education has been sadly neglected to date. I had hoped that Antoine and I…" Charlene sniffed, as a solitary tear plopped silently onto the bedclothes. The thought of losing Antoine so soon was more than she could bear. Her tears flowing unimpeded now. Chas took her hand and held it tightly—he hated to see a woman cry, especially such a pretty one.

"There, there, c'mon, dry your eyes, Charlene. I'm sure Antoine will be okay. You have to stay positive, and maybe a little prayer wouldn't go amiss. We'll get this guy, and that's a promise—and I'm not one to make promises I can't keep. Okay? Here, dry your eyes before Carly comes back and sees you like this." Passing her the box of tissues, he stooped and planted a chaste kiss on her cheek, and picking up his backpack once more he headed for the door.

44

The taxi stopped in front of the hospital and Richard Garner climbed out, and handing the driver a wad of bills, turned, and walked into the hospital. He'd probably overpaid him—but what the hell—it was only money. Strolling nonchalantly up to the Reception area he took out a picture of Charlene and handed it to the girl behind the desk. And, in perfect French, demanded to be taken directly to her room. The girl studied the photograph for several seconds before disappearing, coming back a few minutes later with a burly security guard in tow.

"Mr. Garner?"

"Yes, I'm Richard Garner."

"Can I see your passport please, sir?" Puzzled, Richard handed his passport over to the security guard. Who studied it for several seconds and then handed it back to him.

"Sorry, sir, new security rules. If you'd like to follow me I'll direct you to the Intensive Care Unit."

"Is Charlene badly injured?" The guard smiled sympathetically.

"I'm sorry, sir; I'm not allowed to divulge information about our patients…"

"Don't tell me, because of the new security rules."

"Err, no sir—patient confidentiality actually. You will have to speak to the doctor about Mrs Hamilton-Davies's injuries I'm afraid, and even then, if you're not family, I'd say you'd be pushing your luck." He stopped before a bank of elevators and pushed the button to open the doors.

"Here you go sir; ICU is on the third floor. It's clearly signposted from there." Richard stepped inside the elevator, pushed the button and looked up, but the man had already walked away. Job's worth. Stepping out of the elevator he headed down the corridor.

"Mr Garner? I thought it was you." Richard Garner stared at the man. Who knew he was in France…and then he remembered.

"Agent Denman. I suppose you're wondering what I'm doing here?"

"Not at all, sir." Chas Denman, you are such a liar. "I think it's exactly what the lady needs—to see a friendly face."

"That's exactly what I thought, and the reason I hopped on the first flight into Vannes."

There was no doubt at all in the CIA officer's mind as to why Richard Garner was here—having furtively read the card concealed in the basket of fruit. At a guess, Troy didn't have a clue that his long time partner and his soon to be ex-wife had been playing hide the salami behind his back.

"I'd better be off; I have a fugitive to apprehend, with the help of the French authorities, naturally." Richard Garner's lips twitched in a tight lipped smile.

"Naturally. Good luck, Agent Denman, because from what I read about him in Troy's files you're going to need it. Your fugitive is as slippery as an eel. He has managed to evade capture for almost 8 years, and you can't be certain Sebastian Delamare and your man Bastian Lamare is the same person."

"I wouldn't be too sure of that, Mr. Garner." Denman tapped his backpack. "I have all the evidence I need to prove otherwise in here—thanks to Charlene."

Denman watched as Richard Garner turned and carried on down the corridor without another word. He could have sworn he saw a flicker of the green eyed monster. Strange. Garner had nothing to be jealous of. His attachment to the lovely Charlene was purely in the line of duty. Now the Monroe guy—him, he ought to be wary of, and Troy, most definitely—Chas found it amusing. Three lawyers fighting over one woman, in a country with an abundance of beautiful women—now that took some believing. The doors to the elevator closed and Chas Denman disappeared from view.

"Uncle Richard, what are you doing in France?" Carly squealed—leaping into the astonished lawyers arms as she hugged him tightly.

"Carly! My, how you've grown." Carly groaned.

"Uncle Richard! What did you expect—a five year old with pigtails, scraped knees, and a runny nose?"

"Of course not silly. Here, let me look at you properly." Holding her at arms length and studying her closely. What a doll.

"You look so much like…"

"Please, don't add insult to injury by adding the rest Uncle Richard. It's such a cliché. C'mon momma will be thrilled to see you; after all, if it wasn't for your call to the CIA, momma and Antoine would still be lying in the cellar."

Carly opened the door to her mother's room, dragging a reluctant Richard in behind her. He had hoped for a few minutes to prepare a speech, and beg Charlene's forgiveness, but his god-daughter had other ideas.

"You'll never guess who I found in the corridor?" She moved aside and pushed Richard forward; propelling him with such force he almost toppled onto the bed.

"Carly. Do be careful. Richard—what a pleasant surprise. You just missed Agent Denman."

"No, I ran into him at the elevator—right before missy here spotted me, and almost bowled me over with her welcome. She reminds me of Luna as a puppy. How are Luna and Juno…?"

"Oh my god, Carly—the dogs, they won't have any food or water. Richard, could you do me a huge favour? Take Carly back to the house and stay with her until they locate Troy. Please. There's no one else I can ask. After all, you are her godfather—pretty please, I'll be eternally grateful."

"Please say yes Uncle Richard, otherwise they will send for Madame Champlain again, and take me to the DAS with all the other waifs and strays." Richard looked from mother to daughter and back—two against one just wasn't playing fair. But how could he refuse, it was the perfect way to charm his way back into Charlene's affections. Richard Garner—knight in shining armour to the rescue, for the second time in as many days.

"Okay, you twisted my arm, but I warn you, I'm not very domesticated."

"Hallelujah, lord be praised—that means we can go out for supper, just the two of us—and I know just the place."

"Please tell me it's not McDonalds, that's all I ask. It would be sacrilege to come to France and not sample their 'haute cuisine'. It's such a pity you can't join us Charlene."

"Yes—isn't it just? Never mind I'll be out of here in a couple of days or so, and I'm sure you'll be more than happy to make it up to me. N'est-ce pas?"

"Bien sur! In more ways than you could wish for. And bravo, I'm pleased to note you are making an effort to learn the language, Charlene."

"When in Rome, Richard, when in Rome…"

"And when in France…" Carly coughed loudly. "Hello. I'm still here in case you'd forgotten the pair of you." She could have run naked through the hospital and they wouldn't have noticed. Her mother was amazing, men fell at her feet in adoration—even Richard, a confirmed bachelor and according to her father, a serial womaniser, was no exception. All mother had to do was crook her little finger and they were as putty in her hands.

It was almost obscene, the way she sucked them in, only later to spit them out when she'd had her fill of them. Carly sighed; she had hoped her mother had found 'Mr Right' in Antoine, and then fate had intervened in the form of Sebastian Delamare, and put an end to that. Antoine was dying.

When she'd gone in search of a plastic bag for the fruit she'd accidently eavesdropped on a conversation between the doctor and Antoine's mother. No brain activity could be detected—the doctor was asking permission to withdraw treatment. They were going to switch off the machine and let him die with dignity. It would have been his wish. She had only known this kind, and gentle man, for a very short while, and soon he would be gone.

Richard coming to France was a godsend; Carly knew all about their tumultuous relationship. Just as she knew the real reason behind the break-up, it could be summed up in two words—Vanessa Sumner—the bitch whose sordid affair with Richard Garner, had destroyed her mother. Forcing her to flee her native Georgia, and head for France. So, she was ace at eavesdropping, and even better at keeping the information to herself when needs must, and today was just one of those times.

Antoine's death was unavoidable, and preserving her mother's sanity wasn't something she was prepared to leave to chance.

In the room adjacent silence reigned. The machine still, its function now to stand and wait. A solitary figure sat at the bedside, the silence broken by the swishing of the door as the nurses came, and went. The woman's eyes closed in silent prayer. The man before her seemed smaller in death, than life. Taking comfort from the doctor's words, he hadn't suffered at the end. She had held his hand, and watched him die, her only son—gone forever.

It was time to leave, there were arrangements to be taken care of, people to see, flowers to choose. Bending forward she kissed his brow—he was still warm.

"Goodbye my precious, you will always be with me, until the joyous day we are re-united on the other side."

'Maman, je suis la. C'est moi, Antoine.'

45

His mother looked so sad. But why was she alone—where was Charlene? Surely she should be here with his mother, mourning his passing.

'She can't hear you, Antoine. Your mother isn't a receiver I'm afraid.'

'Annie.'

'Yes my darling, I'm here. Everything will be fine now; I'm here to protect you.'

'And what of Charlene, is she…'

'Charlene is alive and well, see for yourself, she's in the next room, but I warn you. You may not like what you see.'

Antoine reached out and touched his mother, recoiling instantly, as the equivalent of a high voltage electrical charge shot up his arm, sending sparks flying into the air around him.

'Sorry, I should have warned you about the static charge. It only happens when you touch mortals— walls and doors have no energy field to speak of. Here take my hand and I'll show you how it's done.' Antoine hesitated, his hand still smarting from the shock. 'Come on scaredy cat, last one through the wall's a rotten apple!'

Annie held out her hand, impatiently. 'Are you absolutely certain it won't hurt, Annie?'

'Yes, it just feels a little funny when you're between one room and the next. Like someone walking across your grave—it sends shivers down your spine. Now let's go see what Charlene is up to next door shall we?' Antoine took hold of Annie's hand, squeezing it tightly. 'Relax Cheri, it won't hurt a bit—ready? One, two, three, jump!'

The ghosts stood by the side of the bed, invisible to all, they assumed. Watching, as the stranger leaned forward. 'Who is he Annie?' Annie put her finger to her lips.

'Shush, the girl will hear you. She's a receiver.'

'Does that mean she can see me too?'

'I'm not sure. The only way to find out is to try to attract her attention somehow.'

'Oh, no, I'm not going to do that again in a hurry, it hurt like hell the last time!'

Annie laughed. 'You won't have too, here I'll show you.' The curtains fluttered in the breeze, the smell of perfume permeating the air—Annie's perfume. Antoine watched as Carly turned and smiled. She could see him.

"I'm thirsty. I saw a vending machine down the hall, anyone else fancy a Coke. Uncle Richard?"

"No thanks, Carly, not at the moment, but you go ahead."

~

So the man was Carly's uncle. But that didn't give him the right to touch Charlene. Not in the way he was touching her. No, there was more between them than that. He looked around the room at the flowers, and the fruit, his gaze coming to rest on the chocolates on the bed between Charlene and the man. They had once been lovers! Annie took him by the hand and led him through the wall.

'Antoine, we have to go now, Carly is waiting in the corridor beyond. There is nothing for you here now, let them be.'

"Antoine. Are you...dead?" Carly asked.

'Yes, Carly, I am. And the man with your mother, he is your uncle?'

"No, he's my fathers' business partner, and my god-father… and he was my mother's lover back in Atlanta. It's a long story, and not one I think should be discussed here. For one, if anyone comes by they'll think I'm mad—standing here talking to myself. You're dead, remember."

'As if I could forget. Sorry, that was un-called for, it's not your fault I'm dead; your mother's neither. I should have told Charlene about the house, about Sebastian, and the killings.'

A sudden blast of cold air made Carly shiver, reminding Carly of a line from a novel. Who was the woman standing with Antoine? She looked somehow familiar…A little like Amelia.

"Who is she, Antoine…?" Carly whispered, backing away from the woman. "You killed Amelia and Daniel, didn't you?"

'You watch your mouth girl.' Annie hissed…The meddlesome girl needed a lesson in manners, but now was neither the time nor the place for a showdown. It would keep…

Antoine moved in front of the desk, putting himself between the two women. His face darkened—Carly had never seen him look so angry. 'So it was true…it was you. You killed Amelia and her baby, and then buried her body in a shallow grave. It was your fault your children died, Annie. Why, Annie, why? You evil bitch…Run, Carly; go back to your mother and Richard. I'll deal with this now.' Carly ran down the corridor, and flung open the door to her mother's room, slamming it behind her. Sliding to the floor, her hands clasped over her ears.

"Make the noise stop momma. Please make it stop."

"What noise, pumpkin? C'mon, dry your eyes, there's nothing here that can harm you, I promise." Richard shrugged. He couldn't hear anything either.

The lights flickered and the corridor plunged into darkness. In the distance Antoine heard the sound of horses, galloping closer; their breathing laboured…The Horsemen of the Apocalypse. They had come to claim their prize—the soul of the fallen one… Antoine turned to Annie, his eyes blazing with hatred.

'There is no way out, Annie, their word is final. You took the life of your child and her newborn son without remorse, and now you must pay. Justice must be served. Goodbye, Annie…'

'No, please, you have to help me. Antoine, please—don't let them take meeeee............'

The air heavy with the cloying odour of decaying flesh, as the spirit of Annie Delamare was sucked into the vortex. Antoine looked away, covering his ears to shut out the pitiful wailing—the sound of a thousand souls in torment. And then silence. The corridor awash once more with light. A bright white light, so bright it hurt his eyes. It was over—it was time to leave. He would have liked to say goodbye—to kiss Charlene one last time...Alas, it was not meant to be, and sighing he walked towards the source of the light, its bright aura enveloping him. Soaring upwards—high above the clouds now, he kissed his hand and putting it to his lips blew his true love one last kiss.

'Goodbye, Charlene, I will love you forever....'

Carly sat up slowly, wiping her eyes on her sleeve. It was over. Antoine was gone. Annie too. "Momma, there's something you should know—Antoine is dead." She watched as the colour drained from her mother's face.

"No—it can't be true. No, please, no—not Antoine too."

"I'm sorry for your loss, momma, I truly am. He was a fine man. He would have made a wonderful husband—a wonderful father too. Here, dry your eyes. Antoine wanted you to know he loved you, and that he was sorry for deceiving you about the house—and about Sebastian."

"How do you know this Carly?" Richard intervened.

"Because he was here a few moments ago, and I spoke to him. He's at peace now momma. It was his time."

"So where is Antoine now, Carly?"

"His body is in the room adjacent; ask the doctor if you don't believe me. I'm sure they'll confirm my story that Antoine died peacefully in his sleep this afternoon." Carly pressed the buzzer and within minutes a young nurse appeared at the door.

"You rang Mrs Hamilton-Davies?" Charlene nodded.

"Can you ask Dr Marsh to pop in for a moment please nurse?"

"Certainly, is there anything I can help you with in the meantime?"

"No, thank you, not unless you know how Mr Monroe is?" The nurse closed the door quietly behind her, sat on the edge of the bed, and taking hold of Charlene's hand patted it gently.

"Mr Monroe's life support was switched off this afternoon; he died peacefully in his sleep a few moments later. I'm sorry for your loss, Mrs Hamilton-Davies. Would you like to see him, I don't think they've come for him yet."

"No, I'd rather remember him as he was—but thank you anyway. When you locate the doctor could you ask him to prepare my discharge papers and the bill? I want to go home today please, as soon as possible."

"But, Mrs Hamilton-Davies, I don't think that's such a good idea. You still haven't recovered the feeling in your legs. You could cause permanent damage…"

"It's a chance I'm prepared to take. The man who killed Antoine will be back, and you won't be able to protect me. The policeman wasn't able to stop him from hurting Antoine. The only thing that will stop him is a bullet and I'm sure the hospital won't let me have a gun in my room. So the only alternative for me is to go home." Richard opened his mouth to speak, but a withering look from Charlene stopped him dead. He knew that look; there was no reasoning with her when she set her mind to it. "Richard, could you be a love and organise a wheelchair and a private nurse? Carly, pass me my clothes and help me dress."

"Small problem, Momma, the cupboard's empty." Damn, in her haste to escape she'd overlooked one essential thing, her clothes. Now recalling the conversation she'd had with the nurse in the early hours of the morning.

"Here, take my purse, there must be a shop nearby. I'll need undies too, pumpkin, some flat pumps, and something to wear—black naturally."

Richard walked with Carly to the elevators. "I'd better let Agent Denman know Charlene is going home, and perhaps hire myself a bodyguard. Carly, things could get very rough, is there anyone you could stay with until this is over. A friend from school maybe, I'm sure if you told them about the attempt on your mother's life they would be honour bound to take you in."

"Yes, I have a friend I could stay with, but I'm not going to call her. My place is with my mom, Uncle Richard. Imagine how embarrassing it would be for her—for you both, when she needed the toilet. A girl needs her privacy, and mom is no exception, trust me on this. I'm staying put—end of discussion. Okay?"

"Okay. Tell me, does your mother still have her gun?"

"Yes. She keeps it in the drawer beside her bed. Why do you ask?"

"Insurance. I like to know I can cover my back if it becomes necessary."

"You don't think this man will try again, do you, Uncle Richard?"

"I don't know pumpkin. Let's just say I'll be glad when he's behind bars. Tell me, Carly, how do you rate my chances with your mother?"

Carly raised her eyebrows heavenward. "Who knows? Be gentle with her, she's not as strong as she would like people to believe, and she has just lost a friend, and then there's pops... What do you think will happen when he finds out about you and mom?"

"I'd rather not cross that bridge unless I have too, Carly. You know what a temper he has when he's crossed."

Carly shook her head. As much as she loved her mother, she was apt to be unpredictable, to say the least. Who could know how Antoine's passing would affect her—it was the unknown quotient in the equation. No one could have foreseen the cataclysmic events that had lead to his demise...Unless... No; he would never hurt her mom like that, would he?

Deep in thought she stepped out of the elevator with Richard following close behind.

"I'd better see if I can get hold of Agent Denman. Will you be okay alone?"

"Uncle Richard, I'm sixteen years old. Of course I'll be alright..." So angry was she, she didn't take particular notice of the car pulling up alongside her. Nor did she take particular notice of the man inside the car. At least not until he bundled her unceremoniously into his car and drove off at speed towards the outskirts of town.

Richard looked at his watch for the third time in as many

minutes. What was keeping Carly? Perhaps he ought to have gone with her—though when he'd suggested it Carly had practically jumped down his throat. He'd give her five minutes longer, and then he was going to look for her. Checking his watch again, she'd been gone for almost an hour, and Richard was starting to worry.

A small crowd had gathered outside the hospital, as a policeman questioned a small group of teenagers lolling on the wall in front of the supermarket. Richard approached a couple watching from the safety of their car.

"What's happened?"

"A young girl's been abducted, right here, and in broad daylight too." Richard's blood ran cold.

"Did you see the girl, what did she look like?" He opened his wallet and took out a photo of Charlene and Carly, taken before they left Atlanta and showed it to the woman. "Is this the girl?" The woman took the photograph from Richard and studied it carefully.

"Not sure, I only saw the young girl for a second or two before the car drove off. The youngsters over there were the ones who called the police and reported the incident."

Richard turned, and walked towards the policeman, and, photograph at the ready he addressed the man who appeared to be in charge. "Bonjour, Monsieur." The policeman turned to Richard.

"Do you have information regarding the abduction Monsieur...?"

"Garner, Richard Garner, Attorney at Law. I'm not sure, can you ask them if this was the girl please—it could be a matter of life or death. The girl left the hospital over an hour ago on an errand for her mother and hasn't been seen since." Richard passed the photograph to the policeman, who in turn passed it amongst the group of youngsters.

"Was this the girl you saw?"

"Yeah, that's her."

Richard stumbled forward. Troy was going to kill him. He'd let Carly out of his sight for a few moments, and someone had abducted her. "Are you alright sir? Is the girl your daughter?"

Richard took a deep breath. "No, she's my god-daughter;

her name is Carly Hamilton-Davies, her mother, Charlene, is in the hospital. Did anyone get a good look at the man who did this?"

"Yeah, I did, mister. He wore a scruffy jacket, his hair was long and unkempt, tied back in a pony tail, and he had a beard, I saw his picture earlier on the tele. Reckoned he was that murderer that killed his wife and kids a few years back. Said he were dangerous and not to approach him. That's why I called them." He pointed to a man dressed in a smart suit walking towards him, and behind him, Chas Denman.

"Richard. Good to see you again, this is Inspector Malestroit of the Surete Nationale. Did you witness the abduction too?"

"No, Agent Denman, I didn't, but I know who was abducted…"

"Jesus, tell me it wasn't …" Richard nodded, collapsing onto the bench, head in hands.

"Troy will have my guts. I swear I only left her alone for a few minutes. I was trying to contact you, to let you know Charlene was discharging herself from the hospital and going back to the house."

"Has anyone told Charlene yet?"

"No, not yet, but it's only a matter of time before she finds out. See for yourself—there's a film crew just arrived."

"Calm down, Richard. The last woman he captured he exchanged for his freedom—and the chances are he'll do the same again."

"Yes, but what if he doesn't? What if…"

"Don't torment yourself, Richard; Carly is going to be fine." Denman hoped he sounded confident—but he prayed to god Sebastian Delamare didn't subject Carly to the same ordeal Naomi had endured. One thing Denman was sure of was they had to find him, and fast. The clock was ticking now… Delamare was out for revenge and the top of his list was Troy Hamilton-Davies. And Carly, his bait.

Denman figured that having failed the first time round with Charlene he'd gone for the easy option the second time. Or maybe that had been the idea all along, to lull them into a false sense of security and then snatch the girl from under their very noses. Either way, things didn't bode well for the youngster.

Sighing deeply, Chas walked back towards the bench, and Richard Garner. The poor man was beside himself with worry. He'd flown all this way to come to Charlene's rescue—and here he was about to be thrown to the lions. You just had to feel sorry for the guy—intelligent he may be, but he was no match for a killer like Sebastian Delamare. He reached over tapping the lawyer on the shoulder.

"C'mon, we had better go break the news to Charlene, before they do." He said—pointing to the reporter preparing to begin her broadcast to the nation.

46

Troy sat down on the bench, and took off his shoe. His foot was killing him. Pulling off his sock he examined the huge blister on his big toe. He should have listened to his inner voice this morning and hired the bicycle. But no—the man was hard, and the walk from the town to Bangor lighthouse a 'walk in the park.' What he hadn't taken into account was the combination of his new boots and woollen hiking socks rubbing his soft, city feet.

Thankfully the boys were not here to witness his dilemma—they were off river rafting. There was nothing else for it he would have to ring for a taxi. Troy was sure that the lighthouse keeper would have a phone book. But he'd been in such a hurry to get underway that morning he'd forgotten to pick up his trusty phrase book. And the chance of the lighthouse keeper speaking English, he guessed was slim.

Picking up his boot he pushed his sock inside and hobbled down the stony path to the front door of the building—the small granite pieces of the cliff path adding insult to his sore foot.

Troy knocked timidly on the door and waited for what seemed an eternity.

"J'arrive! J'arrive!" Seconds later the door creaked open; Troy stood patiently waiting for an invitation to enter to no avail. And pushing the door open, he called out to the mysterious occupant.

"Bonjour Monsieur...." The door swung in the breeze for a few seconds and suddenly a wiry little man, sporting a long beard, and wearing clogs, flung the door open wide. Reminding Troy of the pictures he had seen as a child in the tale of Moby Dick of the ancient mariner, Captain Ahab.

"Entré. Entré. N'est laisse pas la porte ouverte comme ça, Monsieur, allez vite." He assumed the man meant for him to close the door, and following close behind he found himself in a large room—the only furniture, a large table, and two rickety old chairs. An old wood burning stove and stone sink the only other objects in the room. The man produced a bottle and two glasses seemingly from nowhere; gesticulating wildly for Troy to sit. Taking hold of the chair nearest him, he gingerly sat down, worried it might collapse beneath him.

The old man carefully poured the colourless liquid into the two small lasses and, picking up a glass, handed it to Troy. Troy sniffed—he detected the faint odour of apples; the man picked up his glass and drained it in one go. Oh well, when in Rome…Troy raised the glass to his lips and followed suit; the colourless liquid tracing a fiery path all the way down to the pit of his stomach. It certainly packed a mighty punch. Troy set the glass down on the table, the fiery liquid rendering him temporarily speechless. He watched with dismay as the man filled the glasses once more. On the one hand, he didn't want his host to think he was impolite, but neither did he want to end up in emergency having his stomach pumped. The man slapped him on the back and handed him the glass.

"A votre santé, monsieur—Anglais?"

"American." Troy spluttered finally pointing to the bottle. "C'est quoi ca?"

"Chouchenn—I make it myself. Is good no?"

"Strong, but good, yes. I need to telephone for a taxi, new boots—bad idea." Troy raised his foot for the old man to see.

"L'ampoule is bad, douloureux n'est ce pas?"

"Yes, very much so." He waved his sock in the air. "Also new." The old man grinned—his two remaining teeth, black and rotten. Troy guessed visiting the dentist wasn't high on the list of the old man's priorities—either that or the Chouchenn had dissolved the rest. The old man disappeared into the hallway, coming back moments later with yet another bottle. Troy groaned inwardly. He had promised to take the boys fishing that evening, the mere thought of which made his stomach churn. He pushed the bottle towards Troy.

"Is for you. A gift. You take this to America and maybe your friends come to the island too. Is good for trade, yes?"

"Thank you. I am sure my friends will love it." Searching his pockets for a token to give the old man in exchange—his hand coming to rest on the small flick-knife Naomi had given him for his birthday. His face softened, maybe he had been a little harsh with her, after all, she hadn't asked him to fall in love with her…He placed the knife on the table, pushing it towards the old man.

"For you. Be careful though, it is very sharp." The old man picked it up and examined it.

"Is broken, no?"

"No, to open it you have to press here." Troy pressed the button and the gleaming blade slid smoothly out.

"Pas mal. Pas mal du touts—merci…" He quickly scooped up the knife and put it in his pocket.

"Troy Hamilton-Davies." He held out his hand to the wiry Frenchman.

"Jacques Sauzon, and in France we do it this way, Troy." He stood up and embraced Troy, kissing him on both cheeks. "Now we have been properly introduced. I took the liberty of telephoning Giles—they will be sending the taxi after lunch. Giles will not consider fares that are disrupting his lunch break, Troy. Come, we too shall have lunch. I have ham, bread and a jar of pate from last seasons hunting and of course, a nice ripe Camembert. A meal would not be complete without cheese, the riper the better."

Troy smiled to himself; he couldn't see how he could possibly refuse, after all it wasn't every day the offer of year old pate and smelly cheese came along. He just hoped his health insurance covered him for such eventualities.

"Come, we shall eat in the other room, it is warmer in there. This old house is damp, and even in the summer one has to light the fire." Troy followed the old man through the hall and into the room beyond, it was a room of approximately the same proportions as the kitchen. Or so he presumed. For this room was full to the point of overflowing.

Groaning under the weight of the food upon it was a small, fold away table, in front of which was a huge flat screen television. Several armchairs were dotted around the outside of the room, all but one piled high with old newspapers and magazines—some dating as far back as the war years. The book lined walls boasting several first editions. The old man watched in silence as Troy carefully took a book from the shelf—his father would have given his right arm to be where he stood now.

"My only sin is that of hoarding—and what of you Troy, are you a sinner too?" Troy slid the book gently back into place.

"I like to think not, but as the lord said—'Let he who is without sin cast the first stone.'"

"Ah, I see you have also read the 'good book'—somewhere in this mishmash I have a Gutenberg." The old man said, waving his hand towards the bookshelves, switching on the television with the remote control.

"I only watch the news and nature programmes—especially ones made around these parts." Sitting at the table, he placed the remote control on the arm of the chair.

"For what we are about to receive, may the good Lord make us truly thankful. Amen."

"Amen. This looks good. Is this home made too?" Troy asked pointing to the jar of pate.

"Yes—but unfortunately this is the last jar—and I have been saving it for just such an occasion. Do you mind if I leave the television on while we eat?"

"Not at all." Troy froze as the image of his daughter appeared before him. "Carly... my daughter...the photograph." The old man turned the sound up higher and watched as the reporter showed the area where his baby had been forced into a car—Carly had been abducted. He had to find the boys and get back to the city—back to Charlene. He banged his fist down hard on the table; sending crockery tumbling to the floor.

"If Bastian Lamare harms one hair on her head I will personally see him dead! I have to find my boys and get back to the mainland, Jacques, could you ring Giles and ask him to make an exception to his rule today."

"Of course, I will tell him of the urgency. He has a daughter too; he will understand your anxiety. Here…take this." The old man thrust a battered leather case towards Troy. "It may come in useful. I take it you have used one before?"

He unzipped the case and peered inside. It was antique, and probably worth a small fortune. Troy hoped it was still in full working order. "I most certainly have. I'll be sure to return it—you have my word as a gentleman." "When was it used last, Jacques?"

"La saison dernière. T'inquiète pas, ça fonctionnera très bien—jamais hors sujet. Demande à lui, sur le mur. C'est mortelle—mais silencieux." Troy didn't need a phrase book to know exactly what Jacques said—his facial expression said it all. Silent, but deadly—open season had just been declared on Bastian Lamare.

47

Carly stood up, her movements slow and clumsy; the man had drugged her. The very same man her momma had described to Agent Denman—the man responsible for the death of his family—of Antoine. If only she'd paid more attention she'd be tucked up safe in her own bed, instead of rotting in some dingy attic. Her mother would blame Richard. If only she hadn't been so insistent, Richard would have gone with her. Dejected she sat down—the floorboards creaking noisily under her weight.

"Forgive me father for I have sinned…" It had been a long time since her last confession—too long. She'd not set foot inside a church since leaving Atlanta, and boy, how she'd sinned in the time between. Was this God's revenge for aborting her baby? And Antonio's death—had it really been an accident?

Crawling over towards the door she paused to listen for a moment, but the only sounds she heard were the scratching of mice behind the wainscoting—at least she hoped it was only mice. Carly tried turning the knob—it wouldn't budge, locked, no doubt by her jailer. Had he by some small miracle left the key in the lock the other side she wondered? There was only one way to find out and that was to peep through the keyhole.

No such luck. She had no option but to wait and see what transpired—and hope that when her jailer returned, if he returned, that he would eventually set her free. What if he demanded money? Would her father be prepared to pay a ransom to get his baby back alive?

Carly shivered, pulling her thin jacket closer. The temperature in the attic had dropped, and that meant only one thing—she was not alone. Something or someone was here in the room with her.

"Who's there? Show yourself, whoever you are."

'Tell me, Carly, how did you know someone was here?'

"The temperature changed suddenly. Hello, Amelia, I never thought I'd be pleased to see a ghost. I met your mother earlier in the hospital. She was with Antoine."

'I know; I was there. My mother finally got what she deserved. A mighty fine pickle you've gotten yourself into this time girl. My father will kill you, unless by some small miracle your father does exactly as he asks and judging by the weapon he was carrying onto the boat there's not a chance of that.'

"You've seen my father? Does he know I've been abducted?"

'Oh yes—he's as mad as hell with my father. I managed to get Jason alone and I asked him to ask your dad to re-consider, for your sake, but Jason said he won't listen to reason. According to Jason, 'he's a stubborn old coot.' So I think we have stalemate. Should be interesting to see who wins—I'm sorry about scaring you before, Carly.'

"That's okay I deserved it. I know now, Antonio never intended to leave Sophia. Tell me about his death, Amelia, was it an accident?"

'Poor Antonio never stood a chance. My father told Marcello Senior about his affair with you, and he put a contract out on him. My father 'volunteered' for the post of executioner, after all, he'd spent seven years in exile because of Antonio. Seven long years, waiting for an opportunity to revenge his family honour.'

"Did you know that your father was planning to kill Antonio beforehand, Amelia?"

'Yes, I knew about it, but there was nothing I could have done to prevent it from happening—it was his time you see.'

"Did Sophia's father put a contract out on me too—is that why your father kidnapped me?"

'No, Carly, that's not the reason you're here. Your father got you into this mess I'm afraid, albeit unintentionally.'

"That's just great. Tell me, Amelia—am I going to die?"

'Of course you are—one day. We all have an expiry date. Trust me; it's better if you don't know when, or how—information like that could seriously damage your health. I have to go now, Carly, Sebastian's back. Try not to antagonise him—ask him to pray for you. That should win you brownie points. And, Carly, don't worry, I'll be back later.'

"Promise?"

'Cross my heart and hope to die…Sorry, force of habit. I'm going to check on Jason, and see if I can get him to lead your father here and get you out before the battle commences. Hang in there, Carly, between us we'll figure a way to get you out of here.'

Carly smiled and reached out to touch her ghostly companion's hand. 'Please don't, Carly, it hurts like hell when we spirits make contact with a mortal.'

"Sorry. I guess I have a lot to learn. Thanks for coming to my rescue, Amelia."

The door flew open, catching Carly off guard—her captor pushing her roughly to one side as he searched the room. "Who were you talking to, girl?"

"No one. I…I was praying for forgiveness." Sebastian eyed her suspiciously.

"I hope you're not mocking me, girl?"

"No sir, not at all. Pops—my father was… is a religious man."

His face softened, the girl reminded him of Amelia—she would have been twenty three now…had she lived. "I will pray for your soul, Amelia. Come, kneel with your father and repent your sins my child."

Carly knelt beside him on the hard, wooden floor, her head bowed as if at prayer, but her attention was elsewhere. In his haste the man had left the door ajar. If she made it to the door and locked it behind her perhaps she'd have a chance to escape. But where was she? How would she get help if she was in the middle of nowhere? No, it was too risky, the man had killed for less—he was strong, agile…and crazy with it.

"Lord, I beseech you; have mercy on this poor sinner before you. Show her the path of righteousness, purify her, and save her soul from the fires of hell. Amen. Now, child, tell me how one so sweet and innocent allowed herself to be led into temptation?"

That was the million dollar question. Carly wasn't sure when, or how, it had actually happened, just that it had. Antonio had a way with him, and the moment you let down your guard, the inevitable happened. Antonio was the popsicle you just had to lick! Not exactly what the crazy man was waiting to hear. No, what he wanted to hear was how Antonio had tricked her into sleeping with him. Which was untrue—so desperate had she been to 'lick the popsicle' she'd practically thrown herself at him. She knew the consequences of having unprotected sex, and still she'd said yes. Careful went out of the window, along with her morals, the first time Antonio kissed her.

"What's the matter, girl—cat got your tongue? Speak out, let God hear how the fornicator, Antonio Giovanni, seduced you—an innocent child."

Taking a deep breath Carly whispered. "He made me touch him below. He said if I told anyone he would say that I begged him to shove it inside me. It was then he made me take off my undergarments and lie on the table with my legs wide open, and then he tickled me with the end of it. It was hot, so hot it burnt my skin. He told me next time he would kiss me there, and make me scream out with happiness. But the only thing I screamed with was pain, as he forced his throbbing, hot, thing, inside me. He took the one precious commodity I had—my virginity, my innocence. He deserved to die…"

Closing her eyes, as the tears trickled down her face—poor Antonio. Carly shuddered as the crazy man licked his lips, lustfully. That wasn't the reaction she'd expected at all. Here she was, trapped in the attic with a lunatic, and from the look in his eyes he intended to do her harm. Diversion tactics were urgently required—and flinging herself at his feet she begged his forgiveness. "Father, forgive me…" She lay quite still, not daring to breathe lest the spell be broken.

"Amelia. You have returned to me. I knew God would find a way. Come, we have much to discuss, you and I." Sebastian held out his hand. That was all she needed—now he believed she was the re-incarnation of his late daughter. It was true—God really did work in mysterious ways.

48

Charlene gazed anxiously at the clock. What was keeping Carly and Richard? Surely it didn't take this long to buy a skirt and top. The door opened and closed—and taking hold of the pulley Charlene sat up.

"About time, I was ready to send a search party out to look…Agent Denman; sorry, I thought you were Carly. Richard, at last, what kept you? Where's Carly…" Richard hung his head in shame—Charlene had trusted him, and once again he'd let her down. "Please dear god no…Not my baby, he's taken my baby, hasn't he." Agent Denman took hold of Charlene's hand.

"Fetch the nurse please, Richard, and tell her to bring a sedative for Mrs Hamilton-Davies. He won't get away this time, Charlene, we have all available manpower out there looking for her. We'll have Carly back with you in no time—you have my word."

Inspector Malestroit stood at the back of the room, watching Agent Denman with Charlene Hamilton-Davies—this family had suffered enough, Sebastian Delamare had to be stopped. Malestroit walked to the door pausing briefly beside the bed. "Try not to worry, Madame Amilton-Davies, I will be supervising the operation personally, Sebastian Delamare will be behind bars if it's the last thing I do. Monsieur Garner, I understand you are a lawyer n'est ce pas?"

"Yes, Inspector, that's correct. I am also Carly's Godfather, Mr Hamilton-Davies's business partner, and a close friend of the family. I hope it's not free advice you're after, Inspector—I specialise in Company Law, and I have only a limited knowledge of 'le loi Français'."

"Ah, I see. Then I'm sure you are just the person I need, would you mind sparing me a few minutes of your time please."

Charlene smiled weakly at the nurse; she had to keep her eyes open for some reason…but she couldn't remember how, or why…Carly—it had something to do with Carly.

Floating peacefully away, high above the bed Charlene could see her body, pale and wan, lying on the bed below—she caught her breath… was she dead? Descending for a moment, she watched as the bedclothes moved…she was breathing—thank goodness for that …But if she was up here, and her body was down there, what was going on.

'Hello, Charlene.'

"Antoine—but it can't be you…you're dead—aren't you?"

'Yes, Charlene, I am.'

"But…how can I be talking to you now if you're dead…"

'You're having what's referred to in laymen's terms, as 'an out of body experience'; you will come to no harm. Here, take my hand, there's something I want you to see.' Charlene hesitated, keeping her hand by her side. 'You'll be quite safe with us, Amelia's with me, and before you ask—yes, she's a ghost too. She's worried about Carly. Sebastian Delamare has her, Charlene. He blames Troy for something that happened back in Atlanta, and the reason behind the kidnapping is to force Troy out of hiding.'

"But, Troy's not hiding, he's with the boys."

'No, Charlene, the boys are back at Troy's hotel.'

"And, Troy is where?"

'We don't know, Charlene, that's the problem. We have

to find him before Sebastian does…it's a matter of life and death—his. But in order to get to Carly out of there we need someone to act as bait. Do you think your friend Agent Denman would oblige?'

"Yes…no…I don't know. He'll think me quite mad if I tell him a ghost showed me where Carly's being held—even more so if I tell him the two of you want him to act as bait."

'Yes, but will you at least try, that's all we ask, for Carly's sake?'

"Of course I'll try. Now take me to my daughter." Charlene felt a rush of warm air as her spirit rose higher still, high above the treetops, fields, and rivers. Finally coming to rest in the attic of an old house. Carly lay on a dirty old mattress covered with an old blanket, chained by her ankle to a beam in the opposite corner of the room.

"Carly. My poor baby, what has that animal done to you?"

'She can't hear you, Charlene; your molecular structure and vibrations are different. The ethereal strand binding your earthly remains to your soul is blocking the link. It's the link between life and death, Charlene—and if it should break…'

"You said I would be safe with you, Antoine, and I believed you. It's not my time to die, my baby girl needs me—my boys need me"

'And me, what about my feelings for you, do they not count at all? Why did Richard Garner come all the way from Atlanta; was he your lover too? Did you lie to me that first time, Charlene?"

This time it was Charlene who hung her head in shame.

"I never meant to hurt you, Antoine—Richard and I were history long before you came on the scene; he was the real reason I left Atlanta. I caught him in a rather compromising position, with his then secretary. I'd packed a picnic lunch and gone to the office intending to surprise him—I don't know who got the bigger surprise—him, or me. He begged me to forgive him and I refused—you see I couldn't live with a man I couldn't trust. I thought you were different, but you were economic with the truth too. You could have warned me about the house's history, but you chose not to. Charles Dupont should have told me about the five bodies they found buried under my patio, but he chose profit over truth, and look what that got him…A one way ticket to an Asylum for the mentally insane. I'm finished with men for good—I'd rather spend the rest of my life alone than put myself through that again. You had your chance, Richard too, it's over—you're dead, and I can't bring myself to forgive Richard—end of story. Now, please take me back…"

'I want to check on Sebastian first, and then I'll take you back…and for what it's worth, I'm truly sorry for deceiving you.'

Antoine floated out through the open window to the garden below where Sebastian Delamare struggled to remove a large metal chest from the wheelbarrow. It hadn't been this heavy when he'd put it in the barrow he was certain.

Antoine chuckled to himself from within the chest. Being a ghost had its advantages—this being one of them. The chest was full of coins, shiny, gold coins—hundreds of them, worth a small fortune at today's prices. But what where they doing buried here? Whose garden and house was this—not Sebastian's, that was certain. Something whooshed past him, its energy field sending him hurtling high into the air—there was only one entity he knew of that could do that…and it was pissed off with something—or someone. He had to get Charlene away from here to safety, and fast.

'We have to go.'

"What's wrong, Antoine, you look…" Grinning foolishly to herself—she'd just been about to ask a ghost what had spooked him.

'It's not safe for you here—there are evil forces present, and their numbers are growing. Amelia, I am trusting Carly to your safekeeping—do not leave her side, not even for a moment. Understood?'

'I understand. I will protect her—I am protecting her. Look, she is wearing my cross; god will protect her from the evil ones. Goodbye, Charlene, I will keep her safe. Take care, Antoine, and hurry back.'

'I will, I promise—come, Charlene, you have to find a way to get the policeman here, and quickly, Carly's life may depend on it.'

Antoine took her hand; once again she drifted high among the clouds and back into her room where her body lay unmoving on the bed. 'Goodbye, Cherie...' And placing a final chaste kiss upon her brow, he vanished.

Charlene awoke with a start. Carly was in danger, needed help..."Where are my clothes, I have to go to Carly, she's in danger. Antoine told me...please, I know where she is—I saw the house, and the spirits there are evil..."

"Calm down, Charlene, it was just a dream."

"No, it wasn't...you have to believe me, look..." As she opened her hand one of the gold coins from the old chest tumbled to the floor.   "So, if, like you say, it was just a dream, where did the coin come from?"

Richard bent down, picked up the coin, and put it in between his teeth, biting down hard. "I don't know how you came by it, Charlene, but I do know one thing for certain—it's solid gold, and very rare. A gold ducat, first minted in 1423 in Venice, and commissioned by Fracesco Foscari—the Doge of Venice. They sell for anything in the region of twelve hundred dollars each on the internet. It's exquisite." Pulling the handkerchief from his breast pocket he laid it on the bed, carefully placing the coin on it."This side of the coin depicts Christ, standing, and on the reverse, St Mark, with the Doge, kneeling at his feet. I'd give my right arm for a barrow load of these. It's probably Raubgold—gold stolen by the Nazis during World War two. I read something about this last week..." Richard faltered momentarily as he tried to recall where he'd read about the gold—Troy's files, the ones he'd downloaded from his computer...Surely Troy wasn't involved in anything shady.

"Sorry, I was trying to recall where I'd read about Operation Sundown—I believe that's what it was called. When the Germans realised they were losing the war they shipped looted gold coins and art treasures in sealed caskets, and buried them in the copper mines at Deutschneudorf. They reckon they booby trapped the mines too. Interesting don't you think?" Richard exclaimed.

"Yes but wasn't the 'Raubgold' Jewish gold?" Malestroit interjected.

"Not according to the report I read, no. There are more than ten countries still claiming the Germans looted gold and other valuables during their occupation, and we are talking mega bucks too."

Charlene turned to the Inspector, and, crossing her fingers behind her back began her plea. "Do you believe in ghosts, Inspector? I mean, really believe, not just agreeing with me to appease me because you think I've lost the plot like Antoine and I did when we found Charles Dupont in the cellar." Charlene demanded.

"I believe there are things we cannot explain away by natural phenomena, Madame Amilton-Davies. Charles Dupont mentioned seeing dogs in your hallway—two ferocious black dogs. The man who alerted the police regarding your 'accident' mentioned hearing the dogs in your hallway too."

"Who is he Inspector? I would like to meet him—to thank him for his bravery."

"I am sorry, madame, but that is no longer an option, he passed away in police custody—poisoned, we believe by a hamburger laced with a deadly neurotoxin, distilled from the Hemlock Water Dropwort plant."

"What a horrible way to die, Inspector. But going back to the dogs—would you let me take you to the house—the house I saw in my 'dream state'—the house where Sebastian Delamare is holding my daughter, Carly, captive."

Deep in thought Malestroit absentmindedly rubbed his chin—he needed a shave—and a good night's sleep wouldn't go amiss either. But more than that he wanted an end to Sebastian Delamare's killing spree, and if following a hunch—however crazy it seemed, was what he had to do to end it, so be it.

"Yes, Madame Amilton-Davies, I will go with you—but you must promise me one thing, you will not try to interfere in any way, no matter what. Is that understood?"

"Of course, Inspector, I promise." She'd done it; against all the odds she had convinced the inspector to trust in her—but would she be in time to save Carly…

49

Troy crept around the back of the building; Bastian had said to come alone, but had omitted to mention not coming armed. Taking an arrow from the bag slung loosely around his shoulders, Troy placed it in the crossbow and pulled back the mechanism. Let battle commence…

Antoine watched as Troy primed the weapon. At least now they knew where he was. His task now was to keep Troy out of harms way until the cavalry arrived…

He would be safe for the time being as Sebastian was slightly pre-ocupied—between them, the ghosts had managed to lure him into the cellar, where Ben and Antonio were doing their best to 'entertain him'. But Sebastian wasn't a man who was easily scared—the dogs had worked their magic for a short time. And Annie would have probably tipped the balance in their favour, if it weren't for the fact that Antoine had dispatched her to purgatory for the foreseeable future. Things like that sometimes had a knack of coming back and biting one on the proverbial bum when one least expected it. And this was most definitely, one of them.

Ben and Antonio hovered overhead. 'It's no use, Antoine; we've done everything we can think of to try to scare him, but he's as stubborn as they come—all we succeeded in doing was making him madder than hell. Sorry, but Sebastian is, as we speak, looking for something to break down the door.'

'It's okay, you did your best. We'll just have to keep them apart for as long as possible, perhaps we should have locked the Counsellor in the cellar instead of Sebastian.'

'Now he tells us.' The ghostly duo drifted up into the heavens, then came hurtling back down as if the devil was behind them.

'They're here, Antoine—the police, Charlene, and a big black guy—I wouldn't like to meet him in a dark alley alone.' Ben laughed at the irony of Antonio's words.

'Antonio, you are such a wuss.'

'Okay, you two, that's enough—we have work to do. In case it had slipped your memory we have to get Carly out of here and back to her mother. So which one of you is going to volunteer to keep the Counsellor out of harms way? Ben?' Ben shook his head. 'Antonio?'

'You have to be kidding; if he sees me, he'll kill me!' Antoine shook his head, Ben was right—Antonio was a wuss.

'Antonio, you're already dead, and the chances are he won't be able to see or hear you anyway. Look, I'll give you a demonstration and I don't suppose I was actually his most favourite person in the world—I poached his wife out from under his nose remember.' Antoine hovered a few feet away from where Troy lay in wait—he was barely visible to the untrained eye. Antoine shook the branch above him vigorously and waited—Troy didn't move a muscle.

'See, what did I tell you guys…Ben, Antonio?' He was talking to himself again…

"You finished there, Antoine. I was hoping to stay hidden, and you're not making it easy."

'You can see me?' Antoine exclaimed.

"Yes, and I can hear you too—and if you don't mind, I'd rather I couldn't. Where'd the other two clowns disappear too, anyways?" Antoine was too shocked to answer. "What's up, Antoine—cat got your tongue?"

'Disarm your weapon, Troy, and come with me. We have to get Carly away from this place, and fast. There are evil forces gathering—forces I am not equipped to do battle with, and they're as mad as hell. Whatever Sebastian has done to upset them, it must have been bad.'

"Where exactly is Sebastian?" Troy exclaimed menacingly. "If he's hurt one single hair on my baby's head, so help me, I will cut him in two. I still owe him for what he did to Naomi."

'Never mind, Sebastian, the police are here—Charlene, and Richard Garner, too, and the man from the CIA.'

"Chas Denman is here, in France. And why is Garner here? He's supposed to be holding the fort back in Atlanta. It's coming to something when one can't get even in peace."

"Put down your weapon, Troy." Troy winced as heard the distinctive click of a revolver. "Don't force me to use this." Denman took the crossbow from the counsellors grasp, disarmed it, and laid it on the ground.

"Fancy meeting you here, Chas."

"The deal as I seem to recall, Troy, was that you were going to keep me informed."

"And I would have, if Bastian, or Sebastian, or whatever he's called hadn't intervened—he has Carly in there." Troy nodded towards the house.

"I know, Troy, that's why I'm here. Sebastian's been a very busy man whilst you and the boy's have been away. He broke into Charlene's house, locked Charlene and Antoine in the cellar and left them for dead, amongst other things."

"How'd they get out?"

"A tramp saw Sebastian leaving the house, and went inside to investigate, he paid for it later too, but that's another story. Charlene is waiting in the car, I suggest you go and join her, and let us get on with our work."

"Isn't that Antoine's job—babysitting my ex-wife? And while we're about it, what's Richard Garner's involvement in all this?"

"Antoine's dead, Troy, Sebastian got past the police guard in the hospital and finished what he'd started—revenge for sleeping with his dead wife. Antonio Giovanni, too, seems the mummified remains the boys found in the attic, and Sebastian's youngest son, Ben, had the same father…"

Troy exhaled, loudly. "But, I was just speaking to Antoine, Giovanni was here too, with a young boy...He was as close as you are to me now..." Denman shook his head.

"Looks like you had a conversation with a real, live, dead person then Counsellor, either that or you've had one over the eight..." It was Troy's turn now to shake his head in disbelief... Antoine, dead—Giovanni too...

"I need a drink..." Troy stood up shakily, and made his way over to the police car. Richard Garner sat in the back with Charlene, his hand entwined in hers. They were talking quietly, and Troy sensed this was not the first time the two love-birds had snuggled up together.

"Sorry to interrupt, but Agent Denman said I was to wait here." Richard got out of the car; this was neither the time, nor the place, for a showdown with his partner.

"We thought you were with the boys?"

"So it would appear." Troy replied sarcastically. "You are one class act, Charlene, the other boyfriend is hardly cold in his grave, and here you are, canoodling with my ex-partner."

"It's not like that, Troy; Richard was just comforting me. In case it slipped your notice, our daughter's life is in danger. And what do you mean by ex-partner? Richard said nothing about terminating the partnership."

"No, he wouldn't have, seeing as how I just decided. I should imagine he's as surprised as you are. Ain't that right, Richard?"

"That's fine by me, I'll have Della sort out the necessary paperwork and get your secretary to pack up your belongings. Where would you like me to ship them to?"

"No, Richard, you have that all wrong—you're the one moving out. The lease is in my name, remember."

"But..."

"But, nothing. I have nothing more to say to you...except wish you and my ex-wife all the best for the future. Oh, and I'll be filing for custody of my children too, Charlene. At least I'll know they'll be taken care of correctly."

"I'll fight you every step of the way, Troy. I know all about Naomi—you don't stand a chance. The law always comes down in favour of the mother; you should know that better than I. You'll be hearing from my lawyer." Charlene spat, venomously.

"And for your information, Richard and I are just good friends. I'm in mourning—I loved Antoine dearly..." Dejected, Richard walked over to the fence. He'd lost everything, his livelihood, the woman he loved, his best friend, his self respect.

Richard watched as Denman entered the building, gun in hand. This time he was taking no chances. Payback time was overdue, for Naomi, for Sultan, and for all the innocent people this monster had slaughtered. He seethed with indignation when he thought back to Naomi's ordeal—the doctors said she would never have children. So horrific were her injuries, they'd been obliged to perform an emergency hysterectomy, poor, sweet, trusting, Naomi. Warily he climbed the stairs to the attic.

"Carly?" He whispered. "It's Agent Denman—I've come to take you home."

"Not so fast, Agent Denman." Sebastian said menacingly. "Well, well, we meet again. Drop the weapon...Now. Easy does it, that's right, put it down on the floor and then kick it over to me. No funny business, now, or the girl gets it. Take out your handcuffs and put them on. Now, cuff yourself to that pipe." Denman made his way slowly over to the sink, and attached the other half of the handcuffs to the pipe, snapping it shut. Quickly he tucked the spare key behind his watch strap. "Good, now throw me the keys." Chas threw the keys over to Sebastian. "I wonder how long you'll have to wait until they come looking for you... Pity I won't be here to see the fireworks, gonna love ya, and leave ya. Places to be, things to do, seems I'm to be a daddy again—Sophia will make a lovely bride, don't ya think. Ah, I forget, you don't know the lovely Sophia do you, Agent Denman. Carly does, she was her love rival for a while back there, until I persuaded Giovanni it was time to mend his ways, that is."

"You'll not get away this time, Delamare; the police have the house surrounded."

Sebastian chuckled. "You're a laugh a minute, Denman. Malestroit is no match for me; the counsellor was the only person who might have stood a chance—pity you disarmed him. See you around." Delamare disappeared through the door.

"Are you okay, Carly?"

"He's going to burn the house down isn't he, Agent Denman."

"I don't know, Carly, and that's the truth." Denman reached for the hidden key—it slipped from his grasp and tumbled to the floor, and try as he might he couldn't reach it.

"Jesus, give me a break."

"Would you like me to try and reach the key for you, Agent Denman? There's an old wire coat hanger hanging on the beam above me—if I can just stretch a little…"

~

Richard lifted his head wearily. Smoke. There was smoke billowing under the door from the basement. Jumping up he ran towards the house—Carly and Agent Denman were still inside. He picked up a couple of old tea cloths from the kitchen table and wet them under the tap, and headed for the stairs.

"Carly. Agent Denman…."

"Uncle Richard! We're in the attic. Please hurry, the smoke is hurting my eyes." The acrid smoke stung his eyes, burning his throat, and making breathing difficult. He had to go on, Carly was depending on him—it might be his only chance of getting back in Charlene's good books. He stumbled and reaching out to steady himself he grabbed hold of the banister—the skin on his left hand blistered immediately and he screamed out. "Uncle Richard, please hurry…" Carly coughed, and with every ounce of force she could muster, she yanked hard on the chain holding her captive. There was a loud crack, and the chain slipped free of the broken beam. She grabbed the key, and unlocked the handcuffs holding Denman captive.

"You okay, Carly?"

"Yes, Agent Denman, I'm fine." She coughed, as smoke billowed under the door and into the room.

"Cover your head with your jacket, Carly." And picking up the bottle of water from the sink, he quickly unscrewed the cap, and poured the contents over Carly's jacket. Putting the back of his hand against the door, it was hot, the paint blistering with the heat—but it was this way, or no way. He kicked the door open, sending an unsuspecting Richard hurtling down the stairway.

"Take my hand, Carly, and whatever you do, don't let go."

"What about Uncle Richard, shouldn't we wait for him?"

"He will have turned back, Carly; he's a very brave man for

even attempting to come to our rescue. I'll see to it he get's a commendation."

Denman half-dragged, half-carried Carly the last hundred yards, overcome by the heat and the fumes of the burning paint. The house burned fiercely now, engulfed by bright orange flames with sparks and beads of lead flying in every direction thanks to the boxes of exploding shotgun cartridges.

50

Carly tried to sit up, pulling at the oxygen mask. "Lay still, pumpkin, momma's here." Charlene said, stroking her daughter's face.

"Is Uncle Richard okay mom?"

Puzzled by her daughters' remark Charlene turned to Troy.

"Has something happened to Richard, Troy?" Troy looked down at the ground, wishing there was an easy way to tell her.

"Richard was seen entering the burning building, Charlene. It is presumed he made an attempt to rescue Carly and Denman…He never came out…I'm sorry pumpkin, Uncle Richard, didn't make it." Troy turned away, wiping a solitary tear from his eye.

"No, please, not Uncle Richard too…"

Charlene forced back the tears—this was all her fault. If she hadn't telephoned Richard in the first place he would be alive now…. "And, Sebastian Delamare—is he dead too?" Charlene demanded of Denman.

"No, Charlene, I'm afraid he got away again. He won't get far…"

"You said that the last time, Agent Denman, and look what happened." She hissed venomously.

Charlene came running over towards them. "Carly, Agent Denman—thank god you're okay."

"She'll be fine, Charlene, she's just inhaled a little smoke. Get some oxygen over here please." Denman handed the unconscious girl to the paramedic and sank to the ground. "You're walking, Charlene—miracles happen when you least expect them—talking of miracles, where's Richard? I want to thank him for his valiant effort; even if he did have to turn back, he gave Carly the push she needed to break free." He turned towards the crowd of policeman huddled against the fence and shouted. "Has anyone seen Richard Garner?"

"He was over by the fence a few minutes ago, Chas." Troy interjected.

"Richard was in the building, Troy, I can assure you of that, but he must have been beaten back by the smoke. Surely one of you saw him come out?"

Troy shook his head. "He didn't come past me." Troy said nonchalantly.

"Hey guys listen up—did any of you see Mr Garner come out of the building?" Denman watched as the police officers around him shook their heads. A hand went up in the air hesitantly.

"I saw Mr Denman go in, sir, but as far as I know, he never came out."

"I'm sorry for your loss, Charlene."

"Get out of my sight; you too, Troy, this is your fault—you were the one who brought the madman to my door. First Antoine, and now Richard—I never want to see you again…"

"Please, Charlene—I had no idea Delamare would come after you. You have to believe me, I wouldn't hurt you for the world—I love you…"

Denman pulled Troy away. "Leave it, Troy, you're only making things worse. She'll calm down. Eventually…"

Troy shook himself free and picking the crossbow up took off at a brisk pace over the fields. If he'd learned one thing over the years living with Charlene, it was that she would never, ever, forgive him. His only chance to get back into her good books was to find Delamare, and kill him, or die in the effort.

~

Denman watched as the ambulance drove off. Carly Hamilton-Davies would be fine in a couple of days. He wandered over to Malestroit, standing a few feet away from the now smouldering ruins, hat in hand, as the charred body of Richard Garner was carried out to the waiting ambulance. Denman shuddered; it could so easily have been him or Carly lying in the body bag.

"I took the liberty of asking my office to contact Mr Garner's next of kin."

"Thank you, Agent Denman, can you arrange for his dental charts to be made available too. Poor woman—first Monsieur Monroe, and now, Monsieur Garner, if I were Monsieur Hamilton-Davies I'd be worried. I take it that was him I saw running across the field?"

"Yes, and if I know Troy, he'll not stop until he finds Delamare, and if he finds him, God help him."

"You think he intends to flee the country again—n'est-ce pas?"

"Yes, Inspector, I do, and furthermore I don't think he will be alone. He mentioned a woman called Sophia. He also said she was expecting his child."

Inspector Malestroit whirled round almost colliding with Denman. "I don't believe it…Sophia Giovanni and Sebastian Delamare—if her father finds out the baby is Delamare's, he's a dead man. I think it's time we paid Mario Marcello a little visit—don't you agree?"

"Whatever you say, Inspector, and now's as good a time as any, there's nothing more we can do here tonight."

"Come, we'll take my car, Agent Denman. After all we wouldn't want to alert Marcello of our arrival by turning up in a police car, would we?" "If you say not, Inspector." Malestroit reminded Chas of 'Hercule Poirot', with his funny little mannerisms. The two men walked in silence towards the lane, where Malestroit stopped in front of a red, Porsche Carrera. Denman watched in amazement as the Inspector opened the door and climbed in.

"Agent Denman?"

"Nice car, sir." Bemused, Denman opened the door and pushed the seat back as far as it would go, before sitting down and attempting to tuck his long legs inside.

"It was my wife's. It's been sitting in the garage gathering dust since she passed away. My car was destroyed in a controlled explosion, some three nights since—Sebastian Delamare's handiwork, we believe."

"It could have been worse, sir. You could have been inside when it exploded." Denman caught the flash of headlights in the wing mirror. "Sir, there's a police car behind us, and I think it wants us to pull over."

"Zut, alors! That's the second time this week." Denman chuckled, as Malestroit stopped the car and opened the window.

"Evening, sir. In a bit of a hurry are we?" Malestroit took out his Carte d'Identité and handed it to the policeman.

"Merde. Sorry Inspector Malestroit, I didn't recognise the car. Drive carefully, sir."

The Inspector put the car into gear and indicated to pull back out into the traffic. The policeman ran back towards the car waving his hands in the air. Malestroit lowered his window once more. "What now, officer?"

"Constable Lebrun would like you to telephone him immediately, sir."

"Did he say what about, officer?"

"Why don't you ask him yourself, sir?" Malestroit switched off the engine and followed the officer back to the squad car.

"What is it, Lebrun?"

"Sir, thank goodness we found you. It's Charles Dupont, sir, he's holding a young nurse hostage, and demanding to speak to you. He says he wants to confess to a murder."

"Lebrun, in case it slipped your mind, Charles Dupont, isn't playing with a full deck… Okay, tell the hospital I'm on my way."

"Okay, sir, will do." Malestroit handed the speaker phone back to the officer.

"Would you gentleman care to escort me to Saint Martin's Psychiatric Hospital, please."

"Certainly, Inspector. Ready when you are."

Malestroit shook his head. Of all the times, Dupont had

to pick now to 'confess'. He wondered what it would be this time…The last time he'd decided to confess, Malestroit had high tailed it over to Saint Martin's to hear him confess to killing Charles De Gaulle. He wouldn't have minded, but for the fact, France's former president, had been dead for over forty years, and he died of natural causes.

"Sorry, Agent Denman, it would seem we have to take a detour. A psychiatric patient at Saint Martin's is holding a young nurse hostage and demanding to speak to me. He wants to confess to a murder…"

"Not a problem, inspector, I'm sure Mr Marcello will keep until tomorrow." The Inspector nodded his agreement, he'd hear Dupont's confession, and then he was going home.

~

The police car pulled up in front of Saint Martin's and the officers got out and waited for Malestroit and his passenger.

"You'd better wait in the foyer, Agent Denman. I'm sure you will be able to persuade one of the nurses on duty to bring you some refreshment." Malestroit turned to the waiting policemen. "And you two had better come with me, just in case…."

Denman waved the Inspector away. "I'll be fine, off you go."

Chas sat down on a bench, head in hands. God, he was tired. He'd been on the go since he landed, and so far all he'd eaten were a few pieces of fruit. His stomach rumbled noisily.

"Are you alright, Monsieur?" Denman looked up to find a woman dressed in a white uniform at the side of him.

"Yes, just tired, and very hungry. I'm waiting for Inspector Malestroit, he's visiting a patient—a Monsieur Dupont, I believe."

"Yes, I know. He asked me to tell you he'll be a while, and he understands if you want to make your way back to your hotel."

In the excitement he'd forgotten all about booking himself in to a hotel, and to make matters worse, he'd left his back pack in Charlene Hamilton-Davies's hospital room. "If it's okay with you, I think I'll wait…" He hesitated for a moment… "You couldn't rustle me up a cup of coffee, and maybe a sandwich could you?" Denman smiled at the young nurse, turning on the old Southern charm.

"Certainly, Agent Denman, I'll be right back." She disappeared through the double doors, returning minutes later with a steaming cup of coffee and a plate of sandwiches. "They only had ham, but at least they're fresh—the coffee too."

"Thank you, ma'am, I'm much obliged." Chas picked a sandwich up from the plate—ham had never tasted so good. He finished the last of the sandwiches, placing the cup on the plate, and put it on the reception desk.

"I hope they were okay, Agent Denman."

Chas sat up, rubbing the sleep from his eyes. "Delicious. Sorry, I must have nodded off." The young nurse sniggered. "Don't tell me—I was snoring…"

"I'm afraid so. Are you sure you wouldn't like me to ring for a taxi to take you to your hotel?"

"I'd love nothing more, believe me, but I'm afraid I left my bag back in town, and I haven't actually gotten around to booking a hotel. With everything that's happened today I haven't had the time. I sort of hit the ground running."

"Oh dear. I'm sure the Inspector won't be long now, Agent Denman. Monsieur Dupont is back in his room, and the doctor's sedated him so he shouldn't give us any more trouble tonight at least."

The double doors swung open. "Agent Denman, I thought you'd be tucked up in your bed, fast asleep by now. Did the nurse not give you the message?"

"Yes, sir, she gave me the message, but in all the excitement I left my bag in Mrs Hamilton-Davies' room, and I never did get around to booking a hotel."

"Oh dear, well in that case you'd better come home with me, Agent Denman, in fact I'll be pleased of the company."

"Thank you, sir, it's much appreciated. Did your man confess?"

"Oh, yes, he confessed alright, to the murder of a young woman—a hit and run, a couple of months back. He said he didn't see her until it was too late—but then, the state he was in that evening, he wouldn't have."

Malestroit sat down wearily on the bench beside Denman, head in hands. Shaking his head he slapped his thigh and stood up again. "I don't know about you, Agent Denman, but I could do with a drink. I have a bottle of Bourbon chez-moi, a present from my late wife, and its high time it was opened I think. Come on, we can stop off at the first restaurant we find open and have ourselves a huge steak beforehand. Don't worry, I'm going to leave my car here and pick it up in the morning." He turned to the young nurse.

"Could I trouble you to telephone for a taxi please—it's been a long day, a very long day, indeed…"

"No need, Inspector, we can drop you off at the restaurant." The policeman replied.

"Thank you, Officer Bertrand, it's much appreciated."

The young nurse waved goodbye as they left, and with a last lingering glance, she returned to the desk. It was so not fair. She had been on the brink of inviting Agent Denman home for the evening…Another missed opportunity to add to the memoirs….

51

Sebastian pulled into the driveway of Giovanni's former home, and looking in his rear view mirror, straightened his tie—it was time to claim his prize. He opened the red velvet box—it sure was a beautiful ring. The perfect gift for his princess, the tear drop diamond glinting in the bright sunlight. Closing the box, he put it in his jacket pocket, and climbed out of the car.

The salesman had almost wet himself with excitement, when Sebastian had emptied the pouch containing fifty gold Ducats onto his desk earlier that afternoon. He'd driven the sleek, black, Mercedes convertible, out of the showroom, and down through the town, half an hour later. Grinning, like the proverbial, Cheshire cat—but perhaps he'd been a little hasty in his choice of vehicle. Exactly where would they put Giovanni's brats, when the new baby arrived?

It was right what they said about money talking—thanks to the old couple, and Hitler's greed, Sebastian was now 'rolling in it'.

He knocked briskly on the impressive carved oak door, and waited. Mario Marcello opened the front door.

"Delamare. You're looking very dapper today; to what do we owe the pleasure."

"I've a proposition I'd like to run past you, if I may, sir."

"I'm intrigued. You'd better come in, Sebastian." The old man walked down the corridor to the sun room, with Sebastian following close behind. "Please, take a seat. Would you care for a drink, Bourbon, Scotch—name your poison." The inflection resting heavily on the word poison. But the wily old man didn't intimidate Sebastian. On the contrary, with Mario Marcello, one knew exactly what to expect if you crossed him.

"Bourbon on the rocks please, sir." Marcello poured Bourbon into two crystal tumblers and handed one to Sebastian.

"Okay—fire away, Delamare…" Sebastian placed his glass on the table next to him, and, drawing himself up to his full height, began his speech.

"I have come to ask for your permission to marry your daughter, Sophia, sir." Marcello said nothing, his heavily lined face giving nothing away. Sebastian continued undaunted. "She is, I understand, expecting a child—my child, and a child needs a father—Charlotte and Alicia too, naturally."

Taking the red velvet box from his jacket pocket, he placed it on the table before the old man, who picked it up. Sebastian took a sip of his drink, as the old man opened the box and looked inside. Marcello leaned forward, one hand in his inside jacket pocket— Sebastian squirmed nervously in his seat—was this how his life would end? Shot dead by Mario Marcello in his sunroom—his body rolled, in the old Afghan rug, and dumped into the bay at high tide? Sebastian almost jumped out of his skin as the tight-lipped old man produced two silver tubes from his pocket and handed one to him.

"Celebratory Havana." He picked up a tiny bell. The maid appeared, curtseyed, and awaited her master's request. "Consuela, please ask Miss Sophia to join us."

"Yes, sir, right away, sir." And with that she scuttled back towards the door.

"Oh, and Consuela, could you bring a bottle of Veuve Cliquot please." He waited until the maid closed the door before addressing his daughter hovering in the doorway.

"Sebastian just told me your good news. I had no idea the two of you 'were close'." Sophia winced—her father was furious, Sebastian Delamare was not exactly ideal 'son-in-law' material.

"May I, sir?" Sebastian said, pointing to the small, red velvet box open on the table.

"By all means—you may as well make it official." Sebastian got down on one knee, and taking Sophia's left hand in his, he took the diamond from its box, and carefully slipped it onto Sophia's finger. It was a perfect fit.

"A short engagement would be advisable under the circumstances, Delamare, followed by a quiet, family wedding in Sicily; shall we say two months time, Sophia?"

"Yes, Papa, whatever you think is best." And taking two glasses off the tray Consuela had placed on the table, she handed one to her father, and the second to Sebastian.

"Are you not joining us, Sophia? A small glass of Champagne won't hurt the baby." Sebastian said quietly. Sophia nodded in agreement, glancing at her father for his permission. He was already angry, no point in making matters worse than they were.

Formalities over, Mario Marcello excused himself and made his way to his office. What in the name of God, had the stupid girl been thinking—letting white trash like Sebastian Delamare into her bed? Had she learned nothing in the years married to Antonio Giovanni?

Banging his fist on the desk, sending the photograph of Charlotte and Alicia hurtling to the floor. This marriage would be the shortest in history—if it happened at all. Unlocking the draw of the antique desk, Marcello took out a battered, black leather book, opened it up, and picking up the telephone he dialed the number before him. Replacing the receiver quietly Mario Marcello exhaled. It was arranged—now to break the news to the 'family.

~

Sophia was worried; she had never seen her father this quiet. "How did you find out about the baby, Sebastian?" Sophia hissed.

"A little bird told me." He reached out and grabbed her by

the arm.

"Let me go—you're hurting me, Sebastian." She examined her arm for signs of bruising. "Congratulations, you got what you wanted—I only hope you live long enough to regret it!"

"And what's that supposed to mean, Sophia?"

"Surely you don't think my father is 'happy' to have you as a family member?" She watched as Sebastian digested the last snippet of information. "You're a dead man walking, Sebastian."

"Is that so? Then you're in danger too, Sophia, it's my baby growing inside you, and accidents happen. A toy, left carelessly on the stairs—are you catching my drift."

"He wouldn't hurt me, he loves me?" Remembering the look on her father's face as Sebastian had slipped the ring onto her finger.

"I'll pack an overnight bag and fetch the girls."

"No, there's no time, we can buy what you need. I'll go tell your father we're taking Charlotte and Alicia out for a ride in my new car. You get the girls, and don't forget your passports." Sophia nodded, and running upstairs to the nursery, she grabbed the girls' coats from the hanger and hurriedly put them on.

"Are we going out, Mamma?" The girls said in unison.

"Yes, Uncle Sebastian's going to take us out for a ride in his brand new car, and if you're really good we might be able to persuade him to take us to McDonalds. Wouldn't that be good?"

"Yay, I'm going to have muggets this time, Mamma." Alicia exclaimed, and was instantly corrected by Charlotte.

"They're nuggets, silly!"

"That's what I said!"

"Didn't!"

"I so did!"

"That's enough, now behave nicely, or no nuggets!"

"Told you." Charlotte whispered.

"Charlotte Giovanni." Charlotte bowed her head, her bottom lip trembling—she didn't like it when mamma shouted.

Sophia rummaged through her underwear drawer for their passports—they'd vanished. What if her father had found them and locked them in the safe? Then she remembered—

she'd moved them when Consuela had cleaned upstairs. Taking a deep breath she led the girls downstairs into the hall. Her father and Sebastian were waiting by the car.

"Kiss grampy." Sophia said quietly. The girls rushed towards Mario Marcello, and one by one, he picked them up and showered them with kisses.

"Will you read to us at bedtime, grampy? Pleease grampy, mamma always cups the story short—says we need our boaty sleep." Alicia whispered to her grandfather.

"I most certainly will, girls. Drive carefully, Sebastian."

Sophia bit her bottom lip. She hated deceiving her father, but Sebastian was right—accidents happened.

"Into the car girls, buckle up." Satisfied her daughters were safely buckled into their harnesses Sophia turned and waved to her father.

"Do you think he suspects anything?" She said as they drove away. Sebastian shook his head.

"No—and by the time he realises something's wrong we'll be miles away. Passports?"

Sophia nodded, waving them in the air. For the first time in her life she had disobeyed her father…

52

Xavier Malestroit unlocked the front door and ushered Chas Denman quickly inside—the curse of having nosy neighbours was that they never knew when to leave well alone. Two and two would instantly multiply into double figures and by lunchtime tomorrow the whole neighbourhood would be convinced, that he, Xavier Malestroit, was now gay!

"Make yourself at home, Agent Denman, I'll be right back." Malestroit opened the freezer compartment of the refrigerator and peered inside. Yet another job to add to his growing list of tasks. Spying the ice cube tray peeping out from under a bag of frozen peas he reached inside, and taking hold of the tray he pulled—it was stuck to the bottom of the freezer. Taking a knife from the draining board he ran it under the hot water for a few seconds then slid it under the container. All this palaver for a bit of ice, he muttered to himself. And, taking two tumblers from the cupboard he went back into the lounge.

"Sorry—the ice tray was stuck to the freezer. I'm afraid I don't entertain much these days; Bourbon okay?"

"Fine. Thanks for taking me in, Xavier."

"It's nice to have a little company; it used to be such a happy home." Sighing, Malestroit dropped a couple of ice cubes in each glass, topped it off with Bourbon, and handed one to Denman.

"Cheers—or should I say, santé." Denman took a man-sized drink from his glass—the amber liquid tracing a fiery path down his throat, warming him right to the pit of his stomach.

"Are you married, Agent Denman?"

"Please, call me Chas—Agent Denman sounds so formal, after all we are off duty now. It's a fine Bourbon, Xavier; your late wife had good taste. Sorry, I'm always doing that—changing the subject, that is. Yes, I am married, my wife, Mary-Jo's a Vet'nary back in Atlanta—though we seem to spend more time apart than we do together of late. Work's the culprit—she wants me to take a desk job, maybe raise a family." Denman gazed thoughtfully into his glass.

"We were never blessed with children. Such a shame, my wife would have made a wonderful mother, but alas, it was not to be." Malestroit added quietly, his voice tinged with sadness. The men sat in silence for several minutes, before Malestroit jumped up, almost upending the bottle of Bourbon.

"I'd better see to your room—you must be exhausted, Chas. Please, help yourself to another drink, I won't be a moment."

"Thanks, don't mind if I do, I rarely get the chance these days."

Denman poured himself another drink, and closing his eyes sat back—replaying the events of earlier that day. What had happened in the building to make Richard Garner go back down to the basement? The words 'did he fall, or was he pushed,' uppermost in his mind. He knew it was highly improbable they would ever uncover the truth, though he suspected Delamare may have had something to do with it.

"Bed's ready when you are, Chas." Malestroit whispered softly. Denman opened his eyes.

"Thanks, Xavier, I was just running through the events leading up to the demise of Richard Garner..." His train of thoughts rudely interrupted by the trill of the telephone, on the table beside him.

"I wonder who that can be at this hour." Malestroit muttered as he picked up the receiver. "Malestroit." The policeman listened, nodding occasionally and then finally he replaced the receiver.

"The body in the basement has been identified…" Denman waited as the policeman picked up his glass and slumped into the chair.   "I'm getting to old for all this malarkey, Chas. It would seem the body in the basement wasn't Richard Garner after all…." Malestroit picked up the bottle and poured them both another drink. "They're not sure whose body was cremated—just that it had been dead for some time."

"You're kidding me?" Denman said in amazement.

"I wish I was, because now I have to upset Madame Amilton-Davies once again. She has taken it upon herself to make the necessary arrangements to have Monsieur Garner's body transported to Atlanta."

"Ah."

"Exactly. I'm off to my bed, Goodnight Chas—if I am to do battle with Madame Amilton-Davies again tomorrow I need to recharge my batteries in readiness for the ordeal."

"Me too, I'm all in." Denman said following his host into the hallway.

"Your room is here, Chas, and the bathroom is at the end of the hall. I hope you sleep well."

"You too, Xavier—goodnight."

~

Richard Garner banged his head as he tried to sit up. The last thing he remembered was being dragged from the burning building seconds before it exploded—by whom, he had no idea. Reaching in his pocket for the tiny torch-key fob Carly had given him last Christmas—Carly. She had been in the building, Agent Denman too… He shone the torch around; his saviour had dumped him in the trunk of a car—nice man—he'd remember to thank him personally, that is, if he got out of the trunk alive.

He looked around the trunk for something to use as a lever to prise it open, but found only a plastic scraper, for clearing ice from the windscreen. The noise of an aeroplane passing directly overhead startled him. The man, whoever he was, had dumped the car at the airport—in the car park he hoped, because if he was on the runway....

A second jet passed overhead, he was in the middle of a busy flight path—if he could only find something to bang on the lid of the trunk. Eventually someone would be bound to come over to see where the noise was coming from—wouldn't they? Struggling he pulled off his shoe, and began hammering as hard as he could on the trunk lid.

Over the other side of the airfield the occupants of the camper van were sleeping off the effects of a heavy evening's partying. Emerging from his stupor one of the youths sat up.

"Hey, Jimmy."

"What now, Pete. I was just dozing off..." The young man sat up, rubbing his eyes sleepily. "Well, I'm waiting?"

"I thought I heard someone banging."

"Banging, what?"

"How the hell should I know what? Listen...there it is again..."

Jimmy cocked his head to one side, and listened.

"Yeah, you're right; I can hear it now too. Pass me the torch."

He opened the door to the camper van and shone the torch around. "The noise seems to be coming from a car parked over the far side of the field. I suppose we'd better investigate—Mr Marcello will have our hides if anyone breaks in."

Pete pulled a wrench from under the front seat of the van and joined his friend by the door. They made their way quietly over towards the parked car.

"Try the handle, Pete, and see if it's locked."

Pete nodded, and tried the handle. "It's locked." Pete whispered back.

"Help! Let me out... please, I can't breath." Richard cried out.   The young men jumped back dumbfounded.

"How'd you manage to get yourself locked inside the trunk?" Jimmy demanded.

"How'd you think I got locked in the trunk, asshole." Jimmy looked across at Pete, and then around them—what if the person who locked the man in the trunk was still here...

"Pete, go fetch a crowbar from the hangar."

"Why's it always me that has to go fetch stuff." He muttered to himself. Jimmy was taking the whole seniority thing way too serious; after all he was only a couple of months older than himself.

"We'll have you out of there in a couple of minutes, mate, just relax, okay."

"Thank you, whoever you are." Richard said hoarsely.

"Name's Jonathan, but my friends call me Jimmy. What do we call you?" The young man asked warily.

"Richard Garner…"

"I recognise your accent—you're American, aren't you?"

"I sure am—from Atlanta, Georgia."

"Will this do, Jimmy?" Pete asked handing him a small crowbar.

"Yeah, it'll do just fine. Pete, say hi to Mr Richard Garner, he's an American—from Atlanta, Georgia."

"Hi there, Mr Richard Garner, from America, pleased to make your acquaintance, the name's Pete."

Richard smiled; at least his saviours were polite.

"Hi there, Pete, any chance you can break open this tin can, and let me out?"

"You just hang in there a while, Mr Garner; this here car you're trapped in is a Mercedes cabriolet, and a brand spanking new one at that. Does it ring a bell, you know like—do you know anyone who dislikes you enough to lock you in the trunk of their brand new Mercedes, and then abandon you in the middle of nowhere?" Pete enquired.

"Not that I can think of offhand, no. Where exactly am I?"

"Mario Marcello's private airfield—which is a mere hop, skip, and a jump away from Vannes airport. Does the name ring a bell, Mr Garner?" Jimbo said, crossing his fingers behind his back, hoping this wasn't the work of the Marcello's, or he'd be next in line for a new overcoat.

"Never heard of him. Do you work for Mr Marcello?" Richard asked.

Jimmy breathed a sigh of relief—he wouldn't end up in a supporting role after all. "Yeah, he lets us keep the camper van here, in exchange for keeping an eye on his property. He has a couple of Cessna's, and a private jet, in the hangar."

Pete turned around and walked back towards the hangar. Something wasn't quite right, he was sure when he'd fetched the wrench there had only been the two Cessna's in there…

He ran back to the Mercedes, and handed the keys he'd found on the board to Jimmy.

"These might help."

"Where did you find these?"

"On the board with the keys for the Cessna's..." Pete chewed his bottom lip. "The jet's gone..."

"Are you sure?" Jimmy exclaimed.

"Yep—and I found this on the floor where the jet should have been." Pete handed the small teddy bear to Jimmy. "Maybe Mr Marcello took his daughter and grandchildren on holiday." Pete said nervously.

"Let's hope so, Pete, because if not, we just fucked up big time." He slid the key into the lock and pushed the button and the lid to the trunk rose majestically into the air. "C'mon mate, looks like you could do with a stiff drink." Jimmy held out his arm to steady the American as he clambered out of the trunk.

"Sounds good to me, but could I trouble you for a large glass of water first. My throat's real sore, and I reek of smoke."

Jimmy sniffed Richard's jacket sleeve. "You're not kidding. Your jacket reeks of barbecue lighter fluid and smoke."

Richard raised his arm to his nose and inhaled. Jimmy was right... "I think I'd better take a rain check on the drink, guys. I need to get to a telephone and fast. Do either of you remember hearing a jet take off?" Richard looked from one to the other.

"We had ourselves a party earlier—some home grown weed, a few beers... Chilled out a little, you know how it is."

"More like passed out, Jimmy." Pete said, embarrassed. "It's funny though, I could have sworn I heard a woman shouting—she had an accent—Italian maybe."

"You guys had better come with me." Richard said, as he grabbed the keys to the Mercedes from Jimmy's hand. "Because when Mario Marcello finds out his jet's missing he's not going to be impressed with you guys. So the further away from here you are, the safer you'll be."

The two youths nodded in agreement. "We're right behind you, Mr Garner, sir."

53

Richard Garner parked the Mercedes in the car park outside the police station and waited for Jimmy and Pete.

"Now what do we do, Jimmy? He's only gone and parked in front of the Gendarmerie…" Pete whispered.

"Calm down, Pete. We haven't done anything wrong… Okay, well maybe driving under the influence…"

"And our stash…"

"It'll be fine; we're the one's who rescued Mr Garner, silly, not his captors. Just stay cool, answer their questions as truthfully as you can and everything will be okay." Jimmy crossed his fingers behind his back—well he hoped it would be. The youths jumped down from the van and locked the doors. There was no reason for the police to search their van—their stash would be safe in plain view…as long as there were no sniffer dogs around…

"Follow me, boys." Richard said as he walked up to the door to the police station and rang the bell. The door opened and the three men went inside. Richard walked up to the front desk. "Good morning, Constable, I'd like to see Inspector Malestroit, please, tell him it's Richard Garner…"

The constable disappeared down the corridor and into the filing room. "Lebrun, I've got a guy at the front desk who's claiming to be Richard Garner…Shall I telephone the Inspector?"

"Very funny, Jacques, Richard Garner died in the fire yesterday."

"Well that's what he said his name was—smart arse."

Lebrun stood up, and picking his cap up from the desk he tucked it under his arm and walked out to the front desk. "Can I be of assistance, Monsieur?"

"Garner, Richard Garner. I need to speak to Xavier Malestroit, urgently—it's regarding Sebastian Delamare…"

The buzzer sounded, and the outer door opened and in rushed Malestroit. "Monsieur Garner—you're alive! Mon Dieu, what happened to you…?"

"I don't know, inspector. One minute I was on the stairway to the attic—and the next, someone was dragging me from the burning building, and seconds later it exploded. Tell me Inspector, what happened to Carly and Agent Denman?" Richard asked quietly.

"They are both fine, Carly, is recovering in hospital from her ordeal and Agent Denman, is on an errand for me. Now, tell me what happened after you were pulled from the burning building?"

"Not a clue, inspector. When I came to I was locked in the trunk of the black Mercedes, that's now parked in the car park outside."

Malestroit ushered the men into his office.

"Ah, yes, the car." Malestroit said, closing the door to his office. He waited until the three men were seated before continuing. "As I was saying—Lebrun telephoned the Mercedes dealership in town a few moments ago. A man calling himself Troy Monroe purchased the car yesterday—he paid in cash—with gold coins. I think we can safely assume Monsieur Troy Monroe, is none other than Sebastian Delamare. Agent Denman is on his way to the garage now with the sketch he made with the help of Madame Amilton-Davies yesterday."

"So it looks like Delamare got away again, Inspector; but

this time he may have hostages—Pete found this teddy bear in the hangar at Mario Marcello's private airstrip, and his jet's missing…"

Malestroit turned to the young man. "Is this true, Monsieur?" Malestroit demanded.

"Yes sir, it is—I think I heard a young woman shouting—she had an accent—Italian, I think."

"You think you heard a young woman, or you think she was Italian—you didn't see anything strange, or hear the jet take off?"

"No, sir, I heard raised voices, one of which sounded foreign. I was sleeping—in fact I thought I was dreaming until Mr Garner asked if we'd heard anything strange. We work for Mr Marcello from time to time—the odd job here and there—clean his car, stuff like that. Jimmy used to work for Charles Dupont, until a few weeks back."

Jimmy closed his eyes—he'd told Pete to say nothing, and here he was spilling his guts. He'd be telling him about their stash if he didn't intervene quickly and shut him up.

"Is this true Monsieur?"

"Yes, Inspector, business hasn't been so good recently for Monsieur Dupont. It started going down hill when he put the haunted house up for sale. Though I heard on the grapevine recently that he'd sold it."

Malestroit rubbed his chin thoughtfully. These boys were hiding something, and he intended to find out what. "Okay, if you gentlemen would go with the constable—fingerprints—if you worked at the airfield we need to eliminate your prints from the crime scene. It's routine—nothing to worry about, and thank you for helping Monsieur Garner."

Lebrun led the young men out of the office and down the corridor. Malestroit had said to let them stew, as he was sure they were being evasive with the truth. Another of his famous hunches.

"Would you like me to arrange for a car to take you to your hotel, Monsieur Garner? I'm sure you would like to freshen up before going to see Madame Amilton-Davies and Carly. Naturally, I will telephone ahead and warn Madame—she is under the impression you are dead Monsieur." Malestroit picked up the telephone and dialled the hospital, not a pleasant task, but someone had to do it.

"Madame Amilton-Davies—Inspector Malestroit à l'appareil—I have some wonderful news—Monsieur Garner, he is alive and well…" He passed the telephone to Richard and sat down.

"Charlene, please don't cry—I'm fine, honestly. How's Carly?"

"We thought you were dead, Richard. What happened to you, where did you go?"

"It's a long story, Charlene, one best left until later."

"I'm so relieved you're safe, Richard—Carly's okay. The doctor say's she can go home this afternoon. Would you like to speak to her?"

"Please, Charlene." Richard wiped a tear from his eye.

"Uncle Richard—is it really you? And you're really okay—you're not hurt at all?"

"I'm fine, I burnt my hand when I touched the banister, it's sore, but I'll live…and you, pumpkin, are you okay? Nothing broken?"

"No, Uncle Richard, there's nothing broken—not anymore. Mom wants you to come and stay at the house. Please say you will, Uncle Richard; I'll feel safer knowing you're there to protect us."

"I'd love to, pumpkin. I'll be along later, I need to go freshen up and arrange some transport. I'll see you both later. Bye." Richard handed the telephone to the Inspector and sat down heavily on the chair.

"I think you should let the doctor here take a look at your hand, Monsieur Garner, and maybe ask him to prescribe a little something for your nerves too—you've had quite an ordeal."

"I think you could be right. Thank you, Inspector. For everything."

"It is my pleasure, Monsieur Garner." Malestroit opened the door to his office and beckoned the constable over. "Constable—please escort Monsieur Garner to the infirmary and whilst he is with the doctor can you arrange for a car to take him back to his hotel."

"Yes, sir. Right away, sir."

"Goodbye, inspector."

"Goodbye, Monsieur Garner, take care." Malestroit closed

the door to his office and sat down at his desk—damn Sebastian Delamare…

~

Jimmy wiped the ink off his fingertips. He sincerely hoped Pete hadn't done or said anything detrimental to anyone whilst he'd been with Lebrun having his fingerprints taken. Leaning forward on the bench he watched as Lebrun took Pete's right hand in his and rolled the ink over his fingertips.

Jimmy was worried—Pete had been in trouble with the law as a youngster—he'd stolen a bar of chocolate from a shop in town and the owner had called the police. His furious parents had banned him from everything—including hanging out with Jimmy. He was a bad influence on their son—so they said.

Lebrun led Pete back to the bench and disappeared into the Inspectors office. Pete looked up at Jimmy. "Okay mate?" Pete asked nervously— he hoped Jimmy wasn't angry. He hadn't meant to say anything about Dupont to the Inspector; but his mouth had a tendency to run away from him at times.

"Yeah, fine. I wonder how much longer we'll be?" Jimmy said quietly, as the door to the Inspector's office opened

"Jonathan Larue?" Lebrun asked. Jimmy swallowed nervously, and nodded. Pete had dropped them in the mire once again. He stood up and walked towards the office.

"Inspector Malestroit would like a word with you both, starting with you." Ushering Jimmy inside the office once more.

"Sit down please, Monsieur Larue."

Jimmy sat down and waited for Malestroit to speak. "Monsieur Larue, would you care to explain how your fingerprints came to be on Monsieur Dupont's car? It was found abandoned on waste ground near the station on April 13th by a routine patrol." Malestroit sat back, pen in hand waiting for a response.

Jimmy shrugged his shoulders. "Like Pete said, I used to work for Monsieur Dupont, and I sometimes used the car when visiting properties on agency business."

"I see—and did Monsieur Barton, also work for the Agency?" The inspector demanded cautiously.

"No, sir."

"Then how do you account for his fingerprints on the

steering wheel and the driver door?" The colour drained from Jimmy's face—he had no choice but to come clean.

"The car was parked outside the haunted house. The stupid man had left his keys in the ignition, and the car unlocked—he was just asking for it to be stolen...."

"What time was this, Monsieur Larue?"

"Around midnight, give or take or minute or two. Why do ask?"

"I'll ask the questions if you don't mind, Monsieur." Malestroit replied sarcastically. "Did you notice if the car was damaged in any way?"

Jimbo sat and thought for a moment. "Yes—one of the headlights wasn't working, and the car was pulling badly to the right. Pete pulled on to the waste ground to see what the problem was...He panicked when he saw the blood, dragged me out of the car and said we should abandon it there and say nothing. It wasn't Pete, Inspector—I swear to you, we only drove the car a few hundred metres before dumping it..."

"Thank you for your help, Monsieur Larue. I can't see Monsieur Dupont pressing charges for the theft of the vehicle, not under the circumstances. If you would accompany Constable Lebrun, he will take your statement. You are free to go... for now, next time you might not be so fortunate. Show Monsieur Barton in please, Lebrun."

Malestroit sat back in his chair. Another case solved. Dupont had confessed to the hit and run, and the boys had confessed their part in the affair. The waiter at the restaurant had confirmed that Dupont had drunk a considerable amount of alcohol during the evening. Case closed.

If only all cases were so easily solved—his fingers lingering on the folder gathering dust on the corner of his desk. Sebastian Delamare had eluded captivity once again, and until he surfaced the case would remain unsolved... A knock on the door interrupted his reverie. "Come in, Lebrun."

"How did you know it was me, sir?"

Malestroit smiled knowingly. "That would be telling. Did Monsieur Barton corroborate Monsieur Larue's version of events, Lebrun?"

"To the letter, sir, they had nothing to do with the hit and run."

"Was there something else, Lebrun?" Lebrun looked down at the manila envelope in his left hand and smirked.

"Forget my head if it wasn't screwed on sometimes, sir. It's the autopsy report on the guy they found in the basement."

"Thank you, Lebrun, just put it in my in tray; I'll look at it later. Do you think you could rustle up a pot of coffee and a couple of croissants? I missed breakfast."

"Certainly, sir, I'll get right on it." Lebrun said as he dropped the envelope into the tray.

54

Sebastian tapped the fuel gauge—the tanks were all but empty. He would have to ditch the plane—he scanned the horizon in the vain hope of spotting land. Nothing but water as far as the eye could see. No flight plans meant no one would come looking for them, and even if they did, where would they look. He was sure the tanks were full when he'd checked them that morning—damn Mario Marcello. Time to break the bad news...

"Sophia..." She lifted her head sleepily.

"Are we there?" She asked, yawning.

"Nope, and we're not likely to be now—someone tampered with the fuel tanks—we're almost out of fuel, Sophia, do you know if there's a life raft onboard?" Sophia screamed.

"That won't help. Don't just sit there woman, search the plane." Shaking, Sophia unbuckled her seat belt and made her way to the rear of the plane. She found the life raft tucked into a compartment at the back of the plane along with three life jackets. Three life jackets, for four people—there had to be more. Frantically she searched the cupboards and under all the seats but found nothing.

"Did you find a life raft, Sophia?" Sebastian asked worriedly from the cockpit.

"Yes—there's a raft."

"And life jackets? Snap out of it woman, this is not going to be pleasant for any of us."

"I'm scared, Sebastian…"

"I'm scared too, I'm sorry I shouted. Now answer the question—have you found the life jackets?" Sophia merely nodded. Women and children first—that was the unwritten rule in any shipwreck wasn't it? She looked around for something to use as a weapon, because if push came to shove, Sebastian would be the one to perish in the crash—not her— or her girls. He'd gotten them into this mess, and he would be the one to pay—with his life if necessary. The flare gun—that would be perfect. She tucked it inside the waistband of her jeans and zipped the flares into her inside pocket—her jacket was waterproof she hoped.

Pushing the life jackets out of view she went back to her seat and buckled in, and pulling her rosary beads out of her pocket she started to pray.

"Say one for me while you're about it." Sophia smiled weakly. It would take more than a prayer to save him; he'd need a full blown miracle.

The number one engine stuttered and died, followed seconds later by the other—their survival was in the hands of the Gods now. "Time to put Charlotte and Alicia into their life preservers, Sophia, you too…"

Sophia nodded and did as he asked, her fingers crossed that he didn't ask where his life jacket was until the plane hit the water. Giving her precious time, she hoped, to push the emergency door open and inflate the raft before he found out.

Sebastian stood up and removed his jacket. The son of a bitch was wearing a parachute. "You bastard—you planned this to get back at my father…

"Not at all, it's the survival of the fittest, nothing more—sorry, Sophia, shit happens sometimes…" Quick as a flash she buckled the girls into their seats as Sebastian made his way to the back of the plane. "Ciao, Sophia—oh, by the way, I activated the automatic pilot. Have a nice life, what there is left of it."

With the last cutting remark Sebastian opened the door—depressurising the cabin. Sophia wedged her foot under the seat, unbuckled the belt on her jeans, and attached it and the life raft to the girls' seats. He was leaving them to fend for themselves— there was no way he was getting the raft too. Sophia kicked out wildly, knocking Sebastian off balance; and as he fell he hit his head on the fuselage and with one final kick she ejected him from the plane.

Laughing hysterically she leaned forward—watching as he catapulted towards the ocean—his parachute now rendered useless...

"You were right, Sebastian, shit does happen, the only difference is this time it's happened to you!" She shouted triumphantly. The cabin pressure equalised and Sophia unbuckled her belt moving into the now vacant pilot's seat. If she could just bring this baby down in one piece she would buy precious time to get the girls into the life raft, and safety before the jet sank to the bottom of the ocean.

Sophia picked up the radio microphone, and turning the dial to the emergency channel she began her broadcast. "Mayday, mayday, mayday...this is Charlie-Tango-nine-seven-three-five-alpha, about to ditch into the ocean, position unknown. Over. I am initiating beacon now. Over and out." She flicked the switch and started the beacon—all she could do was hope and pray that someone had heard her distress call.

The nose of the jet hit the water first; she heard a cracking sound followed by a boom as the plane bounced over the water and finally came to a halt.

Sophia quickly unbuckled Charlotte and Alicia and took them to the rear of the plane—quickly reading the instructions for inflating the raft she threw it out of the door and pulled the cord as hard as she could.

"Charlotte, I want you to hold Alicia's hand firmly. Mummy is going to jump into the water, and swim to the raft. As soon as I tell you, I want you to do the same—okay. The life preserver will keep you afloat, baby. Do you understand what I'm telling you, Charlotte?" The young girl nodded, and grasped her sister's hand firmly. Sophia pulled the cord to inflate their jackets and with a final hug, and kiss, she jumped out of the sinking plane.

As she turned—the plane was filling rapidly with water—if the girls didn't jump now they would go down with it. "Jump, Charlotte, Alicia—jump now and swim to mama." Sophia screamed. "Please, God, let my babies live." She looked on in horror as the plane disappeared beneath the waves and sunk to the bottom of the ocean. But where were her babies?

"Mama. Help me…" Charlotte's tiny voice cried out. "I can't find Alicia." Frantically scanning the horizon for her daughters—time was running out, she had to get to the girls—and fast, but swimming against the current towing a raft was difficult… And if she let go of the raft they would all die for sure. Then she caught sight of Alicia's red coat—but the relief was short lived, as the strong current carried poor little Charlotte out to sea.

Sophia climbed into the raft, picked up the oar, and paddled as hard as she could. Alicia was unconscious, her life, hanging in the balance as Sophia dragged her limp body into the raft; and placing her in the recovery position, she picked up the oars once more paddled as fast as her arms would go.

One hundred metres—two hundred metres, she had Charlotte in sight now, she couldn't give up, she had to go on—had to save her baby girl. With one final surge Sophia reached the little blue bundle, her lungs on fire, her heart beating so fast she could hear it above the crashing of the waves, and, leaning over the side she lunged forward scooping the little girl into her arms—her body limp, lifeless. The raft tilted precariously, and frantically Sophia pushed Alicia to the other side of the raft to help balance out the weight; she held her breath as the raft dropped once more onto an even keel. They were safe…for now.…

Carefully she removed the life preservers from Alicia and Charlotte's trembling bodies, and with no blanket to wrap them in, removing their wet clothes was her only option. Sophia sat the girls on her lap and hugged them tightly in an attempt to warm them with her body heat. She leant back against the wall of the raft—the emergency box, maybe there would be blankets inside. And shuffling forward still clutching her babies to her breast—she fumbled with the catch, her hands numb with cold but she persevered until the lid sprang open.

There was a god after all. And silently gave thanks for the bounty inside—three foil blankets. She swiftly opened one of the packets, and wrapped the sleeping girls tightly together in the blanket. Her 'oven ready babies'. Her hand instinctively caressing her stomach and the baby growing inside her. Sebastian's baby—the bastard who had abandoned them when the going got tough—or at least he would have if she hadn't turned the tables on him and kicked him out the plane. Good riddance to bad rubbish. But what if he'd survived...

She pushed the thought to the back of her mind, as she rummaged through the contents of the orange box. First item, a box of Carr's Water Biscuits—hardly haute cuisine, but at least they would stave of hunger pangs. Two bars of milk chocolate followed by a bag of barley sugar sweets—instant energy boost. A first aid kit, a rescue whistle, a signal mirror, repair kit, and a foot pump—she hoped to God she never had to use the last couple of items. She wondered if they packed the emergency box in order of possible necessity—and if that were so, surely seasick bags should come after the seasick tablets. Next out was a bailer, a fishing kit, a water-tight flashlight and spare batteries, a pack of water purifying tablets and a tin opener.

The mind boggled on the logic of adding the last item—what damn use was a tin opener in the middle of the ocean when there were no tins in the box?

Packed at the bottom of the box she found two large containers of water—she wondered how long they had been in the box. Perhaps that was the reasoning behind the water purifying tablets. Two red hand flares and a parachute rocket were the last items in the box—now all she needed was a ship or a plane to come by and end their nightmare.

Sophia peered outside—it was pitch black—the only sounds to be heard—the waves, now gently lapping against the raft. Stripping off her damp clothes she wrapped herself in the second foil blanket and lay down at the side of her daughters—things would be clearer in the morning...

∼

Sebastian groaned, as his stomach heaved—he was going to throw up again. He leaned over the bunk fumbling for the bucket—he was sure he'd seen a young man place there earlier. He sat up slowly, staring into the darkness. Where was he? The door opened slowly and clanged shut.

"Good evening, Agent Childs. How are you feeling now?" The officer asked sympathetically. "You had us worried for a moment back there sir."

"Where am I?"

"On board the USS Washington, sir."

"On board a submarine…But how?"

"You were picked up on our sonar, sir—or rather the jet you were flying was. By the time we surfaced there was no sign of the aircraft, it was lucky you were wearing a parachute, sir. The Commander asked if you would care to join us for drinks, sir. If you're feeling up to it that is."

"Yes, of course, I'd be delighted. Tell me, officer…"

"Lieutenant Fielding, sir. Yes, sir…"

"Were there any other survivors?"

"No, sir, I'm afraid not. I'll send someone down with some clean cloths for you, sir; the shower is down the corridor. Until later, sir."

"Okay, Lieutenant." Sebastian sat down on the bunk. Sophia and the girls had perished in the crash—it was a pity, but like Sophia had said as she'd kicked him out the plane—shit happens.

He walked over to the sink, looking back at his reflection in the small mirror above. The beard and the hair would have to go…he'd spent the last thirty years masquerading as someone else and now it was time to stop. Time to step back into his own life, time to move on, maybe find himself a woman and settle down—buy himself a little ranch up in Wyoming and raise horses, a couple of kids too…He would want for nothing…his secrets safe.

There would be no more killing, no more looking over his shoulder. He'd known the time had come to hang up his gun and badge when he failed to eliminate Xavier Malestroit.

Troy Hamilton-Davies's life would never be the same either. He'd lost his partner, his wife, and his family. He was alone; his bitch of a wife had even taken his dogs…And like the man said 'he'd really missed those dogs.'

And then there was Naomi…Damaged goods and all

because she'd gotten too close to the man. She'd forgotten her pledge to Uncle Sam, and stepped a little too close to the flame…And we all know what happens to moths…don't we.

Barton Childs shaved off the last of his beard, picked up the scissors and started to cut. "Would you like me to ask the barber to help you with that, sir?" Childs watched as the young sailor placed the suit on the bed.

"It's almost as good as new, sir. One of the guys repaired the tear on the sleeve, you can hardly see where it was—not unless you look real close that is."

"You have a barber and a tailor on board the Washington—I'm impressed. Please do, it's not easy cutting your own hair."

The young man smiled. "I'll get him right away, Agent Childs."

~

He straightened his tie, pulled his shirt cuffs down, and with one last look in the mirror Barton Childs stepped out into the narrow corridor.

"This way, sir, the Lieutenant and the Commander are waiting." Childs flicked a piece of lint from his lapel subconsciously—he could almost taste the bourbon, feel its warmth as it coursed its fiery path into his stomach—he hoped there were nibbles too, his last meal having re-surfaced several times in the past few hours, leaving him with a sinking feeling.

The sailor opened the door to the officers' lounge and stood to one side to let Childs enter.

"Agent Childs, Barton, good to see you again—you're looking well. Please take a seat—Steward, Bourbon on the rocks for Mr Childs, please."

"Commander Masters, it's been a long time—a very long time indeed."

"You must be wondering why you're here, Barton."

"The thought had crossed my mind, sir." Childs said as he cautiously sniffed his drink.

So, what was the game in hand now he wondered?

"It's quite safe to drink, Barton, at least for the time being. You have something for us I believe?" The Commander demanded.

"I did, sir, I'm afraid 'it' went down with the plane. I do

hope your team marked the spot with a buoy, sir—after all, the Atlantic covers a substantial distance, as you well know, sir."

"Indeed it does, Barton. I take it you have a sample for us."

Childs took a handful of gold Ducats from a pouch zipped inside the lining of his jacket and handed them to the Commander.

"I think you'll find the goods to be of 'merchantable quality', sir."

The commander picked a coin from the pile and put it in his mouth, biting down hard. "Nice doing business with you, Barton, for a moment there you had us worried, especially when you disappeared with the lovely Sophia Giovanni and her daughters. That was when we called on the help of a friend, to make sure you didn't disappear permanently with our merchandise. Thanks to him you are still alive—I'm sure you'd like to thank him personally."

"Naturally, sir—it goes without saying." Childs sat back, and drained his glass. The man stepped out from the shadows and sat next to the commander.

"Hello, Bastian, long time, no see…"

"Troy…"

"I bet you're surprised to see me here aren't you, Bastian."

"Not at all, Troy, I find little surprises me these days. How's the wife doing now? And Carly, I do hope her little sojourn in the attic didn't perturb her too much. Pity about Richard, though. I'm afraid I forgot to inform the authorities of his whereabouts before I absconded—and I think by now it's a little late. Not much oxygen in the boot of a Mercedes."

"They're all fine, Richard too."

"That's not possible." Childs said nervously.

"Can I get you a refill, Bastian? Four Roses Bourbon please steward for Mr Childs, and I'll have the same. Naomi sends her regards too; I'm sure you'll be relieved to know she made a full recovery from her sojourn in the cabin. Can't have any kids though—thanks to you."

Childs looked from Troy to the Commander—what game where they playing. He'd never have taken Troy Hamilton-Davies for a traitor, not in a million years, the Commander neither. The commander leaned forward.

"Troy has been assigned to 'protect you', Childs, at least

until the merchandise has been retrieved. I suggest you co-operate, it will make the transitional period so much more agreeable."

"And after you have the goods, what then?" Childs asked nervously.

"After that you will be free to leave the service, find yourself a woman, and maybe have yourself a couple of kids. Who knows what fate has in store for us, Agent Childs…Who knows…." Commander Masters stood up. "And now, if you'd be so kind as to follow the Lieutenant, Agent Childs, he will take you to your new quarters. Goodbye, Agent Childs."

He was now formally dismissed, and he new exactly where his new quarters would be located.

55

Malestroit finished his croissant. After dusting the crumbs carefully into the waste basket he picked up the manila envelope and slit it open. He skimmed through the first page and halfway down the second before leaping to his feet, upending his chair as he rushed to the door. "It's not possible, there has to be some mistake… Lebrun—get in here, now!" Malestroit roared.

"Something wrong, sir?"

"Damn right there is. Here—read this." Malestroit exclaimed, tossing the report over to Lebrun. Lebrun scanned the pages, calmly placing them back on the desk neatly.

"But if the body in the cellar was none other than Sebastian Delamare, sir, who dragged Monsieur Garner out of the burning building and locked him in the trunk of the Mercedes?"

"Exactly—and who's been masquerading as him for the past thirty years…" The door to the office flew open:

"Xavier, you aren't going to believe what I just found out…" Exclaimed Denman excitedly.

"Try me—today seems to be my day for surprises." Malestroit tossed the autopsy report towards him.

"Sebastian Delamare was working for the CIA, Xavier—he's been undercover for years."

"That doesn't surprise me—all except for one small detail, Agent Denman—the real Sebastian Delamare has been dead for the past thirty years. It was his body they recovered from the fire." It's all there in the report—heart failure—Sebastian Delamare was literally frightened to death."

"By who, and how? And if that's so, exactly who was posing as him?"

"Your guess is as good as mine on that one, Agent Denman. Perhaps we'll never know the answer to that question. The man we know as Sebastian Delamare is on the run again, and he has hostages—Sophia Giovanni and her twin daughters we believe. We sent a police car to collect Mario Marcello—his jet is missing, and we have witnesses to the kidnapping—Jonathan Larue, Peter Barton and Richard Garner. As I said, today has been packed full of surprises." Malestroit sat down, and beckoned Denman to do the same.

"I'm thinking Sebastian Delamare's death is somehow tied in to the discovery of the gold. They found the occupants of the house too—an elderly German couple, Franz and Heidi Spiegel—Jewish refugees. They survived the Holocaust, only to end their days wrapped in an old sheet, and buried in a shallow grave in their own back garden."

"Do you think they were killed for the gold, Xavier?" Denman asked.

"Yes, I do. I think somehow the real Sebastian Delamare found the gold, and was disposed of to stop him talking—he was, by all accounts, a bit of a 'Walter Mitty' character. A member of a religious cult, the head of which was none other than his mother, Adele Delamare—and before you ask, yes, she's dead too. Died around the same time as her son. The death certificate states she died from heart failure. I'm not so sure it was natural causes, too much of a coincidence—I believe she was murdered in order to cover up the death, and re-birth, of her son, Sebastian. Is there any chance you can dig a little deeper into our friend—find out the where, the when, and more importantly the why the CIA found it necessary to send him undercover?"

"I can try, but I got the distinct impression I was being given the run around earlier. My source at HQ politely suggested what I didn't know, couldn't harm me, and told me to leave it at that."

"That sounds suspiciously like a threat, Chas; perhaps it's best if we just let it go…." Malestroit added cautiously.

"No way, Xavier—that son of a bitch killed my dog. Not to mention what he did to a fellow agent—Naomi Gibbs. And the jury's still out as to who was behind the attempt on my life at the mall after a meeting with Troy Hamilton-Davies. Talking of Troy, does anyone know where he disappeared too?"

"He was last seen running from Madame Amilton-Davies—she told him in no uncertain terms what she thought of him—said he was responsible for bringing Sebastian Delamare to her door."

"Surely you don't suspect Troy had anything to do with this? He barely knew the guy; and Counsellor Hamilton-Davies is a respected member of the community—his family are 'old money'."

"That's as maybe, but it still doesn't explain what he was doing at the house in possession of a cross-bow, and an antique cross-bow at that."

"He was there to rescue his daughter. Believe me, if someone kidnapped your daughter you'd put your life on the line too. Charlene was just overwrought; in the past few days she's been attacked in her home, and locked in the cellar and left for dead. The man she loved was murdered in the hospital, two rooms from where she slept. Not to mention what took place before that between her daughter, and Antonio Giovanni. The woman was at the end of her tether, and I for one would have been worried if she hadn't balled him out!"

The conversation lapsed into silence—Denman watched as Malestroit took the large, yellow file from his pending tray, hesitating before handing it to Lebrun.

"I think you can put this back in the Archives, Lebrun."

"Of course, sir. I'll put it with the others." Constable Lebrun stood up, saluted Malestroit, and shook hands with Denman. "Nice meeting you, sir."

"You too, Lebrun, and if ever you happen to be passing through Atlanta, be sure to look me up." Denman shook hands with the constable. "Time I made tracks too, Xavier, I still have a fugitive to catch—wherever he may be. Thanks for putting me up last night, I hope one day you'll let me repay the favour—I'm sure Mary-Jo and Tata would be delighted for the chance to show you some good old Southern hospitality."

The door burst open and a flustered constable thrust a wad of paper at Malestroit. "It seems like your work may be finished too Agent Denman… Mario Marcello's jet is reported to have crashed into the ocean—position undisclosed—the coastguard received a distress call from a woman with an Italian accent at 1700 hours today. It's not known if there are any survivors."

56

The Limousine pulled in front of the hospital, and Richard Garner turned to his driver. "I'll be as quick as I can, Jarvis. If they try to move you on tell them you're collecting Madonna."

"Okay, Mr Garner, you're the boss—Madonna it is."

Jarvis tilted his cap and raised the window, they'd have Bob Hope of getting him to open it, he was on a mission and he answered to no-one except Mr Garner, they were his orders. This was an undemanding number, with no lifting involved and there was no way he was going to screw this up.

Richard stepped jauntily into the elevator and pushed the button for the second floor. Today was the first day of the rest of his life—and this time round he wasn't going to screw it up. One didn't get a second chance at a 'second chance' often in life.

The elevator came to a halt with a jolt, the doors opened and Richard walked out into the lobby and down the hallway to room 474. He knocked on the door and opened it slowly.

"Are you decent, girls?" Richard asked as he poked his head

around the door.

"Uncle Richard, I thought you'd never get here. We're all ready to leave."

Richard bent down, placing a chaste kiss on Charlene's cheek—he wasn't going to blow it by rushing in, not this time. This time he would take his sweet time; woo her, shower her with perfume and designer originals, anything as long as she agreed to be his forever.

"Richard, I am so glad you're alright, I promise to make it up to you. After all, it's partly my fault Troy dissolved your partnership—if he hadn't got hold of the wrong end of the stick about you and me in the first place he would never have done it." Richard's heart sank.

"The car's waiting, girls. Sorry, Charlene, I never thought to ask do you need a wheelchair."

"No, Richard, not any more I don't—look."

She stood up and taking two small steps she collapsed into his arms. It was all he could do not to kiss her, his whole being longed to be in her arms, her bed…

"I think for now at least we'll get you a wheelchair, until your legs regain their strength. Is that okay with you, Cherie?"

"Don't call me that." Charlene snapped angrily. "Sorry, Richard, I shouldn't have snapped like that, I guess I'm still a little touchy—give me some space, time to grieve for Antoine."

"Sorry, it was tactless of me. Of course, take all the time you need, I'll be right here by your side…waiting, hoping, and praying you'll grow to love me once more, the way you used to. I know I let you down, God knows, I spent months berating myself for my stupidity, and I promise you it will never happen again. That part of my life is behind me, I learned my lesson."

Charlene smiled, who knew maybe one day, she could perhaps come to love him again, but could she trust him… "Okay, let's go home. Take it one day at a time and see where it leads us—no promises though—deal?"

"It's a deal. Shall I push?"

"Yes, you can push, this time; just don't think you're going to get your own way all the time. I'm a woman of independent means I'll have you know." Carly rolled her eyes heavenward and winked at Richard. With a little help the two of them would be cooing like turtle doves before long. They were going home as a family, albeit slightly dysfunctional, but what was new about that. Life with her mom had never been conventional.

"Are you coming, Carly?"

"Yes, Mom, I'm on my way." Richard held the door to the elevator open for Carly—something was worrying her.

"Penny for them, pumpkin?" Carly chewed her bottom lip, a habit of her fathers she'd picked up.

"Do you think the ghosts are gone now?" She blurted out. "I never got chance to say thank you to Amelia and the others…"

"I don't know, pumpkin; I'm not 'clued up' on ghosts and stuff, sorry. Maybe we could find a Medium or…"

"How about using the Ouija board, Carly?" Charlene interjected. "I believe your brother still has the one he found in the attic under his bed."

"How did you know…?"

"I wasn't born yesterday, Carly. I knew as soon as my back was turned he'd go fetch it, or send someone else for it."

"You're not angry with me, are you?"

"No, pumpkin, of course I'm not angry, let's just get home and then take it from there, okay?"

"Okay, it's a deal."

Richard pushed the wheelchair down the ramp towards the Limousine. "Can you get the door please, Jarvis?"

"Yes, sir, sorry, sir, I must have dozed off for a minute. Hello again, Madame, sorry I didn't realise you were—you know—her." Charlene blushed, recognising the obnoxious man who'd delivered her furniture in an instant—of all the drivers in Vannes, and Richard had to pick this one.

"What are you blabbering on about, man…?"

Richard laughed loudly—Jarvis thought Charlene really was Madonna. "Sorry, Charlene, I'm afraid it's my fault—I told Jarvis if anyone questioned his parking here he was to say he was here to collect Madonna. Sorry. You have to admit it is quite funny though…because you look nothing like Madonna…"

"He's right, mom, you really don't, it's the hair I think? Don't you agree, Jarvis?" Carly demanded of the jovial red faced man, desperately trying not to laugh. Poor Jarvis, he couldn't see what they all found so funny. Muttering as he folded the wheelchair and put it in the trunk of the car—no lifting the advert said, and here he was folding up an oversized pushchair.

The last time he'd seen Madame hoity-toity she'd been nimble enough on her pins. He wondered what had happened to the last bloke—women—fickle creatures, always changing their minds…

"Everything okay, Jarvis?" Richard asked.

"Yes, sir, just checking the trunk was secure. Be right there."

"Oh dear, I think we've upset him. Perhaps we should apologise?"

"He's not the only one who's upset, Richard." Charlene said pouting.

"Sorry…Am I forgiven?" Richard asked sheepishly desperately trying to stifle a snigger.

The car rolled to a halt outside the house and Carly leapt out of the car straight into the arms of her older brother, almost knocking him over in her excitement.

"Whoa, steady on there, sis. Hi, Richard, how's tricks?"

"Fine, thanks, Philip, where's Jason?"

"He's just putting the finishing touches to the…."

"To 'the what', Philip?"

"Err…it was supposed to be a surprise, he's spent all morning in the kitchen, promise me you won't let on I told you about the cake, mom."

"Of course I won't." Charlene said, wondering what state her lovely new kitchen would be in, after a mornings' baking with Jason.

Jarvis opened the trunk and took out the wheelchair. "No need to open it, Jarvis; and I don't think we'll be requiring your services again today—why don't you take the rest of the day off?"

Jarvis doffed his cap. "Thanks, Mr. Garner. Is it alright if I take the wife for a little spin, I'll be really careful—I promise?"

"Of course, Jarvis, I'll call you first thing in the morning to discuss our itinerary."

"Right you are, sir. Goodnight all." Jarvis said, and as he drove off he tooted the horn.

"Philip, will you bring the wheelchair inside please while I see to your mother." Richard scooped Charlene into his arms and carried her up the steps and over the threshold of number 55.

"You're taking liberties again, Mr Garner…"

"Yes, I am rather." Richard replied wickedly. "Smile, and don't forget to look surprised when Jason produces the cake… and do try not to dampen his enthusiasm, you never know where it might lead, and the kitchen will come clean… Eventually…"

"Jason, they're here." Philip shouted as he slammed the front door. Charlene pushed open the kitchen door expecting the worse and was pleasantly surprised—her kitchen was spotless.

"In here, mom—close your eyes, and don't open them until I say it's okay." Jason called out from the dining room.

Now what where they up too? She opened the door to the dining room slowly…

"Surprise!" The patio doors were wide open, but instead of leading out onto the terrace, they now opened into a beautiful garden room. Charlene caught her breath.

"But, how did you pay for it—it must have cost a fortune…" Charlene stuttered.

"It's my welcome home gift to you, Charlene." Richard said, handing her a glass of Veuve Cliquot.

"Does it meet with your approval, Madame?"

"Richard, it's beautiful, but you shouldn't have."

"It was my pleasure. Come; sit here by the window, Charlene."

"Yeah, mom, sit down, make yourself look less on the legs and then I can bring you your second surprise." Jason exclaimed, and cake in hand he made his entrance. "I spent all morning baking it…" Charlene suppressed a snigger as he placed the plate on the table. "It's a bit lop-sided I'm afraid—I couldn't get the cream to whip properly, and every time I tried to put it together the top tier slid off onto the table."

"It's lovely, Jason. Wonky cake is my favourite." She was home again with her children. Some things would never be the same again—but with time the old wounds would heal, and the past forgotten. The future was her goal, with that thought in mind she cut the first piece of the cake and handed it to Richard, and smiling happily she picked up her glass.

"To us, our new home, and family life. There is one more thing we have to do before we celebrate though…We have to thank the ghosts of the Delamare family for keeping Carly safe from harm. Jason, the Ouija board if you please…"

Jason hung his head in shame, caught in the act again. "I can explain…"

"I'm sure you can, but there's no need—now fetch the board. Philip, clear a space—I want you all at the table please." Philip cleared the table and helped Jason set the board up.

"Carly, would you like to begin. I think to be on the safe side we'll start with a prayer. I don't intend inviting trouble in the form of malevolent spirits into my new garden room. Though I think it's as much the home of Amelia and Ben as it ours…And if they feel they'd like to stay, well, that's okay by me." They placed their index fingers on the pointer lightly and waited.

"Amelia, Ben…are you there?"

"Yes, we're here…Daniel too, and Antonio…"

"And, Antoine?" Charlene asked quietly.

"No, he isn't here, Charlene, sorry; he's passed over to the other side. He wanted you to know…"

"What did he want me to know, Amelia?"

"That for the short time you had together he was very happy, and he wants you to give Richard a second chance. He said he had a gift for you both, but you would have to be patient, as the cogs turn slowly."

"A gift, but how?"

"Patience, Charlene—remember the cogs turn slowly. I'm sorry Charlene that was all he said."

"Why didn't you tell her the truth, Amelia?" Ben asked accusingly.

"What good would come of her knowing the man she loved had sold his soul to the devil in exchange for immortality."

"But what if he did it for her—so he could be with her once more."

"And when she died, what would happen then…No, Ben, it's best this way." Ben turned towards the light; Amelia had Antonio and Daniel, and she didn't need him hanging around spoiling their fun. He'd find himself a spot somewhere, and with one final look at the old house he let the light carry him up into the heavens.

Charlene sat back, puzzled by the cryptic message Antoine sent her.

"I wanted you to know I'm sorry, Amelia, and I hope that you find eternal peace, all of you…I'll miss you." Tearfully Carly sat back.

"Don't cry, Carly, we're a family now, I'll miss you too, you have my cross and chain to remember us by…Goodbye, Carly, goodbye, Jason, Ben says to say ditto too…Until we meet again…Take care…."

"Ciao, ma belle, fait du bon vent…"

"I take it that was Antonio…" Charlene demanded. Carly nodded, as she wiped away a solitary tear.

"They've gone."

"Is there anything else we need to do to close the door Jason?" Charlene asked quietly.

"No, Mom, just throw the board away, we won't need it again." He said, and taking the board from the table he broke it across his knee and threw the pieces into the wood burning stove, lit a match, threw it inside and closed the door.

~

Damn the boy Jason. Now she'd have to find another way back…Annie slipped into the shadows, down into the depths of hell…One day, they'd slip up, and when they did, she'd be waiting in the shadows, ready to take back what was hers, by rights…

Epilogue

Richard Garner scooped his bride into his arms, and, pushing the door to Number 55 open with his foot, carried her over the threshold. Tonight was a night for celebration, tonight the restaurant would remain closed. Jason, Philip, and Carly, had returned to Paris with Matthew, and his wife Celine—finally they were alone.

The man moved out of the shadows, stubbed his cigarette underfoot, turned up the collar of his jacket, and walked away. It was a done deed; he'd left it too late to claim what was rightly his, and now that part of his life was over. He stopped …He'd almost forgotten the real reason behind his visit, and pulling the dog eared envelope from his pocket he walked quickly across the road, hesitating briefly before pushing it into the letter box, and walking off into the night.

Inside the house, the newlyweds, stripped of their wedding finery, now sat together in the garden room, the dogs, Luna and Juno at their feet.

Richard sat back in his chair, smiling contently—his bride stood up and wandered into the hallway bending to retrieve the envelope lying on the floor. The writing looked familiar somehow. She slit it open and pulled out the contents—curious now she opened the card. Taped to the inside was a key, under which was a number. The letter informed her that the key was to be produced at all times in order to access the safety deposit box. Charlene was puzzled; she didn't have a safety deposit box, and especially not one in a bank in Zurich that's for sure.

The breeze whispered its message to his one true love. "Patience, Cherie, remember the cogs turn slowly…" Charlene shivered—the room suddenly cold. She would talk to Antoine's legal representative next week and give him the envelope and its contents.

Christmas was just around the corner, all the children would be home, and this year Matthew was bringing his wife and child too. A grandmother—who'd have thought it!

The pizzeria would be closed for Christmas—family came first. She'd thought Richard had lost the plot when he'd suggesting buying the restaurant. After all, what had the two of them known about running a restaurant—but business had boomed. Jason's wonky cake had helped choose his career and was training to be a chef in Paris. Carly and her husband had announced today that she was expecting their first child and Philip had taken over the Dupont Estate Agency in town and was doing really well, thanks to him the price of property in the area was rising in value.

Life as she knew it was good, everything in the garden was blooming—including Carly! She'd asked Philip to put the house on the market earlier—it was time to move on, time to let go of the past…

~

The house is empty once more, waiting, watching, and hoping. Its secrets trapped forever within its walls…

Malestroit struggled slowly to his feet, his movements slow and awkward as he shuffled down the corridor to his room. His only regret as he lay down on the bed was that he wouldn't live to see Carly's baby, and as he closed his eyes for the last time his thoughts were of his wife…waiting patiently on the other side.

~

The children are grown up with children of their own, and

Charlene and Richard now live by the sea in the house once owned by the Marcello family. It is said that the ghost of Mario Marcello haunts the seashore, still waiting for the return of Sophia and his granddaughters, lost at sea after the family jet crash landed in the Atlantic. It is un-known if Sebastian Delamare was on the plane, as his body was never found. Likewise the bodies of Sophia Giovanni and her twin daughters, Charlotte, and Alicia. Some say you can hear them calling out for help, when the moon is full, and the wind blows in from a certain quarter.

And as for Troy…

The end

Lightning Source UK Ltd.
Milton Keynes UK
UKHW020610090120
356604UK00002B/14/P